THAT MOMENT

Bernie reached out her hand to catch Lena, who at that moment seemed to be having a seizure. Bernie was horrified. God help this woman, she thought. She opened her mouth to offer a word of comfort, but then her hand closed around Lena's upper arm, and the word was instantly burned away.

She had never touched a live electrical wire, but she was doing it now. A human electrical wire, covered in skin and clothed in a sad prom dress and atrocious black sandals. Bernie went rigid. A sword of current cut through her hand and arm, singeing veins and muscle, coiling and bending and following a line to her very center. Bernie was jerked backward; she tried to scream. But her horror could not find a voice. It was fried in the wake of the sword. And then the current shifted. In a second, it burst out through her back like an alien hatching in a sickening scene from a science fiction movie.

Other *Leisure* books by Elizabeth Massie:
SINEATER

Welcome Back to the Night

Elizabeth Massie

LEISURE BOOKS NEW YORK CITY

A LEISURE BOOK®

November 1999

Published by

Dorchester Publishing Co., Inc.
276 Fifth Avenue
New York, NY 10001

ISBN 0-8439-4626-1

This book is dedicated with love to the wonderful, extensive Spilman family of Waynesboro and beyond, in remembrance of, and in anticipation of, many fun-filled, banquet-fueled family reunions. Of course, dear cousins, aunts, uncles, and such, this is a WORK OF FICTION! Remember that when you read this. Work of fiction. Fictional characters. Get it? Okay? Really. Thanks! I love ya'll!

Welcome Back to the Night

Now I lay me down to sleep, I pray the Lord my soul to keep. If I should die before I wake, I pray the lord my soul to take.

—night prayer, HeartLight

Now I lay off for the night, I know the Truth will bless our fight. Give us power to stop our foes as pure and strong our wisdom grows.

—night prayer, White Eagles

Where the fuck did I leave my stash? I better find that shit in the morning.

—night prayer, Norris Lynch

Chapter One

The only advantage the nigger alien in the Night Room had was that he could see in the dark. At first this had bothered Rex, because when he would climb into the crawl space and close the small wooden door behind him, he wanted to play blind-man games. Blind Alien's Bluff. Blind Alien on the Pipes. Rex wanted to do his tricks in the blackness and have the advantage of knowing his way around by sense of feel and memory. But, of course, after the first twenty-four hours, the chained alien's eyes had picked up what little light filtered in through the seams along the door, and when Rex came in and shut the door, the alien could watch and know what was coming. An unfair advantage.

It didn't really matter. Rex held all the cards. But Rex enjoyed sport. *Oh, God, what fun!*

And so he began to take a flashlight in with him when he went. The alien would see him, and Rex would laugh. He would work his way along the storage boxes to the back wall, bent over so he didn't bang his head on the low ceiling, and when he could hear the panicked, rapid breathing, he would bring the flashlight up before him and flick it on. For a second, in the white glare, there would be the open mouth and the gleaming sweat and the twitching ears as the alien strained and tried to pull his head away. The handcuffs which held the alien's arms behind his back would rattle. The water pipes would complain.

Then, with all visual things equal once more,

Rex would turn the light off. The crawl space would be dark as night.

Once a day, Rex took food and water to the alien in the Night Room. The alien never ate when Rex was watching. On a bad day, Rex would just dump the uneaten food on the floor for the mice and beetles. On a good day, Rex would kiss the alien and feed him with a spoon.

Today was a good day. It was the alien's one-month anniversary. Rex, feeling especially cheerful, had found a present to take inside. He unhooked the crawl-space door and pushed it slowly back against the wall, making it creak. He liked that creaking sound on good days.

Beautiful sounds like crying and singing.

He began to sing one of the songs his old girlfriend had hated with a passion.

"Cupid, draw back your bow-ho, and let your arrow go-ho." Rex bent down to climb inside. A thick smell of wet dirt, molded cardboard, and dusty cobwebs curled about his face. There was a more distant, yet definite stench. Urine. Feces. Old blood. Spoiled food. Rex shifted the wrapped bundle he held into a better position in the crook of his arm. The fingers of his free hand caressed the splinters on the door frame. They were cold; it was late February, and winter was enjoying its stay very much.

"Straight to my lover's heart."

He climbed into the crawl space, then straightened as much as he could. The alien in the back of the Night Room began to thrash about.

"For me."

The thrashing got stronger. It seemed to stir up the stench and throw it in Rex's direction.

"For nobody but me-he," sang Rex. "And for all

the other natives of our planet Earth." He reached back and tugged the door closed. The Night Room fell into night-blackness. Rex began moving slowly toward the back of the room. There was an electricity of sweat beneath his arms. His stomach was full with the weight of gratitude. He loved the meaning of his life. He sang, "Cupid, please hear my cry-hi, and let your arrow fly-hi."

The chained alien, now much closer, whispered, "Jesus, help me." Rex knew the alien could see him, so he stuck out his tongue and grinned.

"Straight to my lover's heart for me."

It was all of the song he knew. With the side of his leg, he recognized the trunk to his right. This meant the rear wall was just three feet ahead of him. He took one more step forward. His shoe came down in something slimy. But it didn't matter. It was a good day.

The chained alien became suddenly silent. Rex imagined he was holding his breath, pressed to the wet dirt wall and the pipes behind him. The alien probably hoped he could disappear by being quiet. *Silly thing*, thought Rex.

"Silly alien thing," Rex said. A rush drove from his heart, full of heat and passion. There was a wonderful sensuousness of the moment. Rex licked the air and it tasted rich and good. He put his package down in the slime. He pulled his flashlight from his back pocket and held it toward the wall. "Good morning, alien." Rex flicked the switch. The alien lurched, and tried to pull away. His eyes were closed, his mouth twisting and gurgling. It reminded Rex of a Three Stooges still shot. Curly bracing for the hammer that Moe was about to bring down on his head.

Get ready. Nyuck, nyuck, it's gonna hurt. The

humor in that correlation made Rex chuckle. "Cointenly," he said. He laughed louder, and his bowels filled with love.

Rex, as well as the other members of the White Eagles, was fully aware that most citizens of the planet Earth had no idea that the being he had in his basement was an alien. Most people, ignorant as they were, thought this thing was a man. But that was because the aliens had been on Earth so long that no one even noticed anymore; no one knew their true origin. But the facts were as plain as the flesh on a body. Citizens of Earth were light-skinned. Citizens of other planets came in other colors, came with bigger noses or slanted eyes. They infiltrated easily, but those humans who knew the truth were in a constant battle to capture and often destroy those who did not belong here. If it was left unchecked, then one day, by the Millennium or not long afterwards, there would be no true white people left.

Only the aliens. Or alien half-breeds. How those aliens loved to fuck.

Rex didn't hate the creatures; those on Earth weren't terribly smart. It was the master aliens back on the other planets who were in control of those on Earth. Sometimes, Rex even felt a love for the pathetic things. As long as they were contained.

Rex trained the light along the alien's body. He was naked and filthy. Bones delineated the flesh at strange places. His right shoulder had collapsed. There were bruises and scabs across his throat and chest. His legs were up nearly to the calves in his own thick, wet wastes and the food Rex had spilled on bad days.

"You smell bad, Billy Bailey," said Rex. "Aren't you ashamed?"

The alien was silent, but his teeth chomped once, involuntarily, clacking like a nutcracker.

Rex turned off the flashlight. The alien gurgled. His breathing was raspy and dry. But it was his own stupid fault. He rarely drank the water Rex offered him. He was most likely dehydrated. Silly, silly alien.

By sense of touch, Rex opened the bundle by his feet. He reached into the cloth and took out one of four slender wooden sticks. It was wonderfully smooth, and Rex traced it with a good sense of pleasure. He felt until his fingers came upon the pointed tip. He pushed his thumb against the sharpness, and his dick rose a little. The other end of the stick was blunt with a shallow notch.

"Got something for you, Billy Bailey," Rex said. "It's been a month, do you know that? Happy anniversary to us."

Then the man once again whispered, "Jesus, help me."

"Silly old alien nigger," said Rex. "Pretending that your kind understands about Jesus. Jesus came to our planet, not yours. Best leave Him out of this."

Rex reached into the bundle again and brought out the second part of the present. It was a homemade bow, ridiculous Rex knew, but it would serve its temporary purpose. He slipped the notched end of the stick against the string and raised it to shoulder height.

"Cupid, draw back your bow . . ."

He stretched the string back into a fine angle and squinted his eye as if he could really see.

17

" . . . ho."

He imagined the sunken shoulder, the protruding ribs, the skeleton-thin arms. The lovely, inferior face twisted in fear.

He saw, in the front of his mind, the scrawny hipbones and the pathetic unwashed penis shaking like a little whipped dog's tail. Rex aimed for the right leg, and let the string go. The scream was beautiful, and Rex laughed aloud.

The man had two legs and two shoulders, just enough for all four of Rex's gifts. The man accepted them all.

After midnight, when the anniversary was over, Rex came back to the Night Room and took the arrows out and cleansed the wounds so the alien would not die.

Chapter Two

In the narrow hallway by the apartment-building staircase, Norris Lynch stood, the lid to his crusty mailbox popped open, the day's collection of mail drooping in his hand. He was leaning against the wall, his heart hammering through the back of his shirt and into the plaster.

He whispered, "Oh, God. Oh, fuck it. They did it."

It was four-fifteen in the afternoon. Except for the invisible apartment wives and forbidden, invisible pets of 6917 West Bruton Street, the nine-unit building was deserted. The manly men who lived there were off doing manly-men things: driving laundry trucks, wielding hammers, greasing the gears of the boats on the James, dragging oysters from Chesapeake Bay.

But Norris was home now, a day of work completed. He was a school teacher in his second year at Bright Creek Institute, having gone into education after yearly stints at everything from convenience-store clerking to cab driving to fast-food french-fry cooking. Good old Bright Creek Institute for social deviants and fuck-ups. Norris taught social studies and remedial reading, and was the unskilled, forced-labor, assistant volley-ball coach. In to work at seven-thirty, out at three-forty-five except during volleyball season, and then he didn't get home until dark.

They had done it.

Norris stared at the envelopes in his fingers. The one on top, with the Henford postmark, would be a reminder of the family reunion this weekend. It would hit the trash before Norris's fingerprints were cold on the kitchen door knob. There was a phone bill, a cable bill, a gritty folded newsprint flier from Wal-Mart. At the bottom of the stack, a large manila envelope with an ink-stamped return address: "We're In the Money. Norfolk, Virginia."

Teddy had said they'd probably do it and they had. May God-who-did-not-exist have mercy on his career. His reputation. His ass, which could easily end up in prison.

He tried to steady his breathing. He counted the air in, the air out. There was a way to handle this. There was a solution to every problem, or so he had told himself countless times over the last thirty-six years of his life. Got to live 'til you die and make the best of it. Take the mail up to the third-floor apartment. Get a beer. No problem. Keep calm. Take it one minute at a time.

Maybe this was Teddy's joke. If it was, he would find Teddy back at Bright Creek, more likely than not sitting in his little janitor cubicle off the boiler room and smoking some of the grass he supplied to Norris and listening to his God-awful country music on his black AM-only radio. On finding Teddy, Norris would torture him on the spot. Beat the shit out of him. Dismember him. Something slow and painful and bloody. Listen to Teddy scream and beg forgiveness. And then they'd laugh because it was only a joke. A pissingly stupid joke, but a joke. A Teddy joke.

After laughing, the two of them would share a hoot and whatever smoke there was left and sit on the oily, cat-piss-stained blanket covering Teddy's lawn furniture and listen to the whine of the black hillbillies on the radio.

Norris's heart, banging away, said, "It ain't a joke, buddy." He shoved himself from the wall with his elbows, and didn't even realize he had made it up the two flights of steps until he found himself face to face with the grimy nameplate on #8. His keys were uncooperative, and playfully slid around and about the keyhole until Norris crammed the mail beneath his arm and jabbed the key in with both hands.

The door opened and Norris went inside. He put the mail on the kitchen table, then lifted the top, suspiciously family-looking envelope and threw it into the trash can by the stove. He slipped out of his jacket and dropped it onto the chair at the table. The shoulders didn't catch and it slid to the floor. Norris did not move to pick it up. He went to the refrigerator and pulled out a Diet Coke instead of a beer. Punishment drink. He popped the tab but did not drink. Sweat trickled under the curly hairs of his black beard and the hairs at the nape of his neck. He rubbed his temple, and looked at the mail on the table.

Please God, Teddy, it's your little big-ass joke and I'm going to hate you and then we'll have a good time over it.

He put the Diet Coke can on the counter, went into his bedroom and kicked off his work shoes. He climbed out of his slacks and shirt and tie. There was a set of gray sweats on the floor. He put them on, then went barefoot back to the kitchen, wishing he'd placed an order with Teddy for something stronger than the pot he had in his bedroom.

"Open the mail, asshole," he said. He went to the table, and one by one opened the envelopes. The phone bill, $32.00. No long-distance calls from this end. The cable bill, $42.90, MTV, Cinemax, HBO, Showtime, and Playboy Channel included. A lazy bachelor's reliable late-night date. Third dimension be damned. The Wal-Mart ad, its front page boasting men's jeans for $18.98. And then he came to the manila envelope. The return address, complete with a little Jetsons sticker to the right, a malign joke to the addressee. The white mailing label, computer-generated.

"Fuck it fuck it fuck it."

Norris slid his index finger beneath the glued flap and tugged. The flap and one-third of the envelope tore. The shiny corners of several color photos winked.

"Oh, Jesus," said Norris, and it was not a swear word this time. It was an appeal. Slowly, he dumped the photos. Several fell face down. Three of them didn't.

Norris stared without moving. Only his lids blinked spastically and the blood of his veins moved with a cold, uncaring haughtiness. He stared at the face-up photos.

Nothing was worth this. Not joy, not any amount of physical pleasure. Certainly not the insane, fucked-up care package that was his life.

Norris stood from the chair and went into the bathroom. He pushed the switch under the sink light. The fluorescent bulb flickered on. He took a razor pack from the medicine cabinet. A new blade tinkled onto the enamel beside the toothpaste tube and a piece of toilet paper with dried blood, left from this morning when he'd cut his throat cleaning stray beard hairs. He licked his lips. He licked the flat side of the blade. It tasted like death.

"It ain't fucking worth it," he said to himself. Screw suicide notes; they were for pussies who really wanted a mama to rescue them.

The blade point moved to the soft skin of Norris's wrist. Cuts parallel to the arm were the most effective. He'd heard that somewhere. It would hurt more but he could do it. He'd really wanted to for a long time.

Thank you, you motherfucking blackmailers. You gave me the incentive I've wanted.

"Thank you, motherfuckers!" Norris shouted.

His reflection in the mirror screamed, too.

The blade edge was pushed into his skin. Blood welled. So did the heat of pain. He hesitated. It fucking HURT.

"Do it."

He tried to pull the blade up his flesh, but his hand shook and the blood began to drip. It hurt like hell. "Don't quit on me now!" He moved the blade. Skin pulled away in its wake. Blood poured. Norris cried aloud. The blade stopped, and fire seared the nerves all around it.

"Goddamn it!"

Norris stared at the blade and the blood. He willed it to move, and to not hurt. The blade's will was stronger. It would not move, and it hurt.

"Pussy!" The word seethed through clenched teeth. The blade would not move.

Norris drove his face into the mirror. It cracked softly. The blade dropped into the sink. A thick string of blood followed it down the side of the bowl. Norris's breathing steamed the glass. Head throbbing, he looked at his arm. It didn't even merit stitches.

He put a thumb over it and sat on the side of the tub. With his bare foot, he pushed the bathroom window open a little to let in fresh air.

When he was able to get up again, Norris found the can of Diet Coke in the kitchen and forced it down his throat. Then he found the family-reunion notice in the trash and opened it. It was a pamphlet, ten pages of stapled boasting from the Lynch family tree limbs. All Norris wanted was the time and date.

Two days from now. Saturday and Sunday. A weekend of wall-to-wall Lynches. Sacrifice for the long-term good, the longer-term survival.

He tore off the bottom of the first page and put it into the dollar section of his wallet. The rest of the pamphlet he used to cover the photos on the kitchen table.

Chapter Three

It was a bad day.

Rex Wells stood in the center of his basement's rec room and slowly drew his hands in and out of his jeans pockets. "Why are you here?" he said finally. "Why do we allow you to stay?"

There was no answer at first. Instead, he heard only the agitated tapping of Dean's cowboy boot on the thinly carpeted floor, and the soft, indistinguishable buzz as Lizzie, on the bottom basement step, whispered to Peaches. In the corner of his eye, reflected in the harsh, irregular light of the room, Rex could see sporadic details of some of Ronald's poster art on the walls. Scenes drawn and colored with bright permanent markers. Talentless sketches of crucified alien women, of impaled alien men, and of boiling alien children. Scenes awash with thick strokes of blood red and bordered with favorite quotes of the movement. In their ineptness, they were only a mockery of the cause of the True Human Race. They made Rex want to vomit.

He looked at the woman kneeling before him on the floor. She was stupid and slow, and she believed in what she was doing. She knew, also, that she must answer Rex's questions with caution. With care.

"Why are you here?" Rex repeated. He swung his boot. It connected with the woman's shoulder, and she lifted her head slightly. But she did not look at Rex.

"To serve," she said.

"Yes," said Rex. "And how must you serve?"

24

Sweat beads trembled in the stubble of the woman's newly cropped blond hair. "With my body, mind, and spirit," she said.

"Yes," said Rex, and he had no doubt that she would do just that. She had been with the organization only five days now, and already had offered herself in entirety to the cause. Bruises on her neck and across her forehead and cheeks attested to her willingness to be whatever the White Eagles would have her be. There had been no Arm Test for permission to strike this bitch at will. It would have been a waste of the Test's power.

Rex had even given Junior, via the Test, permission to fuck her, right there on the basement floor last night, with Lizzie laughing and Dean playing his own designs on his cheap bass. Of course, Junior was slow and stupid as well, and nearly as ugly as the woman. Even Lizzie and Ronald were strikingly unattractive and unimaginative. Rex knew that this did not speak well for the White Eagles.

The White Eagles. Here was a group, young and fresh, all True Humans, all between the ages of seventeen and twenty-three with the exception of the older bitch on the floor, all dedicated to the True Human Race.

There was Dean, the cowboy. Twenty-one, a tall and talented musician. The best of them all.

Joe, one-third of Dean's "Band of Truth." Nineteen, high-school dropout, mediocre on the twelve-string, energetic and enthusiastic, short blond hair so pale that the myriad of emblems carved into the skin of his skull were as clear as paintings on velvet.

Lizzie, eighteen, receptionist at Brandon Building Supplies. Giggly, red-haired, faithful bitch.

Peaches, the beautiful Eagle. Blond, almost twenty, worked at the Henford Parks and Recreation Department as an aerobics instructor. She shared an apartment with Percy.

Percy, the last third of the "Band of Truth." A muscular drummer with a quick joke and a nervous eye. Twenty-three, brown hair. Day job, rural route driver for *The Henford Press*.

Junior, seventeen, quit school at fifteen. A mama's boy, living at home and never worked a day in his life. Black hair, the brunt of Percy's inbreeding jokes.

Ronald, the artist. Twenty-two, lacking much artistic ability, fond of sketching torture scenes. Worked part-time as a security man at Symicon Fiber Factory.

All dedicated members of the cause. Yet four of the nine were an acute embarrassment. It was a puzzle, and one which frequently dug thorns into the space below Rex's ribs.

Rex dragged his fingers upward, raking through the short bristles of his own close-cut brown hair. He traced the outline of the initials "W. E." carved on the right side of his scalp by Dean's pocket knife. He wondered if other groups around the country ever considered the dichotomies of their situation. If they didn't, then they would be caught off-guard, and deserved to be.

But my vision will make me a leader in the final battle, Rex thought.

"To serve," the woman said again, uncertain with Rex's minute of silence. She turned her face upward, a questioning expression squeezing her already homely features into a pudgy ball. "Body, mind, and spirit."

Ugly, so fucking UGLY! Rex snorted silently. She was fat, she had rat's eyes, she had a bad leg that made her limp when she walked. Rex knew this woman's mental and physical weaknesses did not come from alien inbreeding. Rex's uncle had researched each one and found them clean. Yet they did not fit Rex's vision of the True Race.

A puzzle. Sometimes, an infuriation. Rex's hand flashed out and caught the woman across the jaw. She crashed to her side, then blinked, touched her face, and sat straight again. "You're a BITCH!" Rex roared.

The shout caused Rex's alien prisoner, kept in the dirt-floored storage room on the other side of the steps, to cry out. The White Eagles ignored the cry.

Rex brought his foot back and hurled the heavy leather boot at the kneeling figure. It rammed into the softness of her large stomach, and she grunted and doubled over, striking the uncarpeted floor with her face. She coughed once, but made no other sound of protest. Rex kicked her again, and again. She gagged and coughed, but did not try to protect herself. Rex wanted to see tears, to hear pain, to know that she was feeling his righteous, furious anger. Her need for him made him want to puke.

Lizzie giggled. Peaches shushed her.

Rex stopped and knotted his hands together, trying to make the heat of the blood rub away. He stared at the ceiling. A puzzle was only that, he told himself. In time, things would come clear.

No babies, Rex thought, and the thought eased

27

his mind somewhat. She is one of us, somehow, but she cannot reproduce. She will do what she can do best. She will serve. "Yes," said Rex. When he looked back down at the woman, there was a tight smile on his lips. Not a smile of acceptance, nor of resignation. But of compromise.

"You may serve," he said. There was a sigh of relief from somewhere in the room. Someone was glad that it was done. But Rex wanted a good ending to this. Rex wanted the woman to remember who was the man in charge. Who was the visionary. Who was the leader.

"Kiss my feet," he told the woman. She bent over and cupped his boots between her fat fingers. Her lips lapped the leather, making wet streaks in the dust until he pulled his feet away.

"Slow-witted shit," he cried. "Don't you know the difference between feet and boots?"

The woman passed her hand across the dust on her mouth. She swallowed, then slowly reached for the buckle on the side of one boot. Rex winked at the other White Eagles. The woman pulled off the boot, then the stained sock. She unbuckled the other boot and removed it and the sock beneath. Rex wriggled his toes.

"Kiss my feet."

The woman leaned over and planted two long, hungry kisses on the man's feet. Rex crossed his arms and smiled, but he wondered how the man Jesus could have tolerated it. Then he said, "Kiss my ass."

On her knees, the woman crept behind Rex and waited respectfully as Rex lowered his jeans and briefs. Then she cautiously placed her hands on his hips. Rex felt her face press into his buttocks, then pull away.

"That was worthless," Rex said. "Where is the love?"

The woman pushed her mouth to the crack of his ass and he could feel her tongue praying for acceptance. In the corner of the basement, Junior smacked his lips. Rex knew this show of repulsive love was making the boy as horny as a fat-dicked gorilla.

Rex stepped forward and hiked up his pants. He turned and stared at the woman. She would serve. And he would make full use of her.

"You are one of us now," he told her. "A soldier against aliens who have ruled our world for much too long."

The woman smiled. Her mouth curved upward, revealing uneven teeth and a pocketful of saliva.

Rex strode to the steps, and both Lizzie and Peaches scooted out of his way.

"Mind if we play a little?" asked Percy. Normally Percy wouldn't ask, but Rex knew that Percy, like the woman, saw the necessity of caution at the moment.

"Go ahead," said Rex. He took the steps two at a time, easily gliding to the top on his long legs.

Behind him, he could hear the group moving about, now free of the restrictions of the solemn ceremony. The ceremony for each member had been different, tailored to each particular personality, yet each one had been full of pledges and oaths. Each one honed to vivid memory by Rex's deadly threats and horrifyingly calm ultimatums. None had been quite so ridiculous as the one he had just performed, but then, none of the other members was quite as moronic as that imbecile he had left on the basement floor. Tailored to suit her need to serve.

So be it.

Lizzie giggled out loud. Dean plucked on his guitar strings. Joe and Percy and Ronald finished off their beers, picking up threads of a previous conversation that dealt with the niggers parking on Wayside Drive near Joe's parents' home.

"Rex?" It was Junior, calling up the steps. Rex turned and looked down. Junior's foot was wiggling, his shoulders shrugging apologetically.

"What is it?"

"I was wondering if I could do like last night? Remember?" Junior held up his middle finger and, almost apologetically, thrust it up and down a couple of times.

Rex ground his teeth together. "Yes," he said.

Junior, his eyes popping, turned to face the new woman. He said, "Come here, give me a job like last night."

The woman said nothing, and as Rex pushed through the door at the top of the steps, he knew that she would indeed give Junior a job like last night.

In the kitchen, Rex sat and stuck his finger into the bacon crumbs on the paper plate on the table. He licked the crumbs off, balled up the plate, and aimed it at the trash can by the door. It bounced off the wall and went in, leaving another grease-trail on the green paint above the can. Then he picked up the salt shaker. He shut his eyes and listened to the beginnings of music in the basement below. Dean was now picking at his guitar, although through the floor Rex could only hear the lower-frequency notes. Percy had moved to drums, but at the moment Dean and Percy were not making music together.

Rex dropped his head to his crossed arms, letting the salt shaker fall, spilling white grains over the table. He breathed on them, making them scatter. He wouldn't use pepper. It was nasty and black, like the alien niggers.

If it wasn't for the crucial need to purge the country, and then the world, Rex would have nothing to do with the gathering below. They made him crazy much of the time, and that was no way to run an organization. He had to keep his thoughts elevated.

Think only of the cause.

Now that he had enough close followers, it was time to make a concrete plan. No more shitting around doing piddly time wasters. No more ridiculous graffiti sprayed on the railroad overpass, or anonymous phone calls to colored homes. No more bloody notes left in door jambs.

Time to take the status of lone martyrdom away from the storage-room prisoner. The land was soon to be his, a promise of his uncle, a good if worthlessly timid man.

Rex ran his hands in the spilled salt. He bit the back of his hand and then rubbed it in the salt. It burned as it should. He thought for the briefest moment about the girl he had dated just over a year before, and wondered how she would like what he had become. She was pretty, she was smart. She was white—True Race perfection. But she was weak. How would she like what he now

31

was? She would probably scream, and the thought of that scream made Rex suddenly erect.

Below, the sounds of music grew stronger, guitars whining, rapid drums, and Lizzie vocalizing. And beneath it all, the sounds as Junior whooped it up with the woman. *Let her serve*, Rex thought.

He reached for the phone to call his uncle to arrange a quick and private sterilization for the newest member of the White Eagles.

Chapter Four

The woman wandered back home, back to her small apartment over the Sunshine Bread distribution warehouse, aching with the soreness between her legs and shivering with excitement. She was one of them. She was accepted. She was of the True Race. A True Human.

She climbed the steps, clutching the rattly railing and breathing hard with the exertion. She never got used to going up these steep stairs, it always made her heart pound and her chest tighten. Her bum leg dragged slightly.

But soon, she would be with the White Eagles always, and would never have to come back here. They had land in the country, Rex had said, and they would all live together to face the coming alien battle.

The woman lumbered into her bedroom, dropped onto the sagging mattress, and touched herself gently in every place Rex had touched her. She was tingling.

She was blessed.

Chapter Five

Lindsay Hollin finished buttoning the back of her dress and stood before the full-length mirror on the back of the closet door. The dress was old and soft, a comfortable navy blue favorite, with brass buttons and piping, but the added pounds on her hips and stomach pulled it in unflattering places. There was a pucker over Lindsay's rear end, and one where her control-top panty hose squeezed in below her ribs.

"Damn," she said. She turned about, sucking in her gut, trying to make the dress hang better. "Damn it." The figure she'd had ten years ago when, at twenty-seven, she married Hank Hollin was gone. Time and children were her excuses, but she hated excuses.

Hank, in the bathroom, clicked off the hair dryer and came into the bedroom. He was dressed only in his powder blue briefs. His hair was nearly dry, with random strands spiking out like dark, wet thistles. His mustache was newly trimmed; tiny hairs speckled the bare skin of his shoulders. He scratched his eye and reached atop the chest of drawers for his Mennen Speed Stick.

"What were you saying?" he asked.

Lindsay turned from the mirror. "Nothing. Just that my family is going to comment on my extra twenty pounds at the reunion."

"You look fine, Lind."

"What would you know about it?" she said. "You never weighed a pound in your life." She sat on the bed and adjusted the toes of her panty hose. "This isn't your skinny family we're seeing. This is mine. The family who notices everything. Remember the mini-reunion two years ago, when everyone came except some of the out-of-staters? Uncle Leonard waited until the blessing was given and everyone was chowing down before he clinked his glass with his fork and stood up. I thought it would be another toast to the grandparents. But all he does is draw his obese self up and say, 'I just want to point out that I am no longer the fattest one in the room.' Then, of course, everyone scanned the room to find out who, indeed, was the fattest family member. Old Uncle Bennett had Uncle Leonard beat by maybe thirty pounds."

Hank got this shirt from the closet and slipped it on. "I remember. Uncle Bennett was pissed."

"Of course he was pissed. He told everyone he was pissed. Everyone, that is, except Uncle Leonard."

Lindsay bent down and rooted beneath the bed. She pulled out a brown flat shoe and a black heeled shoe. "My other heel?" she muttered. She pulled out a slipper, then another slipper, then one of Hank's jogging shoes. "I told you we should buy one of those plastic shoe-holder things that you hang on the back of the closet door."

They finished dressing. Lindsay put on some pearl pink lipstick. She put on a white jacket to help conceal the dress puckers and found her missing shoe under the nightstand. Then she clopped through the large, cluttered kitchen to check on the two girls in the family room as Hank went out to get the heater going in the car.

Lindsay's daughters were in front of the television, Mandy on the love seat and Grace on the rocking chair. Mandy was giving Grace a running commentary on the cartoon antics on the screen. Grace had a bag of potato chips in her lap. Mandy had a bag of cheese puffs.

"Oh, just great, girls," said Lindsay as she moved to switch off the television. Mandy groaned in protest, and Grace echoed the groan. "We're supposed to be going to Great-Grandmother and Grandfather's anniversary dinner. And here are you two eating like we haven't fed you in a week."

"Mandy give me 'em," said Grace.

"Yeah, blame her," said Lindsay. She took the bag of chips from Grace and the bag of cheese puffs from Mandy.

"We're really hungry, Mom. We couldn't wait any longer. Besides, I don't like that stuff we eat when we get together with Great-Grandmother and Grandfather."

"I hear you." Lindsay tossed both bags onto the coffee table. "Wipe that orange off your face, Mandy. And Grace, you've got a piece of chip in your front tooth. Can you feel it to get it out?"

Grace nodded enthusiastically and dug at her teeth with her fingers.

"Is it gone?" asked Mandy. Lindsay looked her older daughter over. The child was fairly clean, with only a few crumples in the originally well-ironed dress. She was tall, taking after the Lynch family already in that respect. Her blond hair was her mother's, and her round face made her look much like Lindsay did at nine and a half. She was independent, outgoing, and a second mother to Grace.

"You look fine," said Lindsay. "Now just

remember to smile at the relatives, but if anyone tries to pinch your cheek, don't be afraid to tell them to cut it out."

"Okay," said Mandy.

"And me, how I look?" asked Grace. The smaller girl patted her mouth, indicating that the chip was gone now.

"Better," said Lindsay. "Your hair is all in a tangle now. Were you two wrestling while I was getting dressed?"

"Yeah," giggled Grace. "Mandy me did Indanna Jones."

"I bet you did," said Lindsay. She slid the red bow from Grace's light brown hair and fastened it back quickly. "Everyone is going to wonder why we're late. Should we say you and Mandy were playing Indiana Jones?"

"Yeah!" shouted Grace.

"You're a poot."

"Me a poot! Mandy a poot, too!"

Lindsay wiped a smudge from Grace's cheek. The girl had obviously been in the cheese puffs as well. "You don't say 'poot' at the dinner, Grace. Okay? There are a lot of relatives from out of state you haven't met yet. We want to make a good impression, right? Don't call anybody a poot."

Grace grinned and nodded. She was her father's child. Grace had the same light brown hair, the same love of power plays. She was an early riser, an avid storyteller, and she loved music, as did Hank. The only two differences were her mild mental retardation, and the fact that she had been born with no eyes.

As Lindsay ushered her charges out through the kitchen to the hall foyer then out the front door, she allowed herself a moment of truth. It was not the twenty pounds she was truly worried about, although she knew it would not go unmentioned. It was her family's response to Grace.

Granted, they all knew. The relatives in town, not counting Lindsay's own truly wonderful parents, had shared Easter afternoons and Christmas services and family picnics with the Hollins. When Grace was born, they'd had their time of bewilderment, wondering how such a lovely baby could have nothing but cartilage behind her seemingly normal yet fused eyelids. And of course, their sympathetic curiosity was again stirred when it was concluded that Grace would be mentally slow. But familiarity had worn off the shock, and now the in-towners didn't think twice about Grace.

It was doing it all again that had Lindsay on edge. It was introducing Grace to the smiling gawks of the out-of-state relatives, then having to explain again, in spite of the fact that pictures had been sent with Christmas cards, that the child was blind. The child was retarded.

The child was a blessing and a handful and a demon and an angel, like any child. The child was a poot.

Lindsay herded the kids across the gravel drive and into the back seat of the car. She joined Hank in the front. "Grace, get that seat belt," she said.

"Can't find," said Grace.

"Yes, you can. Mandy, don't help her, she can find it. Good. Now," Lindsay flipped open the small lighted mirror on her visor, grimaced, stuck her tongue out at herself, then looked at Hank. "We're off to see the Wizard."

"The wonderful Wizard of Oz," said Mandy.

"Oz!" shouted Grace.

"The wonderful Lynches of Henford," said Hank. "They'll get you, my pretties!"

The car backed out of the drive and onto the road, and Lindsay began tugging at the waist of her dress again.

Chapter Six

Rex's carport was cold but dry. The woman stood there watching out as the icy rain fell to the frosted grass patches of his backyard. It was nearly noon, and she had been standing in the carport, alone, for fifteen minutes. She clenched and unclenched her chapped, gloveless hands and stomped around softly. She watched Rex's back door and listened, hoping Rex would look out through the yellow curtains and see her there. His car was not in the carport, but sometimes he lent the car to a White Eagle. So he might be there.

She wore a formal-length dress she'd found earlier that morning at the hospital's benefit shop on Parson Street. The dress was large enough to zip at her back, but it was too long, and she had gone home and stapled the hem up in six places. Two of the staples in the back had already ripped out, and the dress was frozen and soiled where it had dragged on the sidewalk. Over the dress was her winter coat, unbuttoned, pocked with holes, and stiff with dried sweat. On her feet were black vinyl sandals with buckles ready to give and a pair of soiled knee-high hose.

Since her White Eagle initiation, she had worn

a black knit cap on her bald head to keep warm, but that would not do for today. A blue acetate scarf, found in an accessories bin at the benefit shop, had been an added touch, and she had spent twenty minutes putting the scarf on and off her head, hiding the bristle of her shaved hair, lost to the feel of the soft material on her scalp.

The woman said to the closed door, "Rex, look out."

A gray cat trotted in off the road, licked its butt, and came to sit beside the woman's sandaled foot. It shook its wet feet. The woman stared at it and it stared back. The woman knew it was not Rex's cat. Rex didn't own pets. He was always swearing about the loose animals in the neighborhood. He especially hated cats who whined and howled in the night. One evening, when he was in a very good mood, he had found a little black cat under his car and taken it down to the basement where the Eagles were meeting. Rex had laughed and said he was going to make the cat a gymnast. He said, "This cat can dance just like Nadia." Then he pulled its back legs in two directions until the pelvic bone snapped. Then he danced the howling cat along the rug while he hummed a song. The cat did air leaps, and Rex helped it do splits. White Eagles had cheered. The woman had wished Rex would kiss her.

The woman kicked at the gray cat and it ran away.

It was seven minutes after twelve. The woman ran her fingernail between her front teeth, loosening a piece of breakfast cereal. Rex had not looked out, and she was alone in the cold carport. Soon she would have to leave, because she had somewhere to go that afternoon.

But that thought brought on a shiver of fearful excitement. Somewhere to go today. She brought a clenched fist to her lips. She took several steps across the oily concrete floor toward the back door of the house. Maybe Rex was in his basement. Maybe if she rapped on his back door he would come up and see her through the yellow curtains. Maybe he would say, "Oh, how nice you look, now you must have somewhere to go, don't you?"

She stepped closer to the door. She looked at the greasy glass and the thin curtains behind it. "Rex," she said. "I got somewhere to go today."

Rex did not come to the window. He had somewhere to go today, too.

"Rex, see?"

Rex was not home.

The woman turned toward the road and put her hands into her coat pocket. The gray cat was hiding in the windbreak of Rex's untrimmed boxwood. Its eyes blinked, wet like the grass and yellow like Rex's curtains.

"I got somewhere to go," the woman told the cat.

The cat was unimpressed. It turned its head away and licked its butt.

Chapter Seven

Norris stood at the edge of the overlook, cold Diet Coke in hand, staring down at the city of Henford through the diminishing slopes of foothills. From the high point of Hawk's Roost, on the Blue Ridge Mountains just off the Blue Ridge Parkway, Henford was visible between a "V" in the hills, a small spot of concentrated humanity on the floor of the Shenandoah Valley. Grand town of sixteen thousand. Proud home of Henford High School's Daring Dragons, a seven-story-tall cold-storage building, tallest building in the county, and Symicon Fiber Factory.

The community was cut in the center by the Moss River, which Norris could see as a thin gray ribbon entering town at the north and exiting on the southwestern edge. The foothills were dark; the only trees with leaves in early March were the various species of pines and other evergreens. Trunks of naked deciduous trees made a bleak charcoal picture of the vast scene.

To his right, on a single smaller knoll, was a forest wound, a visible patch of shorter evergreen tree and shrub growth. A patch which covered nearly fifty acres, a patch just now recovering after the fire seven years ago.

Norris could not look at the scar on the knoll.

Seeing his grandparents, the Gs, and talking to them should not be hard, but Norris knew it would be. He had not seen any of his family since he'd moved to the Tidewater area. He had not written or called. Not one Christmas card had been sent to Henford bearing his signature. And most unforgivable of all, he had not come to his father's aid when his mother had run off. Even when his father wrote to him, pleading, Norris had not come back.

Seven years had passed since he'd first attempted to embrace what he knew he was, seven years since he had felt the first, fleeting sensations of self-honesty, and seven years since his honesty had led to tragedy. Seven years had passed since he'd slipped out and moved away. As the Pet Shoppe Boys had once advised, he had run away.

Run away, run away, run away.

41

And he had lived his seven years a coward. Seven years a failure.

I'm sorry, Sam, you know I'm sorry.

And now, he was coming back to a family reunion, the celebration of the Gs' sixty-fifth wedding anniversary, to ask them for a favor.

Ask old Granddaddy for a favor. A granddaddy of a favor, to be exact. Norris was going to be submissive and polite and apologetic and fuckingly genial in hopes of acquiring a monetary loan. A major cash contribution, actually.

Emphasis on major.

Emphasis on contribution.

Because he was a coward, and a failure.

He wouldn't think about what he would have to do if they didn't go along with it.

Norris climbed into his car, looked at the Diet Coke can in his hand, then rolled the window down and hurled the can over the side of the overlook.

"Arrest me for littering," he said to no one. He licked stray drops from his knuckles, straightened the cursed tie he'd put on for the occasion, and lit a cigarette. Then he steered his car down the twisting turns of the road, not allowing himself to glance at the scar on the mountain knoll as he passed it going sixty-three, and entered his old hometown of Henford.

Chapter Eight

When Bernie Lynch arrived at the Henford Hotel, she drove Matt's Volkswagen van around the block four times before stilling her heart enough to look for a parking place. A major headache was gathering steam at the base of her neck. She knew there was nothing she could do about it except take it easy and pray it would ease up. She'd taken four aspirins less than an hour ago. For now, that was as strong a drug as she could afford.

Headaches were something she had been plagued with increasingly, but except for Matt at HeartLight, she told no one about them. Not her mother, with whom she spoke at least once a week on the phone, not the other HeartLight residents, not the housebound she visited in and around Henford. Headaches were nothing compared to the disabilities she tried to cheer others through. She had no right to make any complaints. Everyone had their trials; everyone was confined to their own body and its variations and infirmities. It came with being mortal.

There were several empty spaces at the rear of the hotel's lot, behind the large clot of automobiles she knew had to belong to various members of the Lynch clan. She pulled up next to a dumpster, tugged the rearview mirror down and gave herself a quick look, then locked the doors and slid out. She did not carry a purse; she hadn't in the last eight months. Purses occupied hands which could be otherwise better occupied. In the pocket of her green woolen camping jacket she carried all she needed, her car keys, her driver's license, and a small amount of cash.

She hurried between the cars. A freezing March wind suddenly whipped up out of nowhere. Her long auburn hair spun and threatened to tangle. She tipped her head down, poking her nose into her coat collar. The cold cut through her ears, multiplying the pain of the

43

headache and driving it up toward her eyes. She pulled down into her coat more tightly, and glanced at the other cars in the lot as she passed them. They were undoubtedly relative-mobiles. There were various state license plates. North Carolina, Iowa, Arizona, Maryland, amid all the white Virginia plates. They had all come for the reunion, all drawn to the small town of Henford to see each other again, to soak up the sounds and smells of the Homeplace, to compare physiques and hair loss, and to assure themselves a place in the Gs' will.

Bernie flexed her hands in her pockets, and found the frayed hole in the right one. She had been meaning to sew it up. But she had been busy, doing a gratis housecleaning for a friend whose mother was sick, and helping Sarah clear HeartLight's backyard for a garden. Even Bernie's one prized possession, her horse, Red River, had seen Bernie only at feeding and grooming time, and the time had been pushed later and later into the night. But Bernie didn't complain. God was good, and Bernie did what she could.

Inside the old and stately Henford Hotel, small gatherings of people were clustered about the lobby. Little boys in uncomfortable looking suits pulled at their collars and whined. Teenagers Bernie thought she might recognize if she looked long enough sat on the straight-backed chairs and sofas and stood beside the elevator doors, eyeing each other critically, holding to their well-learned Lynch airs of boredom as if they were life preservers.

Bernie moved quickly to the ladies' room. She eased the heavy wooden door closed, passed the ornate mirror and dressing table, and went to sit

on a toilet lid in one of the four stalls at the back
of the restroom.

She let out a heavy breath. She peered beneath
the stall to her left; a pair of navy heeled shoes
were set primly beside each other. The stall to her
right was occupied by a pair of flat brown pumps
and small dancing Buster Browns. Perhaps a little cousin or niece.

Bernie sat up straight again and leaned against
the cold piping at her back. The heat of the room
did not stop the headache, but changed it to a
dull throb. This headache she deserved, although
it was hard to admit. She was afraid to face her
family.

She was ashamed.

It was stiflingly hot in here. She slipped off her
jacket and put it on the hook on the stall door.
She looked down at her shoes, a clean but scuffed
pair of black hightop sneakers. Except for her
barn boots and some flip-flops, these were the
only shoes she owned. The shelf-ful of shoes she
once had were now God-knew-where, having
been donated to the local Salvation Army along
with most of her clothes. Inside her sneakers
were thick white socks, purchased in bulk in the
fall at the Farm Bureau Co-op. A pair of jeans and
a red wool sweater completed her outfit.

The family would say she was trying to be the
rebel, a thirty-four-year-old hippie. Some would
think that she didn't care enough about the family to dress properly. Some would think she was
on drugs. Even her own mother couldn't understand what she'd been up to recently.

A lance of pain struck at the base of Bernie's
brain. She began to count silently. Matt had
taught her to count while he massaged her neck

45

and talked the pain away. She rubbed with her own hand, pretending it was Matt's.

"One, two, three, four, five. . . . "

The toilet in the stall to her right flushed, and the flats and Buster Browns went out. Water ran in the sink, and the hot-air blower kicked in. Happy mother-daughter chatter ensued, then faded as they went outside. To Bernie's left, the pumps shifted position.

" . . . six, seven, eight, nine. This is just my guilt. Take my hesitation away." The headache flared; Bernie gritted her teeth.

The pot on the left flushed. The occupant left the stall. Bernie buried her face in her hands and rode the current of the headache. "Ten, eleven, twelve, thirteen."

It would be worse before it was better, it always was. She knew a doctor could give her something stronger than a neck massage or aspirin, but neither she nor anyone living at HeartLight had insurance. Insurance was a gamble. They did not have enough money to gamble. And so she relied on Matt, gentle, devout, beautiful Matt.

Ah, what a new life she tried to live. It still hung on her like clothes tailored not quite right, but she was working at drawing the seams up. The fabric was beautiful; she wanted it to fit. She needed it to fit.

Rubbing the bridge of her nose with her thumb, Bernie whispered through set teeth, "Get me through this without looking like a fool, without disgracing You."

God did not answer, or take the headache away, but Bernie felt stronger for the prayer. She went to wash her face and push her hair into place, then left the restroom for the banquet room.

Chapter Nine

The banquet room seethed with relatives. Voices of many ranges and volumes blended together and were stirred into a head-splitting cacophony that stopped Norris dead in his tracks at the open French doors.

God save me, he thought. It was all he could do to keep from turning on his heel and heading back out to his car. He stared at the pulsing crowd, at once recognizing everyone and no one. Faces of the Lynch family. Bodies of the collective Lynch body. Tall and handsome. Slightly upward tilted chins. And the many other relatives, some by marriage only, but all bearing the Lynch air of achievement.

A young teenage girl ran past Norris, bumping his shoulder and knocking him into the door frame. "Sorry," she giggled without looking back. A second later, another girl, about fourteen and already quite tall, ran after the first.

Norris clenched his teeth. He had something in his eye, and he pulled at his eyelid. Where the hell were the Gs? He was surprised there was no dais and no throne, so the family could lay their wants and needs out at the feet of the deities.

A lady with white curly hair and a chicken-wattled neck caught him by his arm as he strode into the room. "Norris!" It was Aunt Marla, Norris's father's oldest sister. "Honey, is that you? My goodness, but you look different. It's a beard, isn't it? It is so nice to see you." She leaned into Norris's face and gave him a dry little kiss on his beard. Her breath was heavy with stale cigarettes and something stronger than reunion punch. "Your daddy said you weren't coming, that you wouldn't return his call last week. When did you get in? My, but we've missed you."

"I just got here," said Norris. Aunt Marla's stale breath passed through his teeth, making him at once ill and in great need of a smoke.

"Hmmm," said Aunt Marla. She stepped back and smiled. Her chicken neck shimmied. "I haven't seen you in a few years. How long has it been?"

"Seven," said Norris.

"Seven years. My." Aunt Marla's eyes clouded over, and she puckered her lips. "Enough time to grow a beard, I suppose. Henford has changed in seven years, Norris. You wouldn't know. It's not the same. More welfare, Norris, and public housing. More non-Americans, more nonwhites, you know what I mean? It's not as nice here as it used to be."

Norris almost asked her for a cigarette, but that would have been too much bonding. "You seen the Grandparents?"

"Oh, they'll be here soon. The newspaper was at the house, taking photos. It's not often a prominent family has a sixty-fifth anniversary to celebrate. It'll be in the paper tomorrow."

So the Gs were really into the celebrating and the fanfare. They had always been used to that, of course. The couple were the founding parents of modern Henford, such as it was. Grandmother and Granddaddy Lynch, Lowell and Mildred Lynch to the world outside the family, had moved to Henford from Maryland after their honeymoon. There, they started the city's small daily newspaper, *The Henford Press*, and a large litter of children as well. The newspaper was a success. Lowell won Press Association awards, Mildred was named Virginia Mother of the Year several years, and each of the eight children grew to be some sort of upwardly mobile adult. Even Marla, unmarried at sixty-two and as close to the edge of loony as anyone in the family had ever teetered, had spun out a profitable life for herself as a public accountant.

All a fairy tale of the golden touch. Happy family growing, expanding, and moving out from the hometown, each member clean as a whistle and straight as a stick.

Funny how the farther out the stick stretches, the more it begins to bend.

"Did you know I retired some time ago?" Aunt Marla said. "Did anyone tell you? But I'm doing fine. I read at the library for story hour. I work twice a week with the little children. I don't mind that I never had my own."

Norris nodded. He knew Marla really didn't mind not having children. She was not the mothering kind. Back when Norris was seventeen, Marla had taken in a foster daughter. Everyone was surprised. Norris's father said Marla had wanted to adopt the girl so she could eventually give Mildred and Lowell more grandchildren and therefore stay in their good graces. But the foster daughter didn't work out. The girl was even more off kilter than Marla was. She wouldn't bathe and she never talked and she pissed her bed at night. After four months, Marla had sent the girl back.

Norris gave Aunt Marla a grin that made his jaw hurt, and moved through the crowd to the refreshment table. He looked back in time to see Aunt Marla confronted by a middle-aged skeleton of a man holding a boy by the hand. Cousin Terrance and his son Terrance, Junior. *Tear-ass and little Tear-ass*, thought Norris.

Norris turned his back to the open room and took a few carrot sticks from the white-clothed table. There were two punch bowls, one for the adults, dubbed by a much younger Norris as the Big Bowl, and one for the children, the Baby Bowl. Norris remembered how when he was a child the Big Bowl had been a point of fascination. He and his favorite cousins, Bernie Lynch and Lindsay Warner, had covered each other at family gatherings as each took turns dipping their paper cups into the Big Bowl. Once, when Norris and Lindsay were thirteen and Bernie was eleven, and dipping from the Big Bowl had become a holiday tradition, Tear-ass, a born-again cousin all of a year older, had spied their crime and reported them to the Gs. Happily, though, the Gs had been busy talking local politics with the Henford mayor, and the serious-ness of the crime had been wasted on them. Tear-ass, indignant that his discovery had gone without punishment, told Norris and Bernie and Lindsay that no matter what, God knew what they had done. Norris had told Tear-ass to take a long leap off a short cliff, a strong state-ment for the times. Bernie had applauded. Lindsay had given Norris a warm hug. It had felt wonderful.

A little girl in a red bow came up to the table beside Norris. She had her fingertips on the table top, and moved along the side with little slide steps. Her eyes were closed, as if she was playing a game. An older girl stood behind her, watching every move. Norris picked up a piece of celery and studied the children. More future doctors and journalists and Mothers of the Year.

"There's cake on a plate there," the older girl said to the younger one. The younger one kept sliding along the table, coming closer to Norris. "Don't you want cake?"

The little girl with closed eyes said, "What else?"

"All sorts of stuff," said the older girl. "Hold still, will you? You're going to run into somebody."

Norris picked up a napkin from the table and wiped his mouth. He watched the girls from the corner of his eye. He wished they'd go. He didn't like children.

"Come on," said the older girl, and she was clearly looking at Norris now. "Just let me get you some cake." The smaller girl tugged away from the bigger girl's grasp and took several side steps. She thumped into Norris's hip.

Norris looked down at her. She did not look up at him. Untrained brat. Where in hell were her parents?

"Say 'sorry,' " said the older girl.

The little girl stuck her tongue out and grinned with cake-coated teeth. She shook her head in a prissy sort of way and the red bow bounced. "Sorr-eeeeee," she said.

"Oh, my God, Norris!" The voice was grown up, female. When Norris looked out over the heads of the two girls, he saw the wide eyes of a smiling blond woman. She was coming toward him, her expression open and surprised. She was taller than Norris, definitely the proud recipient of the Lynch height blueprint. Short blond hair was curled about her face. She lifted her arms to Norris. The older girl pulled the little one away to

51

let her through. "How long have you been here? I had no idea you were coming!"

Norris was caught in Lindsay's embrace, and his face was crushed against the shoulder of her pleasantly scented dress. He almost smiled with the peace the sensation stirred.

Lindsay backed away and smiled, still holding Norris's elbows. Norris was struck by the threads of white in the blond hair, and the faint lines between her eyebrows. "Kids," Lindsay said. "This is your cousin Norris. He's my cousin, too. I don't think you've met him. He's been gone a long time. Norris, these are my kids, Mandy and Grace."

The older girl said, "Hi." The smaller girl, who did not open her eyes, said, "Gone where?"

"Gone away, Grace," said Lindsay. Her eyebrows twitched in apology. She said, "You've got a beard."

Norris shrugged. Then Lindsay said, "Girls, go find your dad. Norris and I need a grown-up talk."

"But, Mom, I helped Grace get her snack," said the older girl. "I didn't get any yet."

"Grab a handful and go," said Lindsay. The girl grunted and obeyed, taking her sister's hand and leaving. Lindsay rolled her eyes at Norris, and patted his shoulder.

"It's great to see you," said Norris. He found it hard to look at Lindsay after her unconditional welcome. She should have been chastising him, rebuking him. Asking him why the fuck he left Henford in the first place. "Why'd you send the kids away?" he said. "Think I'll infect them? I don't have any bizarre diseases."

Lindsay punched Norris on the arm. "You shithead, I don't like to cuss in front of my children, damn it. And it's hard to use proper adjectives when you're around."

Norris put his hands into his jacket pockets. "So I'm a goddamn bad influence, am I?"

"Yeah," said Lindsay. "A fucking shitass bad influence. Ain't it great? We's mature, that's for sure." Then she said, "Have you seen your dad?"

Norris rubbed his beard and took another carrot stick. He did not put it into his mouth. "No, not yet. Kind of hard to come back like a prodigal son when not only have I been gone seven years but I never came to help my dad when he went through a semi-serious breakdown over my mother running off. He called a lot. I ignored it."

Lindsay's smile faltered. "Yeah, not the best move. Or should I say lack of move. You're only a couple hours away. Seven years, Norris. God. You want to tell me?"

"Long tale," said Norris. "Long time and a long tale. Here's not the place." Norris felt a wave of light-headedness coming on. He needed a small sample of Teddy's white stuff, or at least a strong cigarette. He wondered who would be the first to kick him out if he lighted up. "Maybe we can talk a little later."

Lindsay hesitated, then said, "Sure."

A man in his late thirties approached Lindsay and Norris. He held the hands of Lindsay's two girls. Yes, thought Norris. *Here's the husband. Frank. Something like that. If I remember correctly, we don't like each other.*

"Hank," said Lindsay. "Do you remember Norris?"

"Norris," said Hank. He let go of one child to shake Norris's hand. "Of course. Mountain man

53

now, huh?" Hank stroked his chin, indicating Norris's beard. "Your father was just talking about you. Said you weren't coming."

Norris had remembered correctly. He hated Hank.

"I suppose he had no way of knowing otherwise," said Hank. "You aren't much of a writer, he says."

Norris gritted his teeth. Take the crap to get the money. "I suppose not," he said. He put the carrot stick into his mouth and began to chew.

"What are you doing now, down in Norfolk?" Hank asked.

Norris swallowed. A small chunk caught halfway down and made his throat muscles spasm. He wanted to say, "Well, let me fill you in, Hank my smart-mouthed friend. The first year I was a gas attendant, the second and third years I was a janitor at a beach motel, with a few months at the wheel of a taxi and cooking up burgers. The fourth year I lived off my lover Jared, who left to teach para-sailing in Bermuda, then I borrowed some money and took several education classes at Old Dominion University to update my degree while at night I put myself in danger of mutilation or death behind the counter at a gas station." He said, "I'm a history teacher."

"Oh? Where?"

"Bright Creek Institute."

"Isn't that a detention home?"

Asshole.

The younger girl waved one hand around in the air. When she found her father, she said, "Batroom, Daddy."

Hank looked at Lindsay. "You want to take her?"

"Mandy can do that. Mandy, will you take Grace to the ladies' room?"

The older girl stamped her foot and scowled. "That's not fair, Mom. I've watched her ever since we got here."

Hank said, "You go on and play with your cousins, Mandy. I'll take Grace to the men's room."

"All right," said Lindsay. Mandy ran off in one direction. Hank and the little girl went off in the other.

Lindsay smiled and shrugged. "It's not like Grace is going to see anything she shouldn't."

Blind, yes, that's where I've heard of Grace before, thought Norris. *That's the blind child. They sent me a card when she was born. The child with no eyes.* He coughed, and the carrot piece shot up to his tongue. He swallowed it back down. *Retarded, and no eyes. Christ.*

"Kids," Lindsay said. She threaded her arm through his and put her head on his shoulder. "You'll never know how nuts it can be 'til you get into it."

"I'll never get into it," Norris said.

"Don't say that."

"I do say it. There is no way I'll ever have kids." In a way, he hoped at that minute Lindsay would understand, that she would nod and say, "I see, Norris. Is that why you left? The Lynch family couldn't take the surprise?" But he could tell by her silent smile that she was clueless.

Norris took a carrot and put the hateful thing into his mouth. He hated to play the game with Lindsay, but she was a Lynch as much as the others. He said, "So tell me how things are going with you, cousin."

55

Lindsay laughed and began to unravel the finer details about the past seven years in Henford. Norris chewed his fingernails and random carrots in lieu of a smoke and bore the stories out, as well as the stares and brief comments by all the family members who paid a visit to the snack display and began to realize who he was, and who walked away pursing their lips.

Chapter Ten

It was a good day.

Rex stood in a small clearing on his land. His land. Not yet official, but almost. Rex's Uncle Arlen was taking care of that. Around Rex, sleet fell like heavenly crystals, strumming the leaves of the scrubby cedars and pattering the blades of the dead Queen Anne's lace and poison ivy vines. Beyond the clearing, to all sides, trees were glazed with ice, looking like arms, frosty and eager, ready to welcome Rex and the White Eagles.

He had driven south out of Henford an hour earlier, heading into the foothills of the mountains to the pot-holed gravel road and the single chain barrier that separated his land from the privately owned, adjoining campsites. Once off the main road, he'd passed no one at all, in vehicle or on foot. The large camps adjoining Rex's land were deserted, as most camps were in very early spring, and their owners lived elsewhere, in Richmond and Orange. Arlen had told Rex that privacy would be no problem at all.

"This is Night Land," Rex said, his voice hanging on the air in clouds. "My Night Land. All two hundred acres of it."

Rex had been out several times with Percy and Dean, cleaning brush and cutting trees and making room for the proposed buildings. When Arlen gave him the word, then the place would be nearly ready for the White Eagles to move.

Rex stretched his head back and licked the air, tasting the sleet. His sleet. Falling on the dead grasses and the bony trees of Night Land.

Suddenly, this good day seemed too good not to share. Rex went to the back of his car and popped open the trunk.

"Hey, Billy, this is going to be your new home."

In the trunk, Bill Bailey was trussed and bound with yellow nylon ropes and pieces of yellowed bedsheets. His eyes were covered with a single strip of duct tape. Rex, in a moment of sympathy for this alien, had dropped a wool blanket over the man's naked body.

"Exciting, isn't it?" Rex asked. But a gag of bedsheet prevented Bill from answering. "Sorry I can't take off the blindfold. But let me tell you, it's beautiful. Plenty of room. Lots of trees."

Bill groaned. Rex took it for an affirmation.

"We start here," Rex went on. "We train, we learn. We become strong in what is true. We'll build our arsenal and draw in many followers. This is Night Land, where warriors plan and get ready for battle. See that film *Independence Day*? That alien battle's gonna seem like a fucking picnic next to the real battle."

Bill Bailey coughed again. Around the gag Rex could see his tongue clearly, for the first time since chaining him in the Night Room. It was swollen and dry. It was almost black, like the tongue of a chow dog Arlen once had.

"Best get you back," Rex said. "I don't think you've had water since yesterday. But I'll fix you a lunch. We'll see what's in that old house. Something yummy to eat and cold to drink." He slammed the trunk shut.

By the driver's door, he stopped. "Oh, Billy, sorry. Lunch is going to have to wait. I've got some errands to do in town first. Hope you don't mind staying in there a couple more hours."

It sounded as though Bill did a little flip inside the trunk.

Before he climbed into his car, Rex took a blade of icy, dead grass and ran it through his mouth. It tasted like freedom. He chewed it up and swallowed it down, then grinned a happy man's grin.

Chapter Eleven

The woman stood at the curb. In her chest was a tiny electric core, painful and thrilling, a sensation that at once reminded her of the love of the White Eagles and the time she had nearly choked on a Burger King chicken tender. The cold rain had stopped, but the sky hung over her head like a gray sponge.

She shivered with the cold. Her finger punched the walk light button again, and as cars whipped past, she puckered her mouth. A new crack pulled free on her dried lips, bringing out a leak of blood. "Oh pooh," she said to the light button.

She jabbed it again, and finally, on the wire above the road, the green light turned to yellow and then red. Cars halted. The woman hurried across the street as fast as she could with the irregular twisting motion of her bad leg. The torn hem of her dress flapped.

On the other side of the street, she paused in front of the Hallmark store to look at the display of stuffed animals in the window. There were bunnies and a few yellow ducks, all ready for Easter shopping. When she was nine, she had been given a huge white bunny for an Easter gift from one of her foster mothers. Not a stuffed bunny, but a real bunny with pink eyes and twitching little nose. It had been soft and sweet, and all she wanted to do was pet it. She hadn't wanted to go to school or to the talking-doctor place, she had just wanted to pet the bunny. But that was a long time ago. She was now almost thirty-three. She put her hand up to the window glass and traced the outline of a bunny with her thumb. It made a greasy tracing, and when she blew on it, it showed up more clearly, like a frosty etching.

A gust of wind turned her around, and she moved up the street toward the west end of Henford. The knee-highs which had been chafing all morning began to sting like wire cuts below her knees. She stopped to roll them down. Her private parts were still chafed from the sex she had given to the man named Junior. When she began to walk again, she felt down and tugged at her underwear.

The past weeks with the White Eagles had taught the woman lessons she would never forget. How to be quiet when Rex spoke. How to chant and how to hate nigger aliens and Jew aliens and Gook aliens and queer aliens. How not to cry when Junior stuck his thing up her butt. But there was one lesson, one Major Lesson which encompassed all the other smaller lessons and made everything she endured with the White Eagles not only tolerable but welcomed. And that lesson was that she was wanted. She was needed. Her body ached with this amazing truth.

Last night, Rex had told the Eagles that he might have business to take care of on the weekend. Nobody could stay over. There would be no Saturday night meeting. This left the woman on her own to keep busy. Before she had discovered the White Eagles, she had worked on weekdays and slept on weekends. Sometimes, if she felt up to it, she would do a little cleaning on Friday nights after watching *Millennium*. Sometimes on a nice Sunday she would go to the park and throw moldy bread to the mallards. All her time except that at work had been time alone.

But now, time alone was not good time. Being in her apartment drove her to pacing. She bided her time at work until she could go to Rex's house again. Bruises from Rex's fist and random slash marks from Lizzie's nail file were more than acceptable, they were beautiful.

On her way home from work last night she had bought a copy of *The Henford Press*. She saw the notice in the paper. Her heart had leapt, and then had become afraid. But this morning she had felt brave. And so she had bought herself the dress, and stolen the knee-highs from the pharmacy. A new woman, ready for new adventures.

The core beneath her ribs pulsed suddenly, once. The woman put her hand to her chest and felt it. It was fluid and hot. It was bravery. It was need.

A few spatters of icy rain fell to the sidewalk around her feet. She looked up at the solid gray cloud cover. A drop fell onto her eyes, then several drops, then more. The electricity in her chest shifted, pushing her on. She lifted the hem of her dress up to her knees and tried to run. There was nearly a half mile to go, and it would be nice to get there before her dress was ruined or the water made her shiny black sandals fall apart.

Chapter Twelve

As the family was instructed to find their places at the place-tagged tables around the room, and as Lowell Francis Lynch and Mildred Lynch made their grand and wobbly entrances into the room, Lindsay was poked in the shoulder. She looked behind her. It was Bernie.

"Hey, lady!" Lindsay gave Bernie a quick hug. "Thought you weren't coming."

Bernie grinned. "Oh, sure," she said softly. "I live all of thirty minutes away and I'm going to dare not come?"

Lindsay then noticed her cousin's outfit. It was a strange selection for a major family reunion. Jeans, black sneakers, sweater. Bernie's long hair was loose and unadorned. The younger cousin wore not a spot of makeup. Lindsay almost asked Bernie about it, but she held back. G-Mom was giving a speech, and it was a cardinal sin to interrupt.

Quickly and quietly, Lindsay rearranged the

name cards so Bernie and Norris would be sitting near her. Terrance gave her a correctional glance but he didn't say anything. After all, G-Mom was talking. Norris waved silently at Bernie. Bernie waved back and gave him a wink.

The family applauded mildly at something Mildred said. Then Bernie whispered, "I would have been in here earlier but I got caught in the lobby. Terrance Junior must have been on his way to the john, or back out again. He nabbed me by the water fountain. He had to give me the latest on the wages of sin."

"Oh," said Norris.

Lindsay said, "I hope you told him to take a hike."

"I probably handled it better than I used to."

"What's that mean?" asked Norris.

Bernie said, "I wasn't as cruel as we used to be."

"You're kidding," said Lindsay. But Bernie just smiled.

Then there was more applause, louder than before, and G-Mom and G-Dad were escorted to their seats at the head table. At last, everyone had permission to sit.

"I fixed us," Lindsay said. "Got us together. Grace needs to be by me on one side, but I have you, Norris, next to me and Bernie across from you."

Two teenage nieces, Jennifer and Molly, sat on either side of Bernie. They looked at Bernie's clothes and mouthed something behind her back. Lindsay wondered if Bernie noticed, or cared.

Norris sat down beside Lindsay, looking agitated. He glanced about, then played with his fork. Lindsay whispered, "Your father's going to see you sooner or later. You know he knows you're here by now."

Norris took a drink of water. "I just need to talk to the Gs, not to my father."

Bernie raised an eyebrow. "Whoa, Norris, that's a new one. I can't remember any of the three of us actually requesting an audience with the royalty."

"No kidding," said Lindsay. "So what's up?"

Norris shrugged and wiped his mouth with his napkin even though he hadn't eaten anything yet. Bernie reached across the table and thwacked Norris with her teaspoon.

"Lighten up," she said with a grin.

Norris looked at Bernie, then opened his mouth and let out a long, muffled burp. Startled relatives within hearing distance glanced over with expressions of distaste. "I'm a lot lighter now," Norris said.

Bernie stifled laughter. "We's mature, that's for sure!"

The salads were brought in by stern-faced waiters in white tuxedos. The family talk subsided slightly in the midst of the feeding. Lindsay sighed when Grace's salad plate was put before her.

"Whatzit?" said Grace.

"Nothing you like. Lettuce with oranges and dressing. I'll wash the oranges off for you in my water glass."

Lindsay dipped Grace's mandarin oranges into her water glass. Out of the corner of her eye she could see Norris, the fingers of his right hand playing a distracted syncopation on the table-cloth. In her peripheral vision above her brows, she saw Bernie, dressed in farmhand clothes,

63

picking at her own salad. No matter that they had once again sabotaged Aunt Sarah's master seating plan or that they still called the Gs "the Gs" and still shared a need for self-preservation around Holier-Than-Everyone Terrance and Cancer-Breath Aunt Marla, there was something awkward here. Something she had not imagined happening between the three of them. Granted, she had not seen Norris since Mandy was born. Granted, the last time she had spoken with Bernie had been on the phone in August, when Bernie said she was moving from her apartment in Henford to live with some friends in the west end of the county. But, as G-Mom could still command silence of the family with a single glance, and as Uncle Leonard and Uncle Bennett would forever continue the battle of the bulge, Lindsay always thought that the three Mature-For-Sure cousins would retain their comfortable core of single-minded, secret rebellion.

We've all changed, at long last, she thought. *Sad*.

But then Bernie sat straight up and made a face as if someone had stuck her. She asked, "Is Lena coming?"

And the mention of that name made Lindsay's blood go instantly cold.

Chapter Thirteen

The sleet turned into a heavy, freezing downpour that made the woman's sandals skate on the sidewalk and her stapled-hem dress cling to her legs like a scared dog. She was only a block and a half away now, but this was the hardest part in the sleet. The walk was now up, traveling along Main Street to the top of Church Hill. Her head was tucked down, and her chin funneled water into her bra. Her arms were wrapped about herself, holding in a small amount of body heat. She did not have a watch, but she knew she was a little late. The clock at the bank on the corner of Main and Scott Street read one-thirty-seven.

The notice in *The Henford Press* had said that the gathering began at twelve o'clock, with lunch at one-thirty. They would just begin eating by now. She wondered what kind of food they were serving. She shivered, and it wasn't the cold.

A lopsided smile crossed her down-turned face. The electricity in her abdomen turned over and doubled itself again, growing and filling her belly and her throat at once. The hairs on her neck caught the surge, and stood on end like maddened ants. Heat and cold battled it out, and her heart, in the center of it, skipped several beats.

Suddenly her feet scrambled on the ice. One foot twisted and flipped, causing her toenails to scrape the pavement. She grunted, and her hands freed themselves from their embrace long enough to shoot out for stability. Once steady, she drew her arms in again and slowed down a little. She thought her big toenail on the twisted foot might have split. A little shard of pain winked with each step. Heat and cold and pain. Internals, externals, and she felt them all, and it made her feel she might blow up.

A bubble of snot burst beneath her nose and she sucked it into her mouth.

"Oh, pooh."

And then the Henford Hotel came into view on the other side of Lyon's Funeral Home.

Chapter Fourteen

Bernie said, "Lena. Do you remember?"

"No," said Norris. *Lena?* The name made him feel odd suddenly.

"Aunt Marla's temporary kid. Her foster child. Do you two remember how Lena wouldn't eat at the reunion? She wouldn't eat in front of people."

Lindsay dipped another orange and gave it to her blind daughter. "Yeah, I remember. She wouldn't eat anything on her plate. But then she sneaked bread out of the basket and ate it in the bathroom. Aunt Marla had a fit, trying to explain Lena's behavior to the rest of the family.

"It was pretty sad," said Bernie.

It was pretty fucked up, thought Norris.

"Is she coming?" Bernie asked again.

Lindsay shrugged. "I don't know. I don't think so."

"I hope not," said Norris. He turned to Bernie. "Why?"

"I felt something," said Bernie. "I felt her presence." Jennifer, who had been talking to nephew Randy on her other side, caught this comment, and her eyes rolled even more dramatically than before. *Man*, Norris thought. *Bernie's gone off the deep end. It's easy to do in this family, just look at how well I've done with my life, but not Bernie.*

Lindsay was clearly uncomfortable with the comment too, and she tried to change the subject. "Hey, Bernie," she said. "You'll have to give me directions to your place. I'd like to come visit. Your mom told me you had horses. Mandy and

66

Grace love horses. How long have you been out in the country now? Since . . . ?"

"August," Bernie answered. But she was watching the door, her eyes intent.

"And what kind of place is it?" Lindsay pressed.

Bernie said, "A place where we all love each other. I remember Lena from the reunion photo. She had the expression of a dead fish."

"She smelled like a dead fish," said Norris.

"Poor old Aunt Marla," said Bernie. "She tried her best to make Lena a Lynch. She put her in nice clothes, and I know she must have made her bathe every day. But you're right, she did smell."

Lindsay handed Grace her napkin and told her to wipe her mouth. The little girl said, "Can go play?"

"No, not yet, honey. Dinner's not over yet. Now sit still."

Norris looked away from the blind girl. Thinking that there were no eyes behind the closed lids made his skin crawl.

"Where are you staying, Norris?" asked Lindsay.

"The 350 Motel outside of town."

"Free X-rated movies," said Lindsay. "Good choice."

"Only $21.99 a night. Good choice," said Norris.

"Nobody's staying with us," said Lindsay. "We lucked out. We have an extra sofa bed if you'd rather."

"Thanks but no thanks," said Norris.

And then Bernie gasped, loudly.

Norris looked at her. Jennifer and Molly grimaced.

Bernie's eyes were wide; her mouth opened soundlessly. One hand went up to her lips. Norris noticed the plain, unpolished nails. Bernie used to care about the little details. God, everything had changed.

"I think . . . " Bernie whispered.

Norris glanced over his shoulder. He saw another full table of relatives, the buzzing waitresses, chairs along the wall, potted plants, the door to the hallway. He looked back at Bernie.

"Oh, my God," said Bernie. She stood up, her properly placed napkin dropping down from her lap to her thighs, sticking to the rough material of her jeans and hanging there. "I saw her. Peeking through the door at us."

Lindsay frowned. "Who?"

Bernie left her chair and moved away quickly. Norris involuntarily stood up and watched after her. Lindsay did the same. Family members nearby gazed up with mild interest, then continued to eat.

"Is she sick?" Norris said to Lindsay.

"Maybe," she said. "Grace, stay put." Then she pushed past him.

Grace reached over and patted the seat of her mother's vacant chair. "Mom?" she said.

"Christ," said Norris to himself. "She'll be right back," he told the little girl. "Don't go anywhere or do anything, okay?" He followed Lindsay.

The three cousins beelined for the exit. In the rear, Norris still clutched his dinner napkin. At the end of the last table, he glanced to the side and saw his father.

Norris stopped. The older man slowly put his spoon down and gave his son a long, wordless appraisal. The man had aged beyond what Norris would have imagined. His hair had thinned, as had his face. Between a booster-chaired niece and a college-aged nephew, Michael Lynch was old. A worn man.

"Dad," said Norris.

"Norris," said his father.

Norris tipped his head in an apologetic parting shot, then went after Lindsay and Bernie. His heart twisted like the napkin in his hands. His father looked bad. His father looked betrayed.

Screw it, Norris thought. *He brought it on himself. He never liked Mom as she was. No way in hell he'd want me as I am.* As he went through the door into the hallway, Norris crammed the napkin into a standing brass ashcan.

Chapter Fifteen

Someone called the woman's name, and she looked up from the water fountain in the hotel's lobby. A drop of fountain water caught on her jaw and rolled to her chin. She had looked into the banquet room a moment ago, then come back to get water to calm herself. With the sound of her name, the hot core inside had flared. She almost cried out.

The voice came again. "Lena?"

Lena straightened. There were a lot of people in the large room with her, people pushing elevator buttons, people on the sofas and high-backed chairs near the tall, elegant windows. No one seemed aware of her presence. She did not know who was speaking, or if, indeed, anyone had. One side of her face hitched with a hot spasm.

Then there was someone coming close to her, looking at her. Lena stared back. It was a woman with long, dark hair and a pretty, bright sweater. Seeing the face and the red sweater made Lena shudder violently.

The dark-haired woman stopped. It seemed as though she recognized Lena. One of her hands was extended. Behind the woman came another woman and a man. The second woman, tall and blond, came up on the dark-haired woman's right. The man, short and bearded and frowning, moved between the two women. The second woman and the man said nothing. But the woman in the sweater smiled and said, "Is that you, Lena?"

Lena suddenly felt a surge in her legs. It raced down into her feet, her toes. It was all she could do to keep standing. She felt herself nod.

"I know you," said the woman in the red sweater. "You stayed with my Aunt Marla a long time ago. I'm Bernadine Lynch."

Lena trembled with the voltage in her body. She could not remember this woman. And those beside her, their faces drawn and unhappy. Lena did not know these, either. Where were the teenagers she had watched when she had lived with Miss Lynch? Images spun in her mind, memories of her short time with the Lynch family. Well-dressed adults, running children, white tablecloths, bread in baskets, perfumes, a bathtub on feet, cigarette smoke. Lena's body shook. The electricity gripped her shoulders and held her up.

The blond woman said, "Lena. Wow." She wasn't smiling.

"I knew she was coming," said Bernadine. Her hand was still offered in Lena's direction. "Isn't this something?" And then to Lena she said, "I knew you were coming. You're here for the reunion, aren't you?"

Lena pulled her hands to her chest. The surge raced from her arms into her fingertips. Soon she would be filled. But the white heat was not anticipation anymore.

She remembered the teenagers now. They had hated her, they had laughed at her and said she stunk. She remembered them all now. The short boy, the blond girl, and the dark-haired girl. How had she forgotten? They said she stunk.

The excitement was gone. Replacing it was confusion, terror. She did not want this sensation anymore. It was not good. She was helpless with its power. Anxiety swelled up through her tonsils. It grew unheeded. It hissed, a live cable ready to fire bright sparks into the air. "Lynches," she managed.

Bernadine smiled. Lena could not comprehend the smile. She saw eyes studying her. Eyes that did not want her or need her. Lena threw her hands up over her own eyes so she could not see them anymore.

She'd needed to be with them, but they didn't need her.

Oh, no, not at all.

The electricity coiled and slammed upward into her brain, exploding.

She was filled with the dreadful power. Need was, at that moment, its own complete entity.

Lena screamed.

Bernadine reached out.

Chapter Sixteen

Bernie reached out her hand to catch Lena, who at that moment seemed to be having a seizure. Bernie was horrified. *God help this woman*, she thought. She opened her mouth to offer a word of comfort, but then her hand closed around Lena's upper arm, and the word was instantly burned away.

She had never touched a live electrical wire, but she was doing it now. A human electrical wire, covered in skin and clothed in a sad prom dress and atrocious black sandals. Bernie went rigid. A sword of current cut through her hand and arm, singeing veins and muscle, coiling and bending and following a line to her very center. Bernie was jerked backward; she tried to scream. But her horror could not find a voice. It was fried in the wake of the sword. And then the current shifted. In a second, it burst out through her back like an alien hatching in a sickening scene from a science fiction movie.

Chapter Seventeen

The moment Lena screamed and Bernie reached out to comfort her, Lindsay did the same. It was instinctive. Children cry, you offer them help, although the vision of a grown woman in Halloween garb crying out made her wince even as she moved forward to help. Lindsay put her fingertips to the back of Lena's hand, which was pressed pathetically to her face. Lindsay began to say, "Don't be afraid, it's all right." But she didn't have the chance.

Chapter Eighteen

Norris was terrified at the sound of the woman's scream. It was primal and ugly. He saw both Bernie and Lindsay reaching out, and he leaned in as well, not to stop the woman but to stop his cousins. They didn't know what she might do. She might strike out, slashing or biting. With an outfit like that, she might have a snake up her sleeve. The whole scene was pathetic and dangerous. Norris's wrists touched both Bernie's and Lindsay's backs, and he had intended to reach up for their shoulders to pull them back out of danger's way.

But his left wrist was suddenly fused to the back of Bernie's sweater. A lava-hot charge seared from her spine into him. It shot through the length of his arm and spun into his lungs. He could not breathe. His eyes bulged and his knees buckled. The heat found its erratic pathway, slicing up beneath his right armpit, racing down into the nerves of his pelvis. The hairs of his groin sizzled. The charge sped up through the muscles of his diaphragm and cut an excruciating straightaway into his right arm. With a body-shattering burst, it bore out through the base of his wrist. The moment it was gone, he felt Lindsay stiffen.

Chapter Nineteen

Lindsay thought she'd been hit in the back with a red-hot spike. She knew she was going to split open and die there in the lobby of the Henford Hotel. Her eyes snapped open and closed. Then the pain drove forward. Lindsay's chest was constricted by wires of excruciating heat. Her stomach reeled and bubbled. The vision of Lena before her seemed to crackle in electrical colors. Lindsay knew that the sight of the glowing Lena was to be her last sight on earth. She was going to suffocate in the deadly light.

Then in an instant the surge unwrapped her lungs and charged through her arm and out the fingers that were touching Lena's hand. Lindsay's throat squeezed in relief. A terrified whine escaped.

Lena shrieked and folded over. Her blue acetate scarf was knocked off, and the front of her rain-soaked gown was ripped at the waist. Her feet went out from under her, slipping on the rough Persian runner. She hit the floor and lay still, with her hand still hooked to her cheek. Spit pooled from her mouth.

"Dear God," Bernie whispered.

Lindsay stared at the woman heaped on the floor. She was afraid to look at her fingers.

"Norris, Lindsay," said Bernie. "Are you two okay?"

Lindsay slowly put her hands into her skirt pockets. Norris crossed his arms and massaged his elbows.

"Norris?" Bernie said.

"What?" demanded Norris, and in his voice Lindsay heard a plea to let whatever had just happened drop.

"Call an ambulance, Lindsay," Bernie said. She stooped down and said, "Lena, can you hear me?"

Lindsay noticed that Bernie, this time, did not try to touch the woman.

Chapter Twenty

They sat together at Stan's Snack Shop, staring at their hands, the floor, the framed and faded watercolors on the walls. It hadn't been hard for Bernie to convince Norris and Lindsay to skip the evening cocktail party at the Gs' estate, but she knew getting them to talk about what had happened in the lobby with Lena would be another matter.

It was not yet five o'clock. They were scrunched around one of Stan's white round tables. Bernie had gone to the counter to order for all of them. Neither Lindsay nor Norris had been able to decide what they wanted. Conversation between the cousins over the past few hours had been limited.

Moments after Lena's collapse, a crowd from the lobby had gathered. Relatives were alerted, and poured from the banquet room. They hovered, questioning and consoling. Bernie, Lindsay, and Norris were escorted with much sympathetic "tsking" back to their table. Lunch was resumed. Lena's seizure did not remain a topic of conversation at the reunion tables; it was distasteful and inappropriate. Relatives near the cousins began asking inane questions in an attempt to soothe what they believed needed soothing. Laughter around the cousins was artificially loud and frequent. The cousins ate, for the most part, without conversation. Lindsay seemed more than happy to be occupied with helping her blind daughter with her meal. And Norris, who had been sullen the entire reunion, remained sullen.

But Bernie needed to talk. Her heart beat double time at what had happened just a few hours before. They had ridden a train through the dark edge of the supernatural.

At the counter, Bernie asked Stan for two dogs all the way, and a third without onions, having no idea as to what her cousins wanted. She added three large Pepsis to the order. Bernie took straws and the three drinks, one balanced between the pinkies and ring fingers of both hands, out to the little white table.

"Thanks," Lindsay said. She took her cup and pulled the paper from the straw. She crammed the straw into the icy mush and swirled it around.

Norris said nothing, but stared at the paper cup before him. A bent cigarette poked from the side of his mouth. He breathed in and out around it.

Bernie peeled the tip from her straw paper and aimed at Norris's forehead. She blew. The straw paper broke open at the end and made a soft, whispering whistle.

"Don't make straw papers like they used to," Bernie said. She tried to laugh.

Norris said, "Guess not."

Lindsay drew on her straw, swallowed, then sat back and frowned. "This isn't diet, is it?"

"No," said Bernie.

"I'm sorry. I should have said something. I

don't like non-diet drinks." Her mouth puffed at the edges.

"I can get you another drink," said Bernie.

"Nah, it's okay. I'll sip it slowly."

Nobody said anything else until Stan, all smiles in his grease-painted apron, brought the three hot dogs out on a brown plastic tray. "Here you go," he said. "All the way, one no onions." He put the tray on the table. Norris had to move his elbows. An ash fell to the white table top. "Enjoy your food, now. We have a nice dessert menu. Sundaes and cakes."

"Thanks," said Bernie.

Stan went back behind the counter. Norris scowled. "These hot dogs look like shit. Look at this chili, my old dog barfed up better looking stuff than this."

Bernie felt her jaws clench. She said, "I can't imagine what the family photos are going to look like. Could you all smile? I tried, honestly, but I couldn't."

"Why should I smile and ruin a perfectly fucked-up day?" asked Norris. He plucked his cigarette from his mouth, balanced it on the edge of his plate, and took a bite of his hot dog. The taste of the food didn't seem to register. Norris chewed methodically, staring at the napkin in which the dog was wrapped.

Guess shit doesn't taste that bad, after all, Bernie thought.

"I'm sure the photos will be fine," said Lindsay. Bernie caught the tone in Lindsay's voice. It said, *Don't bother me.*

Bernie leaned on her elbows. She said, "I hope Lena's going to be all right."

Lindsay put her cup down. Norris stopped chewing.

Norris said, "How can you care? She shouldn't have even come."

"But," said Bernie, "she was there. She came, she missed us, something. And what happened to us? It wasn't just Lena. Something got us, too."

Lindsay's eyes flickered back and forth between Norris and Bernie. They were tight eyes. *Didn't you catch my meaning? Don't bother me.*

But Bernie pressed, "Didn't something happen to you guys?"

"What do you mean?" asked Norris. There was a spot of ketchup on his beard.

"I touched Lena," said Bernie. "And I was burned."

Norris chuckled then, and tiny fragments of onion sprayed the air. "What the hell are you talking about?"

Bernie held up her left hand and opened it slowly over the table. On the palm of the hand, traveling along the life line for a half inch, was a red, blistered streak. "A burn," she said.

"Cigarette burn," said Norris.

"No."

"Does it hurt?" asked Lindsay.

Bernie nodded. "It throbs some."

Norris picked his cigarette back up. He didn't put it in his mouth. "I burn myself all the time."

Bernie felt her face flush. She wanted to slap Norris. She clenched her will. She said, "My back is sore, too. I've been afraid to look. Will you?"

Without waiting for a reply, Bernie turned in her chair and hoisted up the back of her red sweater.

Stan, at the counter, stopped wiping the soda fountain and cocked his head.

"Well?" she asked.

Lindsay touched Bernie's back. The sore spot, in the center of her spine, crackled, the pain increasing with the pressure. "Well?"

"You've got a spot on your back, too," said Lindsay. "A little bigger than the place on your hand."

Bernie lowered her sweater. She faced her cousins. "Tell me you have no burns. Tell me I'm the only one."

Lindsay picked her paper cup up in her left hand. But she did not drink. She merely rolled the straw about in her teeth. Then she turned her right hand up on the table. On four fingertips were blisters, tiny but distinct.

"I didn't see those at lunch," said Bernie.

"Were you looking?"

"Yes."

"I didn't want anyone to see."

"Why?"

"Why? What a stupid question. This scares the hell out of me. It doesn't make sense." She paused, catching her breath, taking a sip of the drink she hated. "No sense."

"I know."

"I think my back is burned, too."

"Christ save us, will you?" Norris stood suddenly, knocking his chair askew. The cigarette was back between his lips. The chair rattled back and forth as if it was going to go over with Norris's overcoat, but then settled back on its rubber-stopped feet. "I need another drink." He shouted to Stan. "I need another drink, and not some goddamned soda. Don't you have beer?"

"No," said Stan. His smile was gone.

"Sit down, Norris, we'll get you beer as soon as we leave." Bernie reached out for his arm, but he jerked away. "Damn it, sit down!"

Norris sat. He looked as if he was going to either hit her or cuss her out. He did neither. He said, "Screw it all anyway. There's some sort of explanation for this." He shook his head, looked at the ceiling for a moment as if awaiting a deus ex machina escape, then held up his hands. Bernie could see no marks. But then Norris unbuttoned the cuffs to his shirt. "I think I touched you both with the heels of my hands. Here. Above the heel. On the wrists." He rolled one sleeve up an inch. A small, red, bubbling spot was visible. "Something up my sleeve. Presto."

"And the other one?" pressed Bernie.

Norris rolled up the second sleeve. A nearly identical mark scarred the heel at the base of the wrist. "Hurts." He waited, as if counting to ten, then clawed the cuffs down again and buttoned them. "Happy?"

Bernie lunged forward, collecting a handful of shirt-front and pulling her face close to Norris's. The spot in her hand throbbed. "Stop acting like an ass or go back to the beach and quit making us more miserable than we are."

Norris sat back, and Bernie's fingers lost the shirt.

Before she could pursue it, Norris said, "You want to talk about Lena. Let's talk about Lena."

Lindsay said, "I don't want to talk about Lena."

Bernie drove her elbows hard onto the table top and ran her fingers through her loose hair. "Why not?"

"Because I'm pissed," said Lindsay. She looked Bernie in the eye. Bernie felt the anger, glowing, hot. "I'm pissed at you for going out there when there was no need. Someone, security or somebody, would have caught Lena before she came into the banquet room. He would have sent her out. Nothing would have happened."

"But what happened?" Bernie pressed.

"It doesn't matter. I don't want to think about it." Lindsay picked up the last piece of her hot dog, then let it fall to the plate. It bounced like a deformed rubber ball. "She was a wimp, retarded, a smelly low-class—"

"Lindsay."

Norris said, "I don't want to talk about it, either, Bernie. Sorry that you care about me and all that shit. But I have other things to think about. I've got a meeting with G-Dad tomorrow morning. I don't have time to decipher burn marks on body parts. Save that for Colombo."

Bernie looked out the door to the street. There was a lot of traffic on Main. It was near dinner time on Saturday. All the country folk were cruising town, looking for weekend excitement that would take form as an Arby's giant roast beef and a movie at the Henford Twin Cinema. The threat of sleet had passed in mid-afternoon; the streets were drying and the going was easy.

Time to go. Bernie pulled her coat on and felt the pocket for the key to Matt's car. She stood and put a dollar tip on the table top.

"What's that for?" asked Norris. "All he did was bring out hot dogs. He never asked us if we needed anything else."

"Fuck you," said Bernie. She went outside, slamming Stan's blue and orange framed door. The little bell over the doorsill tinkled happily.

Chapter Twenty-one

The wounds were numb.

Lindsay stood in the shower, sweet-scented shampoo running off her shoulders, her eyes closed and her face pressed into the center of the water blast. For the last ten minutes, Hank had been brushing and picking his teeth and chatting. Lindsay had tried to listen at first, then had told Hank she was tired and couldn't hear him anyway. That didn't matter. Hank was feeling amorous, and to him, talk was foreplay.

Lindsay was aware of the burns on her fingers, but the awareness was of the absence of sensation rather than pain. In a way, that was worse. The deadness made her think of leprosy. Tainted skin, playing tricks. The sight of the burns made her sick, and so waterlogged Band-Aids kept them invisible. If Hank asked, which he might during their inevitable lovemaking, Lindsay would blame hot pans.

"Lindsay?" said Hank. He pulled back the shower curtain. He was smiling. He was naked. "Save water, shower with a friend," he said. He stepped into the stall with Lindsay.

Lindsay tried to smile. She knew her tears were hidden by the rush of shower water down her face.

She knew, also, that she would not tell Hank of the afternoon's strange event, and the even more disturbing discoveries at Stan's Snack Shop. Hank, ever the practical one, would brush it off. If she wanted to actually talk about it, to work it out, to decipher it, he would become angry. He did not take to strange events. He did not believe in what was not in the normal, or possible, course of his world. And not believing her would not be the worst part. The worst would be him believing that she believed it, and somehow thinking less of her for it.

As Hank put his arms around her and pulled her face into his shoulder, she sighed out loud, hoping he would take it as passion, not anguish.

Chapter Twenty-two

On the floor of the cold bedroom, Bernie knelt. Her arms were crossed on the mattress of the bed in front of her, her head down on her arms. She had prayed, and now was thinking. In the bed next to hers, Sandra O'Connell, HeartLight's gardener and one of Bernie's two best friends, sighed in sleep and rolled over.

She had to find Lena tomorrow and talk with her. Bernie had gone by the hospital after she left Stan's, but Lena had left. According to an emergency-room orderly, Lena had awakened and refused to be admitted. No one there had been able to get any useful information from her. Lena had collected her torn and soiled hose, which a nurse had tossed into a trash container, and gone.

Bernie had then driven to the Gs' house and apologetically knocked on the huge front door. Uncle Leonard had invited her in for something to eat, forever the polite Lynch, but Bernie had as equally politely declined, and waited in the foyer while he got Aunt Marla from the dining room. Aunt Marla had also offered Bernie some dinner, and again, Bernie declined. Aunt Marla did, however, remember Lena's last name. Carlton. Lena Carlton.

Bernie had looked the name up in a phone book at the East End Wilco Station. There were four Carltons, a Brian, a C. J., a Mary, and a Carlton's Auto Shop, and even though none seemed likely, Bernie drove to each address. No cars were in Brian Carlton's driveway, nor lights on inside the house. C. J. Carlton lived in an apartment, and he had never heard of Lena. Bernie couldn't find the home that matched Mary Carlton's address. And since she didn't went to run Matt's car out of gas, she drove back to HeartLight.

Everyone at the house was asleep except for Sandra's hamster, racing in his wheel in the corner of the living room. Bernie had sat alone on the sofa for a few minutes, listening to the droning squeak of the wheel. Then she went upstairs through the dark, passing the window at the top of the stairs and the rectangular puddle of blue-tinted light from the driveway spotlight, past the closed door of the only married couple at the house, Vince and Meg, then to the open door of Matt, John, and Harner's bedroom. She had stopped, looking into the room, seeing nothing for the blackness, but hearing the gentle and irregular breathing of the men of HeartLight. She had thought for a moment of awakening Matt, but knew waiting until morning would give her time to think.

Thinking wasn't helping, though.

With a silent sigh, Bernie got up from her knees. She pulled off her sweater and jeans, tossed them to the foot of the mattress, slipped into her sleepshirt, pulled up her socks. With a rubber band from the nightstand she tied her hair back. She looked at the single, curtainless window. The shade was drawn. Sandra liked it down; Bernie liked the shade up. Sandra liked the privacy. Bernie liked to be able to see the small piece of world outside in the night. Tonight, she left it alone.

"I'll find Lena," she vowed in a whisper. Whatever had happened between herself and Lena, between Lena and her cousins, it had been something of Power. And even if Norris and Lindsay were too frightened to talk about it, Bernie knew that whatever happened in the world happened with God's knowledge. Good things. Horrible things. Things humans could not comprehend. God knew what had happened between them all, and Bernie would not let fear keep her from seeking the truth.

She looked at the burns on her hand. She tried to feel around to the burns on her back.

What Power had done this?

Climbing into bed and pulling up the sheet and bedcovers, for a brief moment she thought about her old boyfriend. Then she thought about Matt. And for a second, she allowed herself the wish of a thick winter blanket and pair of woolen socks to keep away the cold.

Chapter Twenty-three

Motel pillows sucked. This one was flat, and the stuffing, whatever the hell it was, had separated into large, loose clumps that shifted every time Norris moved his head to see the television. He wasn't watching, but he was faced in that direction. In the ashtray on the phone table a pile of butts and ashes made a tall, lopsided soft-sculpture. Norris lay on top of the bedspread in only a motel towel. The shower had been cold.

In the room next to him, he could hear a late-night cable show of some seedy sort. Sorry organ music and the sound of squealing and smacking hammered the thin wall behind his head like an obscene, begging waif pounding at the door. He wouldn't have minded a porno movie at other times; tonight, though, his nerves were wires of pain. He was reeled in, locked down, afraid to move much in case his skin decided to tear free from stress. On his television, angry men in suits and women in white blouses faced each other off on the topic of the new gubernatorial candidates.

The blisters on his wrists were pink and sore. He couldn't stop looking at them.

A commercial came on. Red Lobster for the seafood lover in you. He thought the spots on his wrists looked freshly boiled, like little lobster freckles.

Norris caught the burned skin between the nails of his thumb and forefinger and squeezed. The pain was mild. Water popped out from the sores and ran down to the sheet.

G-Dad was giving him a one-on-one audience. Generous old fart. If Norris could hold it together, smile on cue, ask the right questions and twist the truth into a plausible lie, then maybe the old man would open his heart and his bank account and give his grandson a sum not unlike what he'd given countless other sad, charitable causes. Tomorrow morning, after church, unfortunately, yet thankfully before another luncheon, Norris and G-Dad were to sit down in the lobby of the Henford Hotel and do the powerful-old-man-needy-grandson two-step.

Norris tasted the fluid that ran out of his wrist. It had the flavor of vinegar.

Eleven hours. He should sleep. The waiting would be easier that way. He could make final speech preparations in the morning. Eleven hours.

And in twelve hours, he would be back on the road again, promise in his pocket. Give the G several days to get to the bank and cough up the cash. Then pay the piper and figure where to go from there. Clear himself on paper, if not in reality.

For a moment, he thought about Jared, his lover of last year. Life with Jared had been surprisingly happy. For about a month. And then Jared had gotten sullen and quiet. Norris, confused, had followed suit. And then Jared skipped out, and Norris had rightly kicked himself for his openness and returned to his life of solitude.

Isolation justly deserved for his lack of courage.

Norris picked at his wounds and watched the talk show on the television until the show was over and the screen dissolved to snow; then he dozed.

He woke again at five, startled from the tangled towel and sheet by a vivid dream fragment. A laughing man Norris could not see had wound something tightly about Norris's throat. Norris had tried to lift his hands to free himself, but the hands were lashed to his sides.

Norris sat up, the sensation of constriction still on his neck. He grabbed at his throat, but found nothing. He sighed and wiped his forehead. On his wrists, the red blisters blazed. "Christ," he swore.

The television was still on. Snow was still on the screen. When Norris got up and opened the door for air, there was snow on the ground as well.

He found an all-night talk show on the dented radio on the table.

At nine, he wrapped his burns and dressed for church.

Chapter Twenty-four

"Morning, sweetie," said Bernie.

Matt beamed, standing at the kitchen sink with his hands deep in bubbly dishwater. "It's all right, I knew you'd be too tired, as late as you were last night."

Bernie pushed the sleeves of her sweater up past her elbows and walked over to Matt. She gave him an affectionate thump on the arm with her elbow. "Let me take over."

"Nah, I'm almost finished."

"I owe you."

"Yeah, I know." Matt turned his attention back to the plate he was scrubbing. Bernie looked at him a moment longer. He was in jeans and a tee shirt, and his feet were bare on the old, scarred linoleum flooring. He was a man of medium height, and at thirty-one was three years younger than she. His hair was pale and straight, and he wore a beard as did all the men at HeartLight, not because of agreement, but because shaving took time and time was better spent on other things.

His eyes were large and dark in his light-skinned face, and above his right eyebrow was a long childhood scar. A fight between a bike and a tree, Matt had joked, but Bernie knew better.

And if Bernie ever allowed herself to fall in love again, there was no doubt it would be with Matt.

Bernie put her palms on the counter and gazed out the window above the sink. The window faced south. The farmhouse's side yard sloped gently downward, and a narrow, well-worn footpath cut through it, past the empty garden and the barren clothesline, leading to the rail fence, a row of spruce trees, and the small barn beyond.

"I have to get down to Red," Bernie said. "I was too tired last night to go feed her. I'm a terrible mother. If I ever decide to have kids, kick me in the butt."

"Will do."

"Did I miss anything exciting yesterday afternoon?"

Matt put the plate into the rinse water, then worked his shoulder to scratch at his ear. There were detergent bubbles in his blond beard. Bernie wiped them off.

"Thanks," said Matt. "Not really. Harner and I got a call from a man up in Mount Sidnor. He heard about the porch we did for the Episcopal retreat. He needs a garage. It sounds good to us."

"That's great." Bernie took a glass from the drain board and filled it with cold water from the spigot. "How much they going to pay?"

"I don't know yet," said Matt. "It'll be fine."

"Ye of mega faith," said Bernie. She went to sit at the table. "You guys are getting a good reputation. What with spring coming on, you'll be busy a lot."

"God willing," said Matt. He picked up another plate and said, "What's that on your hand?"

Bernie looked at her hands, not even remembering until she saw the burns on her palm. She wasn't ready to attempt an explanation. But not explaining was not lying.

"I don't know," she said. "It doesn't hurt much." She pulled the sweater sleeves down, then stood up. "I don't want breakfast this morning. Tell John not to fix anything for me, okay?"

"He'll argue. 'But, Bernie, you're too thin already.' And he has a point."

"I'm still bloated from the Lynch family feast."

"Okay."

"I'll be back in time for service."

"I know." Matt gave her a wink.

On the front hall bench Bernie found her coat. She slipped it on and went outside. The morning sun was dim through thick clouds which were threatening snow or rain. Cold breezes caused the tiny leaves of the walkside boxwoods to shiver like a dog after a cold bath. Trees along the fence line of the yard dripped the remains of yesterday's sleet into the shadows.

Bernie walked the length of the open, wrap-around porch, past the wicker furniture and the hanging porch swing, around the corner and by the stacks of logs that lined nearly half of the south side. She waved in the direction of the kitchen window, where Matt probably wasn't standing anymore, then jumped off onto the pathway and trudged down to the pipe gate that opened to the pasture land.

"Red!" she called.

She pulled her gloves out of her coat pocket

and put them on. "Red, come on, girl, let's have breakfast."

The gate swung wide; Bernie stepped into the mud. Her barn boots smacked noisily as she moved toward the rough-planked side of the barn. Starlings fluttered from the hay-strewn ground and flew off to a tree branch. The first flakes of snow appeared above Bernie's head, and in only a moment, the air was swirling with them.

"Thank you for this morning," she whispered.

The barn, which was actually a small structure with two stalls and a hay and tack room, had been built by Matt and Harner soon after HeartLight opened. It was a good job, made of weathered, sturdy boards and sheet tin. The men had cut large square holes in the roof over each stall and put in translucent skylights so they wouldn't need to run electricity from the house. "We can use the second stall for storage if we need it," Matt had said, calming the last of Bernie's uneasiness with this use of the money she had dedicated to HeartLight.

It had been her father's money. Her dad, Stanley, a prominent lawyer in Henford, a proud Lynch. A loving father, bald pate, Lynch gut line. Clogged arteries. Sky-high blood pressure. Strained heart.

He died at the University of Virginia hospital two years earlier, on the operating table, in the middle of a triple bypass.

Bernie, equal partners with her mother in the will, received $240,000.

Bernie's mother, Carolyn, went on a cruise to ease her grief. She invited Bernie, but she did not go.

Everything had shifted into different perspective. A new camera lens, a new filter called shock. Bernie had never lost someone close, someone she loved. During the day she held it together. At night, she wondered why anyone was ever born in the first place.

She quit her job at *The Henford Press*, where she had worked as a social reporter. She moved into an apartment on the lower side of Henford. She met Shawn, a young and angry employee at a local turkey farm. He moved in with her. Bernie spent many days alone in front of her television or shopping for expensive clothes she never wore. Bernie and Shawn spent many nights wasted and making love or fighting.

It lasted almost a year.

Bernie ended up with bruises she could not explain to her mother, and Shawn had drifted more and more into his own bizarre world.

Last August, Bernie had broken it off. With one of Shawn's guns, she stopped him at the door on his way home from work and demanded he never come back. He had been surprisingly agreeable, had picked up the paper bag of clothes Bernie threw out at him, and had gone his own way. Bernie moved again. This time to an even lowlier place, a tiny trailer park fifteen miles north of Henford.

She felt this was as good a place as any to punish herself for mistakes made. Many of the homes in the park were dented and rusted. Few had a semblance of care; no gardens, no walkways, no window boxes or lawn ornaments. The pine trees shed their needles. The needles stayed where they fell, for the most part. Brooms never saw the outside of the homes of Hart's Trailer Park.

But there was one trailer unlike the others. It

was narrow and plain, but the care of its owners was obvious from the patch of flowers lining the gravel path to the sturdy deck at the back. In it lived six members of a religious brotherhood.

Bernie would always believe that meeting Sandra O'Connell had been the one true turning point of her life. She had joined up with the group, hearing their message and embracing it as her own.

With her inheritance, Bernie had encouraged them to purchase the old farmhouse, along with the surrounding thirteen acres, for $62,000. Advertised as a "fixer-upper," the house became the brotherhood's ongoing project. Most of the rooms were now without serious holes in the walls, and the roof had been repaired so leaks were no longer a problem. There were still, however, many projects to keep the members occupied in between the scheduled outreach work.

With limited domestic abilities, Bernie sewed cotton curtains for the kitchen and living room. Sandra tilled a piece of the ample side yard and put in a winter garden. Vince and Meg had scoured the place, corner to corner, ceilings and walls, attic and basement. John had combed the area, finding secondhand furniture at good prices. The remaining money was then put into a trust to be used for living expenses at times when construction business was slow or emergencies arose or charity demanded it.

They christened the old house HeartLight. The only luxury Bernie had allowed herself was the purchase of a horse. Nearly everything else, clothes, silver and crystal stored at her mother's, and Sony entertainment center, went to the Goodwill or Henford's Salvation Army.

"Red?" called Bernie. She went around to the front and looked into the door of the open stall. Inside, where swallows roosted, there were only the soft sounds of rustling mice and a breeze through an opened back window. Bernie stepped inside. The straw beneath her feet was dry. It was also clean, meaning Red had stayed outside all night. The hay in the net was untouched.

"Stupid, hardheaded horse," said Bernie. "Don't even know when to come in out of the snow."

She went out of the barn and opened the door to the small tack room. Inside, she scooped a handful of feed from the rubber-lidded feed bin and dropped the grain into a feed pan. Red always came at the sound of shaking grain. The horse could hear a rattling corn seed from clear across the pasture.

Bernie closed the tack room door and shook the feed pan. She squinted out across the field. "Red!" Bernie called. "I'm not crossing that mess to come find you."

There was movement from the south side of the pasture. Bernie tipped her head forward, watching. She shook the feed pan. The form of a horse stepped out, head held high, looking in the direction of the barn.

"Trees better than a stall?" shouted Bernie. "You ingrate."

The horse began her slow stroll across the dead grasses toward to barn. "Pampered brat," Bernie laughed.

At the back of the stall, under the small opened window, was a spot of damp straw where the sleet had blown in. Bernie put the feed pan down in the back right corner. She then crossed through the interior gate that separated the two stalls and grasped the pitchfork. Coming back through, she latched the gate so Red wouldn't stick her big nosy nose in with the stored straw and hay.

"One hundred pitchforks of shit in the stall, one hundred pitchforks of shit," she began to sing. "You scoop it out and then you can shout, ninety-nine pitchforks of shit in the stall."

Gripping the fork with her gloved hands, she shoved it into the wet straw, then took it out and dumped the straw on top of the compost pile. Red was closer, her black eyes wide and interested, her pace picking up a bit in anticipation of her long-awaited dinner from yesterday.

"Come on," Bernie said. "Move it or lose it." Back inside the barn, she shoveled another pile of the damp bedding. Her wrists, where the burns were, began to ache from the rubbing against her coat sleeves.

"Ninety-nine pitchforks of shit in the stall, ninety-nine pitchforks of shit, you scoop it out and then you can shout, ninety-eight pitchforks of shit in the stall." She heard footsteps at the stall door, and she spun around to lovingly chastise her animal.

But Red was not in the doorway.

Instead, there was a man. Huge. Sneering.

Bernie froze, staring. All light from outdoors was obliterated by the immensity of the man's body. He wore a heavy coat. A black hat was pulled down over his ears. His eyes were rheumy and threatening. His lips were pulled back into a sneer. He stared straight at Bernie, and his mouth opened wider into an obscene grin. "Baby," he hissed. "Come here, baby, I missed you."

Bernie stepped back, lowering the pitchfork. She said, "What do you want?" Her voice was high and small, like a child's. It was not her own.

"Baby, baby, come here and give your daddy a little lovin'," said the man. He took several steps forward. The straw did not complain under his boots. When Bernie glanced down, she saw that the straw was gone. The floor was wooden.

"Go away," said Bernie. Her heart pounded. *God help me, what is this?* she thought. Sweat sprang out on her arms. The little-girl's voice continued, "Go away or I'll hurt you!" She lifted the pitchfork to prove her threat, but there was not a fork in her hands now. There was a large kitchen knife. The handle was warm and smooth in her gloveless grip. She looked at her own feet, her own clothes, and they were not her own. Her shoes were a child's, and her clothes a thin pink dress.

Oh, dear God! she screamed, but the words did not come out. This was not happening, it could not be. She was not here, she was in the barn, waiting to feed her horse. She stumbled backward into something that gave way with a screeching. She looked; a yellow kitchen chair. Behind it, a table, a sink, filthy curtains against a greasy window.

"Give it to me, baby, or I'll have to take it. You're too ugly to argue. You can't get it from nobody but me 'cause I'm your lovin' daddy." The man strode forward suddenly, as if pushed from behind. His arms spread open to take her into his filthy coat.

"Go away!" Bernie waved the knife, afraid to use it. *God, I can't kill, I can't kill!* The man laughed, and his foul breath hung in the alien kitchen air.

"Put that little thing down, baby," he said. " 'Less you want me to use it on you. You like a little pain, baby? We can do that, too, if you want."

He snatched out, his fingers grasping for Bernie's arm. She jumped back, slamming her back into the table. The knife wavered in front of her. The man laughed at it. He lunged forward again. Bernie dropped to the floor and crawled under the table. There were dead flies there.

"Ha!" shouted the man. "Now don't make me mad. I'm too old to fight for that little ugly pussy of yours. Get out here or I'll give you the spanking of your life."

Bernie trembled, knees drawn up, both hands gripping the knife. *Matt!* she tried to scream. All that came out was a little-girl whimper.

She watched as the man's bulky legs bent beneath his brown baggy slacks. He was coming down after her. Hands clutched; fingers with crusted, blackened nails strummed the air, reaching out, under. She could see his shirt now, the sides of his thick coat, the hair of his neck.

"No!" A child's scream. The knife shook.

His dark jaw was now visible, and his laughing lips.

"Go away!" The knife poised, trembling, ready.

"Baby, baby, baby," cooed the man. His eyes were there then, and he came under the table. Bernie screamed. The man hunched his shoulders and leaned in. "Give Daddy that knife or you'll wish you had." He coughed, spraying Bernie's face with thick spit. Bernie could see the pocks on his face, the unshaven chin, the stain along his cheek from tobacco, drooled some time ago.

The man grabbed for the knife.

With a cry that rushed from her like the wind of a terrible storm, she fell forward. The knife plunged into the man's shoulder. It went in easily, like a spoon into mushroom soup. There was no blood at first, but a look of disbelief exploded on the man's face. Bernie let the knife go and slumped back, hand to her mouth. The man stared at the knife in his shoulder, then suddenly lurched up and cracked his head on the underside of the table. His mouth dropped open and he howled.

Bernie heard herself say, "There you go! There you go!"

"Bitch!" roared the man. Bernie thought he would try to kill her then, but he scrambled out from under the table, holding the handle of the knife, blood slithering out through the slit in the coat sleeve.

Bernie put her palms against her ears. *What is this, dear God, what is this, stop it please!* She heard the man rustling about the kitchen, stumbling in his boots, tripping and moaning. She saw a few drops of blood fall to the wooden kitchen floor.

I've stabbed a man!

Bernie closed her eyes. The man continued to thump about. His moans changed to wet snorts. The heavy bootsteps became muffled. The man's snorts were deep, animal-like.

Bernie knew that to sit under a table and let him die would be wrong. She had to get out, she had to help him. She lowered her hands from her ears and touched the floor.

Straw.

Bernie opened her eyes and looked. Straw. She was in the barn. She was in Red's stall.

"What?" she whispered. She looked at her legs and feet; her clothes were her own jeans and barn boots. She examined her arms, which shook in vicious tremors, and the burns, which were now noticeably more tender than before.

"God," she whispered, and the voice was her own. "Oh, thank God." She pressed her fingers to her eyelids, and only in the brief darkness on closed lids did she see the vanishing face of the man she had stabbed. In seconds, his face blurred and disappeared. She squeezed her eyes tightly, but could not bring his visage back to examine.

Whatever had happened was done.

Then she heard the snorting, and the shuffling. Raising her head, she saw Red before her, great sorrel equine knees buckled, ears twisted back, eyes wide and white and staring.

"Red?"

The horse shuddered and pawed at the straw bedding with weak strokes of her front hoof. She began to pant.

In the sleek, muscular chest, Bernie's pitchfork was buried deeply.

Chapter Twenty-five

Stone House United Methodist let out at twelve-eleven. Fully one-fifth of the congregation had been Lynches, and with Lowell Lynch propped in his front pew with his family horde around him, Reverend Dunn had done what was expected. He took nearly ten minutes introducing various Lynches and extolling the virtues of close family ties. Norris's father had not sat with his son. Norris did not know why, but he knew better than to argue with good luck.

Norris had scribbled on his bulletin throughout the hour. Not like he had done as a child when sitting with Bernie and Lindsay, no stick angels crash-diving from the top of the illustrated steeple, no crafty stick devils peering at the suicidal angels from behind the sketches of landscaped bushes by the church. Instead, he made spirals up and down the margins, round and round like inky Slinkys. Spirals traveled around the front, through the printed order of worship, around the names of the hallowed personnel and the choir members on the back. He had seated himself at the end of the pew, next to Kathy's daughter, who was more interested in her shoestrings than Norris's artwork. By the end of the service, there was not a white breathing spot on the bulletin.

The family was the last to leave the church when the service was over. Most stayed up near the altar to talk with other church members. A substantial traffic jam ensued, and Norris was trapped in the aisle between Lindsay and a large white-haired woman he didn't know but who knew him. Lindsay was cordial, asking Norris how the motel was and how he liked the snow, but it was all surface conversation, no more than he would have gotten from the white-haired woman on his other side had he decided to strike up a chat.

Hank went out of the sanctuary through a side door, to clear any additional snow off the car, he had said. Norris figured that Hank preferred not to have to stand next to him for long. Norris wondered if Lindsay had shown Hank her burns. Bernie had not come to church.

Norris kept away from his father while keeping an eye out for G-Dad. He could see the man's head, topped by the ridiculous hat, down about seven rows, moving with the swiftness of a dying slug. The front doors were open, and snow was still coming down. Norris didn't care if the Interstate was three feet deep in the stuff; after his talk with his grandfather, he was heading out. If G-Dad was magnanimous, Norris wouldn't mind the delay. If G-Dad decided not to give Norris the money, maybe fate would intervene and hurl him off the snowy road into a thick tree somewhere. Quick, painless, bloody death.

G-Dad got outside before Norris could squeeze through the milling congregation. The red plaid hat went on, and was immediately powdered with falling snow. Someone Norris couldn't make out opened an umbrella and held it over G-Dad's head. Another umbrella popped open and was held aloft, probably positioned to save G-Mom's puffy hairdo. Norris turned sideways and forced himself forward. People shook heads and frowned, but none were so un-Christian as to admonish his haste. Norris reached the door, avoided the outstretched hand of the assistant minister, and walked through the snow to the street corner, where the Gs were waiting with Uncle Leonard to cross to the Henford Hotel.

"Granddaddy," said Norris. Snowflakes caught on his eyelashes; he blinked them away.

Uncle Leonard turned toward Norris. Beneath his all-weather hat, his eyes were dark. He looked at Norris for a moment. Then he said, "What is it?"

Norris said, "Let me help him across the road."

"I have him," said Uncle Leonard.

"I could help," said Norris.

"I have him," said Uncle Leonard. His voice sounded to Norris like the voice of a dog if it could speak, declaring that the juicy bone was his.

Tear-ass, elegantly conservative in his black suit and black overcoat, followed by his wife Joan and bug-eyed Tear-ass, Jr., moved up beside Uncle Leonard, holding an umbrella low. G-Mom was scrunched beneath it. Norris couldn't see her face, just the plastic raincoat-enshrouded body and pair of snap rubber boots. Tear-ass gave Norris a tolerant smile.

"Help Grandmother," he said. "I'd like to go ahead with Terry and the wife to make a phone call at the desk. Would you please?"

Norris restrained a snarl. "Well, sure, Terrance," he said. "You go ahead." Tear-ass grinned and handed the umbrella to Norris. Norris slid beside G-Mom, who tipped her head and peered out from beneath to see who her escort was. Tear-ass and family scuttled across the road, jaywalking, Norris noticed, snowflakes swirling about their righteous bulks.

"Terrance?" said G-Mom. "Where did Terrance go?"

Norris said, "He had a phone call to make. It's Norris, Grandmother."

"Norris," said G-Mom. "Why do you want all that hair on your face, Norris?" She squinted in the snow; then her face withdrew beneath the umbrella.

The traffic slowed. Uncle Barry moved to the middle of the crosswalk and raised his hand to stop cars until the family was across. Typical

Lynch bravado. Norris watched as family members took to the street like cockroaches in a kitchen. Aunt Sarah, Paul and his beautiful wife and beautiful children, Cousins Karen and Kathy and spouses and broods. Norris's dad, giving Norris an infuriatingly pathetic stare as he moved on. Aunt Marla, cigarette hanging from old lips, grabbed G-Mom by the arm and practically jerked her out from under the umbrella. Norris followed after them.

It happened in the middle of the road.

The snow was falling hard, slicking up the tarmac and causing Norris to lock his knees to keep his balance. G-Mom, tapping along in her heels, fared much better. The wind began to whip up. Aunt Marla's smoke was sucked out of her cigarette and thrown down toward the pavement. The wind caught itself, then twisted. The umbrella popped free and flew off in a tornado whirl of black on white. Norris looked after the umbrella, made a weak stab at grabbing for it, then turned back to G-Mom.

G-Mom was not there.

Aunt Marla had vanished.

Main Street and the snow and Stone House United Methodist Church on the curbside swirled with the wind and dissipated, then were gone.

There was darkness. There was silence. Norris shook his head and squinted and could see nothing. It was as if his eyelids had been glued shut. He tried to step foreward, but his feet, which were now bare, would not move. A tickle of autumn air stroked Norris's face, and on the air came smells of the woods, smells of dead leaves and fungi and a campfire. "What the hell?" he said, but could not hear his words. His blood sang with fear. He reached out to find where he was.

His hand would move no further than his chest. There was a sensation of rattling metal. He looked down. The blackness veiled his predicament, but he could feel it. His wrists were chained to his waist. He squinted futilely and shook his head in hopes of shaking vision back. The shaking told him something was around his neck as well, something sharp and thin.

What the fuck is this?

Sweat broke out on his arms and forehead. He swallowed, and the something about his throat tightened.

Again he tried to move his feet, but they were held together by something at his ankles. Beneath his feet, he felt the surface on which he stood. It was narrow and hard. He rocked his toes and heels slightly, trying to trace that on which he stood. No more than two inches wide. Rough, edges sharp. Some sort of board.

What the fuck is this!

And then there was another smell mixed with the autumn leaves and the campfire. It was close, crawling up his nostrils like a disgusting, burrowing insect. The smell was rancid breath. Foul and thick, like Teddy's breath in the morning, heavy with stale alcohol.

Norris began to shake. He moved his head side to side, trying to move from the smell, and his neck was cut by what bound it. And he recognized the feel. It was barbed wire.

He was standing on a board with barbed wire around his neck. He was going to hang by barbed wire.

The stench of the breath pulled from his nostrils and trailed down his neck. There was a pumping rush of air, as if someone was laughing.

Ha Ha Ha Ha Ha!

And then the board beneath him was shoved. Norris's feet pawed at the wood in a frantic attempt to pull it back upright. His toes scratched to keep a purchase on the wood. The board dropped clear of his feet.

Norris's silent scream tore the blackness as he fell.

And he hit the road. His jaw slammed into frozen blacktop, shocking his mouth open. Filthy snow filtered in through his teeth. Cold stuffed itself up his coat sleeves and the knees of his Sunday slacks.

Aunt Marla's shoes were visible, the tips crusted in ice. From above, she said, "Norris fainted!"

"Hold the traffic," said an unrecognizable relative. More feet appeared in Norris's line of vision. "Hold the traffic!"

And then strong arms were under his, helping him to his feet. Hands were all over his back, brushing him off.

"Fainted, did you?" It was Uncle Barry. He stood beside Uncle Paul and the beautiful wife. They looked at Norris as though he had become instantly contagious.

"I suppose," said Norris. There was sweat on his forehead, and it was already forming ice crystals.

"You do that often?" asked Uncle Paul.

"Get him out of the road," said Aunt Marla. "We'll kill him out here for sure." She took Norris by the elbow. Surrounded by a Lynch mob, Norris was escorted to the sidewalk in the swirling snow. He let himself be led along, feeling

105

like a weak puppet held by fleshy strings. No one talked during the short distance to the Henford Hotel.

Inside, Norris was put on one of the lobby's red sofas. Uncle Paul sat in a chair opposite. Standing not far behind, other Lynch faces stared, concerned. Norris shivered, and let his head drop against the soft sofa back. He looked up at the ceiling.

"You do that often?" Uncle Paul asked. "Faint, I mean?"

Norris could feel the wet from the snow caressing his skin through his slacks. It made him feel as if he had wet his pants. The texture of the ceiling seemed to spin. He closed his eyes, feeling sick to his stomach. He touched his neck and there was no mark there.

"Do you? Should we call a doctor?"

Norris thought, *I fainted?* He opened his eyes and looked at the arm of Uncle Paul's chair. I fainted, he thought again. *A flashback from some bad stuff, that's all. It caught me off guard. I fainted. No big shit.*

"No," he said. He touched his chin where he had struck the road. There was already a welt. Again he felt his neck where marks from barbed wire should have been, but there was nothing but smooth skin. Bad stuff, that was it. He'd have to try and lay off the buzzes for a while if he was going to get things together in the next few weeks. He could not afford another one of these blackouts. Norris pulled his head upright and let himself actually look Uncle Paul in the eye. What he saw there made him feel suddenly and strangely all the better for his wounds.

There was a cautious sympathy in Paul's

expression. A touch of fear, a curiosity, a concern. Behind Paul, milling about on the large rug in the lobby's center, were other concerned relatives, allowing Norris the space they thought he needed, glancing at him with pity.

Oh, yes, Norris thought. And he said, "No, not usually. Not that often, I mean."

His jaw hurt; his pants were uncomfortably wet, but his mind clamped shut on his salvation. He had planned on telling G-Dad that he wanted a loan for a new business venture, a record-store franchise. But now, he had their concern. He was not a well boy. He needed money for medical bills, for deductibles not covered, for testing on his condition. This fainting condition.

Oh, yes, yes!

He said, "Not usually, but sometimes. We don't know what the problem is yet." He grimaced, partly in real pain, partly in drama. Uncle Paul frowned and nodded.

"I'll be all right, though," said Norris. "I don't want to keep anyone from lunch. I was going to talk with Granddaddy for a minute. You go on ahead. Please."

Uncle Paul reached over and patted Norris's knee. The touch was as distasteful as the wet pants. Paul said, "Is there something I should know?"

Norris said, "Not now, but thanks."

"You certain?"

"No, but thanks."

Paul pulled his hand from Norris's knee. "Take care, there, Norris."

The crowd in the middle of the lobby dispersed along with Paul; most moved into the banquet room, some, who were staying in the hotel, to the elevators to make a quick trip to their rooms. Norris watched them scatter, watched G-Mom go with Aunt Marla to the ladies' room, watched as G-Dad stood in the center of the rug with Uncle Barry, looking lost.

"Let's go to lunch, Dad," said Barry.

G-Dad shook his head. He took off his jaunty beret and rubbed his head. "I had to do something first," he said.

Come on, we had a fucking appointment, Norris thought. *I'm over here, just look. Don't make me call you. Shit.*

"You have lunch with us, Dad. I'll help you."

G-Dad turned away from Uncle Barry's grasp, moving slowly like a man with a dowsing rod looking for the reason he was not supposed to eat lunch yet. Then he saw Norris.

"Granddaddy," said Norris.

The old man worked his shoulders, then tottered over to the sofa. Uncle Barry followed. G-Dad said, "I'm supposed to talk with Norris here."

No shit, Sherlock.

"Thanks for taking time to talk with me, Granddaddy," he said.

G-Dad moved to the chair across from Norris, hovered above the cushion, then dropped. Air whooshed from the cushion and the old man at the same time.

"Dad, do you want me to wait for you?" asked Uncle Barry.

"No, Barry. I'll be in with Norris in a moment." The words were slow and somewhat slurred, but the fact that they made sense gave Norris an added surge of hope.

Now, to strike while the sick boy is still an object of concern.

Uncle Barry left for the banquet room. Only the receptionist, pecking at a computer behind the long desk, shared the lobby with Norris and his grandfather.

"So, Norris," said G-Dad. His long, white fingers hung in his lap. Norris thought it looked as if he was getting ready to play with himself. "Did I hear you fainted?"

Norris stroked the sore place on his face, took a breath, and looked the liver-spotted old man in his pale eyes. "Yes," he said, trying to bring out just the right tone of dignified long-suffering. "And I need your help."

Chapter Twenty-six

Grace hurled a handful of soap suds from the tub. They landed on Lindsay and the mirror behind her. "Poot!" crowed the little girl.

"Poot, yourself," said Lindsay. "Now quit fooling around, we have to get you into bed. I'm tired."

"Not tired," said Grace. "I wanna play."

"Grace, hold still. There's shampoo in your bangs and I can't get it out with you scooting all over."

Mandy, from out in the hall, said, "Mom, Ruffles threw up on my bed."

"Get your dad, I'm still busy here."

"But it stinks! It's really wet and gross. Dad's all the way out in the garage. And you know he hates the cat."

Grace threw soap bubbles out of the tub. They landed on the knee of Lindsay's jeans. "Hold still, Grace. I'm going to pour water over your bangs

109

now. Here it comes." She dipped a pink plastic cup into the bathwater, and Grace squinched up her face in preparation. For a moment, Lindsay let her eyes stray to the dark red burns on her fingertips. They were still tender from yesterday, but the blisters had hardened over. Friction marks, she had decided after awakening this morning. Friction from the cheap, rough material of Lena's outfit. Trying to grab the woman and catching her made small burns the way a simple piece of paper could make a painful slice. It was nothing more.

Grace splashed the water and laughed.

Lindsay tipped up the cup of water, and as it began to cascade over Grace's head, Mandy yelled, "Mom!"

Lindsay flinched, jerking the cup, and water went up Grace's nose. Grace gasped, then clawed at her face.

"Goddamn it," Lindsay said under her breath. And louder, "Grace, I'm sorry. Let me wipe your face."

Mandy stamped her foot. "Mom, I said Ruffles puked on my bed and Dad's in the garage and it really really stinks and I can't go to bed!"

Grace, crying now, drew her knees up and down in the bathwater, making high waves.

"Mom!" called Mandy.

"Mandy, get your father! He's capable of cleaning up cat puke. I've got my hands full."

"But he's in the garage—"

"I said get your father!"

Grace rubbed at her nose with her forearm. Her eyebrows made mad, frantic waves, like the water, over the fused lids of her eyeless face. Her lips blubbered and sucked air. Lindsay dabbed her with the edge of a towel.

"But, Mom . . . " whined Mandy.

The burns on Lindsay's fingers suddenly flared hot. She dropped the washrag into the tub. Somewhere, probably outside but seeming to be deep inside her own ear, she heard the sound of rattling chains.

"Mom, listen to me!" said Mandy.

"Mandy, not now." Where the hell were chains? Did Grace have some, taken from the garage? She bent over to look into the tub.

"Mom!"

Mandy! was what Lindsay opened her mouth to shout, but what came out was "Hurt you!" Her hand, covered with suds, flew to her lips in shock at the words. The burned tips of her fingers were cut with fresh, sharp pain.

Lindsay saw Grace straighten up and turn in her direction, her little-girl's eyebrows arched in confusion, but then Grace was no longer there. Her face shimmered, then faded. The lights of the bathroom snuffed out; the warm smells of the baby shampoo and the Calgon bathbeads were sucked away like water down a drain hole. Muted darkness swirled about Lindsay. A cold dampness assaulted her arms.

Hank! Lindsay's mind screamed. But she felt her lips open and heard a strange voice whisper, "Hurt you! This is what we do!" Other voices, men's voices, women's voices, said the same, only louder.

From the center of the darkness came heavy sounds of grunting. Panting. There was a stench of sharp, foul body odors and mildew. Dampness

111

teased her skin. It felt like a cellar. Not a basement like her own, warm and carpeted, but an old decaying hole in the ground, where silverfish and centipedes made their homes.

No, that's crazy, she thought. She tried to reach out to find the tiles on her bathroom floor or the smooth side of the bathtub. They were there, she knew. Right out in front of her. Her daughter was there, watching her. Wondering what was happening to her mother.

Lindsay's hands would not move.

"We will serve!" shouted someone to her right.

"Yes, you will serve!" called a man in front of her, and the call was followed by a guttural laugh. "This is the will of the way. Obedience and service."

The grunting before her grew louder. A slapping, pounding rhythm. There was a metallic clinking of chains. Someone was being beaten.

"This is the birthright of the inferior aliens who try to overthrow us. This we do to you!"

Lindsay's unfamiliar voice said, "This we do."

The calls to Lindsay's right and left were chantlike. "Hurt and serve! Hurt and serve!"

The unseen victim began to whimper. His voice caught, contracted, his breath wheezing through clenched teeth.

How can they do this? How can he take this?

To Lindsay's right and left, "Hurt and serve!"

Lindsay's stomach contracted. Acid raced up her throat. She folded over and vomited on the floor.

The vomit spattered on tile. Specks of it splashed onto Lindsay's jeans leg. Grace said, "Mommy, don't cry!"

Lindsay caught the next surge in her hand. It

ran through her lips and then through her fingers. It dripped to her knees.

"Mommy, stop it!" It was Mandy.

Lindsay looked up through her fouled hands at her blind daughter in the tub. There was still a streak of shampoo in her bangs, and her face was wet with water Lindsay had splashed from the plastic cup. Then she looked at Mandy in the doorway. The girl's hands were balled into fists. Her face reflected Lindsay's own, ugly terror.

"Mommy, what's the matter?"

Lindsay slowed her breathing. She took the washcloth from the tub and wiped her fingers and then her knees.

"I'm sorry," she muttered. She stood, shakily, and took the cloth to the sink and rinsed it out.

"What happened?" asked Mandy.

"I'm sorry," Lindsay said. "I don't feel well." Her fingertips hurt. She dropped the cloth into the hamper. "Mandy, could you please get Grace out of the tub?"

Mandy looked at her mother and then at her sister. Then she said, "But there's still cat puke—"

Lindsay screamed, "And my puke is on the bathroom floor! Just get your sister!"

Mandy whispered, "Okay."

Lindsay stood. Mandy came into the bathroom and pulled the towel off the bar.

"Don't step in that."

Mandy said nothing. She slipped her hands under Grace's arms and lifted the child from the water, then carried her out into the hall.

Lindsay stared at the vomit on the tiled floor. Somebody at the reunion had had a virus and passed it on to her. Maybe one of the kids had coughed God-knew-what germs into her face when she hadn't been aware. Maybe the roast beef had been tainted.

She looked at the burns on her fingers. Maybe they were infected. That Lena woman had given her a disease.

Maybe she should have told Hank after all. Maybe this was a biotic problem, not a supernatural one.

"Shit," she muttered. Her stomach still queasy, she took the washrag from the tub and wrung it out. Then she wiped the vomit from the floor and rinsed the rag out in the bathwater. She'd see a doctor tomorrow.

Maybe.

Chapter Twenty-seven

The apartment was so fucking cold, Norris left his coat on for a full hour after he got home. He had turned the heat down before he'd left for Henford, but for some insipid reason had left the window in the bathroom open several inches. It was a miracle someone hadn't discovered that free access to all his worldly goods, even on the second floor. But nothing was wrong other than the fact that the bathmat on the floor was frosted with icy rainwater, the toilet paper on the roll was ruined as were several magazines he'd left on the floor, and everything in the apartment was too goddamn cold to sit on.

"You're brighter than even I would have guessed," he said as he threw the toilet paper into the trashcan and draped the mat across the top of the toilet lid. He closed the window, lit a joint, and paced around until he could feel his blood moving again.

He had brought nothing back from Henford but a promise. A promise he'd have to trust an old man to fulfill. G-Dad had seemed as sympathetic as a senile old man could seem, and he had agreed to supply Norris with the money he'd need to research his medical problem beyond what pathetic amount his teacher's insurance would provide. Norris had asked for fifteen thousand, knowing Lowell never gave what was asked. Lowell had said he would contact his bank Monday morning and forward a check to Norris for twelve. Norris had insisted that the money be in the mail by Tuesday. G-Dad had not seemed particularly concerned about the hurry, or that the check would be written out to Norris himself. Norris blessed senility, and hoped that his grandfather's lack of concern was not a foreshadowing of a promise forgotten.

But the danger lay in Lowell's financial advisors, his sons and daughters, if Lowell decided to talk to them about Norris's request. Norris had insisted that Lowell keep it a secret, explaining it was best that for now, no one else be burdened with what not even the doctors understood. He reminded Lowell of his own bout with cancer eleven years earlier how Lowell had not told his family until the treatments were done and the scare was over.

Norris had then suggested that Lowell sign a note saying he had agreed to send the money, and at that point Norris could see a sudden, distant storm brewing in the old man's eyes. He let the note go. He'd have to believe the old man knew what he had agreed to and would follow through.

Oh, what a tangled web we weave. What a fine thread from which we hang.

Or barbed wire.

Norris took a long, deep draw on his toke. He walked to the thermostat and pushed it up another few degrees. If G-Dad's check came this week, he'd have a few spare bucks to pay the heating bill. We're In the Money had demanded only ten thousand. He went to the kitchen and pulled a Diet Coke out of the fridge. Back in the living room, he flicked on the television and settled down to stare at an episode of "X-Files."

On the counter in the kitchen, the phone rang.

Norris struggled from the sofa and caught it on the third ring. Before he spoke, he took a heavy swig from the can, then another draw on the joint.

"Yeah?"

"Man, you've been gone this weekend. We missed you. We would have left a message on your machine, but we like to talk to people in person."

Norris frowned, took another drink, and tried to pinpoint the voice.

"Teddy?"

"Who's Teddy?"

Norris swallowed, and stared at the receiver. Teddy, the janitor at Bright Creek School, was his only friend in Norfolk. Seven years in this city and he had only one fucking friend. And for a fucking friend, Teddy was a pretty bad choice.

Pathetic. Sad. Not a homophobe, a good source of small, illegal pleasures, but still a slob.

"Then who is this?"

"Now, Norris, you know us. We sent you those

lovely photographs. What did you think? Magazine quality, huh?"

Norris dropped the receiver. He found the counter with his hand and put the Coke there. The cigarette went in and out of his mouth rapidly, like the breathing apparatus of a dying man.

A tiny voice from the dangling receiver said, "Norris? Don't play games with us. We're in business. You're merely a client. Don't make this more than it is."

Norris kicked the receiver. It bounced off a table leg, spun around on its cord, then went still.

"Norris?" said the tiny voice after a moment. "Talk to me now or explain yourself later. If I hang up, there'll be nothing more you can do."

Norris took a last, trembling drag, then put the stub of the smoke into the sink. He slowly picked up the receiver and put it to his ear. It was so cold, he thought the skin of his face would stick to it.

"I'm here," he whispered.

"Good, then." The voice was almost cheerful. It was a sickening thing to hear. "Good, good. Did you like the pictures, now tell me?"

Norris said nothing.

"Tell me or I'll hang up. God, I hate a one-sided conversation."

"What do you think?" said Norris.

"What do I think? I think you had a hell of a good time that night, that's what I think. A lot of fun, playful, full of abandon. Like child's play. Oh, don't mean to step on any feet there, Norris. And if I didn't have such high moral standards, I might even be envious of all that fun. But that's neither here nor there."

Norris picked at the scab from his pathetic attempt at suicide four days ago. It began to bleed.

"Are you ready to take care of business, Norris?"

"Not quite."

"And just what does that mean?"

"I'll have money by the end of the week." Norris drew his tongue across the blood. Then he let his finger move to the burned spot just above the razor cut. He scratched it, trying to make it bleed. It would not.

"Hmm. That's pushing it. Our note said payment due ten days from postmark. It really is reasonable. We aren't a shoddy organization. We're a business. Strong reputation here. This Friday will be exactly ten days. Can you afford to put it off until then?"

"I can't afford it unless I put it off until then."

"What's that?"

"I said I'll have the money on Friday."

"All right, then." The voice sighed, a breathy, musical sound. "We trust your sincerity."

"Sincerity, sure," said Norris. He pushed on the burn. It prickled, shooting out sparks of pain. What had been the matter with that bag lady Lena? How the hell had all three of the cousins gotten fried like that? Why didn't he have caller I.D.? Then he could find them and blast them. How did they know he didn't have it?

"Did you hear me?"

Norris pulled his finger away from the burn. "What?"

"I said a member of the business will be with you until Friday. Watching you, kind of like the Lord, or like Santa Claus, you like that? If we suspect any foul play, we'll pull the deal and publish the pictures. And up on the bulletin boards all around town they'll go, with a set to the school to liven things up. We have a man near your place now. Hell, he might even be under your bed."

Norris stared out of the kitchen to the dark hallway. There was no way someone could be there and he not know.

"You'd like that, wouldn't you, Norris? Ha, just joshing you, man. You'll be all right. You remember how to get it to us?"

It was all he could do to make the words come out. His voice sounded like the inhuman computerized voice of the directory assistance operator. "Unaddressed mailbag. Leave it in my unlocked car under the floor mat in the Toys R Us parking lot at eight PM."

"Yes. Good. And you won't go toy shopping, either, will you, Norris? I know you like toys, what with your love of children, but you'll have taken a cab and gone off far away before eight, right?"

"Right."

"And we'll have a shopper or two, milling around the loading zone, or at the store window, or bustling packages to cars, and you won't know them but they'll know you. They'll take care of everything once you're gone. We'll even lock the car when we're finished, so don't forget to take your keys with you."

Norris found a chipped filling on a back molar and ran his tongue back and forth against it. "I hear you."

"Good, good. Thanks for the cooperation. Good doing business with you, man. Bye-bye."

The phone went dead. Norris put down the

receiver. Carefully, he tiptoed into his bedroom to check under the bed. Finding nothing but dust, he went back into the living room and sank down in front of the television. He punched the remote control, stopping on A&E. The show was a western, and a man was sitting on his horse, waiting to be hanged. Norris turned the set off.

Chapter Twenty-eight

"Now I lay me down to sleep."

It was ten PM Sunday. Bernie was on her knees. Sandra was silent in her bed, already asleep.

Sandra had said it was the devil. Bernie, not believing in a devil, did not know what had happened. She had gone through a hallucination, and she had stabbed her horse with a pitchfork. She'd staggered back to the house, startling everyone at the morning service. They'd raced to the barn, and had stood and gazed with amazed horror at the wounded animal. Bernie had followed them and had stood outside the barn in the mud. Vince called the vet. The others stared between the horse and Bernie, wanting, it seemed for that moment, to be distanced from their sister.

Matt was the first to offer comfort. He ordered John to cover the horse with her blanket, then held Bernie for a long time. When the vet arrived, Matt and Bernie waited outside the barn in the mist. The others had cautiously expressed their concern, and had gone back to the house to hold service alone.

"I pray the Lord my soul to keep. If I should die before I wake . . . "

Bernie began to cry. The vet had not saved Red. "I pray the Lord my soul to take."

Chapter Twenty-nine

Rex stared at the reception-room nurse until she flinched unwittingly and scratched her face as if an insect had landed there. This nurse was middle-aged and nondescript; not the young one who, a month before Rex had flirted with and then called several times and ended up screwing in his bedroom in his little house. The young nurse had since avoided Rex. When Rex visited his uncle in the office, she would find business in the back of the nurses' area. Rex didn't care. She had been a shitty fuck.

Most of the women in the waiting room were pregnant. Most were under thirty and already looking like aged matrons. Flat hair. Ugly shoes and pudgy fingers. A few were not pregnant but in for their cunt checks. Such a busy Monday morning for a pussy doctor. Rex stared at them all, thumbing through magazines and rubbing their bellies. Rex thought if he'd not had a more important role in life, he could have enjoyed being a pussy doctor.

The middle-aged nurse behind the counter called for Rex. "You may go in now, Mr. Wells," she said. Rex strode through the door and turned right. Past the lab to his uncle's office.

Arlen Wells was looking out of the window.

121

Rex shut the door and sat in the chair opposite the desk.

"I need a favor," he said.

Arlen drew a fingertip along the flat of the open blind, then held his finger up, looking for dust. He rubbed his fingertips together and looked again. Seeming satisfied, he spun around in his chair.

"I'm busy today, Rex."

"I could help," said Rex. "I know a clean, healthy pussy when I see one. Put me on as an intern."

Arlen ignored this. He stared up at the ceiling, the side of one eye hitching. Rex opened his mouth and belched out loud. Arlen looked back down. He was frowning. Rex loved getting a reaction from Arlen.

"I need a favor," Rex said again. "As long as I have to stay in that little house and not on my land, I need favors." He dropped his jaw and belched. "My Eagles need to be busy with the goal. Our goal."

Arlen scratched beneath his collar and closed a manila folder on his desk top. "What do you need?"

"I need my land. I need space to think. I need room to build the compound, to bring in more Eagles. I'm sick of waiting."

Arlen said, "I've not closed the deal yet, Rex. You know that. I will let you know when it's ready. Another two or three weeks. I'm handling this calmly, with not a touch of urgency. I suggest you try the same attitude. My way, we take the time needed to talk the price down. That money saved will come in handy later. You'll thank me. Until then, stay happy in that house of yours."

"It's hard to keep my thoughts straight in that shit-hole. Shit-hole. Piss-hole."

"Keep them straight."

Rex banged the toe of his shoe against the floor. He burped again, aiming it out toward his uncle.

Arlen's face turned slightly. Streaked light from the window cut his face, making him look like a painted warrior. His eyes, blue like Rex's, were ice cold. "Keep your thoughts straight, boy. You are our arms here. You do what we can't. We can give you what you can't obtain yourself. We are parts of each other. I keep my ideas and ideals clear here." He touched his thin fingertip to his forehead. "So must you."

Rex tossed his head back and laced his hands behind his head. "I need a favor," he repeated.

"You have so much going for you. Don't forget those who have suffered for these same ideals, ridding our world of those who don't belong. It's not a quick fix we seek."

Rex felt a flare in his chest. He leaned in to his uncle. "Don't lecture me. Don't try to convert me, Arlen. Can you convert me to myself? I have the believers and they listen to me. I make the commands. Shut up and give me the fucking favor."

Arlen stood from his desk. "I've got work," he said. "Quickly, what's the favor?"

"I need a fetus. Maybe two or three."

Arlen did not flinch. What was necessary was necessary. "I don't know if I can. How soon?"

"Tomorrow. Day after tomorrow. No later. Can't lose my Eagles for boredom. Nigger fetus, gook, either is good."

"That's short notice. But I'll let you know."

"I need the fucking things."

Arlen stared at Rex. Then, in his rare gesture of what Rex interpreted to be admiration, he nearly smiled, and said, "By Wednesday, then. Keep your persistence. It's a rare and vanishing white American trait, boy."

Rex stood up. He grinned and tapped his teeth together. "Fuckin-fuckin-fuckin A," he said.

Arlen, for a brief moment, seemed to have a trace of isolated longing in his eyes. Rex could feel his uncle licking the inside of his lips, tasting a jealous tang for the center light he could not have. And then the trace was gone, the cold scientific businessman moving in.

Arlen ushered his nephew out to the hallway.

Chapter Thirty

"It's only the right time if you feel like it," Matt said. "Nobody's pushing." He was turned in the driver's seat of his car, one arm resting on the steering wheel. A brown knit hat was pulled down over his ears. Blond hair was flattened against his neck. In the cold, his skin was paler than usual, the scar on his forehead standing out like a seam in a poorly sewn shirt. "With what happened Sunday, I can't see where you'll be any good for anybody today. Tomorrow will come soon enough."

Bernie ran her hand inside the collar of her sweater, searching for a stray hair that tickled. "Three days is plenty of time. I'm all right."

"I care about you, Bernie."

"I know. That doesn't change my mind."

Matt scrunched his nose, looked out through

the windshield, then back at Bernie. He touched her coat; strummed her arm with firm fingers. The touch cut through her, toying with her steeled resolve, sending compassionate messages that she did not want and could not handle at that moment. She braced herself so she would not pull away.

"Matt, don't lecture me."

Matt withdrew his hand. He held it up in apology. Then he said, "Where should I pick you up?"

"Co-op," she said. "Four-thirty. I've got a list, lightbulbs, dish soap, laundry detergent."

Matt scratched his beard.

"I'm not mad at you. Okay?" she said.

"Okay."

"Be patient. Okay?"

"Sure."

Bernie nodded, then climbed out and closed the Volkswagen door. Matt pulled away into the steady traffic of downtown Henford. Bernie watched until she couldn't see him anymore.

She took the sidewalk along Main Street. The sky was clear. Bright sunlight promised warmth that Bernie knew would not be realized. She could feel the heat of the burns on her hand, even though she'd forgotten her gloves and the air was cold. The burn on her back chafed beneath her sweatshirt and coat. But she forced her thoughts away from them, just as she would not let herself dwell on the death of her horse.

It was selfish to dwell on her losses. It was fruitless to go over and over what had triggered the horrific daydream that had led to her killing Red River. If God would clear it up, He would. But until now, no amount of praying, crying, and reliving had wrung any sense from it. So be it.

She had work to do. She had clients to visit, friends to help. She had Lena Carlton to find.

Bernie passed the card shop with the warm, colorful stuffed Easter bunnies in the show window, past Stan's Snack Shop, which, with a glance through the glass door, she could see was having another slow day. At Quick N' Quality Cleaners, she slowed, and pushed through the door.

There was a single customer being waited on, an elderly man in a business-style wool coat, but the woman on the employees' side of the counter waved Bernie over.

"Bernie. It's good to see you."

"Hi, Lisa. Can I come around?"

"You better," Lisa answered. She leaned over to lift the folding portion of the counter and Bernie came though. "Just give me a second here, okay?" And to the man, who had been writing a check but now stood motionless with his pen in the air, "Quick N Quality," Lisa said.

"Oh." The man grunted. "Yeah." He finished the check and tore it off. "I don't usually come here," he said as he handed the check to Lisa. "I usually use Old Dominion Cleaners down on Arch, but they're closed today."

"Well," said Lisa, turning slightly and giving Bernie a humored, exasperated look as the man collected his plastic-shrouded clothes. "I hope you find us to your satisfaction. And we hope you come again."

The man left the shop.

"Next decade," said Lisa. She smiled, and Bernie, who had not smiled much since Sunday, gave in a little. Lisa Pham was a young Vietnamese woman who had lived in the United

States since she was eight years old. Twenty-four, with black hair cut to her shoulders, she epitomized the beauty of her heritage and the independence of an American businesswoman. She and her husband and mother had moved from D.C. to Henford just over a year ago to escape the violence of the nation's capital and to find a place, Lisa said, which would be more suitable for the family she and Peter hoped to begin. Lisa, Peter, and Mrs. Troung had opened a restaurant, The Golden Garden, in Henford, but vandalism, racist graffiti, and scant customers had thrown them into the red and frightened Mrs. Troung so badly that she refused to work there any longer. Lisa and Peter sold the restaurant and bought into the cleaners along with the original owners, Bill and Regina Bailey. Things had gone well until Bill had disappeared a month ago. Regina stoically kept her hand in the business and filed for an investigation with the Henford police.

And then Lisa's mother was diagnosed with cancer of the spleen.

"How's your mom?" Bernie asked.

"Peter is home with her today." Lisa put the check in the register and snapped it closed. "I don't know if she really understands what is happening to her. I don't know how bad the pain is. The doctor gives her a lot of medication. Maybe he knows her pain from her eyes?"

"Maybe," said Bernie. "I've brought her something. Should I go to your home or give it to you?"

"She doesn't want to see people. Sometimes not even Peter or myself. She wants to dream the day away, to sing her songs and pray her prayers when she is conscious. I best give it to her."

127

Bernie put down the paper bag and pulled out a handmade afghan. It was soft and green, with patterns of peach and an edging of white. "Sandra and I made several of these, and they're really very warm. With this March being as cold as it has been, I think it might be a while before we have spring."

Lisa held the blanket to her face. "Oh, she'll love this, Bernie. That's so nice of you. I've said 'thank you' so much recently, I think it's lost its meaning."

Bernie took Lisa's hand. "You don't need to say anything. We just need to be here for each other." She tightened her upper cheeks, a fight against days-old tears. Dropping Lisa's hand, Bernie said, "And how are you doing?" She nodded toward Lisa's abdomen just below the cloth-covered belt of her shirtwaist dress. There was a knot there, a small but proud boasting of new life.

Lisa smiled her steady smile. "Fine. I'm not very hungry, but my mother said she was the same way with me. My mornings are easier. I don't throw up as much."

"That's good," said Bernie. "And where's Regina?"

"In the back."

"How is she? Anything new on the investigation?"

"Investigation? Of course you're kidding. There's hardly an investigation anymore," said Lisa. "Without actually coming out and saying it, the police indicated that black men leave their wives all the time."

"You're shitting me."

"Not at all."

"I'm afraid it's foul play."

"So am I, though Regina won't come out and admit it. She just says he would come home if he could. She leaves most of the lights on in her house all night, in case he should show up at a late hour. Her electric bill was outrageous this last time. She can't afford that."

Bernie leaned her elbows on the counter and gazed out at the street. Pedestrians, so many of them, walking by. Motorists, so many of them, whizzing down the road. So many people in the world. And here she was, having bribed her way into a commune of believers, a sinner of many sins, a convert forever struggling with the convictions, trying to help God help others. There was too much to do.

The door banged open. A man entered the shop. He was young, in his early twenties with unnaturally curly red hair and a tangle of freckles and pimples across his cheeks and nose. He wore dark glasses. The tips of his ears were red with cold. He stomped his feet as if knocking off snow that was not there. In his arms was a white, bundled sheet.

"I lost my ticket," he said. "George Michael. I bought the clothes in last week."

"No problem," Lisa said. She looked through the large vertical file for the name. "I don't see it."

The man turned to face the counter. "I brung them in. Brown coat and pants. You trying to cheat me?"

"Of course not," said Lisa. "Give me a minute." She turned on the clothes carousel. Bernie watched her work, remembering the first time she had met Lisa and Peter. When the Phams had opened The Golden Garden, Bernie had insisted that she and her then-boyfriend Shawn go to the

129

new establishment. But he had made a small scene once inside the restaurant, refusing to order because he just couldn't trust Orientals or their food. A heated argument followed, and he stalked out, leaving Bernie at the table, and Lisa, menus in hand, watching and listening by the cashier counter. This had been the beginning of the end of Bernie's relationship with Shawn. On her own, Bernie began going to the restaurant, originally to try to get herself off the hook, but then because she found the food outstanding and the owners, Lisa and Peter Pham, to be good people. And when Bernie joined HeartLight, the relationship deepened.

Lisa turned back to the counter. "I don't see them, sir. Maybe you were at another cleaners?"

The side of the man's mouth pulled into a half-grin. He said, "Yeah, maybe I was at that." The man licked his chapped lips, then looked behind him as if he were waiting for someone to join him.

"Sir? May I help you with anything else?"

The man chuckled. It was a strange, drawn-out, ugly sound. "Yeah," he said. "I bet you can."

Bernie picked the paper bag from the floor and rolled the top down for a better grip. "I have to go," she said to Lisa. "I'll see Regina before I leave."

"Okay," said Lisa, but her voice was slightly pinched. Obviously she had some reservations about this man. Bernie decided to wait.

The man dropped his sheet onto the counter. He pressed his palms down on top of it. His hands were dirty, the nails coated with grime, not like a man who worked with engines, but like a man who rarely bathed. When he grinned fully,

Bernie could see a green line of tartar across the top of his incisors.

Lisa reached for her pen to make a receipt. "And when do you need this—"

One filthy hand shot from the sheet and came down on the pen, yanking it from Lisa's grasp. Lisa's eyes narrowed. "Wait a second," she said.

"No. You wait a second," the man said. "I got something to say first." That grin again. Those teeth and cracking lips. That strange red hair reminiscent of a poorly performed hair weave or a cheap wig. He sniffed, looked back over his shoulder, wiped his nose with his coat sleeve. "It ain't right," he said.

"What's that?" Lisa's face was hard now, cautious.

"It ain't right," he repeated. The man laughed suddenly, and Bernie's heart tightened. She began to speak, but Lisa said, "Why don't you tell me what isn't right?"

"You," he said. "You ain't right. You and them blackbirds what run this place. You don't belong in Henford. Chinks. Gooks. Niggers. Aliens!" He lifted his hand from the top of the sheet bundle, and Bernie could see that a dingy fluid had leaked through beneath the pressure.

"I'm calling the police," said Lisa.

"Go 'head," said the man. "I said my piece."

Lisa's eyes flashed. "Get out of here!"

The man tossed the pen at Bernie. It hit the counter and rolled off the edge. He spun around and hurried to the door, his laughter and the tails of his coat trailing.

Bernie raced around the counter to the door. She wanted to catch a make of car, a license plate. *Something, damn that bastard!* But the man was no longer to be seen. Bernie stepped outside into the cold. The man was gone. The Wednesday morning hustle had whisked him away.

"Damn!" she shouted. Indignation burned her throat. She went back in to Lisa. The woman was against the wall. Her eyes were closed. "Lisa, he was a jerk." God, it was hard to be calm. Hard to not want to find the man and beat the filthy shit out of him. "He was ignorant. There are people like that everywhere."

Her eyes still shut, Lisa said slowly, "I know."

"Lisa, let's call the cops. He won't get away with this."

"Okay."

"Lisa?"

Lisa opened her eyes. "I hear what you say, Bernie. I should be toughened to this by now. It was bad with the restaurant. But it never stopped. It's getting worse."

"I didn't know."

"Phone calls, vandals. We had the front door replaced three times."

"I didn't know. Why didn't you tell me?"

"We take care of what we can."

Bernie slammed her fist down on the counter. "It's so cruel. This is my town. How dare they do this?"

"I'll toss this out," Lisa said, touching the sheet. "Then I'll call the police, just like we have for every phone call, every broken door. Maybe with time, sheer quantity will get us some protection." She picked up the sheet the man had left. Something inside shifted, and as Lisa tried to collect it better, it fell open.

Lisa screamed.

Cradled inside a fold of the sheet, the arms posed as if in prenatal prayer, its glassy little eyes opened and sightless, the coiled umbilical cord stiff and gummy, was a five-month-old Asian fetus.

A note had been stapled to its tiny head.

It read, "Caught in the nick of time. Love, the White Eagles."

Chapter Thirty-one

"Teddy, you're never going to amount to shit. You don't have to stay here. If I had a choice, I'd run from this place like pus out of an infected cold sore."

"I got what I want. A nice home, a warm bed, cash for extras and women when I'm in the mood. I been to Florida. I don't like it. Too many old people. Get your shoes off my spread."

Norris dug his feet deeper into the stained blue blanket Teddy used on his mattress. "Sue me," he said.

"I might."

Norris stretched his shoulders and closed his eyes for a moment. Then he looked back at Teddy. Old Teddy, old, stinking Teddy, the janitor at Bright Creek.

"You gonna stay here all night?" Teddy asked.

"Maybe."

"I don't want you here. You smell like a drunk."

"I am a drunk. Most of the time," Norris said. He wiped his nose, clearing away the snot from his newly acquired cold and the beads of beer from his beard. Between his fingers dangled a fine, potent joint that Teddy had sold him for a pittance. Teddy was, after all, the closest thing Norris had as a friend in all of Norfolk. Sometimes he put the screws to Norris, sometimes he was magnanimous. He knew what Norris was and what Norris wasn't and he didn't give a shit. He was a hardheaded fucker, but he always had what Norris needed.

Norris looked at Teddy's yellow cat, an unneutered male that had to be, in cat years, the equivalent to Teddy Parsons. Mid, late seventies. The cat was crusty and mean. It hated Norris, and Norris hated the cat. It crapped and sprayed where it wanted, and Teddy didn't seem to care. He would merely kick the little black, dusty shit balls off into corners when they were where he wanted to walk.

Teddy sat on his lawn chair, a bent piece of trash salvaged from the back-alley garbage of Bright Creek School. Around the storeroom that served as his apartment were pieces that could well make a small museum of the school's history. An old flat-top desk, an ancient Underwood typewriter. Boxes of odd, discarded textbooks and magazines. The old man had worked at Bright Creek for nearly thirty years. He lived in the storage room with the blessing of the administration, because he was available in case of emergencies, although none of any interest had occurred in thirty years. He had a lot of money, Norris was certain, but the man was fanatical about it. Norris had once jokingly asked for a loan. Teddy had said he would take the Haitian machete he kept under his bed and cut the balls off any man who tried to take what was his.

Norris decided he'd let some other fool try to part Teddy from his cash.

But it was Teddy's other stash that kept Norris coming back for more. For an old fart, Teddy was amazingly up-to-date. He knew his way around Norfolk like a rat knew its way around sewers. He was friends with no one, but knew nearly everyone and could get anything he wanted or needed.

Norris knew this about Teddy because Teddy trusted him. It was not a trust of love or of soul mates. It was a trust based on an unbalanced quid pro quo. Teddy knew a hell of a lot more about Norris than Norris would ever know about Teddy. Nights of drinking with the old janitor brought out bits of honesty in Norris. Smoking grass on top of it all brought chunks of his soul out with the honesty.

Teddy knew about the mistake Norris had made with a Bright Creek student in January.

"You can't sleep here tonight. I might have company coming," Teddy said. He had a bottle of vodka on the flat-top desk beside him, and a paper cup in his hand. "You got your own apartment. Finish your beer and get out of here. Go find you a skinny little man. You need it."

"Don't kick me out, Teddy. I'll have a wreck. They'll sue you for letting me drive, like they sue those bartenders who kick drunks out and then they end up running over pedestrians. You want that on your head?"

"Fuck yourself, Norris."

"Did that already," Norris said. "Royally." He closed his eyes again. Several times, when Norris had actually fallen asleep on Teddy's mattress, the old man had left him alone. If Norris pretended to

135

go to sleep, maybe Teddy would let him stay. If not, then he could at least hang around and argue with Teddy a bit longer. Anything to not go home. Anything to not think about tomorrow.

There was silence for a moment. Norris didn't hear the bottle gurgle. Maybe the old man was thinking, or picking his nose. The persistent thought pressed his brain.

G-Dad is senile, he probably forgot. Norris opened his eyes to chase the thought away. Teddy was staring at him.

"You being scared is pretty funny," said Teddy. "You never been that way, I guess."

"I never had five jobs in seven years. I never let my fun get me pinned down and sweating like a cow in a slaughterhouse. You're a case."

"I thought he was eighteen. He said he was eighteen."

"Spare me," said Teddy. He stood, arched his back. His spine popped. He walked over to the door that led to the hallway, opened it, and looked out. Cool air drifted in around his feet. Norris blinked and shook his head; for a moment, he thought there were ghosts riding in with the air. Cold, transparent ghosts that would run their clammy fingers through his hair and tickle his shoulders.

A strange smell in the air reached his nose. Wood smoke, cooking meat. Norris frowned. The burning wood smell was edged with a tang of pine needles. The scent encircled his head and made his taste buds rise to attention—making the blood in his veins chill. It was too early for the cooks to be in to make breakfast for the boys. Besides, the kitchen was not even in the maintenance building. How could he be smelling this?

It had been a long time since he'd been camping. But the odors were certain. Some things your brain cells would never shake free. Some things were always there, ready in the memory juke box, waiting for the coin of music. The coin of smell. The last time he went camping, they cooked bacon over a crackling campfire. The last time he went camping, the campfire went out of control.

The last time, there was destruction. He rubbed his nose, trying to rub the smells away. Cold ghosts, wood smoke. He didn't want to remember. He licked his lips, and the taste of fried meat came off on his tongue. There was a trace of pine in the taste.

"You look sick," said Teddy. "Puke elsewheres."

Norris tried to clear his throat, to clear away the taste. "You smell something? Something cooking?"

"You really are smashed. Go to sleep on that blanket on the floor, man. Your babble done give me a headache."

Norris licked his lower lip again. The taste was fading. The cold air, which had brought the scents and the taste, wiped his mouth clean with an icy caress.

"Huh," Norris said. He shivered. He was drunk, that was all. Just a little overstimulation of his pickled imagination centers. Hardly the first time something strange had happened because of the fermented molecules running in his circulatory system. "Shut the door. It's too cold to sleep."

Teddy shut the door. He went back to his chair and flipped the switch on the small set atop a TV tray. It hummed, then came to life. David Letterman was talking to Richard Simmons.

Norris slipped off the cot, dragging the cat-piss blanket with him. He was almost tempted to throw a weak joke in Teddy's direction, "Hey, Grandpa, tuck me in and bring me a glass of water," but no sooner had he thought the thought and found it vaguely amusing than the harsh reality of what could face him tomorrow came ramming up his spine like a skewer in a roasting pig.

The old man might forget. The old man, damn all of life, had to remember.

Norris slept very little on Teddy's storeroom floor.

Chapter Thirty-two

Norris could barely teach Friday. He put a huge textbook assignment on the board, two full pages of chapter review questions, and sat on his stool at the side of the room. The three morning periods of ninth-grade world geography crept by as though the world itself had decided to do a slow-mo on its daily spin. Norris had a mug full of Diet Coke, but couldn't drink it. Several times, his hand shook so badly he spilled drips onto his pants legs. He stared at the clock, and couldn't stop from grinding his teeth. Any student who looked at him funny, he threatened with a white slip.

At lunch, he went to the teachers' lounge, dumped his warm Diet Coke down the sink, and bought another one. To this he added a pack of Van-O-Lunch vanilla cookies. He sat at a table with the science teacher, Bob Thomas, because Bob never had much to say. The cookies went down painfully; the Diet Coke tasted as bitter as dandelion juice.

After lunch, Norris had one class of tenth-grade world history, and two of tenth-grade remedial reading. One of the hardest-core tenth graders, Kevin Sears, in Bright Creek for assault and attempted rape of a middle-school teacher, threatened to stab his reading partner with a compass he'd stolen from his math class. It was all Norris could do to keep from grabbing the broom from his closet and cracking the shit out of Kevin's nose and then claiming the kid had fallen into a wall. Instead, he managed to corner Kevin between the chalkboard and file cabinet, then sent a little toady to the office for an administrator.

All in all, it was a normal day. All in all, it was the worst day Norris had spent at Bright Creek.

Norris climbed into his car at 3:48 and braced his ice-cold hands on the steering wheel. Through his windshield, he watched the other nonresident teachers hit the road with maximum speed, not looking back. He turned the key in the ignition, listened as the engine and the radio popped into life simultaneously, but the clamp on his stomach wouldn't allow him room to lean into the accelerator. There was sweat in his beard.

For a minute, he reconsidered the thought of leaving town and not looking back. Maybe he shouldn't even go back to his apartment. What earthly goods he had accumulated there had no major value. They were utilitarian bits of living which anyone could pick up at any hardware or second hand-furniture store anywhere around the country.

But he knew they had been watching him ever since they had sent the letter. He knew it was

139

worth their while to keep tabs on this teacher, to shadow his footsteps and monitor his goings and comings. The moment he skipped out, they would publish the proof of his indiscretion. Criminal charges would follow. He would be hunted down and dragged back. Nobody could hide forever.

Certainly not a child molester. Even an unintentional one.

Norris slammed his fist into his forehead. It didn't hurt enough, so he slammed himself again. A dull pain played outward like ripples on a pool, then dissipated. The bank was open until seven on Friday night.

He had until eight to complete the transaction in the Toys 'R Us parking lot, if there was going to be a transaction. He pressed the gas and drove home.

Pulling up in front of the shabby apartments, he waited and watched as the mailman delivered his burden and walked off to the next building.

"God," said Norris. He got out of the car and went up the walk. As he opened the door, the invisible wife with the shitty, whining poodle was in the hall, clawing through her stash of mail. Her being there enraged Norris. *Get the fuck out of the hall!* he thought.

The woman gave Norris a look as though she thought he was going to shoot her, quickly scooped up her nappy-coated rag dog, and went back into her apartment.

Norris found his mailbox key in his pocket, pulled it out and dropped it. It pinged on the floor and bounced against the wall. Norris reached for it, missed, cursed, and reached again. He caught it between his fingers. He stood, and put the key into his mailbox. He swallowed. A nail caught in his esophagus. He opened the box.

There were several slick department-store flyers, and a single envelope. He fished it out. The return address was Henford.

Goddamn you to hell if you've failed me. You promised, you old shit. Fuck you to hell if you've screwed me over.

Norris ripped the envelope in half. Inside, a certified check from G-Dad was wrapped in a short note inquiring on Norris's health and spelling out a repayment schedule which Norris was to sign and return.

Yes.

"Oh, yes," Norris whispered. Then he shouted, "Yes! Oh, God, thank you, yes!" He could almost see the flat, bored faces of the invisible wives flinch at the shouts from the downstairs hallway, and imagine their wide eyes moving quickly to press against the peepholes in their sanctuary doors.

Chapter Thirty-three

The March shamrocks that had hung from the nursery-school ceilings were down, and Easter eggs hung in their places. It was the first day of April, almost a week and a half since the Lynch family reunion. Lindsay was more than ready to move on. Everyone seemed happier in the spring.

Bad things didn't happen in the spring.

The weekday nursery class at Stone House United Methodist Church was in the middle of their music time. Laura Hiner, the music director, sat at the piano, tinkling out a rendition of "Itsy-Bitsy Spider" as the three-and four-year-olds, on the rug on the floor, tried to keep up with their fingers. Many of them giggled as they sang. Two boys in the front ran their spider fingers through each other's hair until the head teacher, Carla Myers, a large woman with red hair, went over to sit between them.

At the back of the group Lindsay sat with Grace. Grace, at six, was a full head taller than the other children, and so she had to sit back so the others wouldn't have to crane to see around her. Grace held her fingers lightly against her mother's, laughing as Lindsay made the crawling motions upward.

"Come on, honey, you try it," Lindsay urged, but Grace, after a few jumbled attempts of her own, went back to feeling her mother's fingers. The child seemed to enjoy her mother making crazy motions. A normal little girl, thrilling to her mother making a fool of herself.

The song stopped. All the little hands went down; most of the fingers went still.

Lindsay said, "We're going to sing another song. You try this one, okay?" But Grace was content to feel her mother's fingers and listen to her mother's voice.

Music time ended. It was time for snacks. Grace, knowing this, clung to her mother as Lindsay went into the kitchen with Carla to lay the apple slices out and pour the juice. The kitchen was small and brightly decorated, with flower magnets on the refrigerator and animal sun-catchers on the window. Lindsay took several cartons out of the refrigerator and set them on the counter beside the tray full of empty paper cups.

"What drink?" asked Grace.

"Orange juice, Grace," said Carla.

"Orange juice today," said Lindsay. "Now find a chair while I pour, because I don't want to make a mess."

"I want help."

"Not with this. You can help me pour drinks tonight for supper."

Grace pouted, and reached out for the small dinette table in the center of the kitchen. She pulled herself down on one of the wooden chairs. Carla took the apple slices from the large covered bowl and put them in a single layer on another tray.

"If only it was a few degrees warmer," Carla said. "I'd have these kids outside eating their snacks. They all seem so much happier when they can go outside. *I'm* a whole lot happier when they can go outside."

"Yes," said Lindsay. Small talk. She wasn't best buddies with Carla. The relationship between Carla and Lindsay had always been a bit strained because of Grace's enrollment. Carla thought Grace's needs would be better met with teachers better trained for children like her. Lindsay thought a child with no eyes spooked Carla.

Outside the kitchen, visible through the door, the other children found their places at the long cafeteria-style table. Laura Hiner called for their attention for the snack-time blessing.

Lindsay moved the juice carton over the cups, filling them in nearly to the top. She paused and looked over at Grace, who had her head tilted in

143

the direction of the social hall where the other children were giving thanks for their impending apple slices and orange juice. Lindsay felt a sudden pang of grief for the wider circle of life Grace would never have. Then she shook her head, knocking that impotent anger from her thoughts, because indeed her daughter was doing well. Her daughter was happy and loved. Grace would be, with her help and with Hank's, a child with a measure of success.

She turned back to the counter and tipped the carton to fill the last of the cups.

And her hands flew up and back, dropping the carton with a heavy thump and a splash of thick, terrible red. She cried out and stumbled backward into the table.

Blood.

She thought she heard Carla call her name, and then all was swallowed and narrowed—sounds, smells, sights. Narrowed like the tunnel vision on a worn television set in a darkened room; she could see nothing but the carton of juice. It teetered where she had let it fall, balancing on the edge of the counter and then toppling forward in her direction. The mouth of the carton spewed a wave of dark, viscous fluid.

Blood.

It flipped, spinning the blood outward, an airborne trail like a shiny red comet tail caught in a tornado. The blood hit Lindsay on her skirt and exploded in a scarlet flower.

The skirt wasn't hers. She tried to put her hands to her face to block out the splash of red, but the hands weren't hers, and they wouldn't move. Instead, they hung limply in the air. She looked back at the floor where the carton had landed, and the carton was not a carton now. In was an upended plastic bowl, with blood pooled around it. The floor was bare, cracked concrete. The blood was already forming a rivulet, seeking out a drainhole, trickling by her feet. Feet tucked into black, shiny sandals with broken buckles.

Not my feet!

Lindsay stared at the bowl and the blood. She stared at the skirt, a horrid piece of wraparound corduroy, and at the filthy white hose bagging down around her ankles.

Dear God, what is happening?

"Stupid bitch!" growled a male voice to her side.

She started to turn her head to the voice, but a hand lashed out and struck her on the jaw. Her head jerked to the side with a painful snap. Dizziness and sudden nausea knocked her to her knees.

And, never one to faint, because she was of strong, hardheaded Lynch stock, Lindsay felt her eyes twirl and then roll up into the blackness above her lids. She passed out.

Chapter Thirty-four

"Stupid bitch!" screamed Junior, and the other White Eagles watched in horror as Lena lay on the floor in the blood where Junior had knocked her. She had spilled the drink; she had fumbled when Lizzie passed the bowl to her and had let it fall.

"Stupid fucking bitch!" Junior poised his foot and looked at Rex, and when Rex didn't respond one way or the other, Junior drove his foot into the woman's stomach. Silently, she coughed and folded over, but didn't try to protect herself. Junior kicked her again, then said, "Damn, what are we supposed to do now? Bleed him again?"

Rex said, "We'll do the Arm Test."

Junior hesitated. He was always awed by the Arm Test, no matter how frequently Rex used it. "Okay," he said, his bug eyes twitching. The other White Eagles, standing in a circle on the floor of the basement, nodded too. Rex stepped off the bottom basement step, where he had been standing and watching since taking the first drink and then passing the bowl to Lizzie.

The blood was that of the new alien in the crawl space, the teenage boy named Rusty Nolen. Rex and Ronald had caught the youth at his home last night. It had been a surprising fringe benefit. After dropping the dead chink baby off at the cleaners, they were going to deliver the black grub fetus to the Nolen household and smash a few windows. Rex knew the Nolens. The daddy was a Henford policeman and had once given Rex a ticket for speeding.

"Slow down here," Rex had said, pointing. Ronald, who had at last removed the natty red wig he'd worn to the stint at the cleaner's and thrown it into the backseat, turned off the headlights and parked the car in the pines in the empty lot between the second to the last house on Arch Road and the little gray box that was Paul Nolen's home. Rex told Ronald to stay put, to play getaway driver, and Rex took a baseball bat and the plastic bag with the baby from the rear seat. He sneaked through the trees to the wire fence and wooden gate that separated the Nolens' backyard from the wilderness of the mountain.

It was a good night.

Rex crammed the plastic bag into the Nolen mailbox. He felt around in the dark for the latch on the gate, catching a few minor splinters in the process, and then pushed it open. After stepping into the Nolens' yard, he crept past the well pipe, a swing set, and a storage shed to the back walkway. He stopped, close enough to lean over and touch the glass of one of the rear windows. Someone was home. He could hear the television, playing some bongo shit. He grinned, thrilled to be so close to the enemy on its own territory.

He lifted the bat, ready to smash the window, ready to yell something about the beauty of dead black babies, when the kid came out of the shed.

Rex spun on his toe as he heard the shed door smack shut. The kid stopped, dropping the can of fuel he was holding. His mouth opened, ready to say something. Rex didn't give him the chance.

Instead of the window, Rex smashed the kid.

As he dragged the unconscious boy across the yard and out through the gate, he reconciled the deed with the fact that he hadn't planned on taking more aliens until the White Eagles moved to the land. But this one was a gift, and you didn't look gift horses in the mouth.

The boy was alive, as Rex had wanted. Wounded, dizzy, puking, but alive. Ronald helped Rex get the boy into the basement, and Billy Bailey had an instant roommate. Rex gathered the White Eagles to welcome the new boy the next morning. The Arm Test told the Eagles that a blood ceremony was a good way to celebrate. If silence meant consent, then Rusty Nolen consented to have Dean nick his thigh with a razor and to squeeze out a bowlful of blood for the Eagles' ceremony. That Rusty was bound and gagged the same way as Bill Bailey wasn't taken into consideration.

And now the blood was spilled. Everyone was supposed to have a sip, to taste alien blood and develop an immunity.

Rex walked into the middle of the circle. "Arm Test," he said. "To see if we should get the blood from the nigger or from her." He nodded at the woman on the floor. She didn't see him nod, her face was down, one fat arm bent up and over her face. The blond hair on her head was growing back; it was soft now, baby down.

"Peaches, you do the test."

Peaches stepped out from between Lizzie and Dean and stopped in front of Rex. She tried to smile, but Rex could see the fear and awe in her eyes. The Arm Test. Simple, powerful. Believed by Rex Wells's followers to be the intervention of the power of the Truth. And their total belief almost had Rex believing it at times, and such a strange sensation that was.

"Are we to cut the nigger boy again to drink his blood?" Rex stretched his arm out.

Peaches pulled. The arm came down.

"Can I cut him again?" It was Dean.

"One more question," said Rex. "Lizzie."

Lizzie grasped Rex's outstretched arm.

"Do we cut Lena and mix her blood with the nigger's, so we become immune to inferiors and carelessness?"

Lizzie pulled. The arm came down.

"So be it," said Rex. The Eagles, even the woman on the floor, her arm over her face, said, "So be it."

Chapter Thirty-five

Oh my God my back hurts my head hurts.

"Call 911, Laura, hurry up! I'll stay with her."

Oh God my back hurts my fingers hurt!

"Lindsay, please open your eyes!"

There were the sounds of shuffling feet, the sounds of breathing directly over her, the sounds of panic. And the sounds of children crying. Little children, the shrill wail of children afraid of something, and the sound of someone trying to comfort them.

"Shhhh, shhhh."

One of the children's voices cut through the pain and the confusion. A little girl's voice, sobbing softly. A familiar voice.

Lindsay opened her eyes. "Grace?" Lindsay was on the kitchen floor at the nursery school. Someone had put a folded jacket under her head, and a coat over her lap. Carla was beside her, patting her hand.

"Lindsay, you're awake! What happened? We've called an ambulance, it'll be here in just a minute."

"Where's Grace?"

Laura was there, then, at the kitchen door, holding Grace's hand. "Grace, I'm here. Laura, bring her over."

Laura, her face bunched in doubt, led Grace to her mother. Lindsay sat up gingerly, fresh pain springing up in the back of her head where she'd hit the floor, and wrapped her arms around her daughter.

149

"I'm all right, Grace, I just fell down."

Grace let herself be pulled down. She buried her face in her mother's neck. "You're sticky," she whispered, her voice still hitching from the sobs.

"Sticky? Silly me!" Lindsay forced herself to laugh. There was juice all over the floor, all over her skirt and her arms. When she went down, the snack went with her.

And what had happened?

"Are you still dizzy?" asked Laura. "Shortness of breath? The emergency people wanted to know."

"I think I'm okay," Lindsay said. She held Grace tighter. "Laura, I think I just fainted for some stupid reason. I don't need an ambulance. Please call them back."

Grace rose up from her mother and wiped her tear-covered face. "Don't go in 'bulance!"

"Honey." Lindsay gently moved her daughter off her lap, then grabbed the seat of a dinette chair and pulled herself up. She let the coat drop to the sticky floor. "I'm not going in an ambulance. I'm all right, Laura. Maybe I've got a virus coming on. Please, call them back."

"You scared everyone! We had to do something."

But what had she been dreaming? What had she seen?

"I'm sorry, and thank you, you were right to call. But call them back. Okay?"

Reluctantly, "All right." Laura left the kitchen.

Carla pulled a wet mop from the utility closet and soaked it in the sink. As Lindsay picked the carton off the floor and began to collect the scattered paper cups, Carla said, "Lindsay, what really happened?"

What really happened? I felt sick, I felt the floor drop out from under me. I saw . . .

Lindsay stopped, stood upright, a stack of juice-tacky cups in her hand. "It was nothing." *I saw blood. I saw a bowlful of blood. I saw black sandals and a concrete floor and then someone hit me in the face.*

New pain flared on her cheek. Lindsay caught her face in her hand. Her breath caught in her lungs like a flimsy rag on a thorn bush.

I saw blood and someone hit me in the face, a man I don't know.

She swallowed. She closed her eyes and saw the blood again. Her eyes sprang open. She looked at her fingertips. The burns were bright red, mocking.

And then the tip of her index finger split open. Lindsay gasped. Bright red blood poured down into the palm of her hand.

Lindsay wrapped the finger in a dish towel from the counter, squeezed it tightly to stop the blood and the haunted agony, so she wouldn't have to see it and think about it and understand it . . .

Direct pressure

. . . and Grace sat quietly as her mother tidied up the mess she'd made and mixed a new gallon of Kool-Aid because there wasn't enough leftover juice to go around.

Chapter Thirty-six

Rex's voice was calm now. "This will help protect us."

Lena stood in the center of the circle. Rex gave the knife back to Dean.

Rex kneaded Lena's sliced index finger and the blood dripped into the bowl, mixing with the nigger boy's blood, making one powerful, protective potion for the clan of the saviors of the future.

"Drink this to make us strong in preparation for the coming wars."

Chapter Thirty-seven

The clothesline stretched from T-pole to T-pole, and most of the dried clothes had been removed and were folded in the green basket. Beside Bernie's feet sat a blue basket of clean, wet clothes ready to take their places on the line once the others were down. A cloth sack of wooden clothespins hung around her waist.

It was a sun-spattered morning, April the second. The forecast for the next several days promised clear skies, cool breezes, and lots of sunshine. Matt and Harner had left in the truck at six-thirty that morning, heading off to finish the porch job down the road and hopefully to collect their pay. John was in Henford with Matt's Volkswagen, taking a batch of his homemade bread loaves to the Salvation Army. Sandra was in her newly tilled garden down near the pasture gate, putting out spinach and lettuce. From the clothesline at the side of the farmhouse, Bernie could watch Sandra as she worked, and it was a soulful, peaceful thing to see.

Synchronicity. Harmony. Human and nature. Nature and the Divine.

Bernie shivered. No breeze had stroked her neck, yet she felt a brief tickle. She began to put up the damp clothes. Matt's jeans, Sandra's socks, Harner's work shirt and underwear, John's handkerchiefs. Not a lot for five people. Little fashion with which to be concerned. The way it ought to be. One of the pathways to synchronicity. To harmony. To a closer understanding with nature, and with the Divine.

Bernie dropped a dishtowel onto the line, pinned it down. But what if the Divine decides you need a little testing in your synchronized life? A little trial? It was easier to love God when He was at a distance, smiling on you occasionally, approving your actions for the good of mankind. How much harder when He steps up close.

If that was what was happening. She couldn't be certain.

She slapped wet socks on the line next to the towel. She shook out a washcloth and hung it beside the socks.

After three weeks of searching, she still had not found Lena Carlton. She had flipped over all the town rocks, asking questions, watching street corners, everything short of having a police artist make up a penciled rendition of the white, startled face she'd come in contact with in the Henford Hotel the afternoon of the Lynch family reunion. Finding Lena, Bernie had decided, might be part of a Divine challenge. And the unhealed burns, a reminder.

But were the hallucinations from God? They were hellish and terrifying, even the small ones, the faint ones. The angry, gibberish voices she heard on the periphery of reality each night as she drifted to sleep. Voices she did not recognize. Hissing voices, swollen with emotion, picking at the edges of her consciousness. "Who are you?"

153

Bernie would try to say, but her lips were sleep-numb, and then she would fade into the dark arms of the night.

And then there were the smells. Rotten potatoes, stabbing Bernie's olfactory cells as she drove Matt's car around Henford. Stark scents of mildew and rust as Bernie sat to supper with the other members of HeartLight.

No one else heard the voices. No one else smelled the smells. Bernie was alone with her puzzle, her fear.

You're wasting a beautiful day worrying, she told herself. *You're ignoring God's simple gift*. She wrapped her arms around her waist, staring at Sandra's tilled soil and the pregnant mounds. The breaths she took were deep, drawing in the sweet, muddy scent. Clearing away the surreal with the real. Letting the benign simplicity of a new garden soothe the distress. Catching a moment of stillness, gentle mindlessness.

Riding Red River used to bring her that same feeling. Peace.

Peace.

She felt the sudden change in the air before she felt the impact. There was an audible "swoosh," lifting the ends of her hair, and then a crash between her shoulder blades. She grunted in surprise and pain, and fell forward toward the garden.

The grave?

Her hands couldn't move fast enough; her fingers slashed, grasping for something, catching nothing. Around her, spring sunlight had been swallowed by dark rain. It hissed on nearby trees, hammered dead grass; it sloughed dirt from the grave's sides, funneling muddy rivers down into the dreadful black maw.

Hard, cold autumn rain. Brown grass and trees with dying leaves. Footprints about the grave, deep in the mud.

All this Bernie saw as she teetered, then tumbled into the grave.

The cold blackness rushed upward to embrace her. She arched backward so it would not. She hit the floor of the grave, face down. Her breath was knocked free with the force of an exorcised demon. She twisted her head, dragging the sludge, working her mouth, praying for air. When it came a moment later, mud was sucked in with it.

Above her, there was heavy laughter.

She struggled, gasping, choking mud. She tried to draw her knees up to stand, but one would not move. She found her right hand, caught under her chest, and pulled it free. She wiped her face. Dirt stung her eyes. She spat around a thick clot of gravel and mud and hideous worm-taste.

God!

Above her, closer now, leaning down, a breath hot in the cold rain. "See how you like this, now!"

Bernie coughed violently. She moved her hand down to the immobile leg. Her skirt (skirt?) was hiked up and twisted around. Her upper leg, strangely thin, was numb. Bernie swallowed, a reflex full of terror and impotence. Her fingers crawled further down the small leg. At the knee, she stopped.

Beneath a cold slick of grave mud was a warm flow. Bernie's mouth opened. She spit dirt, and inhaled dirt. "No," she said. It was the little-girl's

155

voice. Her fingers traced the curve where the knee should be. The warm flesh was coated in mud, and blood was gushing out. It was then she found the bone. Slimy and ragged, protruding through the flesh just below the kneecap.

And it was then the sensation of raw, raped nerves and shattered bone kicked into overdrive.

Bernie threw back her head in the rain. She screamed.

A hand took her upper arm and flipped her over. Her eyes, twisted shut in pain, sprang open. Above her, the blue sky of an early spring morning was spotted with distant white cloud puffs. In the center of the sky was Sandra's terrified face.

"Bernie!"

Bernie's scream trailed.

"Bernie, stop it!"

"Help me! My leg's broken!"

"Then don't move. I'll help you."

Bernie wiped dirt from her mouth; she pushed herself up and looked at her legs. In her ears, rain was still hammering. Her jeans were not torn. She touched the spot below her kneecap, the place where she'd felt the slick, oily bone, the gushing blood, the ravaged skin.

"A compound fracture," she said. "My leg is broken. I'm bleeding."

Sandra caught Bernie's chin and turned her around to look in her face. "Bernie, what are you saying?"

Bernie looked at her friend. Her friend? Had she pushed her into the rain-filled grave? Her heart skipped. "Sandra—" she began. She couldn't finish.

Sandra's fingers were a flurry over both her legs. "You don't have a compound fracture," she said. "Can you move them?"

Bernie moved her legs slowly in the dirt of the garden.

"They aren't broken, then?"

"I . . . no."

"I don't see any blood."

"No."

Sandra stared at her friend. Then she held out her hand. "You're going to bed. Something's wrong, Bernie. Let me help you."

Bernie looked at the hand. This was not a hand of violence. She took it.

With her arm around Bernie, Sandra slowly walked her up the yard to the porch of the house. Sandra kept her head down, deep in thought. Bernie said nothing, the rain, the grave, the blood, and the pitchfork in Red's chest taking turns on the back screen of her brain.

At the porch step, Sandra said, "I believe it's the devil at work, Bernie. Hear me out. I really think there's a trial here. Your faith is being tested."

Bernie thought, *A test, yes. But it's not a devil*.

They stepped onto the porch and went around the stacks of wood to the front door. "You get to bed," said Sandra. "I'm going to talk with the others when they get home. We're here to help you. We love you. Let us help you."

Bernie said nothing. She thought, *It's not a devil testing me. It's God*.

And the truth, the resignation, was infinitely more frightening.

Chapter Thirty-eight

The man's house was average, a single-story with paved driveway and new shutters, and as Norris looked through the front door, he felt a peculiar shiver of haughty superiority.

If I wanted, I could have much more than this.

The man, Tom Murphy, wiped his feet on the welcome mat just inside the door, then stepped out of the way to let Norris come in. Tom, a twenty-seven-year-old accountant with a local firm and a part-time musician as well, lived in Chesapeake, a good hour from Norris's home in Norfolk. Norris had met Tom at a club on the south end of Virginia Beach's oceanfront strip.

"If things don't start warming up, I'm thinking of moving to Florida. I wasn't built for cold weather." He shed his coat, waited for Norris to do the same, then hung them in the hall closet. He strode into his living room and flicked the switch. Two sofa-side lamps came on. The living room was small and comfortable, the furniture upholstered in bright Aztec patterns.

Norris, still standing in the hall, said, "Nothing in Florida but trailers, white hair, and three-wheeled bikes."

Tom laughed. He was a handsome man, taller than Norris by a foot, sandy hair naturally waved and almost shoulder length. "Further south," he said. "Key West. I've never been, but I hear it never gets cold. Hot as hell, yes, but never cold."

Norris stepped into the living room. The carpet was dense and cushiony. Tom went around the corner, into what Norris imagined was the kitchen, and came back out with a decanter and a pair of wineglasses. "Have a seat," he said, looking a little confused as to why Norris was still standing. "No bedbugs in the sofa, don't worry. I gave them the night off."

Norris sat on the sofa. He adjusted the collar of his black shirt and ran his hands down the crease in his new jeans. He had worn this outfit three nights in a row now, laundering the shirt and jeans carefully in the afternoons so they would retain their look of new. Three nights of celebration. Three nights of cruising unfamiliar locations, looking for some pleasant company for the evening. G-Dad had come through. Norris had delivered the money to Toys R Us in the mailbag, had taken off in a yellow cab for an hour, then returned to find the store closed, the shoppers vanished, and his own car, unmolested and locked safely.

Story over. End of the scare.

And so celebration seemed appropriate. Norris had driven to the outlying areas of Ocean View and Virginia Beach and Hampton, keeping away from places he'd been before, finding without too much trouble attractive men with good senses of humor and passions needing to be spent. Saturday night had been a burly man named Racer, maybe his real name, probably not. Sunday night was a thin, pale man called Philippe. Philippe had a wild array of body piercings that made Norris wince.

And tonight, probably a mistake because it was the beginning of the school week and Norris did have several tests to construct and give by Thursday, he had found Tom.

"My ears are still ringing from that last band.

Hey, I'm not a musical bigot, don't get me wrong. But I'll take the softer tones anytime. I will never be a head-banger unless I'm reincarnated as one. And I'd still wage a protest, believe me."

Norris nodded. He hated this part. Small talk, discussions on the state of the union or the state of record labeling or the state of the rights movement. Sometimes the other person was good at it and Norris could ride it out. Sometimes the other was as bad at it as Norris, and the silence was impetus to action. Either way, it was wearing. Small talk ranked right up there with the obligatory "Are you negative?" question and the unromantic donning of the safe-sex mini-coat.

"I admire you, being a teacher," said Tom. He sat beside Norris poured wine into one glass, and passed it over. Then he filled his own, took a sip, and put it on a coaster on the end table. "I have a couple of teachers in my family. My dad was. My aunt. Even my great-grandmother taught, grades one through eight, all in the same room. I like kids, but I don't think I have the energy for it."

I don't have the energy, thought Norris. I needed the job. "It's not so bad," he said. "It pays a little better than some other things I've tried. And there are benefits."

"You plan on teaching until you retire?"

"I don't know. Unless something better comes along."

Tom stretched his arm out on the back of the sofa. He put his head back, shut his eyes for a moment, and sighed. "I don't plan on working with other people's money forever," he said. He opened his eyes. "I took it up because it was safe. Shit. Safe. Not much of life is safe. I'm going to become a professional musician if it kills me. I'll never lose that dream."

"You're good," said Norris, and it was true. Tom had been part of one band at the Sea Alley Beach Club, playing strong saxophone to the mediocre pounding and plunking of the drummer and pianist. "You could make it."

"Thanks." Tom took a drink, then picked up the television remote control. "I've got all the cable channels. Something you'd like to watch?"

"Watch?" This was new. "I don't know."

Tom smiled at Norris. The smile had no edges to it, no pressures, no time frames. It was unsettling.

Norris drank the rest of his wine in one gulp, then put his glass down. "You care if I smoke?"

"Ashtray's in the end-table drawer."

Norris opened the drawer and found the lead crystal container in with a number of magazines and Bic pens. He set it on the coffee table, fumbled a cigarette from his shirt pocket, and lit it with a match he'd gleaned from the Sea Alley. He sucked the smoke down into his lungs.

Tom stood up and went out of the living room through the hall. In a moment he was back, carrying a small wooden case. He sat down, nudged Norris with his elbow, and said, "I've been working on this, just as a change of pace. See what you think." A harmonica come out of the case. Tom settled back against the sofa cushion, wrapped his hands around the silver instrument, and breathed into it a slow, haunting melody. A folksy tune. As he played, his eyes closed. It looked as if he were praying to the music.

Norris stared at Tom. This was worse than small talk. It was intimacy. Not mindless banter, not sex, not physical pleasure. It was closeness. And it was frightening. Even with his lover Jared a few years ago, there had been a respected distance between them, an occasional sharing of frustrations and successes, but primarily it had been a relationship of need and convenience. Financially practical. It was easier that way. And here was Tom, getting mellow on his harmonica.

Tom stopped. He shrugged. "I've still got some major problems with it, but it feels so good to play. Seems simple, but it really isn't. I had one as a kid, but when I was a teenager it wasn't the cool thing to play. The sax was, though. Do you play anything?"

"No."

"You all right?"

"Sure," Norris said. "How about some more wine?"

"Right," said Tom. He passed the decanter to Norris. As Norris reached for it, Tom clasped it so Norris couldn't take it.

"Norris," he said.

Maybe he's a narcotics agent and is going to bust me now for the stuff I snorted in the club.

Tom let go of the decanter. "Norris, is this the first time you ever went home with a man?"

Norris felt heat rise on his neck. What the fuck was Tom saying? "No, of course not."

Tom linked his fingers over his head and thumped his knuckles lightly on the wall behind him. "At the club you seemed comfortable enough, but now I feel like I've abducted you. What's the matter?"

"I'm fine."

"Really? Norris, I don't take advantage of people. I don't use people." Tom bit his lower lip, let it out. "Do you hear me?" He put his hand on Norris' shoulder.

Norris nodded. He poured wine; drank it down. He put the glass on the coffee table and took another pull on his cigarette.

Tom seemed to want to start over. "Where are you from?"

"I told you. I live in Norfolk."

"No, I mean before. Before you moved to Norfolk. Where did you live?"

"A small town in western Virginia. Henford. You've probably never heard of it."

"Sure I have. I'm a native Virginian. I know my state. Where did you live before you lived in Henford?"

"I always lived in Henford."

"What kind of family in Henford?"

"Big. Pretty well-off. A bit prejudiced, but all right. Pillars of the community." The hand on Norris's shoulder moved slightly. It was warm, and Norris almost wanted to lean into it, to begin the dance. But Tom, with his soft voice, was setting the rhythm.

"They know you're gay?"

"No," said Norris.

Tom nodded barely. "I've been there. My mother accepted it, but I didn't tell my father. At least not to his face. I told him over the phone. He didn't yell, he cried. That was the shittiest night of my life."

Norris snubbed the cigarette out in the ashtray. A welt was in his throat, and if he could have been rid of it by snubbing the cigarette out in his neck, he would have. He looked at his hand in Tom's.

Goddamn it, he felt like he was going to cry.

"You never told anybody, did you? And you can't even accept it yourself." Tom squeezed Norris's hand. The larger, muscular fingers held Norris's protectively. "Can you accept it, Norris?"

"Of course."

"Say it then."

"This is crazy. I don't have to say anything."

"It's better for you if you do."

"You know nothing! I left Henford because a good friend of mine died."

"I'm sorry, Norris. But was it your fault? Did you kill him?"

Did I kill him, did I, fuck it, did I kill Sam?

"Of course not."

"You weren't really running from his death, were you?"

Norris pulled his hand from Tom's, lit another smoke, drew on it and blew the smoke out his nose. "We're not going to make love?"

"I told you. I don't use people. I don't want it physical unless it's right. Can you say it?"

Norris stood up. "Thanks for the wine and song, Tom. This isn't what I wanted. I think you know that. You're a great counselor. Maybe you should take it up along with your sax and harmonica."

"Don't screw yourself out of a good life, Norris."

"Coat's in the closet?"

"Yes," said Tom. "And so are you."

Norris found his coat and went outside to Tom's front walkway. He lit another cigarette, thinking Tom might come out after him, hoping that the other man might, yet dreading that he would.

Tom didn't.

Norris finished the cigarette in the blackness of the Tidewater night, tossed the butt into Tom's yard without grinding it out, and drove back to Norfolk.

Chapter Thirty-nine

Lindsay stared at the textured ceiling over her bed. There were tiny black cobwebs in one corner, and she made a mental note to tell Katherine, the once-a-week cleaning woman, to put web dusting on her agenda tomorrow.

Hank had taken the girls out to Burger King to pick up some fish sandwiches, then out to the park to eat before it got dark. It was really too cold to be outside for a picnic, but Hank had been pissed to the point of not caring. He hadn't said so; he wasn't the type to verbalize his frustrations, but having lived with him for so many years, Lindsay could read the set of the jaw.

He was majorly pissed.

The hardest part was, Lindsay knew it was her fault. Yes, she'd fainted at the nursery school yesterday. Yes, she had not told him, and of course, when Laura called this morning to see if Lindsay was going to feel like coming in, it was Hank who answered the phone and took the message as Lindsay was in the bathroom.

He wanted to know why she hadn't told him. She told him it was nothing. He asked her again. Again, she told him it was nothing.

"Thanks for letting me be concerned," he had said, then gone off to find the girls. His car had sprayed gravel on its way out of the driveway.

So be it. To explain would be the hardest cross of all to bear.

She thought of Bernie. She wondered if Bernie still had burns on her back and her palm. Probably not. Bernie was living a very different kind of life now, not one that could even compare to life with a husband and a daughter in elementary school and a blind, retarded daughter. Bernie was free to come and go on whatever hippie missions she gave herself, and she had the fresh country air as balm when she came home. Bernie's burns would be gone.

And Norris? Norris, for heaven's sake, was a bachelor. A bachelor teacher, with free afternoons and nights and no one making any kind of demands on him in his after-hours. He probably hadn't even given the Lynch reunion a thought since going home to Norfolk.

And so here she was, the one left with the reminder of the touch of Lena Carlson. Left with her because . . . because of what? Because her life was hardest? Because she had the least ability to do away with whatever gave the burns their staying power? The least reserve to deal with additional troubles?

She began to scrape at one sticky edge of the Band-Aid. What had she seen in the preschool kitchen yesterday? What germ had invaded her brain and festered, causing her to see blood in a bowl? To hear voices screaming at her, to feel a blow against her head? If she went to a doctor, what would he tell her?

She pulled at the Band-Aid; it came up to the cushion part, and she stopped. She didn't want to see the cut.

And there was the blackout in the bathroom.

The voices, the sounds of torture, the groans, the laughter. She bit the inside of her cheek and barely felt it.

The voices, the visions, the sensations were of the same source, she knew. The source had been Lena Carlson, bag woman of Henford, unclean, unkempt, scratching Lindsay and injecting her with something foul.

Although the burns on her back remained, they seemed dormant. They no longer ached. It was the fingers that had her frightened.

The cursed fingers. She pulled up the cushioned pad of the Band-Aid. The cut on the thumb was closing up. The scab was thin and crusted. What if she picked the scab off? What would happen? Back in colonial days, the doctors bled people all the time. Sometimes with leeches, sometimes with little razors. Let the bad blood out. They believed it fixed many problems, from bad colds to fever.

She scraped her fingernail down the length of the scab, pulling the crust up. The blood began to flow. She tugged on the side of the wound, gasping with the sudden stabbing sensation. The wound split open.

The bedroom began to waver, light flexing and bowing like a cheap mirror in a wind storm. The light faded and changed, then came back up again, much dimmer, yellowed, shadowed. Light from cheap bulbs. Light in a cellar.

Nausea swept over Lindsay and she shut her eyes. When she opened them again, she was still in the cellar.

This is stupid, stupid!

She tried to look down at herself, to see if she was still herself, but her head wouldn't move. It

167

was as though only her eyes were alive, trapped inside . . .

Inside what?

. . . inside someone else. Somewhere else.

Ahead of her was a staircase. The door at the top was opened, because she could see strained white light running down the steps and mingling with the yellow. The wall beside the stairs was paneled with cheap dark veneer. Just beyond the bottom step was a small door in the wall, leading probably to some sort of storage space. Some kind of crawl space.

She could not turn her head to see to her sides.

There were footsteps on the upper steps, and the door at the top was closed, shutting off the white light. Then the feet came down the steps, moving slowly and deliberately, as if counting each step.

At first there were boots, then jeans clinging tightly to trim legs. A crotch then, descending, decidedly male. A white tee shirt, arms swinging in rhythm with the steps, a one-man military parade. The shoulders then, and a neck.

Lindsay's eyes were jerked to the left suddenly, and she was looking at a pile of laundry on the floor. On the wall over the laundry was an obscene poster. Homemade. Created with bold paints or markers. A picture of a black man nailed to a tree, a black child in a boiling pot, a black woman with her fat legs spread, and a monkey with an antenna popping out from the hairy hole between the legs.

She could not look away, she could not close her eyes, she could not turn to see the man who had come down the steps and now stood, she knew because of his breathing, in front of her.

"That's right, bitch," said the man. "You best not look at me."

Who is he? Who am I? Come out of this, Lindsay. Get out of this now.

"Who gave you permission to look in the boxes in my bedroom?" The voice was thick like a boil ready to burst.

"Nobody," the lips below Lindsay's eyes said.

"You think you have a right to look where you want? You think I let Dean or Percy or Lizzie look where they want whenever they want?"

"No."

"Silly . . . " the voice was moving down, coming closer. " . . . silly bitch."

Lindsay felt her head drop further. She could see what should have been her shoes now. They were the black sandals she'd seen when she dropped the bowl of blood.

I didn't drop a bowl of blood! It wasn't me, it was her. She who I am now.

And then the man's hands were on her, one drawing in around her throat, one sliding roughly through the neck of her shirt and taking one breast in a painful squeeze. The man laughed. His teeth came together on the side of her face. Lindsay screamed; no sound was made.

"You even taste like an ugly bitch," said the man. His tongue drew up, traveling the length of her face to her temple. She could see that his hair was short, but his features were too close.

The tongue moved down to her ear and probed there. Lindsay's nerves crawled with the invasion, but she could not move away. The hand on her breast pinched and pulled.

"You're going to suck my dick," he said. "You'll keep your eyes closed because you aren't worthy to look. But I'm going to let you worship me with your fat lips."

I'm not here, I'm not here. Oh God get me out of here!

She was shoved to the floor. She saw her hands on the carpet, stubby, fat hands with chewed nails. One thumb was covered with a piece of gauze and grayed adhesive tape.

Her finger is cut too.

Lindsay felt her head begin to lift, and she saw the tops of the boots, the jeans, the belt.

"I told you not to look at me now!"

One boot pulled back and came whistling in a straight line toward her face. It caught her nose. Her head flew backward. Bone and yellowed light splintered.

Her arms were around her face, cradling her nose. She was sobbing, and the sounds were there. Her own voice, her own terror, echoed back to her from the walls around her. What walls were they?

She unwrapped her arms. Her walls. Her bedroom. Above her, the cobweb fluttered merrily in the corner of the ceiling.

"I'm back," she said to the spider's tapestry. She rolled from her bed and ran to the mirror to see if her nose was bruised. There was no sign of any mark. She pressed where the boot had struck. It didn't hurt.

Then she looked at her fingers. The thumb leaked blood. The burns on the others were as red as the tips of glowing matches.

"It was the infection." Her voice steadied as she forced her lungs to inhale and exhale slowly around the shard of fear. "It's woven a fantasy for me. I didn't leave this room."

Her face stared back at her, and she could read the expression in those eyes. The expression said, "It didn't weave a fantasy. It wove a reality."

No.

"This was real. You can't deal with it if you can't accept it."

She touched the reflection of her eyes. They did not blink. They waited. She pulled her fingers back. There was blood on the mirror glass.

The eyes did not blink.

And then fear rushed up and out, spilling in hot sobs. "This is real!" she cried. "Oh, my God, this is real!"

The burns on her fingers throbbed, satisfied for the time being.

Chapter Forty

The phone rang four times, and then the answering machine picked up.

"This is Norris Lynch. Leave a message if you want me to return your call." Then the beep.

Norris sat in front of his TV, remote control in hand, volume cut to mute, and listened to see who was calling.

"Norris, this is Lindsay. I'm calling at, let's see, seven thirty-five. It's Thursday, April third. I wanted to see how you were doing. Thought maybe we'd have heard from you by now. Give me a call and let me know if you made it back in all that snow. And let me know how you are. Please? Bye."

Norris heard the click of the phone, the beep as the machine registered the end of the call.

She had sounded worried.

Norris put the remote control on the arm of the sofa and stared at the silent television screen. Elton John was mouthing a song as dancers cut the sand on a foreign beach. The back of Norris's neck began to hurt, and he bent into it. He remembered Jared's touch, and how sometimes it could ease tension, at other times create it.

He remembered Sam's touch. It was never anything but caring.

Lindsay's voice, even in her reprimand, had held the tone of caring. Like her smile when she first saw him at the reunion. Why did caring roll off him like rain? Why did anyone have to live life when it had nothing to offer but agony?

Norris pulled a ratty throw pillow into his chest, buried his face, and wept.

Chapter Forty-one

The phone rang. The sound was a harsh burr from the kitchen, stabbing the Saturday evening quiet of the farmhouse. Bernie, on the faded floral sofa in the front room, tilted her head and listened, hoping the call was not for her. Supper was just over. Daylight was on its silent retreat, leaving a glowing pool on the floor beneath the western window.

The phone rang again and was caught by Matt, who was in the kitchen doing dishes. The last two calls, within twenty minutes of each other, had both been for Bernie. One was Lisa, with an update that her mother had been diagnosed with depression and near pneumonia. Peter and Lisa had wanted to put her in the hospital, but she demanded that treatment continue at home. The other call had been Crawley Portrait Studios, offering a free sitting and an eighteen-by-twenty-four-inch photo of herself and up to three others if she would merely share names of several friends who might also be interested in preserving the moment in pictures. She picked up her journal to continue her writing. Not for me, she thought. *Good.*

"Bernie."

Matt appeared at the front-room entrance. His pale hair had been plastered back with a wet hand.

"You look most attractive," said Bernie.

Matt grinned. "Thanks. And the phone's for you."

"Not another one."

Matt nodded. "This one's selling magazines."

"Screw you."

"Okay. It's Lindsay."

"Who is it really?"

"Honest, this time. It's Lindsay."

Lindsay. Bernie felt a stirring in her gut, a cold trickle in her veins, a hesitation in her heart. The burn on her palm, for a few days still clearly visible but painless, slowly began to throb. The spot on her back echoed the throb. In her temples, a headache picked up the rhythm.

She knew what Lindsay wanted.

"You make all your relatives wait this long?"

Bernie struggled from the sofa and brushed past Matt at the door.

"You're so popular," he said. "I never get calls."

"Jerk," Bernie said, but the humor she tried to force fell flat. Matt didn't seem to notice.

173

Into the mouthpiece, "Yes? Lindsay?"

"Bernie. I'm so glad you're home." Lindsay's voice confirmed Bernie's fears. It was hesitant. Cautious.

"Yes," said Bernie. "Hi, Lindsay. Not too long a time no see." She glanced back at Matt. He was watching her. She scowled at him, hoping it came across as "finish those dishes, dork, or you're dead meat."

Matt wrinkled his nose and went back to the sink, where he shoved his arms into the steaming water. Bernie looked at the corkboard on the kitchen wall where chores were scheduled. She hadn't been scheduled for over a week now. HeartLight members were monitoring her.

"Two weeks," said Lindsay. "It seems longer."

"I guess."

"How are you doing, Bernie?" The voice was slow, controlled. As if someone might be standing over her shoulder, or someone was tapping her line. Why caution? Bernie knew, but didn't want to know. God was testing Lindsay, too.

"Oh, okay." Not quite a lie, certainly not the truth.

"Really? Oh, I mean that's good. I was hoping so." Lindsay paused. "I was just wondering, since it's been two weeks since we've seen each other."

"That's nice of you to call." *But I want to hang up now, Lindsay, if that's all right with you. I can't understand my own test. I'm not ready to understand how you figure into it*. Bernie's headache found the confines of bone, and pushed outward. She gritted her teeth. She looked out the kitchen window, over Matt's shoulder, toward the path that sloped toward the gate and the pasture. She could see a corner of the spring garden Sandra had put in; it was still nothing but mud clumps and rows of string markers. "How are Hank and the girls?"

"They're good."

"Good." Out past the pasture gate, beyond the barn, which Bernie could not see for the evergreens, was a grave. Red's grave. As cold and muddy and dead as Sandra's garden.

Say it, Bernie. Whisper it if you have to. Reach out here. Reach out to Lindsay. Maybe nothing is happening to her at all. Maybe this was all God wanted of you in the first place, a little familial soul-embracing. A strange method of bringing family members together, but God is famous for those mysterious ways.

Is this all you wanted, God? Watch me, I'm doing it. I'm saying it. Hear me. Help me.

She cleared her throat and dropped her voice. "Lindsay, are you feeling something strange? Hearing anything? Seeing anything?"

"What do . . . ?" Lindsay said. Then she was silent.

Bernie felt the struggle in the silence. She whispered, "You don't know what I mean? You don't know what I'm talking about? Isn't that why you called?"

"Oh, God, Bernie. I don't know I . . . " The voice trailed. Then there was a soft, anxious sigh.

Bernie persisted. "Do you still have the marks?"

"Yes."

Bernie looked over at Matt. He pulled the sink plug and began to chase bubbles around with the water spray.

"Do they hurt?"

"Maybe a little sometimes."

"Has anything else happened? Have you had any odd experiences?"

"Bernie, I thought I could talk about this. I don't know if I can. Over the phone, I mean. Hank might—"

"Can you come out here?" Bernie pressed. "We can talk, okay, Lindsay? Please? You said at the reunion you'd like to bring your girls out to the country. Can you come?"

"We'll see. I'll see if I can."

"Do you need directions?"

"I know it's up Route 287."

"Yes, up 287 from Henford about eighteen miles. Then right on 511 another six. Past the large farm with the pond. We're on the left, a long driveway up through trees. The mailbox says 'HeartLight.' "

"Maybe I can."

"Come soon. Lindsay, please come very soon."

Lindsay hung up. Bernie put the phone into the cradle on the wall. She stared at the floor, and at the tips of her black hightop sneakers. The headache hammered with an acute, pounding pain, and before she knew what was happening, the bran flakes which had been her breakfast a half hour ago were rocketing up her throat. She clenched her jaw and swallowed it back down. She wiped her mouth and glanced back at Matt. He was looking out the window at a robin on the porch railing.

Make some sense of it, God, she pleaded to the ceiling. Then it was a demand, angry and burning and accusing. *Goddamn it, make some sense of this nightmare to me!*

176

Chapter Forty-two

"Celebrate!" cried Rex. He held up a cold bottle of Blackened Voodoo, straight from the cooler between his legs, and waited until all the White Eagles had returned the salute.

They sat on the basement floor of Rex's house. The floor was cold and bare now, the old rug having been rolled up and tied and ready for its relocation.

All the Eagles lifted their amber-black bottles toward their leader. All in a circle, all touching in some way or another, knees, elbows, hips, creating a powerful ring which neither niggers nor gooks nor fags nor weaklings nor any other brand of alien could ever destroy. Dean, Joe, Lizzie, Peaches, Percy, the bitch Lena, Junior, Ronald. And Rex.

It was a good day.

"Celebrate," said the White Eagles.

They all took a drink. Rex watched them as he chugged his own lager. They were here, and they were his. The wheel of Truth and Power made another mighty rotation, and it was time. Today, this very afternoon, the land deal was completed. The deal had been struck between the absentee owners and a knowing, sympathetic real estate agent. The papers were then turned over to a friend of Arlen's, an equally knowing, sympathetic lawyer who, just three hours ago, reviewed the papers and approved them. Mildly curious, the owners, down from Leesburg for the afternoon, had asked how Arlen Wells planned on

using the woodland. Recreation, Arlen said.
Camping. Quiet appreciation of nature and its
wonders. Time away from the stress of his medical practice. The Leesburgers had been pleased.

Arlen called Rex at five-thirty and said everything had been signed. Everything was ready.

Everything in your hands, Rex. Fire at will.

Now, at eight-thirty, the White Eagles had
made visible progress in preparing for the move.
Boxes on the basement floor, cartons in the
kitchen and living room upstairs. Peaches
scrubbed the oven, Lizzie washed scum from the
tub in the single bath. Even the hag had made
herself of some use, scouring doorsills and wall
streaks with a washcloth and spray bottle of 409.

"I don't want anything of myself, of ourselves,
here for the next occupants," Rex had said. "No
scrap of food, no fingerprints, not even so much
as a stray pubic hair stuck in a bathroom tile.
We're free of this place." The White Eagles went
to furious work, following that ideal.

As they worked, Rex had made a run to the grocery store and picked up the lager and some bags
of chips. Now they were on break. A reward.
Even the ugly ones, he would hug now. As they
made their circle on the cellar floor, as they drank
to themselves, to each other, and to the victory of
their cause, a rush of love flooded Rex.

"I hope," he began, swallowing a mouthful of
rich lager and staring at the bare floor in the center of the circle, "I hope we will remain as close as
we are now. I hope our circle will grow as well. I
will lead you. Will you follow?" He looked up. The
Eagles were holding their bottles, watching him.

"Will you follow?"

Their faces hesitated and wavered. They looked

Here's how it works:

Each package will carry a FREE 10-DAY EXAMINATION privilege. At the end of that time, if you decide to keep your books, simply pay the low invoice price of $11.25, no shipping or handling charges added. HOME DELIVERY IS ALWAYS FREE! There's no minimum number of books to buy, and you may cancel at any time.

AND AS A CHARTER MEMBER, YOUR FIRST THREE-BOOK SHIPMENT IS TOTALLY FREE! IT'S A BARGAIN YOU CAN'T BEAT!

✂ CUT HERE

confused. Dean himself had the expression Peter must have had when Jesus said to him, "Verily I say until thee, the cock shall not crow till thou hast denied me thrice."

Lizzie broke the silence with a soft giggle. "Of course," she said. "That's a dumb question."

Peaches gave her a hasty, severe glance, and Lizzie looked down at the bottle in her hands.

"We will." It was Percy. "Ain't nothing more important than cleaning up America. Then, the world."

A knot was in Rex's throat. Such commitment, such dedication. He reached out and took Dean's hand. It was cold with bottle condensation and a fresh sheen of clammy sweat. Dean could not look at Rex.

"I give my life to this," Rex said. He let go of Dean's hand. The hand hung there, trembling, afraid to seem relieved, most likely afraid to be clasped by Rex again. "I give my life to this, and if you can't do the same, leave now."

The White Eagles were silent. They did not look at each other.

"Silence gives consent," said Rex. "Good." He stood, tipped back his head and drained the bottle, then dropped it into a nearby Hefty bag where it shattered at the bottom. He loved that sound. He would have caressed the glass shards for the beautiful sound they produced if a greater thrill wasn't waiting for him.

"I've got packing to do." *Packing; at last the time of Glory is here!* "Enjoy your break, then get back to work."

The Eagles all nodded with various degrees of vigor, and then rose to meet the tasks given them by their enraptured leader.

179

Chapter Forty-three

"Itsybit spider go up water spout."

"Wait, you're going too fast."

"No fast. Do. Itsybit spider up water spout!"

"Grace, I'm not going to sing with you anymore if you don't slow down. It's no fun if you do it so fast you can't get your fingers right. I'm going to just turn around and ignore you."

Mandy, in the front seat of the car beside Lindsay, turned back around in a huff. She crossed her arms dramatically and stared out her window. "She's no fun."

"We all have our days," said Lindsay. "Now, let's enjoy this trip. It's not far. You'll have a good time visiting Bernie. There's lots of space to run and play."

"You said she had a horse," said Mandy. "We better get to ride it. It'll be boring if we can't ride the horse."

"I hope you can, too," said Lindsay. "That would be fun." She stretched her neck and pressed the button for Grace's window and let it ease down several inches. In the rearview, she could see the little girl's hair get caught up in a breeze. Grace turned her face into the wind, seeming to be calmed by the sensation.

Outside the van windows, Virginia countryside rushed by. Henford was behind to the south. To the west were bits of forests and small family farms and out-of-place subdivisions with multi-colored by-levels and school buses parked in yards. The Blue Ridge Mountains were to the east, a steel gray, solid wall of rolling ridges and occasional outcroppings of mountaintop boulders. Lindsay had spent many Sunday afternoons as a child on the Blue Ridge's hiking paths and picnic areas and roadside overlooks. She'd bruised knees, cut her chin, played with dead copperheads, whittled endless hiking sticks, and tossed many smooth stones into mountain streams. Easy, pleasant memories she had never been able to recapture, even as a mother with children of her own. Because try as you might, it's different with a blind child, with a slow child. Grace might not see the slick stone, and might slip and hit her head. She might play around a log where copperheads lie in wait, because not all snakes in the mountains are dead. She might tramp through poison ivy, she might eat a deadly berry before her mother could intercede, she might uncover a brown recluse with her exploring fingers.

Childhood fun had to be monitored carefully when you had a daughter such as Grace.

Mandy pushed a tape into the player beneath the radio. The Chipmunks were caught in the middle of "Wooly Bully." Mandy put her sneakered feet up on the dash and sang along. Lindsay didn't say anything about the feet on the dash, although Hank would have hated it.

Lindsay slowed the car as Penny Brothers' Exxon came into view on the left. Next to the gas station was Route 511. Turn here. Six miles to HeartLight.

Six miles to Bernie and her Jesus-freak friends or whatever they were called these days. Lindsay puffed air through her pressed lips, and tightened

181

her grip on the steering wheel. The Band-Aid was off her thumb, and it was nearly healed. The burns on her other fingers were quiet and numb.

As well they should be.

As well *she* should be. Quiet and numb. She had decided, after talking with Bernie, that she really didn't want to discuss it. Some things did go away if you ignored them. Maybe she hadn't ignored this long enough.

Why the hell didn't I just break my promise and refuse to visit her this afternoon?

The Chipmunks ended their song. A brief interlude, then the Chippettes broke into "Girls Just Want to Have Fun." Lindsay looked in the rearview at Grace, head back, mouth open as if she were tasting the air. In her right peripheral vision she saw Mandy link her fingers behind her head and mouth the words like a true Chippette Wannabe. Directly in front of her, Route 287 slid to the left as the van turned onto the more narrow stretch of 511.

The steering wheel shimmied suddenly, violently, beneath her grip.

Lindsay gasped.

"Mama!" Mandy's feet dropped from the dashboard, smacking to the floor mat.

Lindsay's hands jerked back and up from the wheel. She watched them move. They hovered in the air like fleshy tarantulas, the fingers flexed as if ready to pounce, to kill. She could not make them go back down.

The steering wheel shook wildly, taunting her. "No! she began. "Not—!"

The van's front wheels hit a slight groove in the pavement. It veered left, unmanned, swerving across the broken line.

"Not now!"

"Mama!" Mandy screamed.

"Mama!" Grace, the terrified echo.

Coming toward them on the other side of the road was a rusty pickup truck. Lindsay screamed, pushing into her shoulders to force her hands down on the wheel. They did not move. She saw the truck driver's mouth drop open, saw his hands paw his own steering wheel madly. She strained, willing her foot to lift from the accelerator to the brake, but it wouldn't move.

The truck lurched left, skidding on the pavement, the driver's rusted and scratched door rushing toward the van.

"Mama Mama Mama!"

Lindsay's eyes closed and opened, a blink, a pretense of a blink. And there was a wall, not a truck. A yellow house wall, scarred vinyl siding in lumpy layers, and Lindsay was flying toward it, her own shadow laid out on the vinyl, arms outstretched as if welcoming her, urging her to slam into the wall. But it was not her shadow. She knew it. It was not hers, it could not be hers because she was in her van and her children were with her and they were in the path of an oncoming truck.

Lindsay's scream in the last moment was not her own and was her own. Two voices merged, one in her mind and one in her ears. She sensed the faint but horrible bite of metal to metal, the wails of distant children, somewhere beyond her vision, her hearing.

She slammed into the wall. The world, both worlds, shattered and flew away.

Chapter Forty-four

Norris paced around the telephone, trying to come up with an excuse to call Lindsay. It was too strange just to call. But he wanted to talk with her.

He wanted to hear concern. He needed to feel the voice of care in his ear. He'd never felt so lonely in his life.

He went out for groceries, then came back and looked at the phone again.

He turned on the television and drifted into an uncomfortable, wood-smoke-scented sleep.

Chapter Forty-five

Hank was gone. Her parents had come and gone, too. Thank God. It was all she could do to bear the smiles and the pats and the light, distracting banter of her visitors. She didn't need more. All Lindsay needed was to know that Mandy and Grace were all right.

Amazingly, the girls had come through the wreck with very little damage. They had been treated for scratches and had been released around three-thirty that afternoon. Hank had told her this, because she had not come to until she was in X-ray. She had awakened, screaming, nearly knocking the white-jacketed technician to the floor. Some calm reassurances and a stab of sedative later, she began to believe that Mandy and Grace were, indeed, alive.

Hank was in the hall when she was wheeled from X-ray, and he had stayed with her, down the hall in emergency, and finally to her room on the third floor where she would stay, their family doctor said, at least another day or two.

Hank had sat on the chair by her bed, one arm on the side rail, asking if she needed water, ice, ginger ale. He adjusted and readjusted the pair of crutches next to Lindsay's nightstand. He played with the television remote control when Lindsay's roommate was dozing, and put it down when she awoke. He talked about carelessness in cars and how children have died from such carelessness.

Lindsay finally said, "I need to sleep."

Hank nodded and sat back in his chair.

"I mean you can go. You don't need to stay."

"Supper is in just a little while. You don't want to be moving that arm yet, any more than you have to."

Lindsay, her eyes closed, dragged her head against the pillow in what she hoped appeared to be an exhausted answer.

Hank said, "All right, fine." He trod softly out the door.

Lindsay opened her eyes. Hank was already gone from her thoughts. She let the memory flood back, full force.

A yellow wall. A yellow, dirty wall. An exterior of a house she may well know if she let her mind turn it over long enough. *I think I know this place. It seems so familiar. A filthy yellow house.*

Something bad was going on at the yellow house. And she had become a small part of it. Her heart kicked into gear, reverberating to the snapped bone inside her arm cast, to the acute soreness of her skull.

Elizabeth Massie

Think. Think.

"*Murder She Wrote* all right with you, honey?"

Lindsay looked across to her roommate, an older, gray-haired lady with impending gall bladder surgery.

"Yes, fine, I'm going to take a rest."

The television, mounted on the wall near the ceiling, flashed channels as the roommate punched the remote.

It was a poor house, an ill-kept house, Lindsay thought. She rolled painfully onto her side and faced the window. It couldn't be that hard to find.

"I think Angela Lansbury is a credit to older women, don't you? When you get to be my age, you need to know there's more to life than Ben Gay and porch swings."

Lindsay lay silently, hoping the woman would believe she was already asleep.

Think. Think. A yellow house. Cheap siding, dirty. And there were weeds along the base of the wall. Some sorts of dead flowers from years past, tangled and tall and brown. I drive through a section of Henford with houses like that every day we go to preschool. I could find this house again.

Lindsay's hands spasmed suddenly. She caught one in the other to hold them still.

I could find this house to see what's happening there. To see what connection I have there.

On the other side of the room, the old woman began to snore softly. The television continued to hum. Outside in the hallway, the hospital routine was quieting. In another few hours, things would be settled for the night.

You have two broken bones. You knocked yourself senseless. You aren't fit for moving around.

Lindsay stretched over and found her remote

186

next to the telephone on the nightstand. She shut off the set, and watched the ghost-blue fade to black.

But the house might not even be in Henford.

No, I've seen this house. I've passed it taking Grace to school.

She sat up slowly, gritting her teeth so she would not groan. Nausea swept her, a dizzying, sickening sensation. She held still, waiting for it to pass. Her ankle complained angrily in its cast. When the wave of nausea began to ebb, she lowered the bed rail and, with her good right arm, eased both legs to dangle over the bedside.

This is crazy. You haven't tried those crutches yet. Her lips were dry, but the momentum was going and she couldn't stop to take a drink from her plastic cup. She leaned over and pulled one crutch from the wall. She planted the rubber-tipped base beneath her.

So if you find the house, what then?

"I don't know," she said aloud. She looked to see if Mrs. Gall Bladder had heard her, but the old woman did not move. "Maybe then I'll call Bernie again. But I have to try, for Mandy and Grace and my sanity." A tear welled at the edge of her eye, then ran down her puffed face. "They could have been killed. I have to make things safe . . ."

She pushed up onto the crutch, leaning on her right. Her broken ankle and arm flushed hot. She hopped to the bathroom, then to the door, and back again. Her room was only two down from an exit and a stairwell. With a little luck, she could get down the stairwell before a nurse saw her.

She went back to the bed and sat. It took two minutes to catch her breath. Then, fumbling in her nightstand drawer, she found her watch and worked it onto her right wrist with her teeth and two fingers of her left hand.

In an hour she would call a cab. She would leave the hospital and find the yellow house. She pulled the white curtain closed between herself and her roommate. It would take, she knew, almost the entire hour to find her clothes and get into them without breaking another arm or leg.

Chapter Forty-six

"It's dark," said Dean. "Should we go on and move the things in the bedroom?"

Rex, standing on the back stoop, took inventory of the sky. A toothpick stuck out of his teeth. He wore a black sweatshirt.

"Give it another thirty minutes," he said. "It's still early. We got time. I want it darker."

Dean nodded halfheartedly and went back inside the house. Rex sat down on the stoop and looked out at the carport. Everything was gone now. Today had not been a day of rest, as many religions would have it. Today had been a day of work, of progress and of progression. Rex's car and Percy's truck had hauled endless loads of possessions to the land. Most of it had been stacked inside the trailer Arlen had put out for the White Eagles' temporary use. That which would not fit inside the trailer had been stacked on pallets beside the trailer with tarps thrown over them.

A cat trotted off the street and stopped at the entrance of the carport. It stared at Rex and then sat on its haunches. Rex spit in the direction of the cat. The wad fell short.

"You come here, you're asking for what happened to that other cat. You want to dance? You want to be a gymnast?"

The cat's whiskers twitched. Rex untied the shoestring to one boot. He wiggled the black string on the concrete floor. The cat watched it, instantly intent. Rex wiggled the string. The cat sneaked up the stained concrete floor.

"Go for it, cat."

The cat pounced. Rex grabbed the cat by the nape of the neck and the tail. He held it up. The legs flailed, trying to scratch Rex's arms.

"Just try it," Rex said. He shook the cat so it would try harder.

Percy was behind him; Rex could hear the door shut and then the familiar nicotine cough. "They always keep coming," said Rex. "Like all the slime we have sharing this country with us. They keep coming, more and more, and they're so stupid they don't know what they're up against."

"Cats?"

"Sure, Percy, cats. Whatever you think."

Percy coughed again, then went back inside.

The cat struggled harder. Its neck pulled free of Rex's grasp. "Fuck!" Rex cried, and lifted the cat up by the tail in one fierce movement and hurled it as hard as he could, slamming it into the concrete carport flooring.

The cat wailed, then tried to run off with its broken back hips. Rex stared as it clawed along the floor by its front legs, heading for the road, hissing and spitting.

Rex had slammed the fat bitch Lena against the yellow wall of the house this afternoon, but noth-

ing had broken. She'd fallen in a fat heap on the
ground and had twisted her ankle and sprained
her arm, but she would be a better White Eagle
for it. She would carry these lessons to the Night
Land.

Night Land. Soon enough to reach out and
taste. Rex licked the taste from his lips and
smiled.

The cat fell over, yowled, and staggered back
up again. Rex wondered if he should go and slam
his boot into this cat or let it live, having learned,
and be a better cat.

No such thing as a better cat. But then again, it
made him feel better to see the animal wounded.
The thought of a dead cat brought no emotion at
all. Let the cat live, having learned.

He crossed his leg and retied his boot. Then he
looked up at the sky to wait until it was as dark as
it could become. When the true darkness arrived,
he would call the Eagles together and they would
move the final, and most important, items from
the little bedroom of the yellow house out to their
new home, Night Land.

Chapter Forty-seven

The cab driver wanted to say something, Lindsay
could read it in his eyes in the rearview mirror,
but he had the courtesy not to do so. When she
opened the back door to the vehicle, he mumbled
something that sounded like "need help?" but
Lindsay was already easing her butt onto the seat
and lifting her cast-covered ankle and lowering it
onto the floor mat. She sat still for a moment,

catching air in sharp breaths, trying to convince herself that she needed to move the other half of her body into the cab before they could move on.

"I need to look for a house," she began. She swung her right leg into the cab, eased herself over on the seat a little, and closed the door. The vibration sent shards into her head and ankle. "I'm not sure how long it will take."

The man shrugged, only one shoulder going up. "I'll go wherever you want as long as you can pay."

"Thanks," Lindsay said. She hoped it wouldn't be as long as he seemed to hope. In her skirt pocket, along with her driver's license, was a wadded handful of bills. Thirty-seven dollars from her purse. It had been forever since she'd ridden in a cab. She had no idea if it would be enough.

"So what road are we heading for?"

"I'm not sure. I have a route to follow." *Good, that sounds good. In truth, you sound like a slightly demented woman who has just escaped from the hospital.*

"Sure," said the cabbie. He looked over his shoulder, pulled on a "the customer's always right" expression.

Escaping from the hospital had been easy. The worst part had been worrying between her call to the cab company and hobbling the short distance across her room and to the exit stairway. Her heart had slammed so violently in her chest, she thought she would wake up her sleeping roommate.

But the old woman did not waken. The nurses did not look around when Lindsay maneuvered to the stairway door and pushed through it.

Getting down the steps had hurt like hell, but through the window at the landing she saw the yellow cab in the lot and knew she would make it.

Now, as the cab pulled out of the lot onto the street, Lindsay wondered again what a crippled woman would do once she found the house in her nightmare.

"Go east," she said, and the resolve in her voice amazed her.

Chapter Forty-eight

"It's darker," said Rex.

The White Eagles, who had been biding their time sitting on the bare floors, jumped up and went to the bedroom. The wooden boxes stored there were carefully brought outside and put into the back of Percy's truck. It was all Rex could do to keep from rubbing his hands together with glee.

The weapons here were the best that pussy money could buy. Arlen knew his shit, that was for certain.

It was not time for the guns yet, he knew. They were stockpiling for the war, which was sure to come. But sometimes the thought of opening fire on inferiors was a sweet-tasting dream he could barely contain.

Patience.

One step at a time.

Billy Bailey and the black teenage alien were already out on the land, chained to separate trees, waiting.

If an alien could be patient, then there was no

question that a White Eagle could be patient. The cause demanded it. The Truth could not exist without it.

Rex went into the kitchen and ejaculated his pent-up excitement against the wall as the Eagles continued to move the boxes of weapons outside to Percy's truck.

Chapter Forty-nine

It felt as though the peanuts he had snacked on for lunch had come back up to lodge in his throat. He punched in the number and waited.

Lindsay, I got your call. I got back okay. There wasn't any snow here. There usually isn't. How are you?

"How *are* you?" He tried the words on the air. What worthless words, only on rare occasion truly sincere.

The receiver was lifted on the other end. It was Hank.

Nifty.

"Hank, may I speak with Lindsay?"

A pause. Then, "She's in the hospital. Who is this?"

"Norris."

"Oh. She's in the hospital. Had a wreck today on her way to visit that hippie cousin of yours."

How in the world? The peanut in his throat twisted.

"How is she?"

"Broken bones, concussion." An angry sigh. "She's had episodes I can't figure. She won't . . . " And then Hank stopped. He must have remembered he was talking to someone he didn't like. "She'll be in the hospital a couple days."

"I'm really sorry."

The phone hung up.

"I'm really sorry," Norris said to the dead line.

Chapter Fifty

"Okay, now here slow down."

"Sure."

"I think this is the road. I drive here several times a week."

"Oh."

The road was narrow, lined with chain-link fences and little houses of uniform size and shape. *And they're all made out of ticky tacky*, thought Lindsay. She moved her head back and forth as they passed the homes, not wanting to miss a clue.

White homes, gray homes, green homes, side yards and old cars. One home had an obviously permanent yard sale; bikes, appliances, card tables holding lonely vigil in the night.

"Slower, please," said Lindsay.

"It's your nickel," said the cab driver. He eased back to fifteen.

Chapter Fifty-one

Rex let Peaches drive his car. He wanted to follow in the truck with the weapons. The car pulled out of the carport and onto the street. In it, Rex could see the dark outlines of five heads—Peaches,

Lizzie, Dean, Joe, and Ronald. The truck waited at the curb until the car was clear.

"Go on."

Rex, in the middle of the truck seat between Percy and Junior, leaned forward and put crossed arms on the dashboard. His stomach roiled in anticipation.

In the back of the truck, sitting with the wooden boxes, was Lena. She had not complained when instructed to climb in the truck bed, even though the night air was brisk. She had found an old blanket and was huddled beneath it. Rex didn't care about the blanket. He just hoped she would touch the boxes so he could punish her later.

He kept one eye in the rearview, where he could see her round, silhouetted head.

Chapter Fifty-two

"Slower, please."

"Slower than this?"

"Please."

The cab driver sighed and took his foot off the accelerator. "We could coast. We could even stop if you need to look around."

"I don't want to get out." Lindsay had been feeling strangely uncomfortable for the last minute. It was not the ache of her ankle or the bone-sharp pain of her arm. These she held still, trying to ignore.

But her fingertips had begun to throb. A steady, pounding throb that told her they were close.

"Slower."

The vehicle now barely moved.

"We trying to sneak up on somebody?" asked the driver.

"No." A white car drove by the cab, heading in the other direction. Full of people. Kids it looked like, going out on the town.

The skin of the burns seemed to crawl. *We're close. We're really close.* Ahead, a half-block away on the left, she could see a steel-framed carport, and the outline of a yellow house. She had to squint, because oncoming truck headlights made it hard to see.

It looked yellow.

"Go a little further up," Lindsay said. "On the right. I want to stop and look."

The truck came closer, then was beside them.

Lindsay looked in and didn't know the driver. Her eyes scanned out across the bed of the truck, trying to lock sight back on the yellow house.

There was someone in the back of the truck, hunched over in the cold. Lindsay's fingertips flared. A vision knocked her head back against the seat. A flash of cold, a fetid wool blanket, wooden crates near her knees.

And the vision was gone.

The truck passed and drove on.

This was it! It was here, it was them!

A wave of nausea struck Lindsay like a hammer to the gut. She folded over and vomited on the floor. The driver pulled over to the curb across from the yellow house.

"I shoulda known better than to take no hospital patient nowhere! And I bet you don't even have money for your fare, now do you?"

Lindsay held her head, her fingers screaming, her brain knocked with waves that stole her breath, and she could not answer.

Chapter Fifty-three

He was fucking drunk and he dared anyone to try and say or do something about it. His living-room window was open, and because he couldn't figure out how the side latches worked, he had opened the screen by hammering on the bottom with his fists until it bent enough to give. Now his head was poking out through the bottom and he was waiting until somebody he hated came along so he could spit on his or her head. Hopefully the witch with the yapping poodle who always peeked at him when he checked his mail.

Come on come on come on.

The sun was hard and bright today. All the warmth of an interrogation light in the face of a suspect. Shadows leaked from the parked cars out into the road like so many puddles of motor oil. He thought the air was cool, but he couldn't feel much on the bare skin of his chest.

Norris waggled his tongue in the air, trying to work up some spit for his victim. His mouth was frustratingly dry, though, and the hair on his tongue felt brittle. He had slept off and on since coming home from the Salty Dog Lounge, at times on his bed, at times on the sofa, leaving the television on for nonjudgmental company.

He had looked inside his fridge numerous times, and nothing had caught his appetite's attention but the supply of beer cans in the door. There were two cans left now. He wondered if beer dried up spit glands.

He left the window for the bathroom, filled his mouth with water, and went back to the kitchen window. He stuck his head out through the bottom of the ruined screen and looked at the street. No poodle witch. He thought he'd seen her leave earlier. No telling how long ago. She'd have to come home sometime, unless she and her poodle had decided to elope and take a cruise to Jamaica.

Norris laughed. Water from his mouth simultaneously went up his nose and poured out through his teeth. He coughed and pulled his head back inside. He slammed the window down and thumbed the lock back into place.

He sat on the sofa and stared as the Duracell rabbit careened its way through yet another advertising setup. Then an ad came on for a *Quantum Leap* rerun.

"Sam's most challenging leap yet," said the announcer. "A leap into a reporter bound for Sarajevo in 1992."

Norris dug frantically for the remote control under the sofa cushion and snapped the television off.

Goddamn it. Sam.

Norris lit a cigarette, stuck it in his mouth, and sank back into the lumpy cushions of the sofa.

Sam.

The one friend in his life who truly knew him, who truly identified, who truly cared. Sam, as dead now as the smoldered ash at the end of Norris's cigarette.

Norris pulled the smoke from his lips and studied the tip. What a fucking habit, smoking. Such a simple thing, drawing smoke through paper and tobacco, such a temporary calm to the frazzled nerves. As with many habits, such a pleasure in both the doing and the knowledge that it was there to do. Sam had liked pipes. Norris liked cigarettes, no particular brand, whichever was cheapest.

Maybe now he could put in a payment on the debt he owed Sam. He stuck the cigarette tip down into his navel.

"What did it feel like to burn to death, Sam?"

Norris felt nothing, and he pushed the cigarette deeper. What did it feel like? His family would ask that of each other. Lindsay would cry, and Norris's father would wonder if it hurt like the fires of hell to burn to death. It reminded Norris of a play he'd seen years ago.

Think about the sun, Pippin. Think about the beauty in one perfect flame.

And now it's your chance.

"Payment to Sam, payment to Dad."

He smelled the burn before he felt it. A not unpleasant scent, like the kitchen at Bright Creek School just after breakfast. And then came the pain.

Norris jerked violently, throwing the cigarette to the floor and driving his fist into the pain in his navel. He pounded his fist against the bubbling blister it was becoming. He sucked air through his teeth, and still the pain came, a beeline of furious, poisonous hornets from his gut to his chest to his brain.

"Fucking moron!" he cried. His eyes blurred with tears. Through them, he could see the edge of the blue shag throw rug begin to smolder. He rolled from the sofa and crawled on his knees to the butt. With his fist he pounded out the cigarette and the smoking rug. He fell over onto his back.

He could feel his heart in his neck, he could feel

the cooked nerve endings in his navel. He lifted one wrist and looked at the spots. If he died here, he thought, who would think he was anything other than a depressed derelict?

Lindsay had called and left a message on his machine. When had that been? This morning? Yesterday? Days ago? And Norris had called back. Who had he talked with? Not Lindsay. No, Norris had talked to the husband.

Frank. Hank. He'd said Lindsay was hurt.

Norris clawed at the floor and pulled himself over onto his side. He panted as though he'd just run ten miles. Maybe he should call his poor hurt cousin. She would do that for him. "Fucking-A," he said to the edge of the blue shag throw rug. Norris hoisted himself to his feet, staggered into the kitchen, and stared at the phone.

Why bother? She had a husband to make her feel better. Good old Frank. The asshole.

Fuck him.

He picked up the receiver, thumbed clumsily through the brown plastic file box on top of the bread box under Hollin. Lindsay Hollin. He punched in her number.

It began to ring. After four rings, a man's voice, sounding full of gravel, said, "Hello?"

The asshole husband.

"I want . . . " Norris began. His tongue was thick. He dragged his teeth across it to make it flatter. "Lindsay."

"Who is this?"

"Norris."

A pause, sounding like a soft curse or a clearing of the throat. "Not yet. She had a setback."

Norris felt his stomach twitch. "What do you mean?"

"A setback. The girls are all right, they're home, but Lindsay fell out of bed and stressed her fracture even more. Now, is there something I can help you with, Norris?"

Norris's head was full of cotton. He shook it and the cotton rattled. "I want to talk to her."

"She's not here."

"Put her on the line, Frank." His words tasted funny on his tongue, and they rose to float in the air like soap bubbles. "I'm concerned."

"Hmm, funny, that. You never call. Why bother now?"

"Fuck you."

"What was that?"

"I said fuck you, you pompous turd."

"What was—!"

Norris slammed the receiver into the cradle. Lindsay was in the hospital, injured because she'd had a wreck. Lindsay, the first of the cousins to get her license in high school because she was the most responsible. Lindsay, conscientious mother to a fault.

She must have been sick. Something had taken her attention away. An animal, bright sunlight, a crying child.

Norris looked at the age spots on his wrists. Were hers still there? Did those damn spots make strange things happen to her, too?

Don't think that shit, it's crazy.

Suddenly, something in his stomach gurgled, then began a rhythmic wave. He buckled over and threw up the air from his empty stomach. It felt as if he were barfing up his soul.

Chapter Fifty-four

"Teddy, don't do this to me."

Teddy was leaning on a broom in the gym, like a shepherd on his staff. Norris sat near him on the lowest bleacher, arms crossed, one foot atop the other. A stack of remedial writing papers sat beside him. His white teacher's shirt had come up out of one side of the waistband of his slacks. It was Wednesday afternoon. The students were at St. John's Catholic Church, washing windows.

Teddy sucked at something in his side tooth, then spit into the air. "Sorry, man, it ain't my doing. You get around, you'll be fine."

Norris looked at Teddy's black radio on the bleacher near him. The bent antenna was angled like the feeler of a squashed insect. The station was WBSL, Super Oldies 102. The song, "Nashville Cats."

"Cut this off a minute?"

Teddy shook his head, then grabbed the broom and began one of his long runs down the length of the floor and back. Norris gritted his teeth and watched Teddy. In a minute, the man was back, the bristles of the broom pushing a collection of dirt and dust threads. Teddy pushed the collection into a pile and then leaned on the handle again.

"Teddy," Norris said. "Let's make other arrangements, then. You get around, too. I can meet you."

Teddy stared down the gym, maybe analyzing his attack on the next row of dirt. "I think you ought to shut your face. I think the gym might be bugged, what do you think?"

"Don't play this with me. The fucking place isn't bugged. We need to work something out."

"No, *you* need to work something out." Teddy pulled a pack of gum out of his shirt pocket, peeled paper from a stick, and dropped the paper into the pile of dirt. He put the gum in his mouth and rolled it around a moment. He said, "I can't be your grocery store no more, that's all there is to it. Vice principal Frye knows me, he knows what's up for the most part, and he told me to get things straight because the damn dogs were coming in. He told me I had to do my doin' elsewhere if I wanted to keep living on the grounds. He don't know about you, and if you think I'm going to lose my job 'cause you ain't got no backup, then you the dumbest teacher I ever dealt with."

"You could meet me off school grounds. Shit, how hard could it be?"

"I don't make 'pointments. It worked out here 'cause it was here. Well, no more." He twirled the broom into position and took it down the next length of gym floor.

Norris rubbed his palms together and stood. He watched Teddy reach the far end and turn back around. Come to terms with it, he told himself. Not the end of the world, just the end of a source. There are other sources, maybe not as convenient, maybe not as reliable, but it's not like you're a blubbering addict who can't take his time and find his way. His backup system.

Goddamn it all.

"Nashville Cats" ended. D. J. Morty TimeStop praised his listeners for staying tuned, and popped on Neil Diamond's "You Got to Me." Norris sniffed, catching a sudden scent of pine needles and campfire and cooking meat. He braced himself, waiting to fade out. He didn't this time, and the smells faded.

Shrink might be good, even if he does tell you it's all that shit you've smoked and snorted.

Teddy came back. He pushed the new dirt into the pile. "Go home, Norris," he said.

There were other sources, Norris told himself sternly. It was time to expand his horizons. He could live with that. He collected the stack of papers from the bleacher seat and went outside to the parking lot. It was bright outside. No big deal, the sunshine seemed to say. You do a little cruising, this time for a backup system, not for a one-night stand, although maybe you could kill two birds with one stone on that account.

"No big deal." Norris strolled to his car, opened the door, and sat inside, letting his leg hang out in the sunshine. He found a cigarette in the glove compartment and bent down to light it with the car lighter. He drew deeply, exhaled, then sat straight. He held the cigarette low behind the console in case a kid or an administrator happened along. Smoking on school grounds was not allowed.

"No big deal," he said as he bent for another draw. Sitting up, he began to feel a little better.

It would work out. He'd find his coke and grass supply, no problem. A little less convenient, but he'd just have to make larger purchases so he wouldn't run out when he really needed it.

Norris bent down, took a puff, leaned back against the head rest. He raised his left arm and rolled up the white cuff to expose the burn on one wrist. It was still as red as the day he got it. He'd been through all the possible explanations and had discarded most of them. Not a true burn, and not a bruise. Not a symptom of AIDS, because God knew he was always careful. And God knew he was not that active. Not hives, not an allergy reaction. He'd never been the allergic type.

And so he had concluded that the spots were age spots. The kind of thing old ladies got on their hands and spent fortunes on creams to fade them away.

Norris rolled his sleeve down again, finished his cigarette, and stubbed it out in the ashtray. He pulled his leg inside and moved the test papers under the loose end of the passenger's seat belt so they wouldn't slide all to hell when he made turns. He rolled the window down to let in a little cool spring air.

He left the school and drove to the grocery store, where he picked up a six-pack of Coors, some Diet Coke, a box of Frosted Flakes, and a quart of milk. At the Wilco gas station he bought a thick brochure of the Tidewater area, complete with a listing of restaurants and tourist amusements and night entertainment hot spots.

At home, he would get out a highlighter and mark the places he'd been. Hopefully there would be some good possibilities he'd never visited. Places which sported their own regular customers, places with faces he didn't know and faces that didn't know him. Places just far enough away from where he lived so he wouldn't be caught in a cross-over central Norfolk crowd of regulars. Where he could inquire about a good supplier without risking being identified as "that teacher at Bright Creek" or "that man Philippe left with the other night."

"No big deal," he said as he steered out into traffic again. Screw Teddy.

At his apartment, Norris collected his mail, nothing exciting, nothing frightening, and went inside to his kitchen. He put the groceries away, then sat at the dinette table with his orange highlighter.

No Norfolk places. Too close. Go for:

Ocean View. Small town along the Chesapeake Bay, right off the Hampton Roads Bridge Tunnel. Highlight Starry Tavern. Highlight Bay Shore Lounge. Leave Cape Henry Restaurant and Bar unmarked; Norris had passed it but never been inside.

Virginia Beach. Area-wise the largest city in Virginia. Highlight almost all of them here— Seahorse Cove, Sea Alley Beach Club, The Buckaneer, The Bronze Mermaid, Satin Lounge. A possibility was Hollywood East, listed for its fine dining, after-dinner entertainment, and extensive antique-decorated bar.

Norris looked up from the brochure, pausing with the top of the marker clamped firmly in his teeth. He saw that the red light on his telephone answering machine was blinking. A waiting call. He snorted. It was rare that he received messages. Teddy never called. He didn't fraternize with the Bright Creek teachers, and he hadn't made any lasting friends with the guys at the night spots.

He looked back at his brochure. He had work to do. Check out:

Portsmouth. Across the Elizabeth River to the west of Norfolk. Highlight Dryland Cross.

Highlight Heron Lounge. Leave unmarked the Driver Night Club, although the description left Norris with the certainty it would be one he'd drive past and never step inside.

He looked up at the machine. The red light; blink, pause, blink. His bank, maybe, with a new great deal on extended credit. Or the landlord, telling him an exterminator would be in this weekend for a thorough spraying for roaches.

Norris lit a cigarette.

Blink. Blink.

Shit. Norris capped the marker and dropped it beside the brochure. He went to the phone on the counter, then sidestepped and got the carton of milk out of the refrigerator. He opened the spout, pulled his cigarette out of his mouth for a moment, and took a swig.

Blink. Blink.

Maybe Lindsay was worse. Maybe Hank was calling to tell him. He swallowed, then pushed the message button. The machine whirred, rewinding. It clicked.

"Norris, this is Tom Murphy."

Norris put the milk down.

"I may well have the wrong Norris, but I don't think so. You didn't give me a last name, or a number, and you didn't even tell me the school where you worked. And even though it's been a while since we met, I've been feeling a bit guilty. I thought I should try to smooth it out."

Tom? Musician Tom?

"I got your number through some elementary detective work. You said you lived in Norfolk and you taught high-school boys. So I called around to all the Norfolk-area high schools, private and public, and when the secretaries answered I

207

asked to speak with Norris. I came up with only two. One at Elizabeth South High. I got hold of the guy at his home. He was an old bus driver, so I just feigned a wrong number. The other school was Bright Creek School, that detention school. When I asked for Norris, the secretary said, 'Norris Lynch?' I said of course. You were in class, so I didn't ask to leave a message. I asked for your home number, said I was your brother from Henford. It sounded pretty hectic in the background. Otherwise she might have remembered your number was unlisted. But she gave it to me. Funny how a little work can pay off."

Funny, Norris thought.

"Anyway, my message time is running out, I'm sure. I just wanted to know if you wanted to get together again sometime to talk. We don't even have to come back to my place. It can be a casual meeting, a drink or dinner. Call me, okay? 529-4771."

The beep. The click. The final, softer five beeps indicating the messages were finished.

"Goddamn Emily, how dare she give my number to somebody without asking me?"

Norris jammed the milk carton back into the refrigerator. It nearly tipped over, then rocked back upright. He slammed the door. His eyes closed. The smell of wood smoke grew strong and then ebbed. He took it in, let it out.

Tom lived in Chesapeake. Not close to Norris at all. Maybe Tom would know of a potential supplier that Norris could use without risking his good name here in Norfolk.

"Good name," Norris grunted. He looked at the phone. Tom certainly knew Norris was a recreational user, even if the musician didn't do any of it himself. And the man knew the area. He might be good for a lead, at least. *For some reason he seems to like me. I can put that to good use.*

Nothing to lose but loss itself.

He looked down at the cheerfully colorfully highlighted brochure and then back at the phone. It was worth a shot. He didn't know where else to begin.

Slowly he dialed the number, put the receiver to his ear, and leaned back on the counter to wait.

Chapter Fifty-five

Norris pulled into the small, oyster-shell-covered parking lot outside the Nansemond Lounge in Suffolk. It was almost nine-thirty and only a dozen cars were parked along the weather-worn beams that outlined the lot. Fluorescent lights spread purple pools on the shells.

The lounge was sided with black wood and green shuttered windows. The rear of the building met the steep bank of the East Creek, a medium-sized river, a tributary of the much larger James several miles to the north. Although technically in the city of Suffolk, the Nansemond Lounge had found an unclaimed nook; except for a small fishing pier and cleaning shack to the left and an abandoned car lot to the right, there was no sign of Suffolk civilization within nearly three-quarters of a mile.

Norris sat in the car for a full two minutes before convincing himself to go inside. Then he locked the car, took a deep breath of the fish-heavy air, and crossed to the front door. From the corner of his eye, he saw Tom's Toyota, parked nearest the door. He wondered how long Tom had been waiting.

He pulled the heavy wooden door open and stepped inside. It wasn't as sleazy as he had imagined it would be, given his impression from outside. The smells were strange, a combination of fried chicken and blackened fish and Oriental spring rolls. But the dark wood and candlelight were encouraging. Maybe it wasn't the redneck hangout he'd envisioned. A pleasant-looking hostess greeted him, menu in hand, and asked if he cared for dinner or wanted to have some time at the bar.

A quick perusal didn't reveal Tom Murphy, so Norris decided time at the bar would help him regain his bearings. Yes, he'd agreed to dine with the musician; yes, Tom had likely told the hostess that he was expecting company. But it was easier to play dumb (the ugly girl will go away, the teacher will not ask you about smoking in the bathroom) and let Tom find him. He ordered a white wine and swiveled on his stool to view the wide-screen television at the far end of the bar. Local news, edited-for-television anchorwoman with suit and California accent. Norris sipped the wine, then pulled out a cigarette. As he put it on his tongue, he saw the No Smoking sign.

Unbelievable.

He began to put the cigarette back into the pack. Then he saw the red glow of a tip down near the television. So bars now had smoking sections. How disgustingly up-to-date. He scooped up the glass and sidled down toward the television and his nameless nicotine soul mates.

Someone stepped in front on him, and Norris

stopped. A tiny crest of wine jumped the lip of the cup and splashed somewhere down among the feet and the stool legs.

"Hey, Norris, I've been saving a table." Norris looked up at Tom. The man wore a broad, surfer smile, and a striped, knit sweater Norris thought he recognized from the man on the Infomercials. "Glad you made it. Did you want to sit at the bar first? I could give up the table and bring my drink over."

"No." *No, let's get this done with, Tommy boy.* "You got smoking or nonsmoking?"

"Smoking. I remember you at Sea Alley. Going for the record, I thought. Book of world records."

"Yeah," said Norris. "It's what I live for."

Tom led Norris back around the front to the dining side of the lounge. There were no free-standing tables; lines of shoulder-high inner walls made every dining place a booth. From the ceiling hung fishnets and clamming rakes and a large stuffed alligator draped with Spanish moss. Tom's table was in a back corner.

"The food here is an interesting collection," said Tom as they sat. During the phone conversation on Wednesday, Tom had mentioned several places they might want to try out, places Tom could recommend. Norris had run down his high-lighted brochure as they spoke, latching on Nansemond because, of those Tom mentioned, it was the only one Norris had never visited. "I think it's swamp mentality. What I mean is, here we are, next to the Great Dismal Swamp, not the beautiful Atlantic Ocean. So what are the locals going to do? You have to use what you have to your advantage. So they decide swamps make people think Cajun. Think New Orleans, think snapping turtles and cypress trees."

Norris worked around on his seat, trying to keep his knees from touching Tom's. It was hard; the man was tall and the bench seats barely substantial.

"Take off your coat and stay awhile," said Tom.

Norris shed his jacket and dropped it on the seat.

The waitress was there then, laying paper-bag-colored menus on the table top. "Nansemond Jambalaya," it read on the cover.

"What's with your wrist?" Tom asked.

Norris didn't have to look down to see that one cuff had crept up. "Age spot," he said.

Tom chose blackened swordfish. Norris ordered Virginia ham. With the tossed salads came the time to talk. Norris spooned Italian dressing from the communal caddy onto his lettuce, and said, "You've lived in Chesapeake for long?"

"Sure."

"You know a lot of people around here?"

Tom nodded and lifted his water glass. "Do you want some introductions?"

"I might," said Norris. "Seven years and I've pretty much farted around on the social front."

The waitress came up to the booth, balancing faux-pewter plates of ham and fish. Norris leaned back to give her room. Tom did the same. Their feet touched. Norris jerked his away. Tom seemed to not notice.

"So you've farted around?" Tom cut into his fish, watching Norris with a steady calm that made Norris's neck itch. "What do you mean?"

"No real ties, not that I'm a cling-on or anything. But a friend left me in a bad situation the other day."

Tom was confused. He put his fork down and crossed his arms on the table. "Tell me."

God, he's so sincere, Norris thought. "I'd been able to"—shit, how to put this—"obtain things I needed through this friend. Now he can't help me anymore."

Tom's nod was barely discernible. His brows drew together, and the shadow that formed over his lids reminded Norris of Sam.

Don't think you dare think of Sam, don't drag his memory into this.

Tom said, "What do you need, Norris?"

Norris let out a long breath. "A million dollars, a Lear jet, how about you?"

"Sounds good. But what did you need from your friend?"

"Stuff." Norris looked to the side, out to the other booths and wandering waitresses and waiters. To hell with it, take the plunge. "He supplied me. You know, with the stuff I needed to get going every once in a while. Kickers. It's not that I have to have it. It's just a good boost when things are slow."

"Oh, is that all? I thought you were looking for S-and-M or something. I have friends who find what they're looking for in all the various pleasures."

"No, I'm fairly straight for a non-straight."

Tom grinned. "You almost said it, Norris. Pat yourself on the back. Now, you're looking for simple highs, is that it?"

"Yeah." Man, this was nothing like talking to Teddy. This was like going to the pharmacist and taking out a prescription.

213

"Is this why you decided to join me for dinner?"

"Well."

"Well?"

"Partly."

Tom became intent on his swordfish. Norris sat, forearm resting on the table, chunk of ham speared on his fork. Let Tom have a minute to think. There was a good chance he would change the subject, go on to less substantial conversation. And there was also the smaller chance he would come up with a name Norris could check out. Norris put the fork in his mouth and pulled off the ham. He'd have his answer, one way or another, very soon.

Tom looked up at Norris. "Norris, if you'd accept who you are, you might not need all that reality enhancement."

Oh, fuck. Norris hadn't considered a third option. The man was a righteous convert. This was going to go nowhere but straight down. He snatched up his jacket and scooted from the booth. "I need to get some air, Tom. No offense." The waitress, returning to their booth to check on them, blinked and stepped out of his way.

"Norris." Tom was out of the booth, following. Norris pushed out the front door, pausing less than a second to get his bearings and see his car, then trotted across the shells, pulling his car keys from his jeans.

Tom had come out, too. Norris heard the footsteps behind him. Then the voice. "Norris, don't do this. Give me a break. I'm not trying to tell you what to do."

The fuck you aren't. I don't need another father.

Norris reached his car, jammed the key into the lock. The lock popped, and Norris put his thumb onto the latch. Tom grabbed Norris's arm and pulled his fingers from the handle. With the grace of a martial-arts expert he spun Norris around to face him. The keys flew off into the dark, fish-smelling night air.

"Listen to me." Tom shoved his body against Norris's, thigh to thigh, knees to knees, groin to groin. Norris knew Tom was not thinking sex, but the sudden contact caught Norris off-guard. Blood sang in his veins. He was afraid to look at Tom.

"Listen to me, Norris." Tom did not move away. His breath was on Norris's face, too close, too damn close. "I'm not telling you what to do. But I thought you might need a little help. People need help sometimes, do you even realize that? I'm not trying to drag you into a spotlight. I think you're a good guy. Will you at least listen to me?"

Norris closed his eyes. It seemed as if the oyster shells beneath his feet shifted. He tried to shift his own feet to keep balance, but Tom was pressing too hard.

"Do you want this to end here? Is that what you want?"

The shells were slippery, dipping ever so slightly to the right, to the left. Were there earthquakes in Suffolk? He'd never heard of any.

"Norris?"

Norris felt one of Tom's hands loosen from his own and slide up, brushing the heel of the hand, crossing the wrist, the age spot on the wrist.

The burn.

The burn flared suddenly, red hot. Norris threw his head back with the pain.

"Norris!"

The parking lot buckled violently. Norris felt Tom grabbing at him, at his jacket, his shirt, and

215

then falling away. Norris dropped to his knees.
The smell of fire erupted in his nostrils.

The lounge is on fire?

Norris felt for his car, but his hands fell short.
He coughed, shaking his head. He opened his
eyes, and his car was not there. He looked over
his shoulder. Tom was not there. The lounge,
gone. The oyster-shell parking lot transformed.

He was in the woods. A fire nearby, trees, a
slice of clouded sky above.

There were benches before him, a semicircle of
rough wood planks. On the benches were men
and women he did not know. They were looking
at him. Rows of people, white people, dressed in
plain blue shirts and pants, watching him. Seated
cross-legged on the ground to the sides of the
benches were dark-skinned people, heads down,
hands strung with chains like the galley slaves
from *Ben Hur*.

What the fuck is this?

It was as though he had been dropped into an
outdoor theater. And it was his time to dance.

*Tom, you were right, I don't need anymore god-
damn shit, I don't need this nightmare!*

He tried to slow his breathing. This would pass
as surely as the hallucination of the barbed wire
around his neck. Maybe Teddy's shit was worthless. What the hell kind of crap had he been selling him, after all?

"Hmmm," said a voice to Norris's left. Norris
could not turn toward the voice. He continued to
stare out at the silent collection of blue-clothed
white men and women. At the silent, nearly
naked row of blacks.

This is sick, does this come from my own mind?

"I can't believe that after all this time you

would do that to me." The voice. He didn't know this voice.

Norris tried to lick his lips, tried to talk this fantasy man back into his head along with the zombies on the bench, but his lips would not open to free his tongue. Words formed in his mind only.

The man said, "What were you thinking, can you tell me that?"

Ride it out, this flash can't go on forever!

Above Norris's head, a whippoorwill couldn't make up its mind. "More rain. More rain. No more rain."

Suddenly, without conscious direction of his own, his head spun about. His brain was caught up in the whiplash.

His groans rattled loudly in his mind only. The man who had spoken stood in front of a raging bonfire. Norris couldn't decipher any features, just a glowing silhouette with arms outstretched as in supplication.

"How could you do it? Haven't you learned from the others? Are you truly as slow as I feared you were?"

What did I do?

"You realize, of course, that you can't be part of us anymore. We have to trim the deadweight. Surely you aren't surprised." The man stepped forward, his shadowed body zooming in, Norris still unable to see him clearly. Shadow hands reached down and caught Norris under his armpits. The hands pulled upward. Norris went with them. Then Norris was turned back to face the crowd on the benches. "Is there anyone here who would speak for this traitor?"

Norris watched. No one moved, no one

blinked. Hard eyes, emotionless eyes, stared at him. Behind the gathering, trees heavy with autumn gold and red held silent sentinel.

The man behind him put his chin on Norris's shoulder. Norris couldn't turn to see him. The man's breath was heavy with onions and bacon. The man said softly, "So. we will not hang together, some of us must hang separately. Do you agree with me?"

A young and muscular woman on the front row dipped her head; a slow nod. She said, "We agree with you."

A man beside her, with short hair and tattooed cheek, said, "We agree with you."

"We agree with you," said the people on the benches.

The people on the ground were silent.

Fucking 1984 is it? Wake the hell up! Norris was rooted to the ground. He could not make a single muscle move on his own.

"Give me your hands."

Norris's hands rose against his will, and he was able to glance down at them. They were strange, fat hands. Pale and filthy. Beyond his hands he could see his stomach. It protruded around a tight, alien blue shirt. His feet were pudgy and bare.

The man pulled away from Norris's shoulder and came around to his front. *Look at him, see him.* Norris could not look up from his hands and feet. There was soot on the ground around his unfamiliar, bare feet. Soot of many bonfires, stirred in with the dark soil.

"Penitent now? Too little too late." The man clucked his tongue. "Hang separately. We'll enjoy the cleansing. I'm not so sure you will, but that doesn't really matter anymore, does it?"

"Help me," said the man to someone behind him. Norris tried to look up and beyond the bushiness of his lowered eyebrows. He could not see what was about to happen.

Someone was beside the man now, handing him a coil of wire.

Oh my God!

"Hands together, tighter!"

Norris's traitor wrists pressed together like fat, mindless lovers. The man put the wire to the wrists.

Norris's wrists then understood. They jerked upward, locked together, and caught the man under the chin. The crack was loud, the grunt a millisecond behind. The wire jerked away.

Look now look quickly and see him!

But Norris did not focus, could not focus, because his fat, naked feet were already spinning away from the flailing man, catching up the sooty soil and driving him forward.

Get to the trees!

Norris wanted to scream at his body to move it. He'd never been so sluggish. At vision's periphery he saw his swinging arms, clothed in the short blue sleeves, pale arms swimming for their lives. He saw the people on the bleachers half stand, watching him, watching the man behind him. Not moving but waiting. Waiting for directions. Norris's bare feet clawed the ground, taking him toward the thick rim of trees beyond the outdoor theater. He stumbled across a log bordering the theater. He ran into the undergrowth. Thistles bit his feet.

And then he heard the man coming after him. Calling out in a horrid, patient voice, "You know you can't get far, you fat cow."

Norris ran. Rocks and pine cones slipped under his steps, threatening to throw him on his face. He could hear his rapid breaths; they were high-pitched and whistling. His heart was already aching. *Fucking body!* He crashed down a knoll, through a clutter of dense cedar trees. At the bottom was a stream. His knees locked. His feet slipped on the humus-slick bank and he went down on his butt. He slid into the stream.

Get up!

His hands did not go out to grab at the roots on the stream's edge. They, instead, went to his face. He heard his own sniffles. He heard his own insane sobs.

Behind him, the rustle of boots on the bank. The humored reproach.

"Farther than I thought," said the man. "What do you know?"

The man walked down to the stream. Norris saw his shadow coming, swelling, engulfing Norris's own stupid body sitting in the water. He saw shadow arms reach up. He saw the shadow wire flexed between them. He saw the wire come down over him, and shadow became substance. Barbed wire looped his neck. It snagged, cut with first contact.

"I don't want to tighten this yet. But you come with me now. An extra few minutes of life are worth it, don't you think? An extra few minutes to think of how you betrayed us and shunned the truth?"

Norris shot his arms out behind him, surprised that they obeyed him this time, and he locked his elbows around the knees of the standing man. Then he quickly fell to his side, bringing the man down with him. The wire bit into his neck, drawing a sharp circle of bright pain and blood.

The man hit the water, and the wire loosened around Norris's neck. Norris clawed at the wire, ducking his head from under it, nearly scalping himself, leaving chunks of hair and skin on the barbs. Agony. He shrieked, lunging forward, blood pouring, commanding his feet to get a purchase on the smooth stones of the creek. Sending a plea for help along the telegraph system of his nerves, down to his hands. *Grab the root!*

Grab the root!

He grabbed the root. And pulled. He went up from the water, screaming, then teetered and fell face down in the slimy, dead-leaf carpet of the stream's shore.

He panted, trying to regain his breath. The man would be up, after him. Norris swallowed, and turned his head sideways.

It was night.

There were the sounds of laughing, of talking, of a car engine somewhere beyond the stream.

The smell of dead fish was strident. The rush of water below him, just beyond the reach of his toes, his shoes—he could feel them!—was much louder than that of a stream.

Norris worked up onto his elbows. The sleeves of his shirt were torn. Scratches were visible through the holes, thin lines of red like unpaved county roads on a state map. Little blood. He dabbed at his neck, searching for the wire cut. His neck was unblemished. He bent his head down so his fingers could trace his hairline.

His scalp was not torn. There was no blood.

He was lying on the bank of the East Creek.

The goddamn Nansemond Lounge is up there. My fucking car is up there on that shelled lot.

There was mud on his upper lip. He swiped at it with his knuckles. He shivered. His pants were wet up to the knees. He worked his knees up under him and stood.

The lot was now visible. The purple glow of the lights, the fronts and rears of cars at the lot's edge. Several small shrubs on the side of the lounge.

There was a groan behind him. Norris turned, grabbing a small branch of a shrub to keep from slipping. Tom was lying on the bank, arm over his head, one foot in the water. Norris gripped the shrub more tightly, took a single step down toward the creek.

"Tom?"

Tom shivered, his face digging into the damp earth as if trying to speak, or to cough.

"Tom?"

What was he doing here? Someone had hurt him, someone had knocked him down in a struggle.

Someone, perhaps, who'd been in a drug-induced world and had been fighting mind-demons with barbed wire and blue-shirted followers.

Norris stared at the man for another moment, then scrambled up the side of the bank to the shells of the parking lot and ran for his car.

Run away. Run away.

Run away.

Chapter One

The last day of school for the Bright Creek criminals was May 23. For those who were civil enough
to have earned a pass home, there was a week's
leave before summer session began on June 2.
Most of the Bright Creek teachers had a week's
break as well. Some stayed at time-and-a-half to
monitor those who had not earned passes.

This year, Norris decided he could use the
money and the diversion, and agreed to stay on.
The days were spent in remedial classes and
sports. In the afternoons, the boys went on work
details around the school grounds. On occasion
the administration was called by a church or
business, and the boys were bused to clean yards
or paint or sweep. Norris, who came in on
Saturday and Sunday mornings, was relieved of
the weekday-afternoon chain gangs.

The flashes Norris had been having since
returning home from the reunion in Henford had
been increasing in frequency. There had been
weeks when he'd had more than one. Sometimes
he had even blacked out for more than a minute.
He awakened, still standing or sitting where he
had been before the flash, but frightened and dis-
oriented. Each time, he could smell the scents of
camping. Each time, he heard voices, crying,
chanting. Almost every time, he came out of the
spell with the sense that there had been barbed
wire on his neck, ready to choke him.

The incidents occurred equally at work and at
home. At least when he was at school, he had less

time to worry about them, to wonder when another would come.

When he had moments to think about it, he broke out in nervous sweats. He wondered if he should take his teacher insurance and see a shrink.

He hadn't heard from Lindsay since her phone message in April. He assumed she was out of the hospital and doing fine. Norris had even sent her a get-well card the day after he spoke with Hank. A gesture to show Lindsay that he wasn't as self-centered as she surely believed he was.

Not quite.

So, how are you, Norris? Not horrible and self-centered anymore, is that it?

Confucius say, "If you're alive, you gotta live unless you die, and death is painful."

Confucius say, "Do what you gotta do, be it horrible or self-centered."

Chapter Two

June 3.

Dear Bernie,

I know you've tried to call me several times. Hank passed on to me your get-well wishes. The phone is no longer in our bedroom because Hank doesn't want me disturbed. It's been helpful.

I'm much better since the accident. I'm out of my ankle cast, and only two weeks to go with the arm cast.

Lindsay stopped and pressed the end of the pen

against her forehead. She shifted on the chair, arms leaning on the desk top, gazing at but not out her bedroom window. She had to word this right. Everything was happening so fast; everything was so intense. Sometimes she could barely bring herself to go to the bathroom alone. She never knew when or where the visions would strike her. She knew she was not insane, but she felt her husband thought her so. And wasn't that the way it was with all insanity? The insane were the last to know?

Aunt Marla has been with us since I came home from the hospital. I'm sure Hank told you. She's been wonderful with the girls. She takes Grace to preschool now, and stays with her. In the afternoons she plays with Mandy and Grace. They cook up a storm in the kitchen.

There was a cup of hot tea on the desk beside her letter. She picked up the cup but then put it back down because the spasm in her hand was too strong. She wished she had a straw. At the hospital they had straws and you didn't have to hold your cup. Here, at home, it was strange to ask for a straw. At home, you were supposed to be well enough to hold your own cup. And so she didn't let them know. When she was alone, she often bent to her cup and drank from the desk.

I look forward to summer weather. As Norris would say, "It's the best goddamn season of the year." It was great seeing him at the reunion. Have you heard from him?

Elizabeth Massie

Lindsay bent to her teacup and sipped a little down. There was a tapping on the bedroom door. Lindsay flinched. "Who is it?"

"Grace and me."

Lindsay wiped her face, fearing there might be tears there she did not want her daughter to see. "Come on in."

Mandy led Grace through the door. She held a plate covered by a paper towel. "We got something for you, Mama."

Lindsay made her mouth pull back at the edges. A smile. Hopefully, Mandy would believe. Hopefully, it would help mask the twitch that nestled in her left cheek.

"Good stuff!" said Grace. The girls moved over to the bed and sat side by side, looking at Lindsay. Mandy, holding the plate to her stomach with both hands, watched her mother as though waiting for a formal go-ahead.

"Let me see what you made," said Lindsay.

Mandy grinned. "They're really yummy!"

"What are they?"

"They're brownies," said Mandy.

"Nig cakes!" squealed Grace.

Lindsay took the plate and pulled up the paper towel.

Evenly cut brown squares, four of them, sat on the plate.

"What cakes?"

"Nig cakes!"

Mandy nudged Grace and frowned. "Shhh, Grace."

"But Marla said!"

"And I said no, be quiet, don't you remember?"

Lindsay put the plate beside her cup of tea, and

228

pushed it back so she wouldn't inadvertently knock it off.

"Remember what?"

Mandy stood and pulled Grace up by her elbow.

"Oww!" Grace jerked away.

"Nothing, Mama. Hope you like the brownies. We didn't put nuts in them, just like you like."

"Thanks. You two are so thoughtful."

"And Marla!"

"And your Aunt Marla. Tell her I said so. And I'll see you before bedtime."

Mandy took a step toward her mother, then hesitated. Lindsay felt her eyes brim. Her daughter was frightened of her. It was so unfair. What was her life at this moment if it wasn't for her daughters?

"You aren't going to come down to supper tonight?"

"Not yet. I want to, you have to know that. I miss sitting at the table and watching everybody eat with their mouths open and knock over their drinks." Her eyebrows went up, once. "I'm joking, Mandy."

Mandy smiled. It was as happy a smile as the one Lindsay had produced when the girls had come in the room. She took Grace out, and pulled the door closed behind them.

"Finish this letter," Lindsay told herself. She picked the pen up. This letter would go out to Bernie tomorrow. Lindsay would get down-stairs when everyone was gone and put it in the mailbox. She couldn't ask Hank to do it. He would suspect Lindsay was spilling the family beans.

I'm not ashamed, Lindsay, don't misunderstand me. But this has been hard on us all. There really is no concrete reason why anyone has to know beyond Marla and us. You'll get better, and then it will be water under the bridge.

Hank had been horrified when told that Lindsay had left the hospital in a cab. He threatened at first to sue the taxi company, but then his cooler head talked him out of it. The cab driver couldn't be blamed. The man didn't know Lindsay was going through a stress that was causing her to do things over which she had no control. Besides, a lawsuit would just draw attention to Lindsay's behavior.

Back in her hospital room, Lindsay had been delirious, or so Hank had told her. He said she had babbled about angry people and blood in cups and of being thrown against the outside wall of a dirty yellow house. Lindsay remembered that she had broken her promise in that hour, begging Hank to hear her vision and help her through it. At that moment, she thought her fervor would reach out to him and bring him in. She thought he would understand. And then she remembered herself, and said no more. It was best not to say anything to anyone. Ever. Not to Hank, not to Bernie. She had to ignore it and let it go away. For Mandy. For Grace.

Lindsay's doctor suggested a week on the hospital's fourth floor, for observation. Hank said no, that wouldn't be necessary. They would take care of Lindsay at home. They would get live-in help. They would get her through whatever it was that tormented her.

Lindsay put the pen to the paper. She pushed it with effort.

I must close here. Take care of yourself and tell everyone at HeartLight hello for me.

She had to send this letter to Bernie. If she didn't, she would try to come instead of call. And the last person she wanted to see her like this was Bernie.

Because maybe Bernie was experiencing it, too. And this, doubled, would be way too much to bear.

Love, Lindsay.

She folded the letter and slipped into an embossed Hollin envelope. In the desk drawer was a roll of stamps. When the letter was done, she slipped it in the drawer and lay down to take a nap. She prayed she would not see the nightmare woods tonight.

But she knew she would.

Chapter Three

"Well, Junior, they're looking better, what do you think?"

Junior didn't say anything. He looked at the ground.

"Well, I think they are. Not a bit of baby fat on the bunch. Muscles I never even knew they had. Watch them."

Junior did not look up.

"I said watch them."

Junior's head snapped up.

Rex and Junior, beneath a tall black walnut tree, watched as the White Eagles went through their morning drill. Dean was leading this morning. Leg stretches, jumping jacks, arm pumps, leg lifts. The women and the men of Night Land. Sweating and training. The exercises took place in one of Night Land's manmade clearings near the bunking trailer. Warmups first, then the Eagles took the exercise trail they had hacked up and down the width of the mountain-side acreage. All in all, a good three-mile run. Still, two months into life at the camp, most of them struggled to get around without strain. Peaches hated it most. She was always near tears on her return. But they all did as they were told. They had learned that once in Night Land, Rex bore their burdens of choice for them.

They had learned that options were no longer an option.

Rex left Junior at the tree and walked past the exercise clearing to the pet shed. It was a wooden structure, twelve by twelve, built with wood Arlen had supplied in mid-April. Joe and Junior had put it up in two days, complete with a single hole at the back with a hinged window that could swing and latch open, and a heavy door that bolted from the outside. There was no solid flooring; bales of straw stored under tarps outside were changed once a week, and the soiled straw was thrown into a compost pile several hundred yards into the trees.

Glancing back at the clearing, Rex watched as the Eagles took off on their jog. Peaches, in pain, face red and grimacing, picked up the rear.

The only one not with the pack was the fat bitch Lena. Rex did not demand that she run with the rest. She was not a warrior, but she did serve.

She cleaned the trailer, she mucked the pet trailer. She obediently helped with meal preparation at the kitchen tent. She seemed content with her position. She did not seem to miss the fact that Junior was no longer allowed to fuck her. Now, she was chopping poison ivy at the edge of the common grounds.

As it was a good day, Rex had let her have a pair of work gloves for the job.

"Hey, Billy Bailey," said Rex. He tapped on the locked shed door. Inside, the man would be asleep, or pretending to sleep. Billy slept a lot now. Rex wondered if this was what clinical depression was all about.

"Billy, cheer up, man. You aren't alone anymore. I got you some friends. Now don't be a Scrooge."

As always, Billy Bailey did not answer.

"Fine, then," said Rex. "I had a nice warm doughnut for you this morning. Sorry you're such a sourpuss."

Inside the shed, there was no sound. Since early May, the White Eagles had added two more. A girl of nineteen, chubby at first but slimming down quickly. Another boy about Rusty Nolen's age. They might have even been friends, but they were kept in gags, so friendly banter was out of the question. They were chained so they could sit. Rex had felt magnanimous when deciding where to bolt the eye screws.

When nearly finished with the shed, while putting the latch on the door, Joe had asked why they wanted to keep aliens on Night Land after all. He said he didn't like being near them. Joe learned that questions were no longer a given part of life. After an Arm Test was performed to

233

determine consequences, Joe had spent that night locked inside with the aliens. The next morning, when he was let out, he seemed willing to accept Rex's explanation.

Rex was sometimes amazed at how many lessons the White Eagles still had to learn. He went back to the tree, stood beside Junior, and waited.

One by one, the White Eagles finished the trail and struggled over beside him, panting, coughing, beautiful.

"Sit," said Rex. They sat. Lizzie, rubbing the tail of her shirt across her dirt-streaked face. Dean, barely breathing hard, scratching a scab on his shin, the Eagle who had come the furthest physically and mentally in this time. Ronald, the artist, the hands he had deemed so talented now covered with grit and sticky pine sap.

Rex smiled down at them. His recruits. His army. Their job, to clean up Henford. To clean the streets of the unearthly. To continue to post their posters in town, to secretly leave flyers on car windshields and then return to the safety of their compound. To let the people of Henford see and learn and know the glory of cleansing.

Arlen kept his ear to the town's pulse. He shared with Rex the newspaper articles on the disappearances and the investigations by the police. Arlen and his friends in the police department, the law offices, and the clergy downplayed it when speaking to other Henfordians who were concerned. The missing had run off, as that kind of person always did. They would be happier elsewhere.

The white Humans of Henford would come

around, they would see the benefits with time. Perhaps it would be a bloodless war. Conversion by Truth. Revelation by revelation. But if not, the crates in the storage trailer were brimming with weapons, ready for Rex to distribute.

No matter which path it took, it was a war whose victory Rex already felt in his veins. They were learning.

Peaches came trudging out from the trees. Her face was puffy. The soot on her face was streaked as though tears had been shed in the privacy of the forest cover. But she would not cry here. She joined the others, seated at Rex's feet.

Rex then crossed his arms and said, "Truth."

"Truth," the Eagles repeated.

"Truth demands obedience," said Rex, nodding at Junior.

"Truth and obedience," said the Eagles. They looked at Junior, who had been tied to the tree, arms above his head, shirt peeling from his back, for almost two days.

Junior had walked half of the trail and Rex had cut through the trees and found him strolling along, eating an unripened mayapple he'd found.

"Truth demands obedience," Rex said.

"Truth demands obedience," said the Eagles.

Rex picked up the braided whip at Junior's feet and in turn, each Eagle gave their brother in Truth a severe lash across his back.

Junior grimaced and groaned, and his teeth bore into his lip and made it bleed, but he did not cry.

They were learning.

Chapter Four

"Mail, Bernie."

Bernie sat on the porch swing, her toes dragging the rough, warped boards of the flooring. Back and forth, back and forth. Comfort in repetitive mindlessness, peace in a moment without thought. For the moment, no haunting voices or scents. For the moment, no men after her beneath a kitchen table, no rainy graves and shattered legs, no dark night visits by a skinny old woman with bony hands and a greased rubber glove.

Matt joined her on the porch, holding an envelope. "You've got mail. Postmark is Henford."

"Letter from Mom."

"It doesn't smell like your mom's letters." Matt put his arm around her shoulder.

How do my mom's letters smell? she was going to ask, but it was a stupid question, and it died on her lips. Much of her life now was a stupid question.

Bernie sat forward, pulling away from Matt. Matt let his arm fall to his lap. Bernie thought she saw despair, discouragement, in his move, but she did not acknowledge it. She was too weary to take on any more than her own hell.

"Want me to open it?"

"If you want."

Matt tore the envelope. Bernie closed her eyes, instantly picked up a strong smell of ammonia and spoiled milk. Her vision smells, not scents from the envelope. She opened her eyes.

The letter was from Lindsay. She was fine, said the letter. Healing, looking forward to a good summer. Matt folded the letter and put it back in the envelope.

"That's nice," said Bernie.

"Bullshit. You don't think it's nice." Matt leaned forward slightly, throwing a deep shadow across his eyes. Bernie sensed the anger in them, even though she could not see it. Beautiful, angry eyes.

Matt, don't be mad at me. I can't have you mad at me and God mad at me, too.

"No. You don't think anything's nice. And you think what's not nice shouldn't be shared."

"Don't start this, Matt."

"Talk to me, Bernie. I want to help."

"I can't even help myself."

"Talk to me. Tell me what you see. You've never done that. All you've ever told us was that you see things. Ugly things. Take me in with you. Let me help steer you out."

"I can't."

"Bernie, I love you."

I love you. Was that "I love you, sister in faith"? Was it "I love you, I want you"? Or was it both?

A rabbit raced through the tall grass of the front yard. Behind it streaked one of the yellow, feral cats that had taken up housing in Red River's empty barn.

She couldn't share her visions with Matt. She couldn't open up her most intimate experience for him. Matt understood unconditional love. When he was ten, he had almost died for the life of a friend. He had jumped from his own bike to shove the friend from the path of a drunk driver, and had sustained multiple injuries himself. The only reminder now was a vicious line across his face, the mark he referred to casually as his bike accident scar.

Bernie had seen this love many times, she had felt it. But if she gave this to him, he would know her love for him. He would see her need for him. And then she would fall short. He would see her true weaknesses. And worse, she would be dragging him into whatever danger she was poised at the brink of; she would be pushing him into another drunk driver, a supernatural driver she did not understand.

"Thanks," she said.

Matt got off the swing and went into the house.

Bernie watched the rabbit circle around, the cat on its tail. Her own blood began to race in fury, in rage at God for playing games with her like a vicious cat and a tiny-minded, frightened rabbit.

She stood suddenly. The swing moved back and forward, slamming her legs. She stumbled and stepped forward.

"God! Give it to me! Give it to me now! Give me all you've got, damn You!"

She stretched back her head and screamed at the porch roof and the white June sky beyond it. "Give me all You got! What are you waiting for? I'm sick of this!" She clapped her hands at the sky.

The red burn mark on her palm began to tingle. Bernie clapped harder.

Bring it on, kill me now if this is what You've intended all this time! The red spot caught fire, like a piece of dry tinder.

"Give it to me! Give it to me!"

God, it seemed, was listening. A hand caught Bernie behind the neck, driving her down toward the floor. She fell forward and cracked her head. Lightning exploded in her brain. She panted, working against the pain. She drew her elbows up, moving them to her chest, groping the floor to see if it was her floor. It was not the porch.

"Uglier 'an life and twice as dumb." It was the voice of the kitchen man. She was back in the kitchen.

I've done this before, God! I said give it to me! Is this all You've got?

Bernie's child body turned over on the floor and looked up at the kitchen man. He smiled at her, his tongue drawing across his chipped teeth. He had on an unbuttoned shirt that hung down over his wrinkled slacks.

"Where'd you get this one, Susie?" said the man.

A woman's voice from outside the kitchen said, "I tole you we had one coming. Social services called me and said could we take one on short notice? I said, sure, why not, they's always short notice, ain't they?"

Bernie drew up into a kneeling position. She saw that she wasn't wearing the pink dress. She had on a pair of flowered shorts and a sleeveless top.

I haven't done this before.

"Well," said the man. He took a step closer to Bernie. Bernie could feel the welt on her forehead growing and throbbing. "Susie makes money with you kids. Pisses me off she don't go find no real job." He scratched his belly through the opening of his shirt. "Why does she always get the ugly ones, though?" He took another step closer. He

239

leaned slightly, letting out a whoosh of air as his lungs compacted against his massive waist. "I got secrets with the other little girls here. You like secrets?"

Bernie said nothing.

"Well, you don't have to like 'em," said the man. "You just have to keep 'em. You understand me?"

Bernie said nothing. The man's fist flashed out and caught her across the ear. The ringing stung like a laser. "You understand me?"

It was hard to hear through the ringing, but Bernie knew the question. Bernie's child's voice said, "Yes."

"What I decide to do with you or the other girls is my secret. And you'll keep 'em or I'll kill you. Now. Tell me, little ugly girl. What's your name?"

Bernie said nothing. The fist went up again. He screamed, "What's your name?"

Bernie felt herself trembling madly, and the man and the kitchen were gone. Now she was in a bedroom. Small, dark. She wore a flannel nightgown, and her body was no longer that of a child, but of an overweight adolescent.

I've seen this bedroom. I know this place!

There was a woman standing over her, holding a wooden spoon. "I asked you to say your name! You better learn to talk or I'll crack open your head, you idiot! I won't have you embarrass me in front of my family!"

It was Marla. Aunt Marla with the spoon.

And Bernie's mouth opened, and in the pinched teenage voice she heard herself say, "My name is Lena. Lena Carlton."

Chapter Five

Donald Frye's office was sterile. A desk. Two chairs, one for him, one for the visiting dignitary. A window with a shade and no curtain. A bookshelf with a dead cactus in a sand pot and stacks of photocopied monthly school calendars, student handbooks, and dust.

Norris had found a memo in his mailbox instructing him to drop by the vice principal's office before leaving today. It had unnerved Norris. The students were back from their week leave. Summer school had begun. Norris fretted profusely that afternoon. What could Frye want?

Donald Frye had been at his desk looking over a paper when Norris had come in. He motioned to the chair, and Norris sat. Now he was still reading. Norris wanted to reach over the desk top and slap the man.

At long last, Donald put the paper down. He sighed.

Norris's heart sank with the sigh. This was not going to be good.

"Thanks for coming in, Norris. Hope I'm not holding you up from any after-school appointments?"

"No."

"I'll get to the point, then."

Please do.

"I don't like the way things have been going for you recently. Last, say, four or five weeks."

Oh, shit, wake me up. "What do you mean?"

"I mean what I say. Mr. Franklin doesn't always

take the bull by the horns, as we know, although he's a good guy. But he's vacationing, as you know. Back in July. Then it'll be my turn, thank heaven."

Norris crossed his arms. He would not let this man see him worried. Sweat broke out on his neck.

"Anyway," said Donald. He picked up a pencil, tapped it twice, and let it fall back. "I'm the buck-stops-here guy. I have to do what I have to do. Norris, I've noticed it. Your students have noticed it. Some have even come to me. And they never come to me about anything."

About fucking what?

"You got some problems you want to tell me about?"

"What do you mean?"

"Norris, give me a reason to reconsider."

"Reconsider what?"

"Letting you go."

Norris's scalp tightened. Letting him go? No fucking way, they had no right, they had no reason. He said, "What do you mean, 'students have noticed it'? Noticed what?"

"Your . . . I don't know . . . trances. Are you epileptic?"

"No."

"Too bad. That might have saved your job. Are you sharing Teddy's stash?"

"Teddy? The janitor? What are you talking about?"

Remember, Frye knows about Teddy. He told the janitor to clean it up. Maybe this was part of the housekeeping, finding the abusing teachers and sweep them out.

"Drugs, Norris. The just-say-no kind."

"Of course not."

"Whatever. Actually, it's not here nor there, anyway. I have to let you go."

Norris felt the sweat collect on his sternum and drip to his stomach. "What?"

"I've walked by your classroom and seen you staring into space. The students say sometimes you talk to yourself. It doesn't last long, they say. But how long does it take one mentally unbalanced juvenile delinquent to stab another unbalanced juvenile delinquent with a pencil?"

"You can't let me go."

"Of course I can. This isn't a regular school with a regular grievance procedure. We have drastic students, we have the legal right to take drastic measures to protect them from each other or from incompetent supervision."

"That's not true. I'm not incompetent."

"Maybe you don't want to be, or don't think you are, but you are."

Norris balled his fists against each other and held them against his thighs. A strong scent of pine smoke circled his head. Smells of cooking meat, of hot coffee.

Not now!

"I'm sure there are jobs which don't require so much intense, constant vigil. You're an intelligent man, Norris. We would be happy to write a reference."

Don't say it, Norris, don't burn this bridge, too.

Norris stood from the chair. By Donald's sudden expression, he knew the red he felt in his eyes was clearly visible. *Don't burn the bridge, Norris! You might need it later!*

243

"You can take the fucking reference and shove it up your fucking little pompous white ass."

As Norris slammed out of the office, he could smell the wood smoke again. And the smell of a bridge up in smoke.

Chapter Six

The evening sky was superb, a crisp summer blue unstreaked by clouds. It was seven-thirty and dinner was over. There was no wind. The leaves of the oaks and maples held as still as the gathering of White Eagles in the outdoor arena.

The White Eagles looked beautiful. This afternoon, when Arlen brought out a truckload of food and supplies, he also brought a box of blue shirts and pants. A woman, one of Arlen's patients and a sympathizer, said she wanted to help in her own way. She had heard rumors that friends of Arlen's were the ones who had been getting the blacks off the streets of Henford and was very grateful.

Rex saw the blue uniforms as a new bond between the Eagles. Other groups had their uniforms—the Nazis, the Klan, many of the Identity Christian groups. From now on, at important gatherings the White Eagles would wear their blue uniforms.

The Eagles sat on the plank benches. Lizzie, Dean, Junior, Lena, Joe, and Ronald had been given permission to sit wherever they wanted in the semicircle. All except Dean had chosen to sit on the back row of benches. Dean had been practicing a new Eagle song he'd written, and the guitar was cradled in his lap.

However, at supper, when Rex had announced an important meeting, Percy and Peaches had been instructed to take front-row seats. Percy had gone visibly pale. Peaches, however, proving her stupidity, had perked up, likely imagining honors in Rex's order.

Indeed, an honor. He had thought of it as punishment, but in Truth, it was an honor. He knew he would tell Peaches this, and in telling her, make her honor greater.

Percy, ashen-faced, and Peaches, grinning, sat side by side on the front bench in the outdoor classroom. Rex stood in the center of the semicircle, his boots deep in the black soot of yesterday's campfire. His hands were in his jacket pockets. Also in his pockets were the tools of the honor.

"This morning I took a walk in the woods," Rex began, and Percy gasped and put a hand to his mouth. "I saw a sparrow chasing a crow. Funny, the sparrow being so much smaller, but it was right. It was nature's way. The black crow flew off, intimidated by that sparrow." Rex's hand closed around a tool in his pocket; the thrill of the impending honor made his dick stir. "I also saw the remains of a chipmunk in some dead leaves. It had been killed by a predator. It gave its life to provide food for another. It was natural. It was the way things are."

Peaches linked her fingers around her knees and grinned at Rex. Rex had an urge to jam his hands up her skirt but the Truth gave him willpower, and he used it.

"This morning I also saw something out near

245

the wire fence, near the boundary, out where I guess nobody would even think to look. Or so two of our members thought."

Percy's eyes closed in horrified submission. Peaches blinked in sudden confusion. Other White Eagles didn't dare to turn and look at each other.

"I have set down rules. I thought everyone here knew the rules were to be obeyed. But . . . " Rex shook his head. It was an oddly good day, and he was not going to get angry. "Two of you decided that what you wanted was more important."

Percy's eyes popped open and moved back and forth as if he were mentally working out a path of escape. Rex said, "If you try to run, it will only be worse for you."

An involuntary whine escaped Percy's mouth. Peaches, hands gripping knees, now, finally, the truth of the situation dawning on her, began to tremble.

"We can't break the rules," Rex said. He patted Percy's head. Percy grimaced as if the touch were full of acid. "The United Power will suffer if we're disobedient." He stepped to Peaches, and likewise stroked the top of her head. Peaches began to sob softly.

"Stand up," Rex said to Peaches. She obeyed, hands covering her face. "We will do the Arm Test." Rex looked at the White Eagles in the back. This was more for them than anything else. "You and Percy fucked without permission. The Arm Test will tell me what I should do."

Peaches' knees clapped together. Her head bent down chest-height, heavy with sobs.

"Should this disobedience be forgiven?" Rex asked.

Peaches sobbed. Rex leaned over and yelled in her ear, "Should this disobedience be forgiven?"

Peaches moved her hands to Rex's outstretched arm and pulled down. Rex nearly laughed. It felt like two sparrows on his forearm. The arm did not go down.

"It can't be forgiven," Rex said. Lizzie, on a bench in the back, drew her own arms tightly, protectively, about herself. Beside her, Junior gaped, his ball cap hiding his eyes with shadows. Dean, on the second row, looked around as if he wanted to sneak to the back with the others.

Rex took Peaches' shoulder and directed her to the sooty center of last night's campfire. He forced her down to her pretty little knees, and then with the effort of blowing away cattail down, laid her out flat in the ash.

To those in the back he said, "Can you see?" All nodded. Yes. The homely bitch Lena played with her fingers in her lap, but her buggy eyes were open and watching.

Rex kneeled by Peaches. He took the first of the tools from his pocket. Peaches stared at him from the ground.

"Open your shirt," Rex said.

Peaches cried out. Rex slapped her and said, "Open your shirt."

Peaches drew her sooty hands from her side and clumsily worked open the buttons of her blue uniform shirt. Rex knocked the loose edges aside. Her flat, white breasts stared at the sky with nipples as wide as red eyes.

"Shh, now," Rex said. He nestled the tip of the serrated knife into the soft flesh beneath Peaches' right breast. At the touch, the nipple went hard, a surprising reaction of fear. Rex bent and kissed

247

the dark nub. "What you did was wrong, but to be punished is an honor."

Peaches twisted suddenly, trying to pull away. Rex motioned for Percy to hold her arms over her head. The musician did as instructed, squatting in the black dirt. Rex straddled Peaches' hips.

"Now," said Rex. "I'm not going to do this messy." He pushed the tip of the knife down quickly. Peaches howled. Birds, startled, rose from the tree branches above. Rex said, "Honey, honey, shhh," but Peaches was beyond hearing.

When the right breast had been carved from Peaches' chest and flung into the weeds, Rex demanded Percy's shirt, and pressed it over the raw wound, tying the sleeves around her back to hold it in place. He pulled Peaches to her feet. The woman wavered between awareness and unconsciousness. Holding her under her arms, he moved her to the front bench. She dropped over, her shoulder hitting the bench with a smack and her face twisting into the splintered wood. Rex left her there. On the back row, sets of human owl eyes could not even move enough to blink.

Rex turned to Percy. The skinny man shook violently. He looked at Rex as if he hoped helping with Peaches' mutilation was penance enough.

But Rex said, "Arm Test, Percy. Do you deserve the punishment I think you deserve?"

Percy stepped up to Rex and put both hands on Rex's outstretched arm. He pushed with very little force. In the musician's eyes, Rex could see a futile, wild prayer that the arm would stay erect.

The arm went down. Percy said, "Oh God."

With a flick of the knife, Rex directed Percy to lie where Peaches had lain.

"No," said Percy. He flinched, looking horrified

that he had spoken, that his own voice had dared challenge the leader of the White Eagles.

"Lie down, Percy."

"No."

Rex sighed heavily. Patience and pleasure were waning. With a swift motion he lashed out with his boot, catching Percy's ankles with a heavy blow. Percy dropped. He stayed on the ground, but lifted his head, spitting ash.

"I've got a choice for you, Percy," Rex said. The Eagles on the back bench seemed to lean forward a little. Terrified fascination held them, thrilled that it was only Percy, not them.

Percy said nothing. He stared at the ground.

"We can't lose Peaches, no matter what she's done. She's a warrior-breeder. But you, you are dispensable, do you know that? You became so the minute you disobeyed me in the woods. I should kill you."

Percy began to cry. Rex kicked him with his boot, catching his chin and driving his head back with a loud snap. Percy gagged, choked. The crying stopped.

"But I've never killed anyone. I've never had to, and I really don't want to. I think we can do what we need to do without death. You can keep that from happening, Percy. I don't have to kill you. You have a choice."

Percy sniffed. There was a string of drool from his lips to the ground.

"Do you want to know your choice?" Percy was silent. Rex kicked him in the teeth. He bunched up like an accordion. "Do you want to know your choice?"

Percy gibbered, "Yes."

Chill bumps stood out on Rex's arms. Punishment, honor, power, choices. Obedience. It was all beautiful. He held the serrated knife out to Percy. Percy's eyes were huge as he took it and held it just above the dirt.

"I can kill you, that's choice one," said Rex. "Or you can fix it so you can't fuck anymore."

It seemed as if the White Eagles all caught their breath at once. A dry, sucking breeze pulled around Rex's shoulders, caressing his shaven head, spinning ash crumbs into a temporary whirling.

"Do it yourself," said Rex. "If you don't, I have no option but to slit your rebellious throat."

"Oh, God, no," Percy said. It was a gritty whisper. His head turned, and he looked at Dean. Dean looked at the ground. Percy's eyes tried to catch the gaze from the Eagles on the back row, but they all were watching Rex. Their faces were awash with horror and admiration and utter, dumbfounded relief that it wasn't them on the ground.

Percy looked back up at Rex. Rex looked down at Percy with expectation. He loved this sinner. "Your choice." •

Percy, weeping, fumbled with the fly of his blue uniform slacks. He managed to work his hips out of his slacks and underwear at one time, his white butt coming down on the soot, his pants stopping just above the knees.

"That's too hard, let me help you," said Rex. He grasped the waistband of the underwear and slacks and yanked them all the way off. He lifted the pants, shook the ash free, and draped them gently across his arm.

Percy put the blade to his testicles. "I can't," he whispered.

"Your choice," said Rex.

Huge tears cut the dust on the musician's face. He looked up at Rex. "I can't!"

"Give me the knife. You decided."

Then suddenly, with a scream, Percy grabbed the skin of his scrotum, arced the serrated blade up and around, and drove it into the flesh he held. His head whipped back and he howled. The knife sawed three times. Then Percy's blood-slicked hand dropped the knife. The balls still hung to his body, bleeding voraciously, half-amputated.

"I can't!"

The cry was no longer human. No longer honorable. Rex stared at the groveling half-man in the soot. Rex felt anger now. Love of this sinner was fading. Rex felt sickened now. He looked at his Eagles. They needed to see leadership, they needed to see his power now more than ever.

Rex grabbed the knife from beside Percy and with his boot unceremoniously forced the musician's head back. And as unceremoniously slit his neck from hairline to hairline. Percy writhed, bubbled, and then was still.

Silly man. I've killed him now. And it wasn't hard.

Pointing the knife at the others, he said, "Does anyone not understand?" He almost hoped someone would nod. He'd never killed before, but now he knew it was a good thing. He hoped someone would nod, because he was ready to make another example. "Anyone?" he shouted.

All the White Eagles shook their heads.

"Think about why we are here," said Rex. "We've done well so far. But I have a new rule. A week will not go by that we don't increase our alien .pet population by three. We will have

251

Henford cleaned by winter. Understand me. I will know those who aren't pulling their weight. We must increase our momentum. Does anyone have a question?"

No one had a question.

"Go to bed."

The White Eagles moved quickly. Rex watched them go, then looked at the unconscious woman in the front, and the dead man in the ash. He licked his hand, tasting both Peaches and Percy. He counted breaths, calming himself somewhat. And knew that even in its badness, this night was a good night.

Chapter Seven

The morning after Norris lost his job at Bright Creek School, the morning after Rex killed his first person, Bernie stole Matt's car and drove into Henford. It had been two days since she had had her revelation. Her mind had spun and reeled, and she had gone into her trances with new and surprising impatience. She didn't have time for the vision nonsense now. She had to get to Lindsay.

Bernie's palm burn predicted and accompanied her visions. The burn had come from contact with Lena Carlson. Lindsay, too, had touched Lena. She too, had been burned.

Lindsay had been in a freakish accident. Even though Lindsay refused to speak with Bernie on the phone, Bernie was certain that a trance had caused the accident.

Matt was at the back of the pasture this morning, mending a fence downed by a tree branch in May. After Vince and Harner had gone to the new construction job, after Sandra and John had walked to the farm next door to pick up potatoes the farmer was donating to the commune, after Meg had been picked up by the woman for whom she was baby-sitting, Bernie had told Matt she wanted to get a new horse.

Matt had seemed surprised, but he had said, "That might be good. I miss Red, too."

"There's one in the Buck Saver," Bernie said. "A quarter-horse gelding. I'm going to give it some thought. It might be a good thing."

"It might," Matt had said.

She gave him a hug then, letting for just a moment her feelings stir and rise, savoring his gentle closeness, his beard against her cheek. She then stepped back and said, "But there's a hole in the pasture fence."

Matt gave her a playful chuck on the arm and asked if she wanted to come out with him. The air was nice. He would be with her if something happened. Bernie declined. She would be all right in the house. If she even thought a spell was coming on, she would call him.

"Sure?"

"Sure. Fix it good. I might have a horse delivered this afternoon."

Matt took tools from the back storeroom and went out to the pasture.

Bernie prayed, "God, I'll drive slow. Don't make me lose control of the car." She put the keys in the ignition and drove down the driveway to the road.

She did not drive over thirty-five, although keeping the speed down made her hands cramp.

Trucks and automobiles honked and sped around her. Three kids on bikes almost kept up, for a short distance. Once, ten miles into the trip, she felt her eyelids flutter and sensed a film tickling at the edge of her vision.

"No!" She shook her head violently. The fluttering stopped. Her teeth, on their own, bore down until they ached. She steered on toward Henford.

Chapter Eight

It was not quite lunchtime when Dean pulled Rex's white sedan up to the supply trailer. Rex, inside caressing a rifle, heard the crunching of the tires and immediately sprang for the door. He saw from behind the small curtained window in the door the musician hop from the car and do a little skip-jump. Something had happened. Something was good. He put the rifle back into its box and went outside.

Dean, clothed in a pair of jeans and an electrician's shirt, grinned when he saw his leader. "Got somethin' for you," he said. "In broad daylight."

Rex ran his fingers across his short hair, then down the side of his face. "Yeah, what did you get, Dean?"

"In the trunk. Watchin' Peaches and Percy yesterday just got me fired. We ain't playin', Rex. Not that I didn't know that, but now I feel it in my gut. We're here, and we mean business. This shit's for real."

"It's for real, Dean," Rex said.

The two went back to the trunk. Dean inserted

the key and popped it open. There was a brown blanket inside. Something struggled beneath it. "She's old and sick," said Dean. "But hey, remember, this was broad daylight. Another step up the ladder."

Rex pulled the blanket back.

"Her name is Houng Troung. Goddamn mouthful of a name if you ask me. Probably ain't saying it right. But I know that's her name 'cause I checked her mail on my way in."

"Checked her fucking mail." Rex felt a small swell of admiration in his chest. Another good day.

"Yep. Went in the side door. Lots of bushes and shit. Door came open with no problem. Lady was in bed, TV was on. I left the TV on and rolled her up in her blanket like a Little Debbie Swiss Roll. Damn, I'm good."

Rex looked at the old woman. She had her eyes shut, and her eyebrows were arched so high up they were nearly swallowed in the wrinkles on her forehead. Rex poked her to see if she was dead. She grunted. She was not dead.

"Man." Dean paused for a breath. Rex wondered if Dean might end up writing a song about this adventure. "This is about as high as I've ever been!"

"We might need another stall," said Rex.

"No problem," said Dean. "We're going to need a whole fleet of stalls by October. Thanks to you."

Rex looked at Dean and then away. He'd never seen such devotion in any White Eagle's eyes before. It was a scary and wonderful thing. Rex helped Dean carry the new pet to the stall with the others.

Chapter Nine

She blessed the Lord as the Volkswagen passed the Henford city limits sign. Past Charlie's Imports, past the IGA, turn onto Spring Road heading for Henford Hills. Bernie remembered Lindsay's house. Not far now. To the left, third house from the corner, large brick with sloping front yard and double-car garage. The Hollins' house.

The garage door had been left open. There were no cars inside. Bernie slowed the Volkswagen. She hesitated. Who would leave the door open? Aunt Marla, not Hank. So Aunt Marla was not there. And with no cars, Hank was gone, too.

Good good good. All I need is five minutes.

Bernie drove the bug up the driveway to the garage doors. She hurried to the door inside the garage. It seemed safer than the front stoop.

She knocked. No one came to the door.

She pulled the end of her ponytail out from where it was stuck inside her shirt and shook it free. She knocked again, much harder, then put her head against the door and listened. She heard nothing.

She drove both fists into the door. "Be home!"

A voice came from directly behind the door. A breathy voice, muffled through the wood.

"Who is it?"

"Lindsay, it's Bernie."

Silence. Then, "Go away, Bernie!"

"I have to talk. We have to talk. I've had visions. I'm sure you have, too. I found out mine are of

Lena Carlson, about her life when she was young. Her foster homes, the abuse she went through."

"I don't want to talk."

"Lindsay, please open the door. I think you know about Lena, too. What you know could help me find her."

"Why do you want to find her?"

"To help her. To help myself. This is hell, Lindsay. To help you!"

Silence. Bernie could picture Lindsay's head against the door. Afraid Hank would come home and find her hippie cousin prying into their private dilemma. *But it's not private, Lindsay.*

"Can you stop this?" The voice was barely audible.

"I'm going to try. Tell me what you've seen."

"Tell me what *you've* seen, Bernie."

"I've seen Lena stab a man who tried to rape her. I've seen her shoved into a grave by her foster brothers and her leg breaking severely. I've seen . . . " Oh, God, should she share this? Yes, there was no need to hold back. "I've seen what Aunt Marla did to her when she stayed there."

There was a long pause. Then, "What did she do?"

"It was ugly, Lindsay." Bernie's head began to pulse. A headache was coming. A bad one.

"What did she do?"

"Molested her."

"I don't believe you."

"Lindsay, Lena has been molested all her life. If there were any good times, I didn't see them. Let me stop this for us. Tell me what you've seen."

"A yellow house for a while. But now it's woods."

257

"Woods? Where?"

"In the woods, what do you mean where?"

"Lindsay, please open the door."

"No."

"Tell me what you've seen in the woods."

"A wooden building. A trailer. A huge campfire like we used to have in Girl Scouts. They have a white car. And a truck. Once I saw a chain across a dirt road."

"What else?"

"Another time I saw, from the back of the truck, a mailbox, then a long stretch of woods and then that chain across the road."

"What was on the mailbox, Lindsay?"

"A name, a picture. What's usually on a damn mailbox!"

Bernie's headache was pounding now. *Just not the palms, please. I'll bear the head to stop the hands. Hurry, Lindsay. I can't stay here. Another vision might come. I might never get to Lena, to stop them and to help her.* "Think, please."

"A duck. Flying ducks."

"Good. And a name?"

"Something like ducks."

Bernie heard a car. She turned around. It drove on by. She turned back. "Like ducks?"

"Ducks, something. Damn it. I don't want to think about the trances. I'm always hurt, Bernie."

"What do you mean?"

"I mean I get hurt. I get kicked. Hit."

"Are you seeing what's happening now?"

"Now? What do you mean?"

"I'm her past. Are you Lena's present, Lindsay?"

"I don't know."

"What about Norris? Is he affected, too?"

"I don't know. Please stop this. I'm afraid for Mandy and Grace. They've been hurt, too."

"The mailbox. Ducks. Is that right?"

"Swans. The Swans. On a mailbox with flying ducks."

"Thank you. Thank you. And call Norris, Lindsay!"

"I hear you. And, Bernie, please, whatever you do, be careful." And then Bernie sensed Lindsay moving away, back to the safety of her home.

Chapter Ten

Norris dialed Tom's number.

I'm sorry, Tom, it was bad shit. I didn't mean to hurt you. Are you all right? The phone was picked up on the other end. Tom said, "Hello?"

Norris hung up. What a fool, what a coward not to talk to Tom. Tom might be moralistic, but he wasn't far off base. Tom had really seemed concerned at the bar. Would he be concerned now?

Norris walked back to his living room. He turned the television on, then off. He walked to the bedroom and got a hairbrush. He went back to the living room, turned on the television, and sat down to brush his beard.

Tom doesn't really care. Norris, you are just a short little shit who fucks everything you touch. Get used to it.

On the television was a commercial about some stupid new show beginning this summer. Norris drove his foot into the screen. The television cracked, fell over, and lay sputtering on the floor.

Can't even kill a TV right.

He found a hammer in his bedroom and finished the job. Then he got a six-pack of beer from his fridge—forget the self-admonishing Diet Cokes—and began his search for oblivion.

Chapter Eleven

Swans. Woods.

Great. Needle in a haystack.

Bernie had just gone through the phone book at the 7-11's pay phone. Listed in the book were five Swanns. Two in the city of Henford, three in the county. Two Route Ones, one Route Three. Then she'd called the post office and gotten the real route numbers.

The first Route One Swann was on county route 704, and the second one on a smaller road, county route 430, off 704 west. The Route Three Swann was on county route 998, in the far northeast corner of the county. The post office woman had given tentative directions, read from a map. South of Henford, past the Symicon Fiber Factory, following the Moss River for a mile before crossing and turning toward the mountains.

The countryside was lined with wire fencing and cattle, silos and fields. In a pasture just before the bridge, a chestnut horse stood with her head over the fence, ears up, tail twitching peacefully. Bernie mouthed, "Hey, Red," and steered across the span.

The burns on Bernie's palms stayed still, as if holding their breath. "It's not just a job," she said over the headache. "It's an adventure."

Three miles past the bridge was the intersection of Route 11 and 704. Bernie turned right onto 704, ahead three-tenths of a mile, and then off the side of the road.

This was not the right road. The burns were silent. She strummed the steering wheel, waiting to be told otherwise. Word didn't come.

She pulled back onto the road and drove another few tenths of a mile. Then she stopped again.

This was not the road. There might be a Swann but it would not be the right Swann, not the one in Lindsay's vision. If it was, she knew her fingers would be screaming.

She turned the car around and drove back to the intersection. She drove east, toward the mountains.

Several minutes later she slowed. A small white county route sign sat at an angle on a dented pipe post. Route 430. It seemed to be pointing down to hell.

Sandra would have had a field day with this premonition, Bernie thought. *Demons, hold my tail while I chase it*. She steered onto 430.

This was the road.

There was nothing unusual about this road, but she knew. This was right. The burns told her so.

She drove slowly, no longer thinking of a possible vision but watching for ducks. Two miles from the turn-off, a lone mailbox stood on the left side of the road. Purple-blossomed thistles kept it company. It was a white box with a picture of Canada geese on the side.

Geese, ducks. Close.

Under the geese, "Route 1, Box 943. The Swanns."

261

A car was then visible, coming toward Bernie on the other side of the road. She stuck her arm out of the window and waved at the driver, hoping he would stop. He might know about a camp nearby. The white car slowed, then stopped beside her. Inside were two young men, both wearing ball caps. The driver grinned.

"What'cha need?"

Bernie tried to smile back, but the smiles on the faces in the car seemed to be smirks. *I've seen the driver before. Where have I seen this guy*?

"I'm trying to find a woman, a friend of mine."

"Ain't we all?" said the driver, looking over at the passenger for a laugh of approval. "No, no, tell me. Maybe we can help you."

Bernie steadied her breath. Maybe she should let it go. No, give it a try. They might know. "Her name is Lena Carlton. I have information that she lives near here, or spends a lot of time near here. Do you know her?"

"As a matter of fact," said the driver, "I think I do. Lena. Lena what did you say?"

"Carlton."

"Carlton."

The driver put the shift in park and hopped out. The passenger leaned forward, smiling and watching. The driver came around the front of the Volkswagen and put one hand into his pocket. He pointed up the road, in the direction that Bernie was headed.

Did Lindsay mention a white car?

"Why you looking for her?"

"Why are you asking?"

"I haven't seen her for a while. We're old friends." The man made a smacking sound with his lower lip and moved a step closer to Bernie's car. He took his hat off, revealing a short-cropped head of light hair, and wiped his scalp with his palm. Bernie instinctively began to withdraw her arm into the Volkswagen. "Up there, then," the man said, again pointing up the road. Bernie watched his hand, as though she thought it might lash out and grab her.

But she watched the wrong hand. The other pulled a small revolver from his pocket and pointed it at her face. "Up there," he said, "but I don't think you made a good choice coming to find your friend."

Bernie stared. *Please make this another vision!*

The cold mouth of the gun moved in and pressed against her cheek.

Chapter Twelve

Norris pushed the receiver into his cheek until it hurt. He waited, on hold, listening to the silence.

Pick up pick up!

The phone was picked up. The voice was harsh and comforting in its familiarity.

"Who's this?"

"Teddy, I lost my job."

"Like I didn't know that."

"I'm going to run out of money. I'm supposed to be paying my grandfather back for the loan he gave me in March, but now I can't. And I need to get some stuff to tide me over, but—"

"So get another job. Who am I, your father?"

"I will. When I pull it together. But I'm having a hard time, you got to know that. I'm having these spells, you see—"

"Good-bye, Norris."

"Teddy, please, wait. Just let me borrow—"

"No. Don't call again."

The phone slammed down. Norris's only friend in Norfolk had become a thing of the past.

Chapter Thirteen

The blanket over her made her gag. She breathed through her mouth, through the aching throb of her broken front teeth, pulling in hot, musty air and taunting strands of fiber. Her jaw chattered uncontrollably. She tried to count so she would know how far they had gone, but the numbers twisted themselves up in her mind.

The driver had tied her hands behind her back with a coarse piece of rope from the floor of his car, grinning and shaking his head all the while. "Aren't you something?" he had said. "A burr trying to get under our saddle. But we nipped you in the bud."

Bernie had remembered hearing that victims died much more often if they let themselves get put into the car with the kidnapper. She had dropped down, trying to pull away, thinking she would run into the field screaming for help.

But the young man had been faster than she had hoped. He had kicked her onto her side and put his foot on her neck. The second man, almost a carbon copy of the driver with his short hair and youthful face and ball cap, had climbed out of the passenger seat and said, "I'll follow you up. Rex'll tell us what to do."

Bernie turned her head and looked up at the

driver. *I know this man*! He had grinned at her and said, "You came along at the wrong time, honey."

She had met this man before. But where? And then she remembered. But it was the voice rather than the face that gave him away. He had said, "It ain't right. You ain't right." Lisa's cleaners. This man had brought the dead fetus wrapped in a sheet, stapled with a warning. The man Bernie had described to the police had been freckled, with red hair. They had never found the man.

Dear God help me now save me now! Her heart banged like a spoon in her throat.

"Yeah," the driver had said. "Rex'll know what to do."

"Let me up," Bernie had said then, and the driver had kicked her in the teeth. The last thing she saw before the wool blanket was taken from the trunk and dropped over her was the second ball-capped man getting into Matt's car and reaching for the key in the ignition.

And now they were headed toward Rex.

Rex. Who is that? The name was dreadful, not unlike a devil's name. Over the drone of the engine and the whistling of the air through the open driver's window, Bernie's thoughts screamed in her head, amplified by pain and fear. She thought of Sandra's warning.

"The devil's under this, Bernie. You've got to see this for what it is. Don't go with it, fight it."

But there is no devil. There is only God. Father, help me now please help me now!

The car slowed. Bernie tried to hold her breath but it only came in faster, shallow gulps. She tried to count again, knowing the futility but needing its mindlessness. The smooth hum of pavement

265

beneath the car tires became a crunching of gravel. An unpaved county road? A driveway?

What kind of man staples a note to a fetus as a warning? What kind of man openly kidnaps a woman and kicks in her teeth?

What kind of man is the leader of that kind of man? And is Lena Carlton involved with these people?

God, who had authored all the questions, did not answer. •

Chapter Fourteen

The car slowed. The sound beneath the seat was no longer the snap of gravel, but a thumping of soft earth. The driver cleared his throat. He shifted in his seat. He said, "Rex's gonna love this twist."

Bernie opened her lips, wanting to talk to this man. She'd read of a woman who survived a kidnapping by showing no fear, only boredom. Through the blanket, around the stinging tightness of her jaw, she said, "This is stupid."

The man clucked. "Yeah? You're the stupid one, sister. Looking for that fat retarded bitch. Maybe you're her friend, being so stupid and all."

The car stopped. The gear shift was shoved into position with a soft grating sound. The driver's door popped open. The driver said, "You wait there. I'm going to see if Rex is busy."

"I'll take a nap," said Bernie, straining her voice to make it sound bored, unafraid.

God, what am I to suffer here?

The driver's door closed. She was alone in the

car. Rex was coming. Rex. The name of a tyrant. The name of a demon king. The name of Satan. Her heartbeats were mad dogs, beating themselves to death in fear of the king of devils.

Chapter Fifteen

"Honey, you go lie down now or I'm going to call the police on you, you hear me?"

Marla had a cigarette, unlit and crumpled, hanging from her mouth. She did not smoke in the Hollin home, but it seemed to be a pacifier for her, the touch alone enough. She was dressed fashionably, as usual, in a slim gray skirt and white blouse. Over one arm was a dish towel; in the other hand was a pan of chicken.

Lindsay stood in the doorway, gingerly holding to the sides. Mandy and Grace were in their own rooms, supposedly picking up their toys before supper. "I'm okay," said Lindsay. "I feel better being up."

This was a lie. It felt like shit being up, it felt like shit being down.

"Then would you at least sit, then? It's unnerving having you hanging over me like a buzzard."

Lindsay limped across to the kitchen table, leaned on her good arm, and sat on one of the wooden chairs. Not much longer with the ankle cast, thank God. Already she had lost a bobby pin down its recesses in an attempt to dig at a tormenting itch.

She looked at Marla. What a smiling old mask of a face could hide. It was frightening and sobering.

"The lettuce in the refrigerator was not good," Marla said. She opened the door to the oven and slid in the tray of chicken. Lindsay thought of Hansel and Gretel. How would it feel to push a witch into an oven?

"I threw it out. I'll get more tomorrow, if you'd like." Marla stood, turned, and smiled.

"Aunt Marla, do you remember Lena Carlton?" Lindsay felt adrenaline cry in her veins with the question. She had to know but did not want to.

"Lena Carlton?" Marla seemed genuinely perplexed for a moment. She went to the sink and rinsed her hands. "Is that the woman who came to the reunion in March? The one who had the attack in the hotel lobby?"

"Yes."

"She was the girl I took in, wasn't she? That strange teenager who lived with me for a little while back when you were . . . how old were you?"

"Norris and Bernie and I were mid-teens, I think."

"That's right. Lena. Oh, what a peculiar thing she was. I tried, you know that. What can one person do?"

"Did you know she had problems when you took her in?"

"Oh, I don't think so. The social workers told me she had some trouble adjusting, but I don't think I had any idea of the immensity of the problems."

"Would you have taken her in if you'd known?"

"Of course not. She was nasty, she was smelly. It was like having a dog instead of a daughter. It was like trying to manage an animal, trying to train a pet."

A pet. What a harsh comparison. Marla had always hated animals. She never owned one. She detested their need, their dependence. Marla would never abuse a person. She might abuse a pet. Bernie might have been right.

Lindsay worked her shoulders. Her neck was beginning to throb along with her left arm. "The brownies the other day were nice. The girls were thrilled to surprise me."

Marla brought her glass to the table and sat beside Lindsay. The cigarette breath was heavy, easing in and out through the parted smiling lips of the old woman. "We had a good time making them."

"Grace said something funny. I didn't quite catch it. I thought you might know what she meant."

"What's that?"

"Grace called the brownies 'nig cakes.' What is that?"

"I don't know."

"She said you called brownies 'nig cakes.' "

Marla ran her bony fingers gracefully beneath her chin and turned her old, dignified eyes to look at Lindsay with a stern, direct stare. "Have I said something offensive to your children? Are you asking me to leave, Lindsay?"

Lindsay, suddenly hesitant, shook her head.

Air in and out through the noble Lynch nose. Was there such a bigotry that Lindsay had never seen before in her own family? Such elitism? Was it worth pursuing? The woman was old. She was not staying at their home indefinitely. What

Bernie had seen was a very long time ago. Old water under an old, forgotten bridge.

"Of course not. Forget it," said Lindsay. She straightened as much as she could, and said, "That orange juice sounds good."

Marla smiled and got up to do her auntly duty.

Chapter Sixteen

The back car door opened. Someone leaned over the seat, a knee in the cushion making Bernie feel as if she were going to roll off onto the floor. The edge of the blanket was grasped and pulled with great force. Bernie scooted across the seat and bumped through the door, landing on the ground. She opened her mouth, drawing frantically at the air that oozed through the material. It was as though if she did not get oxygen now, she wouldn't get another chance.

Insanity. She prayed for the oblivion that madness would bring.

But her senses remained clear. The smells of the woods, and of a campfire. The sounds of chopping, the coolness of the ground beneath her. Chills, as sharp as cuts of a razor, ran over her shoulders. Rex was coming. Footsteps were audible, coming closer. A pleased chuckle of the driver standing beside her.

The footsteps were at her head now. She braced herself for a swinging foot to destroy what was left of her teeth.

Help me help me help me or kill me now.

"What the fuck are you doing back here? You

had a job to do in town." An ugly voice, a dark voice, a voice that kicked Bernie in the face on its own accord because she knew it. It was familiar, much more familiar than that of the fetus-bringer.

"Got a snooper, Rex," said the driver. "Came looking for Lena. Got to nip it in the bud, you ask me."

"Roll it out."

The blanket was grabbed and jerked. Bernie rolled over several times and came in contact with grass and dirt, face down. Her tongue automatically went to her front teeth. One was chipped off, one wiggled freely. It stung supremely. She tried to twist the hair from her face.

"A woman," said the familiar voice.

I know you. I knew the driver, but I KNOW you. I don't remember you, but I know you.

"Untie her hands." The rope was cut with a small blade. It nicked her wrist as it sliced the cord. Pain upon pain, amen.

"Roll her over. I want to see what kind of fucking imbecile would dare challenge our order." A hand clawed at her shoulder and slammed her over onto her back. Her head rang, her teeth sang. She saw sky over her head, blue laced with clouds and fringes of tree branches.

"I'll be damned," said the man named Rex.

A face moved into the center of the picture of sky. Bernie looked at it. She knew it. Tears of terror and laughter of confusion erupted, and she began to shake.

"Shawn."

Rex?

Shawn her old lover. Shawn the wild, the bright, the mad.

271

"Oh my God, Shawn."

"If it isn't the old love of my life," said Rex-Shawn. And into Bernie's tortured mind raced images of fetuses and nails and dead horses and blood and violated little girls and guns. Then all thoughts faded, taking, for the moment, the pain with them.

Chapter Seventeen

He looked at her, bruised and unconscious. She was different. She was plain, she was thin and pale. If she hadn't spoken, he didn't think he would have recognized her right away. But the voice was the same. He'd once been enthralled with that voice. It had been the voice of a rich bitch who loved him and fucked him to snub her family, the voice of one who could have been a breeder of fine warriors.

But there had been a weakness in her. She'd become critical of him, and hadn't appreciated his blossoming vision as it was coming clear to him. She had dumped him.

For what? For whatever she was now? For whatever had her looking like a scraggly, long-haired feminist with a chipped tooth and bloody lip?

She was coming around. Her face twisted against the cushion of the sofa on which she lay. Rex and Ronald had untied her hands and carried her into the supply trailer. In the trailer's front room was Rex's office, off-limits to the other White Eagles because it was his place to sit and dream and plan. There was a portable phone on a wobbly table beside the sofa. There was a battery-powered radio next to it. Several lanterns hummed about the room, on the floor, on crates, emitting their purpled light. There was no electrical power here in Night Land. They needed to be self-sufficient. Arlen Wells supplied what was needed.

Bernie groaned. Rex watched. His head spun in a confusion of pleasure and anger. Her eyes opened.

"Bernie," said Rex.

Bernie tried to sit up, holding her jaw in her palm.

Rex sat in the chair beneath the window. He watched her face in the lantern light. Outside, through the window, he could feel the June insects tuning up for the night. Dinner was in the works; the Eagles were tending the grounds and tending the captives. A smile crossed Rex's face. The smile triggered a rash of emotions on Bernie's face. Watching them play with her features increased his excitement and agitation.

Was this going to be a good night or a bad night?

"You look uncomfortable."

Bernie struggled, her elbows pushing on the soft cushions. One set of fingers went to the front of her mouth. Then she looked at him.

"Do I, Shawn? I can't imagine."

Rex crossed his arms and studied her. "It's not Shawn. It's Rex. I have another life now. I have another name."

Bernie flipped her ponytail over her shoulder, out of her way. The impotent defiance was curious. "Rex? After what? Tyrannosaurus Rex? You

273

into lizards, Shawn?" Whatever fear was on her face did not show up in her voice.

Rex almost leaned over and slapped her across her broken mouth, but held himself back.

Play it out this will be good very good.

"What are you doing here?" Rex asked.

"You tell me. I was brought here at gunpoint."

"You had no business playing detective."

"I had no business driving on a public county road? What is this, Shawn? Is this a drug dealership? Have I run onto your moonshine-running organization?"

Rex slapped Bernie in the face. She fell back, grabbing her mouth with one hand and throwing a fist out in front of her in a defiant threat.

"Going to hit me?" he said.

"Whatever this is, you have to let me go." Bernie's voice was now edged with renewed pain. "I have nothing to do with your life now. I haven't seen anything. I don't know where I am. That's good for you, I'm sure."

"You are in Night Land."

Bernie shook her head sharply. "Don't tell me."

"Night Land, home of the White Eagles. And our little family grows."

"I don't want to have anything to do with this. Let me out, now, Shawn, do you hear me?" And then he saw tears in her eyes, enraged tears, terrified tears, and it was, indeed, a good night.

"But," said Rex, stretching one arm over his head and tapping the window glass absently with his fingers, "you are part of my life now. Again. No one comes here and gets out. So welcome, Bernie. Welcome back to my life. Welcome back to the Night."

Chapter Eighteen

She did not want to take the tour. Her mind swam, her teeth ached, her chest throbbed. But she went. She followed Rex's lead out of the storage trailer, and shadowed his footsteps along the outdoor classroom and the clearing next to it that Rex described as the exercise area. Bernie stared, comprehension hanging just outside her reach, and listened as Rex gave his spiel. He was frightening in his sudden euphoria, swinging his lantern before him as he linked arms with Bernie and trotted along. Bernie's feet snagged on roots and stones with which Rex was obviously familiar. She wanted to scream her prayers, but kept them inside her head.

"We only have a few trailers," said Rex, flipping a lantern in the direction of a stubby silver structure. Faint streaks of light stroked the trailer windows from the inside. Whoever the others were, they were inside. "The Eagles bunk here. Boys in one room, girls in the other. No fucking around, that's reserved for me. Perhaps one day one of the others will prove himself and I might give consent, but for now, the women are subject only to me."

Bernie's mind scrambled for a retort and came up empty. "What are you creating here?"

"We are the beginning of the salvation of the world. It begins here. We cleanse our town. We grow. We send out offshoots to other places and do the same. It is the beginning of what we've been destined to all along."

"I don't understand."

He pulled her up in front of a dark, uneven structure made of logs. "Here, see this building? We built this ourselves. In fact, it was the first thing we put up. So don't let yourself think we don't care about the pets."

They stepped closer. The place smelled like a barn.

"I never believed killing all the aliens was the answer. Even the worm has a place if it knows its place."

Aliens?

"But I will kill if I have to, don't think I won't."

"What do you mean, aliens?"

Rex let go of Bernie's arm. In that flash of an instant, she turned her head to find a way of escape. As she did, Rex slammed the lantern into the side of her face. Pain burst open in her ear. She groaned and bent over.

"I know what you're thinking!" he screamed. "Don't be a bitch! I have too many of them here. I don't want to kill you, but I can if I have to. We know these woods and you don't. Don't be fucking stupid!"

Bernie grabbed her ear. "You couldn't kill anyone," she hissed.

"Should I show you the burned bones of Percy? I cut his throat and we roasted his body. His bones are buried under the storage trailer. Should I show you Peaches? I sliced off her breast for her disobedience. Now look!"

He unlatched the shed door and tugged it open. He leaned in and held the lantern for Bernie to see. Bernie looked. Inside was the scene of a concentration camp. Bony, naked people were chained to the rough walls. Straw littered the floor. Some eyes were closed, others stared at her in supreme hatred and terror.

Victims. Captives.

"Aliens," said Rex. "Cleaned from our hometown. You think they'd be missed. But so far, not so much as to cause concern. The network of sympathizers help smooth it over for us. In time, the others will see the benefits of having them gone. Nonhumans parading as humans." Rex shut the door and latched it.

How can this happen?

"You mentioned Lena," said Rex. "Why were you looking for Lena?"

"I need to see her."

"Why?"

"It's none of your business."

Rex held the lantern up, ready to strike her again. He repeated, "Why do you need to see her?"

"You wouldn't understand," said Bernie. "Shawn."

Rex lowered the lantern. "Don't take me lightly."

"I don't think I should take you at all."

Rex seemed to falter slightly. *God, yes, let this be my foothold.* Suddenly Rex shouted, "Lena!"

It only took a moment. A shambling figure came out of the shadows, carrying a flashlight and smelling of feces. She stood beside Rex, staring at the ground as though it held the fascination of the face of God Himself.

"Lena!" cried Bernie. Bernie wanted to reach out to her, but hesitated.

"Have you moved the compost pile where I told you?"

Lena nodded, barely.

277

"Tomorrow morning, you can move it even farther," said Rex. "I've decided I don't like where you've put it."

Lena nodded.

"Again," said Rex, facing Bernie. "Why do you need to see Lena?"

"Lena," Bernie said. "I have something of yours. And you have something of mine."

Rex pressed his face into Bernie's. "What?"

"I knew she was here." *Tell him, Bernie. Perhaps the truth here will set you free.* "I've had visions. I've seen part of her life through her eyes. We became fused, back in March, when we touched. I have seen parts of her past as though I lived them myself."

Lena did not move. She stared at her feet.

"Lena," said Bernie. "Lena, have you felt anything? I've blacked out, and I've seen pieces of your childhood. I wish there was something I could do to erase what you've been through. I wanted to find you to talk with you, to help you."

"You've seen her past. How sweet," said Rex.

"Have you felt anything, too, Lena? Talk to me."

"No," said Rex. "You talk to me, Bernie. Now. Tell me. How did you know Lena was here?"

"I wasn't sure. I've only seen Lena's childhood. When she was very young. But I'm not the only one who's linked with her now."

"What do you mean?"

"There were three of us." Bernie tilted her head, trying to see up into Lena's unblinking eyes. "Lena, there were three of us, remember? At the reunion. There was me, there was Lindsay and Norris. We all touched at the same time. We linked with you."

Suddenly, Rex threw his arm around Bernie's

neck and shoved a blade to her throat. "I've had enough of this fucking game-playing! Answer me carefully or I'll take out your vocal cords! Now, you plain little bitch, I have one question to ask of you. How did you know Lena was here?"

Tears pooled in the corners of Bernie's eyes. Cold steel probed teasingly at the skin of her throat. Her eyes flicked upward, looking for the eye of God, and seeing only a swarm of swallows, darker black against the sky of paler black, circling like vultures awaiting a taste of blood.

Maybe the truth will set you free.

"Another," Bernie began, "one of us." Heartbeats in her neck made talking difficult. "Another one who linked with Lena can see her present. What she is doing as she does it. I see only the past. Lindsay sees the present."

The blade at her throat tapped her flesh. Rex sat in the dirt, crossed his arms, wanting more.

Bernie continued. "We're linked. Me with Lena's childhood, Lindsay with her present. I think Norris is linked, too, but I don't know. I haven't talked with him."

Lena shuddered, and Bernie thought she might be crying.

"How did you find us?" demanded Rex.

"A vision led me to Route 430." *No more,* thought Bernie. *I'll say no more.*

"Your connection with her mind showed you where we were?" he said.

Bernie said nothing.

Rex looked at Lena. "You've done bad," he said. "You've brought spies to us. I should kill you now."

Bernie said, "Shawn, you don't need to do that."

"Got to shut off the brain waves," Rex said. "Death or drugs, I can't think of another way.

279

Drugs might be the best choice. I could give Arlen a call for medical advice. But I would need incentive for that. I would need something to keep my mind off the image of happily cutting out the heart of this bitch." He looked back at Bernie and winked.

Bernie clenched her teeth. She knew this man. She remembered his pleasures. The thought made her nauseous, but she said, "I'll fuck you, Shawn."

"Call me Rex."

"I'll fuck you, Rex."

"Will you, Bernie? How nice. That would be a suitable diversion. But first, you will write a letter to these friends of yours. You will tell them you've gone off seeking employment elsewhere. Henford has you bored. I'll have Dean drive the letter to D.C. and drop it in the mail. This might stave them off. At least long enough so we can find them ourselves and bring them here. Then, Bernie, you will fuck me. Oh, yes, better than you ever have before. Say you'll suck my cock."

"I'll suck your cock."

"Ahhh, to bed, Eagle!" he said to Lena. His voice was high and lilting as if he was having a good night. As Lena wandered off, Rex took Bernie's hand and gently lifted her from the bench. They walked the path to the supply trailer.

Chapter Nineteen

Lindsay's fingers had decided before her mind had. Trembling wildly, burns freshly throbbing, they punched the number for HeartLight. *Someone be there, be there!*

It was eight PM. She still sat on the living-room sofa. She had just experienced a brief, terrible vision. She had seen Bernie seated on a wooden bench, a knife at her throat. Her mouth was bloody. She had been beaten. And before the vision faded, Bernie had said, "A vision led me to Route 430."

Bernie had not been careful. "Someone please answer!"

The phone was picked up. A male voice said, "Hello?"

"Hello, this is Lindsay Hollin. I'm Bernie Lynch's cousin and—"

"Thank God! This is Matt. You've heard from Bernie?"

"Yes. No. Not exactly. I'm not sure where she is exactly. But I think she's in trouble."

"I knew it. I felt it." The voice was pained, full of urgency. Lindsay knew hers sounded the same.

"She's in the woods. A place like a retreat. It's off Route 430. Do you know where that is?"

"South of Henford," said Matt. "How do you know, Lindsay?"

"I just do. Go find her."

"But where off 430? It stretches several miles."

"I don't know anymore than that. Please, hurry!"

"Yes, right away. Will you come with me, Lindsay?"

"I can't."

"But you seem to know—"

"I have my daughters here."

"I think I shouldn't go alone. The other HeartLight members are out looking for Bernie. Lisa Pham, I'll get Lisa to come with me."

"Would you shut up? Bernie's in trouble, I don't think it, I know it. Now go!"

She slammed the phone down. She folded over and covered her head with her aching arm, trying to draw in and away from the nightmare.

She had done all she could do. "There's nothing else I can do, Bernie! I've sent help. Now leave me alone!"

Chapter Twenty

She awoke, nude and cold. A spot of sunlight was on her stomach, and she stared at it, confused.

Where am I?

She was on a lumpy sofa. Her hair was a tangled mass beneath her shoulder blades. She shifted to pull it loose. Across the small room, on a table, was a lantern. On the floor were her shorts, shirt, and underwear.

Night Land.

A blanket was balled up next to her clothes. She clawed it up and wrapped herself. Then she sat up and looked at the room. The supply trailer. Shawn's hideaway. Shawn's little love nest.

Suddenly she bent over and emptied a stomach full of bile onto the tiled floor. Her shorts were spattered, but she was beyond caring.

Every point of her body ached. Her mouth. Her ear, which still bore the indentation of the lantern. Her breasts and her privates.

She was mortified. She was terrified.

She slipped on her clothes and found her shoes under a stand beside the door. Looking out of the small window, she could see people milling about, several exercising in the clearing, some bringing wood to the center of the classroom.

There was no question about it, she had to escape. She would tell the authorities and send them here. Alone, she could do nothing for Lena but get the woman killed.

And this is what You had in mind, isn't it? She directed her inquiry to the cracked ceiling of the trailer. Now get me out so I can do my job.

Sitting back on the sofa's edge, she slipped on her shoes, leaving the socks wherever they were hidden. She glanced at the window in the rear wall. It was too tiny to climb through. She peered out of the window. Rex was not in sight.

Heart hammering, she slipped down the narrow hall to another room. The door was closed. She pushed it open.

It took a moment for her eyes to focus. The only window here had been covered over will black paper. She took a step inside. There were stacks of large wooden boxes on the floor. On the walls were obscene, homemade posters of torture and blood and death.

Bernie's head swam, but she held to the door until the wave passed. Slowly she moved to a column of crates. She pushed at the lid of the one on top. It shuddered, creaked, and then moved back.

Inside were guns. Long, heavy, shining guns stacked like cords of wood for an impending fire. Stockpiled here for what? What was this group? Her skin prickled.

"Are they at war?" she whispered.

She stepped back and counted the crates. In this room alone there were fourteen. Each one could have held as many as twenty guns. And there was another room next to this one, at the end of the hall. What did the White Eagles have there?

"Yes." The voice was behind her, in the hallway. Bernie spun around.

"We are at war." Rex had his hands on his hips. A bemused smile was on his face. He came into the room. "You like these? Sleek, cold metal at our command. Look." He took a gun from the open crate. He ran his hands down the barrel, then pointed it at Bernie's crotch. "You want to feel real power between your legs? Lizzie screams when I fuck her with this. She must really like it, don't you think?"

Bernie did not move. There was fresh sweat on her collarbones. It trickled down beneath her tee shirt.

Rex put the gun barrel to his cheek. "Oh, Bernie, I have such a surprise for you. Those names you mentioned last night. Lindsay and Norris, right?" said Rex. "Well, my dear, it's such fun. They found us!"

Bernie barely found her voice. "What do you mean? That's impossible."

"Is it impossible that you found us but they couldn't? Are you such a better detective than they are? Are their visions less than yours? But, silly you, you've slept most of the day away and missed the fun."

Bernie tried to catch her thoughts. They buzzed her head, slamming, echoing, making no sense. "They can't be here." She tried to imagine Lindsay and Norris captured by the White Eagles. Bernie had given no clues to Lindsay's identity. And Norris, he was still in Norfolk.

"But they are. They saved me the trouble of finding them, I'll say. How handy! They won't talk to us, they haven't said a fucking thing, but they're here, big as life. Two exciting days in a row now. Nyuck nyuck! We'll have to have a new shed, as sure as we're talking here. A new pet shed! Come."

Rex grabbed Bernie by the forearm and with the tip of the gun he nudged her out of the trailer door and down the two steel steps. He steered her down the short path to the outdoor classroom. He nearly skipped as he walked. To a man stacking wood on the ashes of a previous fire, Rex said, "Get the new captives out now. Bring them to me."

The man immediately dropped his load of logs and strode to the dark shed. He went inside. A moment later, he came out with a man and a woman.

"God, no," said Bernie.

The man and woman were dazed, their clothing torn. There were bruises on their faces as though they had been severely beaten. Their hands were lashed behind their backs. The White Eagle brought them before the benches.

"Dear God, no!" Bernie began to weep.

Matt, his mouth a split and bleeding wound, said, "Bernie, thank God I've found you."

Lisa Pham, hanks of her beautiful black hair ripped from her head and scarlet cuts hashed into her arms, stared at Bernie. The stare was dreadful. And then her head folded down, and she began her own, silent sobbing.

Rage flared in Bernie's chest. "I'm not with these people!" she cried to her friends. "I have nothing to do with them. I didn't mean to lead you here. Forgive me!"

Don't let Rex know who they are. This might be the out. Watch your words.

Rex tapped the front of his teeth with the

285

mouth of the gun and said, "Now, Bernie, you can write a letter on behalf of you three. We'll mail it and have it taken care of. Three birds with one note. Then back to business as usual."

"I won't write it," Bernie said.

"You'll write it," said Rex. "You have no power here. See what I mean. Joe, an Arm Test."

The Eagle who had brought Matt and Lisa from the shed immediately stepped beside Rex.

"The Power will tell us if the newcomers are to die if Bernie writes no letter." Rex's right arm went up, straight out from his body. Joe reached up and pulled down on the arm. The arm came down against Rex's side. "What does the Power tell us, Joe?"

"The answer is 'yes.' "

Bernie stared at Joe. Who was this mindless follower?

"Yes," said Rex. He smiled at Bernie. "The Power never lies to us. It guides us, its truth through me. They will die if you don't write the letter."

To Joe Rex said, "Take them back with the others." To Bernie he said, "Come back to the trailer with me. You silly girl, you've lost your socks. We'll find them, and then some paper for your letter."

Joe took Matt and Lisa by the arms. Bernie said, "I want to go with them."

"Now, Bernie. We're old friends. You may be ignorant of the things we represent here, but I don't want to see you in with those other . . . those other things." He kissed Bernie on the cheek.

Bernie gritted her teeth. They chattered against each other. "I want to go with them."

Rex threw up his hands like an exasperated

parent. "Fine, then fine. Joe, take this silly woman with the others. She'll find it's much more pleasant to accept hospitality when it's offered than to spit in the face of the host."

Joe's lip twitched once, then he gestured with his head for Bernie to come move in behind Matt and Lisa.

"But," said Rex, "don't chain her until her letter is written. I want to send Dean up to D.C. shortly so we can clean this matter up behind these three fools."

Joe nodded.

Bernie, Lisa, and Matt were ushered silently, like sheep, to the small, dark shed.

Chapter Twenty-one

It was hell on Earth. The smells, the sounds, the grayed traces of bodies twisted in anger and helplessness and horror. Bernie cried for a long time before she was even able to hold the pen, paper, and envelope Joe had found and brought to her here in the shed.

There was a single window in the back wall, and it had been opened and latched. Flies, hornets, and sweat bees flew in and out of the window-hole. When there was a break in the whispered whimpers and groans from the captives, the breeze could be heard through the window-hole like a child learning to whistle thought grass blades.

Hissss. Hisssssssss.

Evil children, mocking, playing their taunting, musicless tunes for the victims of the White Eagles.

287

The floor was a thin layer of soiled straw. The smell was rank and heavy; bowels and stomachs twisted with fear had all been emptied on this bedding. Bernie had counted the victims once her eyes had adjusted. All were seated, all were naked, all had arms stretched above their heads in obedience to the chains that held them there. On the right wall, Bill Bailey, a skeleton, his eyes closed. Beside him, a young black teenager Bernie didn't know. He snarled frequently through the gag between his teeth. A troublemaker for the White Eagles.

On the left wall a middle-aged woman Bernie thought she'd seen in town. Next to her was another young black man, who grunted frantically and unintelligibly and gestured with his head. Beside the man, hanging against the wall as if she were already dead, her pathetic, wasted, cancer-ridden body shuddering with not even a blanket to cover it, was Lisa's Pham's mother, Houng Troung.

Joe had chained Lisa and Matt but had not removed their clothes. For some reason, they had been rated a step above the others. Bernie herself had not even been chained.

When Joe left, Matt was the first to speak. He leaned his head toward her, and she let her face fall against his bruised chest. "Thank God you're all right."

Bernie sobbed, unable to answer. Matt allowed her time, whispering, "We'll all be all right."

And then Lisa spoke. "My mother," she said softly. "What have they done to my mother?"

"I don't know," Bernie said.

Bernie was afraid to see, but she slid over to the

chained woman. Before touching her, she removed her tee shirt, in the face of this human degradation unaffected by exposing her breasts, and draped the shirt over Mrs. Troung. "Mrs. Troung," she said. She reached out her fingertips and touched the woman's face. It was warm.

"She's alive," Bernie said. She then crossed her arms, covering herself before Matt.

"What have they done to her?"

"I don't know. Lisa, listen. We will get out of here. Your baby, Lisa. Is it all right?"

"I think so. I feel the movements."

"We won't have to endure this very long. I know it."

"I think this is beyond us all."

Bernie's words seemed foreign to her at this moment, but she said, "It's not beyond God."

"Write your note quickly," said Matt. "I don't want to face what'll happen if it isn't done when they come back."

Bernie pressed the paper against her knee and wrote,

Dear Sarah,
    I'm fine. Please don't worry about me. I've relocated to D.C. and am looking for work. Norris and Lindsay are with me, too. We think we might start a new HeartLight up here. Wish us luck.
    Love, Bernie.

She addressed the envelope to HeartLight, and breathed a silent prayer over it. Then she moved between Matt and Lisa, bowed her head, and held their hands.

The shed door slammed open. Rex came inside. Behind him was a young woman with a hard face and a tray of food.

"All done?" asked Rex.

"Yes," said Bernie.

"You didn't seal it, did you? You know I want to read what you've written."

"I didn't seal it," she said.

The woman began setting bowls of food out on the floor in front of the captives. Rex stepped through the soiled straw. Bernie pulled the letter from beside her and handed it to him. Rex tipped his head and said, "Where's your shirt? Flashing the aliens?"

"You're sick."

Rex's mind was elsewhere already, reading the note. "Good," he said. "Dean's got the car ready for his trip. Your tracks are covered, as well as your buddies' here."

The woman put a bowl down in front of Matt and Lisa. She looked from Bernie to Rex. "What about her?"

"She can feed herself, Peaches," said Rex. "Then she can feed the pets. Tell Lena she won't have to come in for that job today."

The woman nodded and left the shed. Rex put the note into the envelope and licked it shut.

Suddenly, Houng Troung began to moan. She threw back her head and her lips opened and she drew in a long, rattling breath. Her chest began to hitch, knocking the tee shirt to the floor.

Matt and Lisa and Bernie stared. Rex said, "Maybe there's some life in her after all."

Mrs. Troung's eyes flickered, then opened. She

stared in front of her, then slowly her head pivoted until she was facing her daughter.

"The miracle," said Matt. "She's come around."

"Lisa!" Mrs. Troung said. "Lisa!"

Rex frowned. "Who is she calling?"

Mrs. Troung uttered something in Vietnamese, and then, with the few words of English she knew, she said, "Daughter, come to me!"

Rex dropped the letter. "Who is she calling?"

"Lisa, come to me!"

Lisa began to cry.

"Who is she calling?" Rex kicked Matt on the side of the head with his boot. Matt cried out.

"This isn't Lindsay?" said Rex. "Tell me."

Bernie said nothing. Matt said nothing. Lisa said, "She is my mother. You bastard!"

"You aren't Lindsay? I'll kill this man if you don't answer me. And if you answer me wrongly and I find out, I will torture everyone in this shed before killing your mother and then you."

"I'm Lisa."

"And is this Norris?"

Lisa said nothing. The boot swung, cracking Matt's bleeding cheek again, streaking his beard with blood.

Lisa said, "His name is Matt."

"Ha!" said Rex. He laughed and shook his head. "What fakers we have! Thought you'd catch the Eagles in a trick? We have more tricks than you can count. And we'll let you see them, one at a time. Oh, Bernie."

Bernie's heart dropped, a stone in her chest.

Rex said, "First, you will write another letter to your home. This time, you will tell of your safety and the safety of Matt and Lisa. I'll bring you fresh paper. Then I'll call Arlen and see what to do with Lena to end the connections. Feed 'em, Bernie. Feed 'em with your hand, one at a time. It's one of Lena's jobs, but you did such a good job feeding me last night, I think you'll enjoy this, too." He went outside and latched the shed door.

Chapter One

Lindsay steered her station wagon out of the Gs' driveway as Mandy and Grace honored their great-grandparents with a flurry of waves through the windows. When out of sight of the house, Mandy, in the back seat behind her mother, turned around and adjusted her seat belt.

"Grace," she said. "You can quit waving now. They can't see us anymore."

Grace, in the front passenger seat, said, "Maybe. I wave some more."

"Your arm'll fall off, see if I care," said Mandy. "Mom, I didn't like lunch. Can we go by Lee's Chicken?"

"Honey, I have a lot of laundry to do this afternoon. I don't think you have any clean clothes for church tomorrow. We can get a snack at home."

Lindsay turned onto Main Street and drove up the hill past Stone House United Methodist Church and the Henford Hotel. "Thank God that's over," she said.

"What?" asked Grace.

"Nothing. I said no Lee's."

Lindsay flexed her fingers on the steering wheel. Her burns, the one on her back and the one on her hand, were almost gone. It had been months since they were red. It had been since mid-June that Lindsay had last experienced one of the nightmare visions.

The vision of Bernie with a knife to her throat. The night she had called HeartLight to tell them to find her where there were woods.

295

How strange it all seemed now. How fragile her mind had been at that time.

Now she knew that the visions had not been real. In spite of the certainty she had felt after her accident, in spite of the clarity and the intensity of the sights and smells and the blood and the violence, she knew now that it had been her over-burdened mind, her motherly instinct gone haywire in order to keep her daughters safe.

And if Lindsay's visions were unreal, so were Bernie's. Like cousin, like cousin.

Everything was fine now. Bernie was safe.

HeartLight had received a letter from Bernie in June. Sandra, a young red-haired woman, and John, a soft-spoken man with long brown hair, had come by Lindsay's home on June 16th. Sandra brought with her a letter, written by Bernie and mailed in Washington, D.C. It had said,

> Dear Sandra,
> Hi. I hope we haven't caused too much worry. The Lord works in mysterious ways. Here we are, on the streets of D.C. Matt is with me, as is Lisa Pham. We plan on starting a new offshoot of HeartLight here. There is a great need. A lot of crime. A lot of hate. We will contact you when we are settled. Pray for us, Bernie.

Sandra had waited until Lindsay had read the letter, and then said, "Not even a phone call. What do you think?"

"I think they're okay," said Lindsay. "It might be a little irresponsible, maybe, but then Bernie was never one to do things the conventional way."

"Lisa Pham's mother disappeared not long ago," Sandra had said. "She hasn't been found. I'm suspicious."

"I remember reading about her in the paper," said Lindsay. "It said she was not in her right mind at all times. People wander off. When I was in high school, a retired teacher with Alzheimer's wandered into the Moss River and drowned. They didn't find her for a while, but there was no foul play."

John had said, "We miss Bernie and Matt. They were such strong members of HeartLight."

"Do you want to drive to D.C. to try and find them?"

"I want to," said Sandra.

"I think they're fine," Lindsay had said, and she knew she was right. She might have been wrong about the visions' reality, but she knew she was right about Bernie this time. Her cousin was safe in the capital.

The car drove up the long rise of Spring Road. Yards of the Henford Hills homes blazed with Indian paintbrush and blue and purple asters. Boxwoods were neatly pruned. Lawns were mowed to golf-green perfection. Another few weeks and the riding mowers would be delegated to the garages until spring.

Life was good again.

"Lee's," said Grace.

"We're not going to Lee's, Grace, we're home," said Mandy.

"I know. But I like Lee's."

Lindsay pressed the remote for the garage door and then drove inside next to Hank's new Infiniti. The girls hopped out and went into the house through the kitchen door. Lindsay walked back out the garage door.

Hank was at the side of the yard, putting pine needles around the azaleas. Black plastic lawn bags were scattered down the fence line. The red wheelbarrow sat beside him, nearly empty.

"Hi," she said as she came up behind him.

"Hi. How was lunch?"

"Fine, I guess. I made your excuses. The Gs said they hoped your cold was better. Aunt Marla wanted to know if there was anything she could fix for you."

Hank straightened and wiped at his nose. He leaned one arm over the top of the shovel handle. "Thanks, Lin," he said. "You know I love your family and all . . . "

"I know."

" . . . but this cold just has me laid up and I can't get out of bed." He winked.

"I know. You look pretty bad to me." Lindsay leaned over into Hank, and he put one arm around her. She waited, hoping he would make it a full-fledged hug, but he didn't. If anything had lingered from the initial contact with Lena Carlton, if anything concrete had occurred because of that bizarre reunion, it was the increased distancing of Hank.

Lindsay stepped back and looked down the row of shrubs. "Got them almost done, I see."

"I like being outside. I'm inside so much. After I throw these bags out, I think I'll prune those branches from the new maples."

"You want some lunch?"

"I had some leftover casserole a little while ago."

"Hank."

"Yeah?"

Lindsay crossed her arms. She hesitated.

Hank put the shovel into the wheelbarrow. "Yeah?"

"It's Marla. Something about her has been nagging me, and if it was just me I'd let it go, but it's the girls."

"What?"

"She's old, I know. She grew up in a different era. Her values are different in some ways."

"Whatever it is, Lindsay, I can't imagine you getting upset over something Marla's said or done. We all know she's a little strange when it comes to the mainstream."

"This, unfortunately, isn't so different from the mainstream of her time. What she said didn't seem to upset anyone in the dining room but me."

"Who was at the luncheon?"

"The Gs, but G-Mom was nearly asleep and G-Dad had all he could do to keep his roast beef on his fork. But there was my mom, and Jeff and Rebecca Matheny, the judge Ralston Ayers and his wife Emily, and the doctor Arlen Wells. Nice little pre-Labor Day get-together with the neighbors, but damn if Maria can't say things that bug the hell out of me."

"So what dreadful thing did she say?"

"She said 'nigger.' "

Hank tilted his head, waiting.

"She used the word 'nigger,' Hank."

"A lot of people her age use that word."

"It's not right. I don't want our children hearing relatives talk like that."

"I hear you."

"I don't want the girls to say things like that."

"We don't let them say things like that."

"Am I overreacting?"

"What do you think?"

"I think Aunt Maria is a prejudiced old woman."

"What brought the subject up at lunch, anyway?" Hank scooped up an empty lawn bag and balled it up.

"Brief mention of the recent articles in *The Henford Press* about all the blacks who have left town."

Hank walked down the fence line, snatching up the empty bags and balling them together. When he got back he said, "And Aunt Marla said, 'nigger.'"

"Yeah, she did. Said that it was silly to worry about the niggers leaving town."

"And then?"

"Then what?"

"Did everyone whip out their white sheets and hoods and say, 'glory hallelujah the niggers are gone'?"

"The conversation moved on to something else."

"Here." Hank handed the bags to Lindsay and took hold of the wheelbarrow handles. "It's no big deal, Lindsay. We raise our kids how we want. Don't sweat the small stuff."

Lindsay frowned. She swept a strand of blond hair behind her ear and followed with the lawn bags to the garage.

Chapter Two

Tossing the apple core into the grass by the sidewalk, Norris stepped into the apartment foyer and reached into his uniform pocket for his mailbox key. The uniform he hated, but he'd grown to accept it as a fact of life, at least for the present. The present was all he could handle for now. And for the past months, the present had been enough.

It was late September now, only a few days away from October, and Norris's life was tolerable.

He made his payments to the Gs on time. He went to work, he bagged his groceries, he collected his weekly check. A female cashier there thought he had a good sense of humor. He no longer had the flashes that had plagued him in the spring. His burns were hard to trace now, and only rarely did he feel a benign buzz in his head, residue of the old visions. Sometimes he even felt what might have been normal. At times, he thought of calling up Tom Murphy to apologize.

Norris put the key into the hole and opened the mailbox. Between his teeth was a bit of apple skin. With a free finger, he picked it out. When September had come around, he had had a brief wave of anxiety, thinking he should be teaching, thinking that at least teaching was a job that didn't insult his education. But September slipped along and Norris went with it, and now he was looking toward January. In January, he was going to Key West and see if he could pick up a job in a restaurant or guest house. Tom Murphy had mentioned Key West. Maybe, if Norris had the courage to call him, he would mention his plans.

Who knew what the near future held in store?

The mail came out of the box. Norris took the steps, looking through the stack as he went. On the top step he stopped, and nearly stumbled back down the flight. This was impossible. Goddamn it, this was impossible!

Fucking damn it all, this is impossible!

All the mail fluttered from his hand except for a single envelope. The return address was stamped in ink. "We're In the Money. Norfolk, Virginia."

Norris ripped the envelope open. He would kill them. He would find those assholes and rip their goddamn eyes out and then kill them.

> Dear Norris,
>
> We understand you are no longer at Bright Creek. What a shame. You had such a way with kids. But we see now that you are working for the Kroger store on Heron Road. In fact, you bagged groceries for us several times in the past week. Nice to know you landed on your feet.
>
> We've been wondering how Kroger would like to see photos of their new employee with a seventeen-year-old boy? Some 8x10s of you and that child, stuck up on the advertising cork boards with the store's daily specials? True, we said we'd leave you alone after March, but we're in tough times ourselves. Tell you what, you have another $10,000 to us by October 5th, and we'll give you the negatives. All thirty-six. Surprised you didn't ask for them last time, but hey, you're new at this, aren't you?
>
> Toys 'R Us parking lot, before eleven PM, October 5th, same set up as last time. You leave the bucks, we'll leave the negatives.
>
> Give us a double-bag next time we're in your store.

Norris slid down to the floor. Numbness caught his soul like the gossamer fibers of a cobweb. He hung, suspended, unable to think. He stared at the letter until it was too dark to see it anymore.

And then his mind cleared. He knew what to do.

The feeling was different this time. This time it was not fear that fueled him. It was anger. Hot and deadly.

He would play their game once more.

Slowly Norris stood and went inside his apartment. He packed a pillowcase with a few clean clothes. There was no one left to ask for money. He could not approach his grandfather again.

There was only one solution. It would not make him any worse than he already was. It was no different than the dozen other sleazy things that made up his past.

He knew his grandparents' house by heart. He knew the rooms, the stairs, and the hallways. He would rob the Gs and get what he needed.

October 5th he would have the money ready. He would leave it in his car and hide. He would wait. When We're In the Money came collecting, he would, too. He would follow them and kill them. He didn't know how yet. That was yet to be decided. But he would rid Norfolk of the parasites. This was his new purpose. And if they blew him away as he did the same to them, so be it. Maybe some omnipotent power would forgive him at least part of his great sin because he had removed another great sin from the earth.

Norris stopped by Kroger on his way out of town and picked up some snacks and a few small tools. The cashier smiled at him as he went through with his cart, and he smiled back.

Who knew how and when she would next see his face? Let her say to her family and friends when he was written up in the paper, when a gray photo was published showing him mangled after a showdown on a back street in Norfolk, that he was a friendly guy. He had such a good sense of humor.

Who could figure?

Chapter Three

Beautiful fall colors surrounded his head like a crown, reds and golds of royalty, standing silently and respectfully above the king of the Truth. Rex stretched his arms and took it in.

He stood alone in the center of the outdoor classroom. The eternal campfire burned next to him. Around him, business was carried out obediently. The alien pets were out for a walk. Rex had thought fresh air and a little stretching would not be a bad thing. Lizzie and Peaches had them out now, walking around the jogging trail, all tied together on a rope, looking like a class of nursery-school children on a field trip.

Rex told the women to let them pick up brush from the trail as they went and throw it off to the side. Might as well let them do a little something for their keep.

The number of pets had grown steadily, although not as quickly as Rex had hoped. In June they had added three, in July another two, and in the weeks of August and September, an additional three. This had not been what Rex had commanded, and on Joe's birthday, September 9th, Rex had beat him to death before the other Eagles to show that slovenliness would not be tolerated.

He had reduced the original number of Eagles by another, but by doing so the loyalty of the others had increased a hundredfold. Ronald, Dean, Lizzie, the no longer beautiful Peaches, Junior, and Lena now worked with a fervor that would have amazed even a nest of army ants. The trade-off was acceptable. In addition, Arlen had carefully selected and presented Rex with five new Eagles. Four men and one woman. They had been committed and sincere. And since Joe's execution, they, like the other Eagles, were more than eager to please.

Both Lizzie and Peaches were now pregnant with Rex's strong, white seed. While the other men were reduced to masturbation and mute but obviously lustful jealousy, Rex worked at impregnating the new woman, Judy, as well.

The battle was good, the cause undaunted.

The chink alien girl, the daughter of the old woman who had died in July, carried a chink baby due in a matter of weeks. When it came, he would decide what to do with it. The two white pets, though, were another matter. Bernie continued to insist that she stay in the shed with the others. Rex did not insist that she or Matt have their clothes removed, but just for fun he would not let Peaches wash them. Matt was no longer chained. Rex had hoped he would catch them fucking some night. They remained unbathed as did the others. The close quarters had brought on an outbreak of lice, and when not eating, the pets constantly rocked against the wall, digging at their skin.

Several times Rex had felt wonderful and had brought Bernie out to his supply trailer. He smelled her rank body odor, he sucked on her filthy hair, and he kissed the sweaty breasts. Other times, when the day was a bad one, he brought Matt and Bernie both outdoors and tied the man to the large black walnut tree and lowered Matt's shirt so he could receive a whipping. Watching Bernie whisper silent prayers as Matt was beaten made Rex feel stronger.

And stronger was better. Strength was Truth. The Truth was in the battle. And the battle was on.

Rex sat on a bench and waited until Lizzie and Peaches brought the pets back around from their trail-clearing duty and put them back into the shed. Behind the shed, thirty feet into the trees, Junior and Dean and one of the new men, Ricky, were working on a new shed. They would need it soon.

When Lizzie came out of the shed, Rex called her over. He smiled at her as she came. There was a small bulge showing beneath the waistband of her gray Eagle pants. This, he had decided, made the ugly Lizzie less ugly. Perhaps her baby would be beautiful.

"Come with me to the bunking trailer," he said. Lizzie's eyes flinched; no doubt she was expecting a humping although Rex had no arousal at that moment. At least, not an arousal for sex. He had another idea at the moment. If anything had a hard-on, it was his mind.

Inside the bunking trailer, in the tiny third bedroom, Lena Carlton lay on a bare mattress. Her face was blubbery and lifeless, pressed into a thin pillow. Her body was draped in a cotton sheet; it was too hard to turn her over in her clothes. One arm hung from the sheet, tied down and pierced with an IV tube through which Arlen's supply of nutrients flowed. He had instructed Rex how to use it when the fat woman was too lethargic to eat the smashed vegetables and bread they offered her.

She had been drugged since early June, when Bernie had told of the amazing visions that had brought her to Night Land. Rex had feared the visions even though he found them hard to believe and infinitely fascinating.

"I want to get her up," said Rex.

Lizzie glanced at him, then at the woman on the mattress. "Get her up? Why? She's all drugged."

"She is now. But I'm going to stop the treatments. I'm tired of caring for her like this. It will be more fun if she was back with us like she used to be."

"I don't think she'll ever be like she used to be."

"You may be right," he said. "But I think I may have been missing the benefit here. If she can truly do what Bernie claims, then perhaps I should let it happen. Let the others be called, let them come. When the challengers come, we will defeat them. The sooner we clear out the thorns, the sooner we will solve our town's problems. And the sooner we solve Henford's problems, the sooner we can move on to other places that need us as well."

Lizzie nodded. It was obvious she didn't understand. Rex shut his mind once again on the dichotomy.

"Get her up. No more drugs. I want to see what we have left of her."

"She's too heavy for me."

Rex yanked the IV from Lena's arm. A spot of blood welled where the needle had been. The tube swung free. "I'll help you," Rex said.

"Sure," said Lizzie.

"We'll walk her, wake her up," said Rex as he pulled Lena's legs to the floor. "This will be great. We'll spice up things here, we'll give the battle a nudge. This will be as exciting as those damn fetuses used to be."

"Yeah," said Lizzie.

"We'll do more creative things in town, too. We must sit down and brainstorm. This will be a good fall!"

Lizzie groped but could not get a purchase on Lena's arm.

It took Junior, Rex, Lizzie, and Dean to finally get the large, stupored woman from the bed and out to the fresh air of the autumn day.

Chapter Four

It was Monday morning, the last day of September, and Lindsay's day to put out the decorations and craft items at nursery school for the week. From the backseat of her car she got a box of small pumpkins she'd picked up at the Farmers' Market on Saturday. In a paper bag were construction-paper leaves with the names of each of the children. With Grace's assistance, she planned on taping the leaves to the table so the children would know where to sit for craft time. In her purse, Lindsay had thrown several packs of Hallmark leaf stickers that the children could use to make cards for their parents.

"Grace," Lindsay said as Grace hopped out of the passenger's seat. "Take my hand. Now, I'm giving you the paper bag with the leaves. I've got to carry the pumpkins."

Grace took the bag and shook it. Lindsay pulled on her other hand. "Don't drop it, please."

They moved across the parking lot toward the church's sidewalk. A car pulled into the lot, but Lindsay didn't look around until someone called to her.

"Excuse me!"

Lindsay stopped. Grace bumped into her mother.

In the car was a young woman with blond hair, her eyes shaded by black sunglasses. The woman put her car in to park, but continued to let it run. She hopped out of the car, looked briefly both ways, and trotted to the sidewalk. In her hand was a plate covered with plastic wrap.

"Listen, I'm in a hurry. I'm Cindy Cross, Deana Jones's daddy's girlfriend. I promised Deana I'd bring her a snack today. We had an argument yesterday, and I wanted to make up with her. She's a sensitive thing, you know? This is my way of making up. Could you get it to her?"

"I do have my hands full," Lindsay said. "Why don't you bring it on up?"

Cindy grimaced, then grinned. "I'm late to work again today and it's my butt, majorly. Here." She balanced the plate on top of the pumpkins in the box. "It should be okay in there. Thanks." She hurried to her car, climbed in, and spun out of the parking lot.

"Great," said Lindsay.

"What-zat?"

"Nothing, poot. Let's just get upstairs before I drop something and say something I shouldn't."

"Like nig?"

"Don't say that, Grace."

"See?" said Grace happily. Lindsay groaned, and walked down to the church door, which she hooked open with a single finger and a well-placed foot, then dragged her mighty load up to the social hall.

Chapter Five

The 350 Motel hadn't done any renovations since March, and Norris could swear the towels hanging on the rack in the bathroom were in the exact same position he'd left them when he had been here for the reunion in March.

He'd arrived in Henford late last night, and had spent all of today planning and pacing. He wondered if the Gs had videotaped their possessions as so many people did these days. He wondered if he could get rid of the things and get the money before the list was out on the police hot wire, so the guy holding the goods would be the one with the loss, not Norris.

Around two o'clock in the afternoon he got very hungry. Driving into Henford would be a major mistake, though, because so many people could recognize him.

What difference would it make if you're going to go back to Norfolk and get yourself killed, Norris?

Because maybe he didn't want to go back and get himself killed. Because getting killed would hurt. Because maybe there really wasn't something worth dying for. Maybe now the light of day had spoken some sense in his ear. He'd pay up and get the negatives and go to Key West and change his name. Let the do-gooders do good and rid the world of criminals.

He slipped out of the motel around three and went next door to the Exxon station where he picked up a Hostess cherry pie and a sixteen-ounce bottle of Diet Coke. Then he went back to his room, turned on the soap operas, and doodled on his legal pad, waiting for night.

Chapter Six

Because it was Lindsay's week to bring the decorations and crafts, it was also her week to stay after and clean. Mothers and teachers only had their turn come around once in two months. But today, Lindsay would have paid someone a hundred dollars to do the job.

Grace sat at the end of one of the tables, surrounded by a snowfall of construction-paper crumbs and bits of string. Lindsay brought over the trash can from the wall.

Laura came out of the kitchen. "All done in there, Lindsay. Sorry I can't stay to help with the mess here. I have that dentist appointment in fifteen minutes."

Lindsay began scooping scraps from the table. "Go on. This isn't too bad except for the pumpkin Joey smashed on his way out."

Laura nodded. "I'm going to talk with his mother when she brings him tomorrow. He knows just how to do something at the last minute so we can't stand him in the corner. If he was my kid!" Laura got her coat from the hook by the door to the stairs. As she slipped into the sleeves, she said, "There's a small plate of cookies on the counter in the kitchen, with a note for Deana Jones. Was she supposed to take that home or something?"

"I can't believe I forgot to give those to her. Some woman came by this morning and asked me to get the cookies to Deana." Lindsay moved around Grace and swept the string bits the girl had been piling up into the trash can.

"Hey, play those!" Grace complained.

"Who was the woman?" asked Laura.

"Deana's dad's girlfriend. She was a white woman. Deana's dad have a white girlfriend?"

Laura pulled open the door and frowned. She looked back at Lindsay. "Deana doesn't have a father. He died last year of cancer."

"A stepfather, then? Is her mom remarried?"

"No."

"That's really strange."

"No kidding."

"I'll talk to her mom tomorrow morning."

"Absolutely." Laura flicked her hand in a quick wave. "Gotta go. Bye." The door closed behind her.

Lindsay and Grace were home in half an hour. Lindsay parked Grace before the stereo in the family room, with a Chipmunks tape in the player. Then Lindsay went into the kitchen with the plate of cookies and took out the note. It was folded with Deana's name on it. The message inside was written in loopy, female cursive. It said, "Deana, honey, sorrey about the argment." *Great*, thought Lindsay, *another literate model for our next generation*. "This will make you feel better. Love, Cindy."

Who was Cindy Cross?

Lindsay sighed. She shed her jacket and dropped it onto the back of a kitchen chair, then went to the front door and got the newspaper from the stoop. She took it upstairs, sat on the bed with a propped pillow, and settled back to read.

On page five, next to Ann Landers, there was a story about the missing people of the town.

Brandermill Church Expresses Concern Over Missing Members.

Reverend James Veney of Brandermill Baptist Church reported his continuing concern over the disappearance of six members of his congregation at a press conference he called yesterday afternoon. "Since March," Reverend Veney said, "we've had members leave their homes not to return. The lack of concern from the city of Henford is inexcusable. The investigative job the city police have done is sloppy, and we demand that if they can't help us, outside help be obtained."

This reporter spoke with police chief Paul Burns shortly after the conference. "What Reverend Veney failed to mention was the fact that of the people he has determined as missing, some of them have written to family members about the reasons they left home. Some of the notes have cited family problems. Although there are several cases we are still investigating, it is the belief by many here at our station that these people might also have decided things could be better elsewhere. The economy has hit our town hard, and with the laying off of almost one hundred workers from Symicon, Henford might well be considered a scary place to stay by people whose jobs aren't that secure."

Dr. Arlen Wells, member of the Henford City Council, was quoted as saying, "We grieve for the worry of the families. But our police department is doing all it can, and if there are people who don't want to be found, there isn't much we could, or should, do about it."

Reverend Veney said that the inflammatory graffiti found on the paved road outside his church, the paint sprayed on the windows of a Jewish-owned bakery, and the harassing mail received by some of his congregation members are linked to the missing citizens. Police, on the other hand, have found no correlation of the two.

"We'll find the kids who messed up the road and painted the windows. We'll get them down with rags and turpentine. But we see no relation between the two situations. It's overreaction to force-fit them together."

Lindsay rubbed at a spot over her eye where a mild throbbing had begun. Reverend Veney had a genuine concern. She'd met the man; last year his daughter attended the nursery school at Brotherhood Methodist. He was a person who did not seem prone to hysteria.

She thought of Deana Jones, a little black girl whose father died last year. Now a strange white woman wants to give her cookies.

Lindsay put the paper down with the mail and dropped one foot off the bedside. Was the woman telling the truth? Or was she lying? If she was telling the truth, it could be determined by a single phone call.

She found the phone book in the drawer beneath the phone and dialed Deana's mother. Stacey Jones was the mother's name. Lindsay remembered because Deana, when exasperated, talked about her mother by her first name.

The phone rang four times before a child answered. "Hello?"

"Deana, is that you? This is Mrs. Hollin from nursery school. Deana?"

"Yeah."

"Deana, is your mother there? May I speak to her?"

The phone was put down, and Lindsay shut her eyes, trying to see what the background noises were painting. A kitchen. Dishes in a sink. And then, footsteps.

"Yes?"

"This is Lindsay Hollin, a helper at Deana's nursery school. Is this Stacey Jones?"

"No, this is Deana's grandmother. Stacey isn't home from work yet. Could I take a message?"

This was extremely awkward. "This morning a woman came to the church with a plate of cookies she wanted me to give to Deana. She said her name was Cindy Cross."

The voice on the other line was suddenly guarded. "I don't know anyone named Cindy Cross."

"She said she was . . . well, that she was Deana's father's girlfriend."

It sounded like swearing, muffled behind a hand, and then, "That's sick, Mrs. Hollin. Is this a joke?"

"I'm a helper at the nursery school. I don't know any more about this than what I've told you."

"Why did you feel the need to tell me? Do you enjoy spreading harmful lies?"

"No, of course not. I'm concerned about Deana. If Cindy Cross doesn't know Deana, then why would she want to give her cookies?"

"I don't know. Throw them away. Don't call here again with that kind of thing. We have a fine family here, we've had our share of grief. We don't need more."

The line went dead.

Throw the cookies away? No. Take them to those sit-on-your-butt police and have them analyzed. Better safe than sorry, with all the strange things going on in Henford recently.

Lindsay went downstairs and into the kitchen.

Grace was on her knees in a chair, leaning over the plate of Cindy Cross's cookies, one cookie in her hand.

"Grace, drop that!" Lindsay rushed over and pulled her daughter off the chair. She pried the cookie from the stubborn fingers. "You can't have that cookie. Grace, can't you ever leave anything alone? Can't you just stay out of trouble?"

Grace burst into tears and dropped onto her butt on the floor.

Lindsay put the cookie back under the plastic wrap and put the plate of cookies on top of the refrigerator.

"Did you eat any of those?" Lindsay demanded.

Grace wailed louder. Lindsay got on her knees and held her daughter's face in her hands. "Did you eat any of those cookies, Grace?"

"No! But I want!"

Lindsay gathered her daughter to her, buried her face into the blond hair, and wept quietly. Grace, still feeling unfairly treated, struggled. "Grace, shh," said Lindsay. "Shhh. It's just close to supper, that's all. I don't want you to ruin your appetite."

Lindsay helped Grace from the floor. If Hank was here, she would take the cookies to the police this very minute.

But, of course, Hank was working. She would give them to him when he got home tonight. He worked near the station, he could take them in tomorrow. Let Hank have some idea of what fun, everyday things she got to deal with. If he thought it was silly, then she would insist. If he refused, then she would not take Grace to school tomorrow. The two of them would take a trip to the police station.

"What would you like me to fix for dinner, Grace?" asked Lindsay.

Grace shrugged. "Cookies after sup."

Lindsay said, "Wash your hands, Grace. Then you and I can both make a fresh batch of cookies for after supper. How does that sound?"

Grace didn't answer, but she washed her hands, and so Lindsay knew the bait-and-switch had worked.

Chapter Seven

"Name that Bond movie," Norris said to himself as he parked two blocks away from the Gs' house. He stared through the steering wheel for a moment, watching the sputtering of the street light, looking at the blue "This Street Protected by Neighborhood Watch" sign. He was dressed in black jeans and a black sweatshirt. It wasn't enough to keep him warm, but his jacket was white and he would rather be cold than be caught.

Lights on porches were lit; window light sifted soft beacons as far out as the sidewalk. It was nearing midnight. What were all these people still doing up? He sat and waited. Ten minutes, fifteen, twenty. Soon after midnight, most of the house lights went off. People going to bed.

Norris climbed out of his car, shut the door but did not latch it so it would be a quicker escape, and moved down the walk toward the long driveway of the family homestead. The driveway was marked with tall, ancient brick pillars patterned with ivy. Glass-globed lamps stood atop the pillars. Their lights were powerful.

Norris paused at the base of one pillar. Panic rushed up his throat and he swallowed it back. In one front pocket was a pick he'd been taught to use by Teddy when he locked himself out of his classroom. In a back pocket were a compact flashlight, an Exacto-knife, and pliers. Stuffed under his sweatshirt and secured in his waistband was a small cloth laundry bag.

He'd go in through the back porch door, which led to the small hallway and the den and library. A few small antiques there would bring money worth his worry. Forget the dining room; silverware was too rattly, and he wasn't sure of its value anyway. And then up the stairs to the bedrooms.

Where G-Mom kept valuable bits of jewelry.

He even knew which steps squeaked. He and

Lindsay and Bernie had played musical steps when bored at family reunions. There was no way the Gs had dismantled the steps to chase away a few squeaks.

Go for it, asshole.

He ran up the driveway, keeping to the side. His feet were disturbingly loud on the pavement. He ducked beneath the glare of one spotlight aimed at the center of the drive near the garage, and hopped off into the bushes beneath the dining-room window.

And then he heard the dogs.

The barks were sharp and loud. Norris froze, his head turned toward the sound, certain this couldn't be coming from the Gs' yard.

He looked out between two woody branches.

The next bark was very close, not more than a few feet away. Norris craned his neck around and saw them then. Two jet-black dogs, bodies sleek and stiff, straining and staring from the end of matching chains, teeth reflecting the white of the driveway spotlight.

The Gs had gotten watchdogs.

Norris threw himself back, deep into the teeth of the brush, hitting the brick of the house. The Gs had gotten some fucking watchdogs. What was the world coming to?

And then it all broke loose. The two dogs began growling and screaming, tugging at their chains so that the spikes in the ground which held them squealed like old train brakes. Norris held against the bricks, his fingernails digging into the grit, clenching his teeth.

You don't run now your ass is dead.

The dogs snapped and wailed, banshees of doom.

You don't run now you'll wish you'd chosen the razor.

Norris sprang from the hedges and ran down the driveway. Behind him, the dogs spun on their clawed feet, and lights turned on in the upstairs bedroom.

Run you fuck!

A window opened with a *shhhuck*, and an old, quavering voice, surprisingly strong, called out, "I've got the police on the line! I see you!"

Norris reached the brick pillars, grabbing out with his left hand and bringing himself around, nearly spinning off on the slick ivy, catching himself again and racing toward his car.

The dogs howled. They were on his heels, following, showing who the intruder was to the whole neighborhood. Norris picked up his speed, looking back to kick the dogs, to break them to pieces and shut them up.

They were still chained in the Gs' yard, foghorns of warning, barking down the driveway. And the light in the Gs' front hallway was on now.

He never knew they could move that fast.

He reached his car. He jumped in and slammed the door, catching his ankle with the first slam, cursing and pulling his foot in and slamming the door again. He grappled for the keys in his front pants pocket. They didn't come out. He cried out and clawed again. His finger caught the ring and he tugged them free, stabbed in the ignition key, and spun in a U-turn.

Eight blocks away, he pulled into a Hardees' parking lot. He lit a cigarette, put his head back, and let the tremors come. Few customers frequented the fast-food place at this hour. He would not raise suspicion.

Ten minutes later, he opened his eyes, checked his watch, and tried to regroup.

No luck at the Gs, and they were the best bet. There was always Norris's father, but the old man had sold so much of what they had owned when his mother was around. There was no jewelry there, and Lord knew how the old man might have rearranged the furniture.

Who then?

Lindsay?

Impossible. Norris had never visited Lindsay at her home. He knew even less of what she had where than he did of his father.

How about a visit? A drop in and want to chat visit? Lindsay would be glad to see him. *And it's twelve-thirty-nine, asshole. Oops, Lindsay, sorry, I never was good at keeping track of time.*

Then how about a visit of distress? *I went to visit my dad, Lindsay, and it was all right until he got off on Mom. He kicked me out and I need to talk. Talk her into letting you spend the night. When they're in bed, take a quick perusal and take what you can and get out. Yes, they'll know it's you. But if you're good, they won't notice right away. And by then you can be about your business. Don't leave a forwarding address. It could work.*

It could work.

Chapter Eight

"Daddy miss cookies," said Grace.

"Yes, he did, poot. And they were good, too."

"Left?" Grace turned on the sofa and put her head against her mother. On the floor, with a pillow and blanket, Mandy was watching David Letterman.

"Yes, there are some left for him. You comfortable?"

"Uh-huh," said Grace. She snuggled closer. Lindsay couldn't believe she was letting her girls stay up late. It was a Monday night, for Pete's sake. And all three of them, Lindsay, Mandy, and Grace, had school the next morning.

What would Hank say when he came home and found them all in front of the television set?

That was Lindsay's point. Let him see them, up and waiting for him, bleary-eyed and groggy. When else were they to see him? In the past months, Hank's schedule had been more and more burdened. Late nights, many weekends, dinner times. He wasn't a doctor; how many emergency calls were lawyers supposed to have? After ten years of marriage, Lindsay still did not have a good answer to this one. She was certain he was not seeing another woman. He didn't seem distracted in the way a man in love would. But he was certainly a busy man.

Lindsay closed her eyes. Richard Simmons's voice, taunting David with threats of silk shorts and pink socks, drifted down the tunnel of her consciousness like the voice of a comic character in a well.

And then Lindsay was shaking. Something, someone was shaking her. Grace was crying, "Mama! Mandy! Mandy!"

Chapter Nine

As Norris put one hand over the other, pulling the steering wheel to the left to turn onto Spring Road, he was thinking about rich people and how he had once been one and now he hated them even though he still felt he was one, or could be one if he really wanted to.

And then the smell hit him. His nose had begun to tickle, and the nearly invisible burn scars on his wrists began to throb. His knee drew up involuntarily, cracking against the gear shift, knocking it into reverse. Norris grappled and threw it into park.

He licked his lips and waited. His heart picked up a beat.

Deep behind his sinuses he could sense something woodsy. A sensation, a taste of smoke. Then it grew. The smell crawled forward, causing his mouth to water obscenely, teased by the scents of cooking bacon and hot coffee.

The burns picked up a heavier throb.

"This isn't possible," Norris said. "This is over. This doesn't happen anymore. I refuse!"

The vision of the dark street outside the windshield fluttered, and through it Norris could see a mob of people, laughing in his direction. They were lower than he was, as if he were standing on something several feet high. Someone was beside him, but he could not turn to see. There was something tight and cold around his neck.

Barbed wire.

"Goddamn it, no! This is over!"

The vision ran wet and rolled away. Daylight and trees and grinning faces bled into the night of Norris's car. He sat shaking.

It was starting again. Life was the cruelest bastard there could have ever been created.

Carefully he dropped the shift into drive. He was going to Lindsay's. If she thought him insane and wanted him committed, so be it. It might be that Western State was the only place he could be safe. Or perhaps her hug would be there, that hug of the past, the warm, simple sensation of love. "Fuck it!" he cried.

Lindsay, help me!

Chapter Ten

Lindsay's brain screamed at her to awaken, but her body was not as willing.

Mandy?

Grace sobbed, close to her, on her shoulder. "Mama!"

Lindsay sat bolt upright. Her head spun. She looked at the floor where Mandy had been mesmerized by a late-night celebrity she'd never seen before.

Mandy was thrashing and moaning on the rug. One foot was entangled in the blanket; her free foot lashed out, beating a horrific, rhythmic tattoo on the base of the television stand.

"Mandy!" Lindsay fell to the floor and grabbed her daughter. Mandy went stiff, her teeth gnashing and drool spilling down the side of her jaw. "Mandy, God, what's wrong? Mandy!" Lindsay shook her daughter. Mandy's body convulsed violently with a single snap, throwing her head back at an impossible angle. Her eyes flashed open and they were wide with terror and incomprehension.

On the floor, crushed into many pieces by the thrashing body, was a cookie from the plate Lindsay had brought home. Mandy had found the plate. She had taken a cookie and stuck it in her pocket, probably, to eat later. Had she remembered it as Lindsay had drifted off to sleep?

"Mandy!" Lindsay thrust her arms beneath her daughter's head and tried to bring it up so she could look at it, so she could command it to stop this, so she could force her daughter to let go of this demon and be all right.

"I'll kill you, Cindy Cross!"

Mandy's head came back up, but the eyes were already easing shut. The trembling eased. The foot slowed its tapping.

"Grace, call 911!"

On the sofa, Grace was beyond knowing where the telephone was.

"Grace, call 911! I can't leave her!"

Grace wailed louder.

Lindsay felt Mandy's temples, felt the soft skin below the blond hairline. She could feel no pulse. "Grace, help me!" She slid her hands down and picked up a wrist. On the wrist was a braided friendship bracelet from one of the little girls at Mandy's school. There was no pulse at the wrist.

A soul-tearing sob ripped from Lindsay's throat. She put her fingertips beneath her daughter's nostrils. There was no movement of air.

She forced herself to her feet and stumbled into the kitchen and reached for the phone.

And then her fingertips blazed white hot. She

drew them up to her mouth. What was this? No, not this.

Not now!

Her body seemed to inflate, to fill with a drug-like lead. Her arms went limp, her face bloated. The kitchen wavered and disappeared as she watched. Forms took shape before her, and another kitchen. But this was a dark kitchen, an ugly, tent-kitchen. Through eyes that seemed cloaked in a thin, rippling film, she could see a lantern hung on a nail in a wooden beam beside an opened tent flap. A man was nearby, across a table covered with filthy pans and bowls. He wore a John Deere cap. He was young. Lindsay thought his arms and hands looked familiar. She had seen them in previous visions. Here was the man who had abused her.

Had abused Lena.

Oh God Mandy is dying and I'm here. Take me back before she dies!

"Don't even need to be pulling out that arsenal," said the man. "Just keep it safe and warm. We may never need it. To us." He held up a glass of something clear and took a long drink. Another man came into view to Lindsay's right. He was taller than the first by several inches. He stared down the length of the table, but Lindsay couldn't turn to see what was down there. It sounded as if someone were washing dishes. There was a gurgling sound, and the clatter of plates being stacked.

Lindsay's body, Lena's body, struggled with a deep and dreadful heaviness. The film on her eyes fluttered, and one pudgy hand moved up to wipe at it. The man shook his head, and his mouth twitched in an ugly grin.

Someone said, "Rex, I think she's brain damaged past help. How we gonna use a brain-dead fat woman?"

Rex, the man across from her, said, "Don't know yet."

A crash came from down the table. Rex's head snapped around. Lindsay felt Lena's head slowly turn in the direction of the sound.

The tent was longer than she had thought. A woman was near the far end, washing dishes in a large plastic tub. She was staring at the ground.

"Waste is a sin, Judy," said Rex. "You haven't been with us long, but that's one truth you know!"

"I'm sorry." The woman looked up briefly, and through the film across her eyes Lindsay could recognize the woman's features.

It was Cindy Cross. Judy.

Mandy is dying stop this I don't want to see this!

"I'm sorry. I won't do it again."

"The Truth tells the truth," said Rex. Then he linked his fingers on the tabletop and looked at the man beside Lindsay. "And truth is, Dean," he said, "you got to meet those new Eagles in town in half an hour. Key's in the trailer. I won't be going with you, but you pick them up for me. Arlen said Deno's parking lot."

"Two of 'em?"

"Two," said Rex.

A third voice came abruptly from behind Lindsay. It said, "I won't need a ride with you after all, Dean. Junior will take me out to my car later. Paperwork's done, Rex. Now I think I'll take you up on your offer."

Rex smiled in understanding.

The third voice went on. "You have a nice little

get-up here. Arlen's been on me to come visit, and I'm glad I finally have. It's heartwarming." The voice laughed. "It's encouraging. With all the work Arlen and I have been doing in town to keep the bugs out of your hair, it's nice to see the product of the effort."

Lindsay knew the voice. More than any other voice besides her own or her children's.

"But you didn't want to visit the alien pets," said Rex. "I'm insulted."

"I might appreciate what a surgeon does, but I don't want to see the incisions."

Rex said, "Junior is taking you out later?"

"An hour or so. You offered Lizzie, and I don't want to be ungrateful. So head on, Dean. I have a bit of nonlegal business before I call it a night."

Lindsay knew that voice. Her soul, in silence, screamed.

Rex stared past Lindsay's shoulder. "Offer's good," he said. "Got to keep our respectable members happy. You just keep doing what you do best when you get back, Hank. Keep 'em calm down on the homefront."

Lindsay's knees gave out but she did not fall. Lena's knees were locked and felt no shock or betrayal.

Hank.

Rex looked across the table again. Lindsay thought the demented smile itself was enough to stop her heart. "And you, bitch, you stop staring at us or I'll have you back on your bed or worse. You used to have good manners, but they all seemed to go bad."

There was a pounding on the door.

There were no doors to the tent.

The film over Lindsay's eyes fluttered and

thickened and drew her back and down. Her mind spun, her soul dropped, falling as though to the bottom of a damp, rancid well. From beyond, the pounding on the door continued. With the pounding, a high-pitched screaming.

Come in come in I'm here help me help my daughter!

Lindsay's eyes snapped open to her own kitchen. She had slumped to the floor against the wall. Beyond the kitchen, Grace was screaming her sister's name.

Lindsay pushed herself up against the wall but could not reach the phone. Her knees buckled and she slid back. The pounding, down the hall to the front of the house, continued.

"Help me please! I didn't lock it, come in! I can't call. Help me, Mandy is dying!" The pounding stopped, as if listening. Lindsay screamed, her throat tearing. "Help me! Help me! Help me!"

The door crashed open. Footsteps were on the runner of the front hall. They raced to the kitchen.

Lindsay let her head fall back. She looked up. Norris stood gaping, panting, his eyes wide. He was dressed in black.

"Norris!"

Norris dropped beside her. There was sweat on his face, in his beard.

"Call the ambulance, Norris," Lindsay's words were tangled in thorns of horror. "Mandy," she said.

Norris stood and picked up the receiver and jabbed 911. Then his eyes flicked back toward Lindsay.

"What happened?"

From the family room, Grace wailed again.

Norris threw his hand over the receiver. "What happened!"

Lindsay caught her breath and her words. "Poison," she said. "The cookies were poisoned!"

Norris spoke into the phone. "We have a child, poisoned. Hurry."

"Hurry," sobbed Lindsay.

"Yes," Norris said to the receiver. "Yes, hurry!"

Lindsay lifted one hand and pointed toward the doorway. "Mandy," she said. Norris let the receiver swing free and dashed out of the kitchen. Lindsay pulled herself to her feet. She wavered, then pressed her palms to the wall and worked herself to the door and into the hall. She could hear Norris speaking to Mandy and Grace. She could hear Grace's cries reduced to thin, reedlike whistles.

She didn't want to see. She shuffled past the hall table and plant stand. She could see into the family room now, the bookshelf, the window, the edge of the sofa.

Norris was saying, "Mandy, come on, Mandy."

Lindsay closed her eyes and followed her hands to the family-room door. She opened her eyes again. Norris was on his knees. Grace was on the floor beside him, her fingers in her mouth. Norris hunched over Mandy, his linked hands pressing her chest.

"Mandy!" Lindsay screamed. She fell down beside her daughters and her cousin. The vision was horrible, worse than any vision she had had from the burns on her fingers.

Norris looked at her. His eyes were red. His teeth were clenched. "I can't, Lindsay. It's too late."

"No!"

"I can't help her."

Lindsay shoved Norris aside. She looked down at the face of her older daughter. The girl's face was blue. Her eyes were open and rolled up. Thick strings of drool hung from her lip to the carpet. The blond hair was matted.

Lindsay fell on her daughter's chest, pounding and screaming, "Wake up, Mandy!"

Norris said, "This way." He reached over and linked Lindsay's hands together. "No, Lindsay, try it this way, but I don't think it's going to work. It's too late."

Lindsay, fingers linked, began pressing between Mandy's ribs. She stared at the girl's face. Yes, this would work. It always worked. She had seen *Rescue 911*. And then, to Norris, she said, "You have to get them. Stop them. They'll kill more!"

Norris's face twitched in what seemed a mixture of confusion and understanding. He drew back. "Who?"

"The bad guys! The ones who hurt Mandy! One's coming into town. His name's Dean, tall with short hair. A blue shirt. Dean is coming into town to pick up two new men. He's taking them back to the place where they stay. Pretend to be one of them. Meet him at Deno's, you hear me? Get in there and stop them."

"How do you know?"

She pumped Mandy's chest.

"How do you know about this man Dean?"

"Visions, Norris! Bernie and I have had visions ever since touching Lena Carlton at the reunion." Her hands moved, rhythmically, desperately, punching what she prayed was life into the still form of her daughter. "We've seen things.

331

Bernie's seen things that have been, but I see things as they happen. Lena is with these people, these murderers! I know Dean is coming to Henford tonight, to pick up new recruits. Go with them. Stop them!"

"I can't leave you."

Lindsay's head snapped around. She felt fire in her eyes. "You aren't doing shit here! Stop them, Norris."

Lindsay looked back at Mandy. Her hands continued their rhythmic pressing. She heard Norris withdraw, heard his footsteps on the hall, and then heard the front door pull closed. From the kitchen, she heard the burr of the voice of the emergency operator, shouting for her to pick up the phone again.

Chapter Eleven

Coward.

I'm not a hero. What the fuck am I doing?

As Norris had driven back into the mainstream of town, heading for the convenience store called Deno's, he had heard the wail of the sirens. He hoped they would get there and save the girl, but he knew it was already over.

Mandy was dead. She was pathetic on the floor, victim of a group of people Norris couldn't begin to comprehend, even as he rode in the car with some of them.

He sat in the cramped backseat of a white sedan, pressed against the right window next to two other people he'd never seen before, driving in the country to a destination of which he didn't have a clue.

What am I doing?

I want to stop the visions, for you, Lindsay. You hugged me when I was a teenager. You hugged me when I came home in March. But I'm not a hero.

The car hit a bump and Norris's head hit the ceiling.

Lindsay's child was murdered. If he could get hold of Lena, he could stop the visions. At least that much he could conceive. Norris hoped he would know what to do when he saw the woman. Maybe talking to her would break the spell. Maybe touching her again would withdraw the power she had thrown over them.

And what would he do, then, about the murderers?

It hurt to breathe.

Just get rid of the visions. It had priority over stopping killers, because he was not police, he was not military, he was not trained in crime prevention. But he could stop the visions. It would be a gift to Lindsay as well as to himself. Maybe it would help ease the loss of the girl.

Stopping the visions even had priority over We're In the Money. How could he even see straight to solve that problem if his thoughts had an agenda of their own?

How was there anything more terrifying than the loss of one's mind? The loss of one's child?

Beside him, in the middle of the backseat, a thin young man with a ducktail and bug-eyes hummed "I can't help falling in love with you." No one talked. The driver was alone in the front.

For some reason he wouldn't let anyone sit up there with him. His name was Dean.

When Norris had arrived at Deno's, he waited under the light until he saw a tall man in a blue shirt pull up and hop out of his car. The man had looked about furtively. In a matter of seconds, two others had gotten out of cars and joined him. Norris had strolled over, his face set in a mask of calm that quivered just below the surface.

Dean had said, "My name's Dean. But Rex said I'd find just two of you." He looked them all over, as if waiting for an explanation. Norris had put one hand in his pants pocket and stared at the man with the ducktail.

There's your extra. He isn't supposed to be here.

His heart thundered.

"Rex said two," Dean said again.

The other man, chubby with a denim jacket stretched around his middle, looked at the duck-tailed man and at Norris and said, "Maybe Rex made a mistake."

Dean's chin tilted upward. "Rex don't make mistakes."

"I'm supposed to meet you here," said Norris. "I don't know about these others. I thought there was just going to be me."

"One, two, three," said Ducktail. "Three's better than one, ain't it?"

Dean finally nodded, then had them all follow in their cars to a warehouse near the Symicon factory. They parked their cars in an empty garage, side by side, and Dean pulled the door down and locked it. "We'll get these as we need them," said Dean, and the explanation seemed to satisfy the fat man and Ducktail. All three were ordered to sit in the backseat.

They had been driving nearly twenty-five minutes. Norris had watched carefully, tucking into his memory the turns and the night-clothed scenery. Lights from occasional country homes glistened on the window glass, then faded into fields of stubbled corn.

Soon the car found a gravel road, and the pastures were swallowed up by forest. The road angled up slightly, indicating they had reached the foothills of the mountains. Ducktail stopped his humming, and leaned over Norris to have a look out the window. Norris pressed back against the seat so he would have room. He wondered if the man could smell the fear on his breath.

Dean turned right, stopped, and hopped out. Through the windshield, Norris watched him unlatch a single chain barrier that hung across the road, and let it drop. He climbed back in, drove over the chain, then got out to put it back. The car lights stared ahead into the thick, shadow-heavy woods.

Where are we? What have I done to myself?

The car moved along the rutted road, beneath the canopy of branches, then pulled into a clearing. Norris saw spots of lights about the area—lanterns, flashlights, a bonfire.

Bonfire. Sam had died by a campfire. It had been Norris's fault. They had gone camping as a celebration of Norris's acceptance of himself, and Norris had not watched the fire as he should while Sam slept.

Stop it. You don't need those visions. Things are too fucking complex now to deal with any more.

Sam died because of fire. It was your fault,

Norris. You couldn't be a hero if Jesus came down from heaven and gave you a million dollars and a promise of life on a throne.

He was here. This was where Lena Carlton was. This was the place of his visions. It was here they would end.

"Get out," said Dean.

Norris felt a cold trickle of ice run backward in the veins of his arms. He let out a breath against the window glass before he took the handle to open the door.

He was not a hero.

Chapter Twelve

Grace sat on Lindsay's lap in the back of the ambulance. Technicians swarmed around Mandy like insects intent on a societal chore. Their faces were as expressive as insects', vacant, set, emotionless. One woman in a white pants suit and green windbreaker sat on the cushion beside Lindsay, patting her hand. The woman's demeanor was a combination of professional strength and hard-edged terror.

"Just hang on," she said. "We'll be there in a minute. Hang on, honey."

She didn't say, "She'll be all right. Your daughter will be just fine."

A liturgy played and replayed in Lindsay's mind. *Hank killed Mandy. Hank killed Mandy.*

Lindsay clutched her only live daughter and stared out past the technicians to the blur of Henford's street lights.

Chapter Thirteen

All four men climbed out of the white car. Norris was last. He stood, rubbed his neck, and shoved his hands into his pockets. Dean, the driver, strode immediately toward a large tent to the left of the clearing. The other two men came around the back of the car and stood beside Norris.

"Isn't this cool?" said the fat man. "I always knew the whites would rise up. I can't wait to be part of it. Guns, power, what we should have been doing all along. They's damn tootin' that the darkies ain't of this earth."

Ducktail nodded.

Norris caught the end of that comment and pulled at the raveling thread. *I'm at a camp of survivalist right-wingers, Lena's a part of this. These are the killers.*

Dean came back from the tent and waved his hand in the three men's direction. "Everyone wants to meet you," he said. Norris followed fat man and ducktail over to Dean. Dean took them around the tent toward a large area which had rows of benches at one side. Before the benches, like a flaming altar, a bonfire roared and spat at the sky.

"Sit," said Dean.

All three sat on a front bench, side by side. Norris crossed his arms. *Okay, here's the deal. Play the game. Grin and agree. Fit in and don't stick. Play dumb and the ugly girl will leave you alone. Fuck the niggers. Kill the Jews.* He could do it.

These people killed Mandy Hollin.

Cold sweat, thick under his arms, began to run.

A trickle of men and women, wearing the same blue shirt as Dean, came from all directions and stood near the bonfire. A dreadful nostalgia emanated from them and made Norris shiver. Their faces were hard to see, but Norris could read their minds.

Are they loyal? Are there any infiltrators? We'll poison them if they lie to us.

We have to trim the deadweight. Surely you aren't surprised.

No, that had been from the vision. The vision at Nansemond Lounge. Christ. How did his visions fit here? Bernie had seen things of the past, Lindsay had said. Lindsay saw things as they happened.

Dean stepped into the group before the fire. Beside him was another man in a ball cap. He crossed his arms and came up close to the three on the benches.

So what of Norris's visions? Were they of . . .

"There are three here, Dean," said the man in the ball cap. "I said you were to pick up two."

. . . the future?

"I thought I might've misunderstood, Rex," said Dean.

The man named Rex took his cap off and scratched the crown of his head. He said, "There can't be any misunderstanding now, you know that."

"I know that," said Dean.

Norris felt his scalp tighten. This was the man who had put the barbed wire around Norris's neck. This was the man who had said, "Some of us must hang separately."

Oh my god oh my god oh my god.

338

Play dumb play stupid play supremacist.

"Is one of these a faker?" Rex stood before the fat man. "Are you a faker? Who sent you here?"

The fat man opened his mouth, but Rex held a finger before his lips. "No, whisper it to me."

Rex leaned down his ear to the fat man. Then he stood back, looking satisfied. He moved before Ducktail. "And you, who sent you?"

I don't know who sent me. Lindsay sent me. Lena brought me. We're In the Money drove me. Fuck you all!

Rex stepped back from Ducktail, a satisfied near-smile again on his face. Then he looked at Norris. "And you, have you got a good answer for me?"

Norris wondered where they kept the barbed wire.

Chapter Fourteen

Matt was asleep. He slept a lot these days. The days were shorter and colder, and Matt saw less and less of each one. The lice no longer caused him to dig at his skin with vigor, because vigor was sucked from him like water down a bathtub drain. The deep red scratches were fading even as his arms and legs shriveled and drew up.

Bernie sat beside Matt, her arm around his shoulder, his head in its familiar position on her breast. She looked out the window of the shed, out at the same heavenly sky she had viewed from her upstairs bedroom window at HeartLight. The stars and the moon had not lost their friendliness. They shone in glory and strength and timelessness.

But here, through the small, unlatched window, through the uncaulked boards and the straw on the floor, friendliness did not seep in. Cold did, and fear and despair, but no paternal or fraternal spirits from beyond. The spirits that lived here stirred slowly or not at all. The spirits here were dying.

Dinner was late. It was after midnight, and the scraps they were given each night were usually brought around ten. There was something going on outside the shed tonight. Bernie feared it was more captives, or more converts. Either was equally bad.

That afternoon, Lena had come in with Peaches to muck the straw. Bernie had not seen Lena in months and had been sure she'd been banished from the compound, or had died.

It was as if God had decided to wake up. To speak.

"Lena!"

Lena had lost weight, and her skin was bagged like old socks. She had moved with pain and an aura of lethargy way beyond her normal shyness. Her gaze was dulled, and when Bernie had called her name, it had taken a few long seconds before the eyes had flicked in Bernie's direction.

"Lena, how are you doing? I'm so glad to see you!"

Bernie had tried to smile. It was hard to do; her lips were unaccustomed to pulling out and up.

Lena had not seemed to register who Bernie was, and had looked down again, back to the shovel in her hands and the chore at hand. Unlike Peaches, Lena did not wrinkle her nose at the stench in the shed.

Is this the time, God? Is it time now that I will

*at last do for Lena what you have brought me here
to do?*

"Lena, are you all right?"

Surely Bernie had not experienced Lena's
childhood for no reason.

*You have not forgotten me. Now Your will be
known. The time had come around.*

"Lena, please talk to me. Look at me. I have so
much to say to you."

Peaches had screamed at Bernie to shut up
then. Pets had no right to speak without being
spoken to. Bernie leaned back into the wall, dug
at the raw patches on her arms, and watched
Lena until she left.

Now, it was very late and no food had come.
Bill Bailey, like Matt, was sleeping, his thin arms
seeming almost small enough to slip through the
cuffs, but not quite. Naked, he lay against the
dark wood of the wall, seeming to be a part of
the wood, like ivy became part of stone. He was
lice-ridden as they all were, and coughed constantly. It was a wonder he was still alive.

The food had to come. Bernie's stomach
cramped, and she knew the others felt the same.
The Eagles could not forget them.

More captives were there now; once every week
or two, a new one was brought to Night Land to
the loud acclamation of the White Eagles. With
each new arrival, they would stoke up their fire,
and Shawn would bring out a gun to fire off
rounds of celebration. Some had been trans-
ferred to a new shed behind the first. Alien Pen
Number Two.

They would never forget to feed the pets,
though. Sometimes it was late, but they never
forgot.

Rusty, the teenager, dug his heels into the straw and twisted his head back and forth in agitation. Bernie said, "Shh, Randy, hang in there," but Randy did not want to listen. He had been planning escape ever since Bernie, Matt, and Lisa had arrived. As the weeks had crept on, his plans became more incoherent as weakness drew the edge off his keen intelligence. Bernie listened to him, though, when he spun his plans. It seemed to calm him a little.

Lisa hummed softly in the corner. She spoke rarely now, and stared at the floor most of each day until sunlight withdrew from the tiny window, and then she would sing herself to sleep.

Days without end, amen.

Don't forget our food!

Bernie had been counting Matt's breaths. She put her hand on his forehead and stroked the bridge of his nose. It was later than usual. Even later than the late nights. Matt needed his supper.

Is this what the end is? To see Lena and then to die of starvation? This is why you brought us here?

Matt groaned, and Bernie held him closer. She put her face down against his, and felt the scar against her cheek. If they got through this alive, she thought she would ask him to marry her. By then, her dues would have been paid. By then, her love would have been purged.

Where is the damned food?

"Where is the damned food!" she screamed.

Matt jerked upward with a grunt. Lisa stopped humming. Bill Bailey mumbled, "Regina?"

"Where is our food, damn you, Shawn!"

342

Outside at the gathering, Peaches shouted, "Shut up or we'll let you go another day!"

Bernie rolled her lips back between her teeth and bit down so she would not call out again. She held Matt, and she waited.

Chapter Fifteen

Norris whispered in the hairy ear of the leader of the White Eagles, "My gut told me to come. I been puking up nigger shit too long and I need help getting rid of it."

Rex stood straight then, leaning back slightly, and gave Norris a look of amused surprise. *He's going to kill me. I can't take pain. I hate pain. Don't let it hurt*.

"Your gut told you to come?" Rex stuck his pinky in his nose, dug around, then pulled it out and looked at it. "You been puking up nigger shit? What's it taste like?"

Norris felt his shoulders twitch in what might have been a shrug. "Bad," he said.

Rex put out his pinky. "Suck this," he said. "See if this is what it tasted like."

Norris felt bile in his throat. He felt the eyes of the Eagles watching him with extreme pleasure.

"Are you a faker?" asked Rex. "Suck my finger, boy."

Norris tightened his jaw and opened his lips. And then a scream came from a small shed beyond the tent.

"Where's the damn food!"

Rex spun about and stared at the shed. The

other Eagles watched the leader and the new-comer with the open mouth.

"Goddamn it," hissed Rex.

And then a second scream came, and Norris felt the words sting his flesh like bees. The voice was Bernie's.

"Where's our food, damn you, Shawn!"

One of the women called back, "Shut up or we'll let you go another day!"

Rex shook his head and looked back at Norris. "We have pets, did you know that? We have been cleaning Henford out. Good idea, don't you think?" Rex looked at his pinky again. "Now. Your gut told you. You're not a faker, are you?"

"Of course not."

Mercifully, Rex shoved both hands into his pockets. He pointed at the woman who had shouted. "Get the aliens their supper. Give the complainer half ration."

The woman nodded. She walked to the tent and went inside. Rex pushed up his sleeve and looked at his watch. "Get to bed. We have orientation in the morning for these three new men. No one will be late to the classroom, no one will be less than razor sharp for me tomorrow."

The Eagles dispersed. Norris and the other two newcomers stood by the bench, a waiting directions. Rex watched until all the Eagles had gone into the trailer. Then he spoke to the fat man.

"What is your name?"

"Gerald."

"Arlen put a word in for you. You go to the trailer. Sleep on the floor."

Gerald left. Rex looked at Ducktail. "And your name?"

"Pat."

"Arlen vouched for you, too. Go with Gerald."

Ducktail followed the fat man. Rex grinned at Norris. Shadows cut his teeth, making them sharp and deadly. "And your name?"

"Jim."

"Jim, is it? I don't remember Arlen mentioning a Jim. But you say you aren't a faker. Do you believe in Truth?"

"Of course."

Rex leaned closer. His breath was foul. "You're all dressed in black. Does that mean something?"

"No."

"Does it mean you want to look like a nigger?"

"No."

Rex lifted his right arm. "The Arm Test makes clear what is true. If my arm stays up, something must be done because it is true. If it goes down . . ."

Norris watched Rex.

"Tell me what it means if it goes down, Jim."

"It isn't true?"

"Precisely. I want to know if you are supposed to go to bed with me tonight." Rex put his right arm up. "Push on my arm, Jim. If you aren't a faker, and you believe in the Truth, you can't argue with it, you can't fight it. I ask this of Truth, should Jim go to bed without me tonight?"

He can make it come out as he wants. He will make it go down. There is no way out of this.

Norris pushed lightly. The arm went down. Rex laughed and put his hand against Norris's crotch. "I want to know if you enjoy this. It disgusts me, but if you get hard, you're queer, you're an alien and a blasphemy to the Truth. But relax, Jim. Just see this as a test."

345

Norris clenched his teeth. *God don't let this happen!*

"A test," said Norris.

Rex moved his hand to Norris's hand and grasped it gently. "My trailer is over here. This shouldn't be difficult for a true White Eagle."

Norris followed Rex to the trailer. Glass cut his throat. If he knocked Rex down, he could run away. He knew the direction they had come. He could hide.

They all know these woods by night. They'd be on you in a minute. He stopped at the bottom of the trailer step as Rex went up and pounded on the door.

"You best be done in there, counselor. I need my sleep," Rex called.

I can get through this. Play asshole macho murderous bigot. I can get through this. Sweat burned his eyes.

The trailer door swung open and a man stood in the center, buttoning a jacket. He was tall and thin. When his face angled toward Norris, it caught the faint light of the moon. Norris recognized him.

And the man recognized Norris.

"Well, I'll be damned."

Rex looked back at Norris. He said, "What?"

"I said, 'I'll be damned.' Is this your newest man?"

"Shouldn't he be?"

"Keeping things in the family could be a benefit at times, but not this time."

"What do you mean?"

"He's my wife's cousin."

Rex's eyes narrowed. "Oh?"

"Yes. Good to see you, Norris." Hank stepped

down one step and stopped beside Rex. Behind Hank, a young woman appeared, buttoning a plain blue shirt. Norris swallowed around the glass but nothing went down. Even air snagged and caught.

Rex turned to Norris. "What's your name, now? I must have not heard you right."

Norris swallowed again. Air and saliva went down in a clot and filled his belly with fire. "Norris," he said. "Norris Lynch."

"And you lied to me?"

Norris said nothing.

"Good God, Norris, why are you out here? I thought you lived in Norfolk. Take a wrong turn on the Turnpike?" Hank stroked his mustache. "I really am sorry to see you, I think you must know that."

Rex patted Norris on the cheek. "Are you a faker?"

Norris said nothing.

"He's not of like mind, if that's what you're asking," said Hank. The man stepped down to the ground. "Are you spying on us, Norris?"

"No. I'm not a faker."

"No, but you're a fag, Norris. I don't think fags are allowed in this club."

Rex tipped his head back and looked at the sky. Norris watched between him and the woman in the doorway. She seemed suddenly interested in the conversation. Her tongue went out of her mouth, then back in.

"Queer?" said Rex. He looked back down. He was smiling. Norris gritted his teeth.

"I live in Henford," said Hank. "I know more of what goes on than most. I've friends in the force, friends on the bench. There are members who, along with myself, keep tabs on the actions of those who don't have the family values that we need in our town. Such a man was Sam Connors. Oh, we knew he was abnormal. But it was a shock to find you had the hots for him, Norris."

Don't talk about Sam!

"I know that Norris was having a dandy time camping with old Sam Connors a number of years ago. They started a fire in the woods. Must have been a hot old time, right? Like rubbing two sticks together. Rex, you remember the forest fire on the ridge east of Henford."

Rex said, "Maybe." His eyes were alight, fascinated.

"Cousin here was responsible. In truth, Norris, it was better you moved to Norfolk. We'd have found ways to make your life miserable, to encourage you to leave."

"You talk as if you were the town," said Norris.

"Bold words, cousin. But I don't think the words are so true. A good number of Lindsay's family agree with these traditional values. Your grandparents would shit if they knew about you. And Marla, she's a traditionalist from the get-go. And your father, have you considered him? They would do what they could to keep our town clean. Protected, if you will."

"Not if they knew about this place—" Norris began, and Rex punched him in the gut. Norris bent over, spitting bile.

"Norris," said Hank. "I'd never have bothered you if you hadn't bothered us. God, I can't believe you're here, and I don't want to hear the story of how you came. But you've put your nose in. A cat and the fan, so to speak. And Rex had the right to know the truth." He shrugged and sniffed in mild apology.

Rex laughed then, loud and long. When he quieted, he said, "They find us, don't they? Maybe it's destiny, if you believe in that sort of thing. Some we've gone out and caught. Others stumbled along, as though their inner selves knew they belonged here. What do you think?"

"You could be right," said Hank. He took off toward the tent. "And I'm out of here. Junior best be ready. It's nearly two-thirty. Lindsay'll skin me alive as it is."

Norris croaked, "Lindsay sent me. Mandy is dead."

Hank spun around. He retraced his steps in a flash and drove his fist into Norris's jaw. Norris doubled over and stumbled back, tripping and dropping to the trailer step. "Don't you dare!" said Hank. "You try cheap shit with me and you'll find out what cheap shit really is. You're calling your own shots here, cousin." He straightened and rubbed his knuckles. "Sad, but true."

Norris cradled his jaw in his hands. Shards of pain radiated out toward his ears.

Hank walked to the tent.

"Lizzie," said Rex on the step beside Norris. "Let's tie this man up tonight. Over at Junior's tree. Then I'm going to get some sleep and think things over."

Here comes the barbed wire, this is where they'll strangle me, they'll hang me.

Norris struggled upward, to run and get away. It didn't matter where now as long as it was away. There was a creek somewhere. Maybe if he got to the creek he could wake up again at Nansemond Lounge.

Rex caught Norris's arm as he went up, and jerked it around behind him. Norris twisted, but the pain in his face threw him off balance, and Rex caught the second arm as well. The woman was behind him now, too, and rope was quickly and expertly looped and knotted at his wrists. "Hold still," said the woman. Her words were soft and gentle. It was sickening, like a mockery of a mother lovingly putting her child into a pair of mittens or a new snowsuit.

Rex and the woman led Norris to a large tree near the clearing and the bonfire. A long piece of rope was attached there as if others had suffered this fate before. The rope went around Norris's waist and then his neck. To allow enough room to breathe, Norris pressed the back of his head into the scabby, insect-busy bark. Above, the stars winked and counted the minutes of the night.

And the night was full of many, many minutes.

Chapter Sixteen

Rex gazed at the face of the man tied to the tree for a long time, holding a cup of piss. It was a normal face, not the face of an alien scum. It was a face with a beard and an average nose and dark, straight hair. But it was the face of a pervert. The misleading face of danger. The face of morals gone wrong, America gone to hell.

He flicked the glass at Norris. The piss caught him full-face. Norris's head, pressed into the tree and tilted toward his shoulder like the head of a shy child, jerked erect. The eyes flew open, and Norris began to sputter.

"Morning, cousin," said Rex.

Norris's tongue came out, touched the lips, then withdrew. He began to cough and spit. His eyes opened. He focused on Rex. The hate and fear were exciting for Rex. It was still early. The forest birds were just beginning their calls, the Eagles were barely stirring in the trailer, but Rex already knew this was going to be a very good day.

"Do you know that this is my whipping tree? Eagles learn their lessons here."

Norris's face drew up, then went slack.

"Tell me, cousin, why did you come here?"

Norris blinked and said nothing. His breathing was hard, his chest straining at the ropes.

Rex leaned into Norris's face. He licked the man's face in a long, wet stroke. His piss tasted acidic. "Talk to me, queer. I can bite your nose right off your face."

Norris said, "Lindsay sent me."

"Lindsay?"

"Hank Hollin's wife."

Rex sucked his forefinger and then stroked the bridge of Norris's nose. "Talk to me, cousin. You stop before I tell you, you'll be smelling with your taste buds."

"Untie me, I can't breathe."

"Sure you can. Talk to me."

"I've had visions."

"Visions!" shouted Rex. Bernie had talked about visions. This was surely a good morning. "Go on."

Norris took a heavy, guttural breath. "I thought it was the drugs, it could have been. But others had them, too. Others who had touched the bag woman."

"Bag woman?"

"Lena Carlton."

Rex clapped his hands. "Yes! Tell me more!"

"I need a cigarette."

"We don't smoke here. Do go on."

Norris closed his eyes and continued. "We all touched Lena. Bernie. Lindsay. Me. I thought what I saw was bad drugs. I think it was the future."

"What about the future? What do you know?"

"Bernie saw Lena's past."

"I know that! She told me!"

Norris opened his eyes. They locked on Rex. "You talked to Bernie?"

"Bernie is here, with the pets. Go on."

"I want to see her."

"Later you can." Rex tapped his teeth together and wiggled his tongue. "Talk to me, faggot."

"I thought"—Norris hesitated—"I thought if I could see Lena, if I could touch her or talk to her, the visions would stop. For me, for Bernie, for Lindsay."

"I see! Tell me of the future. What's in store?"

"No."

"Silly, don't you know the future is what we make it? I can change it with a whim, and so can you. It's nothing more than a dream that we work into being or steer clear of. Tell me, and tell me the truth or I'll know you are lying."

"You hanged her."

"I hanged who?"

"You said, 'We have to trim the deadweight.' "

"Who's the deadweight?"

"It must have been Lena."

"It wasn't you?"

"I thought it was me, but now I think it was Lena."

"How convenient."

Norris said, "Please untie me."

"Why? We're not through yet. I said I'd tell you when to stop talking."

Norris cleared his throat. It sounded like a mule braying. "You hanged her, with wire. That's all I know."

"Why did I hang her?"

"I think she betrayed you."

"Did she? How did she betray me?"

"I don't know."

"It's a good idea, though, isn't it? She may well have betrayed us, she might not have. Who would need to know but you and me? It will be a good demonstration to the new recruits, the two genuine ones from last night. Lena brought me you and Bernie. I guess she is deadweight now."

"You said the future was what we would make it!"

"Yes, and I like what you've seen. My power grows, and no one can stop me. Thank you, Norris."

Norris rolled his head, digging into the bark.

A good morning demonstration, yes!

Rex grinned. "I'll have you untied to watch, then I'll see what to do with you. You're our first queer."

Rex went to the bunking trailer to see that the Eagles were rising. The morning was getting better.

353

Chapter Seventeen

Their chains were all strung through with the long yellow towing rope. Dean held the lead end, and Lizzie and Peaches made certain all were secure. They were brought from the shed to the outdoor classroom and made to kneel to the sides of the benches on the cold, sooty soil.

The captives from the second shed were brought in the same manner, led by Junior and Ronald. Oliver Worley, the man with no tongue, wailed and grunted, but the others were silent. It was not uncommon to have early morning programs in the clearing. It was not unexpected, and it was always something terrible.

Bernie sat between Matt and Bill Bailey. She would have given the man her shirt if she could, but she had tried once, and Rex had beat the soles of the man's feet for it. Now, she did what she could. She leaned into him, her arm around his back, her hair over his chest, trying to block the October breeze from his flesh.

Matt was awake. His eyes were puffy. Poor food had loosened both their teeth, and last night, as Matt was eating what had finally been brought, a molar had come out in the bowl.

I've led you into the path of the supernatural drunk driver, Matt. And He's crushing you to death.

Bernie put her free arm around Matt.

They sat, watching Dean and Ronald stoke up the bonfire. The larger the bonfire, the larger the lesson to be learned. Bernie watched carefully. The fire was unusually high this morning.

354

Soon, the other Eagles appeared from various places around camp, dressed in their full uniforms of blue shirts and slacks. They sat on the benches. Bernie watched the kitchen tent. Rex was in there; she had heard his voice droning on to whomever was with him. Some major production was being planned.

And major productions usually involved punishments.

Bernie pulled Matt and Bill closer.

The kitchen-tent flap was thrown to the side. Rex came out, followed by a man and a woman, neither bound but both moving in obedience. The man had dark hair and a beard. His head hung low. The woman was Lena Carlton.

Above, in the trees, a whippoorwill called, "More rain. No more rain."

The three came closer. Bernie stared, and then cried, "Norris!"

Chapter Eighteen

She sat in the chapel, a small room on the hospital's second floor. The staff had asked if she needed her minister and she had said no. Mandy was downstairs in the morgue. An autopsy was soon to take place.

Her little girl, her baby, was on a gurney now, while men of science probed and prodded and prepared to cut.

Grace was asleep on the padded pew next to her mother. Every few minutes she would cry out in her sleep and tremble, making to roll over. Lindsay concentrated on keeping Grace from falling.

Her mind refused to let much more filter through.

The police had come and gone and come and gone again. Lindsay told them what she could. They had asked if they should call her family. No, she told them. She would do that. They should take care of business. They should find the Swanns and the nightmare camp in the mountains nearby.

Lindsay did not call her mother. She did not call the Gs, or Aunt Marla. She called her house, and Hank did not answer. She left a message on the machine. "Call the hospital."

Lindsay dozed off, and awoke when the hospital chaplain touched her shoulder. Her watch read six-fifteen. It was barely light outside, and the stained-glass window's glow was tepid and pathetic. The chaplain prayed with her, and offered to take her to his house for breakfast and comfort. No, she said. She was waiting for her husband.

Goddamn you to hell, Hank.

At six AM Lindsay left Grace and went to the nurses' station. She asked if Hank had called.

The nurse frowned. "He was here several hours ago. He checked with me, and I told him what I could about Mandy."

"He was here?"

"Yes. He said he was on his way to the chapel to be with you."

"He said that?"

"Yes. Didn't he come in?"

Fuck you, you bastard! You know you're responsible and you can't face me! Didn't you ever love me? Didn't you ever love Mandy? Where are you, you goddamn monster?

"Yes," said Lindsay. "Yes, of course he did. I'm sorry, I'm just not feeling very well."

The nurse wiped tears from her own cheeks, and put her arms around Lindsay.

Chapter Nineteen

He heard the voice, the joy and agony in the voice, and he looked up. He didn't see her at first. They all looked the same, bound together with bright yellow rope and chains. And then she was there, her long hair filthy and blown against the chest of an old naked man. She was thin, her cheeks drawn and her skin ashen.

Bernie. No.

He lifted an untied hand to call her back, to cry for help, and a uniformed woman stepped in front of Bernie and kicked her solidly in the ribs.

Lena and Norris were put at the edge of the clearing, facing the crowd on the benches. Rex presented himself before the bonfire. He raised his hands in greeting.

"Much we have to do this morning! New Eagles to swear service. And a traitor to be rid of."

The people on the benches shifted, but no one spoke. Norris let his gaze move to Bernie. She looked at him.

Bernie, I've screwed it up. I sealed the future. I saw it and I shared it. I'm responsible for it.

Bernie moved her head slightly, and her mouth trembled in a small smile, as if trying to say something. She was trying to comfort him.

No, Bernie, don't. This is my fault.

Rex swept his arms, reaching out to the crowd

before him. His eyes were huge and white. "Morning of Truth!" he cried. "Morning of destiny. I awoke today and knew the power was complete, and there is no stumbling block to our glory. Look at me." He turned around, arms out, graceful, pivoting in circles before the bonfire. "See what I am? It is what you will become, the purest of humans! Swallow your jealousy, because I am here to worship."

Norris's hands flushed cold.

"Today I awoke with a vision of the future. And I act on the vision, because the future is mine. Come with me and enjoy the glory of what I am and what the Truth is in me."

Beside Norris, Lena began to pant.

She can't know. God, let me change the vision.

Rex moved to the captives on the left of the benches. "You, I almost envy you in your duty. To see me and glorify me. What joy to have the Truth to bless!"

He walked to the captives on the right, and stood before Bernie. "And you, as well, I would want to know your awe, as I would want to know the worship the woman has for the man who enters her secret nest."

GODDAMN ME!

Rex then came to Norris and Lena. He touched Norris's cheek, and then took Lena by the arm. He led her to the center of the clearing. They stood before the fire. Norris looked at her blue uniform shirt. It stretched around the sad bulge of her stomach. He looked at her feet. They were bare. Lena looked down at the ground. Norris remembered the helpless feeling of bare feet, standing there in front of the congregation of demons.

358

Let me change the vision!

Rex said, "You've betrayed us, woman. Do you know how?"

Lena did not move.

I deny authorship of this nightmare!

"You betrayed us because of your slowness. Your dim-witted mind. A true Human, by definition, must be quick and sturdy, and have free will. Therefore, I see that you have chosen to be slow, and in this you have betrayed us. There is a dichotomy no more."

"No!" Norris cried. "Don't, please!"

Dean stepped from beside the captives and grabbed Norris by the beard. "Do you want what she will have?"

Norris felt water on his forehead, in his eyes. Wire—she will hang by wire like the Nazis who betrayed Hitler. I know that, I created it by sharing it. Norris shook his head.

Dean let go and stepped back.

"What were you thinking?" Rex asked Lena.

Lena turned her head and looked at the fire.

"How could you do it?" asked Rex. "Haven't you learned from the others? Are you as slow as I feared you were?" Rex stroked his chin. "You realize, of course, that you can't be part of us anymore. We have to trim the deadweight."

Rex moved closer to Lena, took her under the arms, and turned her to face the crowd.

"Is there anyone who would speak for this traitor?"

Norris looked at Bernie. Her hand was over her mouth, her face twisted.

No, Bernie, don't speak.

"So that we will not hang together, some of us must hang separately. Do you agree with me?"

Voices of Eagles said, "We agree with you."

"Give me your hands," Rex said.

Lena put her hands up. They were balled together in what seemed like supplication.

"Penitent now? Too little too late. Hang separately. We'll enjoy the cleansing. I'm not so sure you will, but that doesn't really matter anymore, does it? Help me."

Dean came over to Rex. He held a coil of barbed wire.

Oh my God.

"Hands together. Tighter!"

Dean carefully unwound an end of the wire and brought it to Lena's wrists.

And Lena drove her fists upward, catching Dean under the chin. He backpeddled, the roll of wire flying. Lena ran from the clearing into the woods. Her arms flapped like the fat wings of birds. It was an awesome thing, watching her run.

RUN LENA RUN!

Rex snatched the coil of wire from the ground and ran after her, calling, "You know you can't get far, you fat cow!" He would catch her at the creek.

And then what?

Dean straightened his uniform shirt and dusted his pants. He winked at Norris. He knew.

The congregation sat silently, waiting. A few of the Eagles whispered, but most sat without talking. The fire also waited, leaping and hissing and throwing out its red arms in imitation of Rex, its king.

Let her get away, let her find the root and get away.

And then there was the sound of footsteps on the forest floor. Norris strained. Two sets or one?

Listen, make it what you want. Have a vision of one and let it be so.

He listened. It sounded like one set of feet.

He looked up. Rex led Lena by a strand of wire around her neck. Her hands were wired together, and blood seeped along her arms in thin red tracks. Her clothes were wet and streaked with mud. Her scalp was bleeding. Rex's hands were bloody; his uniform, soaked, clung to his body. Their footsteps were in grotesque unison.

He'd caught her at the stream. He'd looped her neck and she fell away and climbed up by grabbing the root. She didn't make it to the Nansemond Lounge. *There is no Tom to bring her back to the real world. She is damned here to this world.*

Rex took Lena to the front of the bonfire and turned her again to the gathering. Norris looked at his hands and pushed his wrists together.

Barbed wire on her wrists hurts. What will it feel like to hang and strangle by wire?

And the burns on his wrists, rubbing together, suddenly flashed hot. Norris grunted, and ground his teeth together.

No vision, not now, I can't take any more of this!

The outdoor classroom disappeared, and Norris was looking down at his feet, at Lena's bare feet, hobbling across briars and leaves and root knots on the ground. He saw the bleeding, bound hands. He saw the backs of Rex's legs as he led her to the place of her death.

Bring me back. The prelude is terrible but not as much as the opera itself.

The bare feet moved on, human cattle feet, led to slaughter. Someone was behind, pushing with a stick, urging her to keep moving. And someone was walking beside her.

And the hand of the someone beside her reached over and touched Lena's arm gently. A soft voice said, "It's all right. I'm with you. Don't be afraid. This is not the end, only a transition."

Norris tried to shake, to jerk himself free of the vision. He did not want to know.

I don't want to see!

And then he was standing on boards, several two-by-fours propped between two large rocks. The wire about his neck was cutting deeper, having been stretched up and tied to something above. A tree branch, most likely. The two-by-fours were several feet off the ground. Leaves on the ground were stirred by the breeze into a moving kaleidoscope of oranges and scarlets. There was life beneath the leaves, insects and worms and tiny mammals preparing themselves for the onset of winter. Life went on in spite of death and pain. Life was communal. Death was individual.

Rex stepped into view, on the ground before the boards, crushing the tiny life beneath his boots.

He laughed. "Ha ha ha ha!"

Lena began to cry in great, whooping wails.

There was someone beside Lena on the boards. In Lena's peripheral vision, Norris saw another set of feet. Smaller feet, also bare. The owner of the feet said, "Bind one hand to my belt loop, Shawn, but leave one free."

Rex said, "Why now?" He stepped to the boards.

Don't look over! Norris's mind screamed at Lena. I don't want to see her!

Rex stepped back. A soft, small hand reached

362

out and worked between Lena's bound hands. The fingers folded over in a comforting grasp.

"We're together. Don't cry. I'm going over with you. God is with us." The voice, though trembling, was strong.

Bernie.

No.

Rex laughed again, then jumped up and kicked the boards. They fell backward, sliding from the boulder supports. Lena screamed. The bare feet, the wired wrists, the warm, loving hand, and the world dropped into blackness.

Norris opened his eyes and they were thick with tears. He looked at his cousin, who was now rising on her knees, facing Rex and Lena as if she was going to say something.

"Bernie, don't do it, please," said Norris.

Bernie looked at Norris, her gaze etched in surprise, as if he was brailling her thoughts even as she had them.

Bernie looked at Rex again. She said, "I don't want her to die alone."

Rex, who was putting on a clean uniform shirt, studied her, his head tilting. "What?"

Bernie, don't do it.

Chapter Twenty

So this was it all along. This is why I was brought here. To bear her to the other side and to seal my own faith.

Matt, crumpled beside Bernie, his chin down on his bruised knees, suddenly struggled against

363

the weight of his weakness and lifted a hand to her. "Bernie?"

"She can't be alone, Matt."

There was movement among the chained people on the ground, a silent, dreadful shifting in unison to look at her. She could hear their hearts hammering the air in sudden understanding. It amplified the agonizing terror in her own heart.

Matt looked at her. His hair hung in dirty lanks, the scar on his forehead vivid against the pallid skin.

His face. I want to remember his beautiful face.

"We need you, Bernie," Matt said. "You keep us going."

I always loved you, in all the ways of heaven and earth. I will see you again.

And she was sure now. The suit of love and the clothing of faith now at the moment of her death fit her like something tailored by divine hands. It was what held her together in spite of the human anguish.

The clothes were warm against the cold and the hatred around her.

"God will protect you all," she said. "I know it. I trust Him. But this I have to do." Bernie took a breath, an agonizing contraction of lungs, and said, "The spirit keeps us going, Matt. I was brought here to help Lena. I know that now. I've waited to know, and now I do. I saw her life through the visions. Her need was a living thing. A force. It touched three of us and fused our souls. It burned us, it was so strong. I didn't choose this, it was given to me. I have to see it through."

She reached for his hand.

I love you, Matt. His fingers caught hers, and a soft current of need emanated from them. An intimacy; a marriage.

"I love you, Matt."

Bernie turned away from her best friend on the ground, from the other gentle and beautiful victims of the Eagles, and offered a prayer that they be protected in this den of violence. Her head began to pound, an old headache on a return visit.

After this there will be no more headaches, she thought. *Thank you*.

She walked to Lena and Rex and lifted her open hands.

She said to Lena, "I don't want you to die alone. You've always been alone, but no more. We'll go together."

Rex stared, his eyes wide in amazement. "Well, then, is this what you want? Hands together then. As an old friend, I'll give you this one wish. Just call me generous."

I'm not afraid of death, only pain.

Bernie lifted her hands. *Make it as quick as possible*.

Rex began to sing, "Cupid, draw back your bow-ho, and let your arrow flow-ho, straight to my lover's heart for me."

Bring us into your kingdom where love is the only truth and peace the fusion of our hearts.

Rex wrapped Bernie's wrists with the wire. The fire in the barbs sent tortured laughter through her body. Dean picked up a stick and poked Lena in the back as though he were a cowboy with a stubborn calf.

Behind her, Bernie heard Norris begin to cry.

Chapter Twenty-one

Lindsay, in the hospital's chapel, slammed her fists into the wooden cross at the altar. It fell to the floor and rolled off the step of the dais. Lindsay's mother and grandmother and Aunt Marla, who had been summoned by the nurse, grabbed at her and tried to bring her back around.

She had just come out of her last vision.

There would be no more.

Lena was dead. Dropped from a wooden plank in the woods with a noose of wire around her neck. Lindsay had been Lena as she had hanged. And beside her, she had also seen Bernie hang.

Chapter Twenty-two

The alien pets were taken back to the shed for the rest of the morning. Norris was tied back against the tree, rope at the waist and the neck. Bernie and Lena had been hanged alone, in the woods several hundred yards behind the supply trailer. But afterward all the Eagles and pets had been paraded out into the woods to the scene of the execution and forced to look upon what punishment of dim-wittedness and stupidity had called for.

Norris, against the tree, wished he could claw his eyes out, to rid himself of the memory of the sight. He thought of Lindsay and her dying daughter and the look of hatred thrown at him when he'd hesitated to help.

Rex is mad, what will he do to me?

Norris's heart thundered erratically. Sand etched his throat raw. He thought of Sam, and the charred shoe he had kept as a souvenir for the first year, that scrap performing the part of both penance and solace.

What is it like to die?

He thought of Tom Murphy. The harmonica music caught in his ear and twisted into a squeal of torment. If he survived this, he would get in touch with Tom. He would call Tom. He clung to this thought, a tiny, tenuous life preserver in the sea of fear.

White Eagles bustled about the camp, exercising, doing laundry, fixing the midday meal. Norris drifted in and out of consciousness, his legs aching from the burden of holding his body up. Rex came by often, slapping his face and waking him up, and telling him that the day had just begun.

"I've got more bees to swat today!"

Norris was awake when Lizzie and Peaches mucked the captives' sheds. He wished he knew what to do to become one of them. It would be better to be naked and subhuman than clothed and tortured on this tree. He lost track of time and dreamed he was smothered by ants. They swarmed in his nose and his mouth and he could not breathe. He awoke to the choking rope and a termite crawling on his tongue.

Slowly he turned his head as far as it would go. He could see the outdoor classroom. Dean was at the fire, tossing on new logs. Rex was on a bench, holding a bolt-action rifle like a baby. The grin on his face was madness.

Norris shut his eyes and pretended that the ropes about his waist were Lindsay's arms.

And Dean was there then, slapping his face and untying the ropes. Norris's legs gave out from under him, but Dean jerked him up. They went to the clearing. The Eagles were regathered. The captives were not there this time.

Am I the entertainment now? Norris felt his legs buckle again, and again Dean lifted him up and carried him effortlessly and stood him before the fire.

Rex sat on a front bench, caressing his gun. The Eagles about him were cold-faced and intent.

Norris licked his lower lip. "Whatever you want, I'll do. Tell me. Anything. What do you want?"

"I want you to be a bee," said Rex. He grinned.

Norris began to hum, trying to sound like a bee.

"Silly!" cried Rex. "You are a good bee, aren't you? I've got a new game. We need some fun. We've rid ourselves of deadwood this morning. It was tedious, but it was necessary. We have a lot of pets, and some pets are silly little moths and some pets are bees. You are a bee. You need to be swatted. That will be our entertainment."

He is going to beat me?

"You remember Hank. Good man, a lot of help to us here, keeping us covered and in business. He said he wished you hadn't come here. Does he like you?"

"No," said Norris.

"But he wouldn't kill you, would he?" Rex played with Norris's beard. Norris felt the skin beneath the hair crawl. Rex put his hand down. "I've got a chance for the bee to escape. Do you like that idea? Hank might like that idea." Rex looked back at the Eagles. "Do you like that idea?"

The Eagles, a unified mass of white faces, nodded.

"Then these are the rules. A race, do you think that's good? See our jogging trail, the entrance over there?"

Norris looked. The path left the edge of the clearing and disappeared around a curve between the heavy growth of trees. "Yes," he said.

"I give you a two-minute head start. Then I'll come after you. A fair footrace through the beautiful autumn woods. I'll have no advantage over you except that I'll have clothes. But if I catch you, Dean will kill you. You, little bee, will be swatted cold and dead with this." He lifted the rifle, kissed its barrel, and handed it to Dean. "If you make it around the trail before I catch you, you will be set free. Free to go home to your boyfriends."

Norris shook a fly from his face.

Rex wiggled his eyebrows. "Free to go home and cook a few more fags on camping trips, sound good?"

And then Norris's heart made a strange, sudden turn. Anger swelled, growing beyond the ache of fear. He stared at Rex and saw the truth of what was there, a demented man, an evil man who held all the cards.

But only a man. Nothing more. Holding the power of life and death but of nothing else. Norris knew at that moment that whatever happened, he would not let the memory of Sam be spit upon by this bastard.

"Shut the fuck up, you stinking asshole," Norris said.

"Getting brave? Don't you wish you were more like me?"

"I'd rather die than be like you."

"Your wish is my command." Rex laughed. "Unless you make it around the trail. I play by my own rules, you see."

Norris's anger drew his muscles up, preparing for the race. He knew he would die either way. There was no way the White Eagles would let him live. Like the Arm Test, this was rigged. But he would not let them drag his spirit down again. He would not be their bee. He was a man, god-fucking-damn it, and he would live his last minutes in respect of those he loved, and those he had loved.

"The Eagles will wait at each end of the trail. If they hear me call, they will know you're caught. And they will come and hold you down. Then Dean will shoot you." Rex crossed his arms. "Bang," he said.

I'm going to die today. Sam, if there is something on the other side, be there for me.

"Strip," said Rex.

Norris undressed. He hesitated at his underwear, but Dean yanked them down for him, and he stepped out. The air was brisk. His head swam from his lack of sleep.

"Run," said Rex. "Run, you queer!"

Norris ran. He dashed across the clearing and over the low plank boundary and into the mouth of the trail.

Chapter Twenty-three

It was a very good day. So much going on. And tomorrow would be better, and the next day better than that. It was falling into place, bubbling to a head.

Rex, counting down the two minutes, danced by the fire. Joy rushed up from his gut in loud shouts. The White Eagles, rightly amazed, sat still and said nothing.

"One two three four five six seven eight nine!" cried Rex. "I can run like the wind today. Dean and Peaches and Judy, to the beginning of the trail. Ronald and Lizzie and Junior, to the end of the trail. Listen for me, for I will call. You others, stay here and watch and learn. See what bloody treasure we bring back! I will have him in a matter of seconds, because today I am the wind."

He skipped, digging up puffs of sooty soil with the toe of his boot. The Eagles obeyed, stationing themselves at the opposite ends of the path.

"Forty-five forty-six forty-seven forty-eight," said Rex. "That's almost a minute. One two three four five six seven eight."

Dean, by the path entrance, carefully opened the bolt, looked inside, then shut it, satisfied. Beside him, Peaches and Judy stood, feet planted apart.

Soldiers in the cause. We grow. Nothing can deny us!

We are True Humans, dedicated to cleaning the world!

It was this thought that stopped Rex at a minute

and fifteen seconds, and sent him racing after Norris Lynch.

He was Rex.

He did not have to count, even if he said he would. And there was no way the queer would make it out alive, even if he made it all the way around the trail.

Chapter Twenty-four

Thirty-three thirty-four thirty-five thirty-six!

Norris pumped his arms, trying to make up for the carelessness of his legs. He was already sucking air, and his feet were already scraped raw on the irregular, rocky footing of the trail.

Forty-five forty-six forty-seven.

He would never make it around the trail, he knew this. He would never outdistance Rex.

If he ran off the path, he could find the creek and find a way out.

They'll catch you easily. This is their home.

If he could climb a tree, they might not see him and at night he could slip down and get away.

There are no trees with low branches. This is the woods. Branches are high, reaching for sunlight.

Norris's hands stretched forward, cupping air and dragging it back. He tried to think of Native Americans. They used to run naked, it made them part of the earth, it made them swift. Like him, they were not bees, they were men. Norris's legs drove forward in ungraceful, ponderous movements. He was slowing down.

Move!

He bent over. He stretched his arms out even further, lifted his knees higher, and he slowed even more.

Now what?

A Lynch with a tall, graceful body could have run the race. Norris's short legs could not cover the ground fast enough.

There was a thick patch of brush to the right of the path. A pile of timber covered with vines and shrub growth. Dense and spiny. A small person could hide there.

A fucking short Lynch could hide there.

Norris skidded to a stop. His breathing was so loud he was sure it was a beacon to Rex.

I'm here, I've stopped.

Find me.

Norris jumped from the trail behind the clot of brush. A thistle comb dragged his chest as he squatted down and peered out at the trail. Acorns and cones, nature's glass, bore into the soles of his feet. He caught the slimy side of a log with his hand and worked down into a coiled, springing position. With the other hand, he felt around for a weapon.

Chapter Twenty-five

Today I am the wind and tomorrow the sky. The beautiful blue sky, blue like the eyes of the whole people, the right people, the lords of creation. There is no power higher than me because I hold the Truth and the Truth is what I will have it.

Praise the Truth.

Rex laughed, and ran up the trail, watching for the back of the bee and anticipating, on his tongue, the delightful taste and thrill of seeing the life running like sludge from the eyes of a pervert.

Chapter Twenty-six

He heard Rex before he saw him. The man panted loudly; perhaps he was not in as good shape as his followers. Norris dug his nails into the bark of the log to steady himself. In his other hand he held a squared-off rock the size of a grapefruit.

Norris watched down the path. There was a slight turn just before the patch of brush where he hid, which would give him a single second to catch Rex by surprise. If he hesitated, Rex would be gone up the trail, and Norris would run down to the creek to be caught by the military precision of the White Eagles.

The choice was death by gunshot or death by torture. This way, he would at least have a moment of advantage. A second of power over the king of the devils.

He was not a hero. But he could have this time before death.

For you, Sam. I'm not a cause; no one will ever know what went on here. But I will at least, at last, hold up my head for you. And for Lindsay, for Tom. And for myself.

And then he saw a flash of light and shadow, and Rex was around the turn, passing in front of the patch of brush where no tall Lynch could have hoped to be hidden.

Chapter Twenty-seven

Cupid, draw back your bow-ho, and let your arrow go-ho, straight to my lover's heart, for me.

For nobody but me!

Rex's heart was ahead of his body, flying up the trail in search of Norris, like a scout sent ahead by a wagon train of pioneers.

And then something rushed from the right side of the pathway, slammed into him, and knocked him to the ground.

Chapter Twenty-eight

For us!

Rex passed the brush with a heavy pounding of boots.

Norris sprang from the hiding place, locking his teeth because he had to be silent, and hit Rex with the full force of his body.

Rex grunted once, not loudly, and crashed to his side. Rex's hip caught Norris in the balls, and the air and will whooshed from him in an explosion of pain, but he didn't double over, he couldn't do it, his mind kept him on track because it was life or death here. His death. His life.

Rex's head rolled around, seeking the face of his attacker, and his body began to follow.

No, I don't want to look at you!

Rex almost smiled, and he said, "I should have—"

And Norris brought the rock up and then down

on the man's head. Blood burst from the skin on his scalp.

Not hard enough!

Rex's smile did not disappear, but seemed to lock on his face. Rex bucked, trying to throw Norris off. Norris caught Rex with his legs and lifted the rock again. Rex's grinning mouth opened, ready to call for the White Eagles.

For you Sam Lindsay Tom Bernie Mandy this is for you this is for us! He brought the rock down into Rex's face. The nose shattered beneath it, and Rex's demon eyes fluttered upward, and closed. He shuddered beneath the grasp of Norris's legs, and dropped back onto the path.

He's dead, God, he's dead, I've killed someone now do it do it do it.

Norris ripped at the buttons on Rex's shirt, popping them free and sending them in a spray. He rolled Rex to his side and pulled one sleeve off. Then he rolled the bulk the other way and jerked the other sleeve off. With a tug, he had the shirt in his hands. There was blood from the wounds on the front, blood of the demon man, and the smell and sight almost made Norris lose his concentration.

He slipped the shirt on. His skin crawled at its touch but he went on. The pants were harder. There was a belt to unbuckle, a fly to unzip. Norris's fingers, spastic in fear, could not catch the zipper tab.

How long until they come after me? How long is the trail? How long should it take to run the trail?

He caught the tab and drew the zipper down. He scooted back on his butt and grabbed the pants legs. He bore back, peeling the pants from the dead man. They caught on the boots.

"Fuck," Norris hissed. He cupped a boot heel in his hands and pulled. The boot shifted, stopped, then slid from the man's foot. Norris tossed the boot aside and grabbed the second. It fit Rex's leg more tightly than the first. He straddled Rex's shin and put his weight against it, then tugged at the boot.

Hurry up goddamn it hurry they're going to come.

Two hands grabbed the boot, one by the heel, one pushing the underside of the toe back for leverage.

Come on come on!

The boot came free of the foot, and Norris pulled it off. He dropped it by the first.

Norris stood and grabbed the bottoms of both pants legs and tugged, lifting Rex's legs from the ground and leaning back with all his strength. The pants slid off, and Rex's butt hit the ground. Norris backpedaled, then caught his balance. He stared at Rex, undressed now except for his underwear and socks.

Fuck that.

Norris climbed into the pants, snapped them shut, then stripped Rex of his underwear. He threw them into the weeds on the side of the path. Then he squatted down and reached for the socks.

Rex sat up with a roar, his eyes snapping open, the blood on his face a mask of painted fury, his hands grabbing Norris around the throat.

"Dean!" Rex cried. "Dean, come now! I have him!"

Chapter Twenty-nine

He had been dreaming of red leaves and flowers and then there was a dull pain, opening and growing at the top of his head, pounding like water from a waterfall, or from a Chinese water torture. Then there were sounds, birds, rustling leaves, and light at the edges of his vision.

His eyes opened and he knew where he was and who was there.

He screamed and sat up, and the enemy was there with wide eyes blinking at him as though they had never seen something so terrible, so powerful before.

Rex grabbed the queer around the neck and called for his Eagles. "Dean! Dean, come now! I have him!"

He threw his body on top of the faggot's, knocking the small man down, and tightened his grip on the bony, struggling throat. The face was splotched with purple. Rex lifted his ass and then dropped his weight onto Norris's stomach. Air and saliva spewed from the man's mouth. It was then that Rex realized he was naked.

The queer was wearing his clothes.

He dug his nails into Norris's neck as he squeezed.

"Dean! Shoot him!"

Chapter Thirty

He couldn't breathe. Rex's fingers dug his throat, seeking out muscle and nerves and the core, his trachea. Norris twisted his head back and forth, trying to loosen the fingers, but they only closed more tightly.

He caught Rex's hands with his own and clawed and pried at the fingers, but they were iron and would not be loosened.

He couldn't breathe.

Death by torture or death by shooting.

Or death by strangulation.

He thought he could feel footsteps pounding up the trail, Eagles coming to the rescue of their god.

This is it, this is the end.

He twisted his head again, and through the filter of leaf dust and the lightning specks that were closing in around the periphery of his vision, he saw the boots.

Get rid of the boots.

He flailed his foot, freeing one from Rex's leg-lock enough to jab out at the boots. He caught one and knocked it to the path side. Rex's breath was hot on Norris's neck. The face was an ecstatic clown's mask. The tongue that dangled just above his face was like a serpent's tongue, hot and taunting and deadly. Drool dripped onto Norris's cheek. Norris struck out at the second boot. It skittered off the path into the briars.

The footsteps on the path were louder.

Now his face. Get it down so they can't see. A moment is all you'll need. Pull it down.

Norris let go of Rex's hands and grabbed the back of the man's head. He pulled. The periphery of his sight shrunk to a tiny circle, the hated, sparkling eyes all he could see.

But he pulled them down toward him, close enough to kiss his killer. Norris shut his eyes. See us now!

And there was a blast, a crack in the fall air, and the hands on his neck stiffened and drew up slightly.

Someone cried, "We got the faggot, Rex!"

The hands fell away. The weight of the body on his was instantly heavier. A head dropped to Norris's shoulder.

"Got him, Rex, you bet!" It was Dean. And then, somewhere from over Norris's head, a female voice said, "That ain't the faggot."

Norris looked up. Rex's face was next to his. Norris twisted his back and worked up onto his elbows.

The king of the Eagles, naked, was on him like a rapist.

Dean said, "Oh fuck it oh shit!"

A woman said, "You shot Rex."

Norris struggled from under Rex's body. He sat up, his head spinning. He looked back at the Eagles on the path. They stood, staring. Dean and two White Eagle women. Dean handed his rifle to one of the women, and slowly walked over to Norris and Rex. Norris touched his neck, working air back into the windpipe, and watched.

Rex lay with his face down in the leaves. Blood coated the base of his scalp. Dean touched the man's back with his boot toe, then bent and turned him over. There was a large bullet hole just above the bridge of his nose. Dean's shot had been clean, traveling through the angle of Rex's skull and out the back. Rex's eyes had exploded. Blood trailed from his nose and lips.

"God DAMN it!" screamed Dean. He looked back at the women. "He was naked, I thought it was the fag!"

The women were silent. Dean was trembling. He raised a finger and pointed it at the women. "You saw it! I thought it was the fucking faggot! I didn't mean to do it!"

One woman, the younger blonde, turned her head away and looked into the shadows of the trees. The other, with the rifle, stared unblinking at Dean.

Then Dean looked at Norris. "I didn't kill him, Peaches. This queer killed him. He killed him sure as he shot him with that rifle."

The woman with the rifle said, "Sure he's dead?"

Dean said, "He's dead. Eyes blown out."

The woman said nothing.

Dean said, "Guess I'm in charge now."

Norris sat in the dirt and leaves of the path. He rubbed his neck. His vision was clearer now. Now he would be able to see what death they had in mind.

"Give me the gun, Peaches."

Norris looked at the woman. She looked at Norris, she looked at Rex's body splayed out on the trail.

"I'll do it," she said. To Norris she said, "Stand up."

Norris stood, shakily. He could run. A shot to the back might hurt less than a shot to the chest.

"Don't move," Peaches said. Norris didn't move. Peaches went to Rex's body, cocked the bolt, and fired a shot into Rex's genitals. Then she looked at Dean.

"He cut off my boob."

"He was our leader!"

"Fuck that," said Peaches. "He cut off my boob."

"Kill the fag," said Dean.

Peaches spun on her heels and studied Norris. "You got Rex killed," she said coldly.

Norris said nothing. His heart hammered. Let death come quickly. Bernie only asked for the same.

Peaches said, "I was real pretty. You should've seen me. Even a queer would have wanted me, you can bet. He cut off my boob, the fucker."

"Peaches, you bitch!" said Dean. "Listen to yourself!"

"I say, screw this shit." Peaches cocked the gun and lifted it to Norris's face. Then she pointed it at Dean. "Let the fag go."

Dean gaped. "No!"

"I said, let the fag go. He didn't ask for this shit. Neither did I."

Dean stepped toward Peaches. She fired past his ear. He stopped, and she cocked it again.

"You let him go," said Peaches. "Or I'll kill you."

"You let him go," said Dean, "and I'll kill you when he's gone."

Peaches almost smiled then. "Don't matter. I'm gonna shoot myself anyway."

Then the other woman, the younger blonde, said softly, "If a fag found us, then the police gonna find us, too."

"That's shit, Judy!" said Dean. "The Henford police are on our side. Arlen Wells said so."

"Think so?" said Judy. "Arlen Wells gonna care about us now his nephew is dead? Rex was the one he trusted. Rex was his man. Now Rex is dead, the police gonna slip through. Arlen gonna want to find who killed Rex. Arlen gonna drop us quicker than a hot coal."

"That's shit," said Dean. "I know what to do. I can be as strong as Rex."

"Think so?" Judy walked over and stood beside Peaches. "I say let the fag go. Then we go. Far away. Never come back. That's what I say."

"And we got the gun," said Peaches.

Dean stared between the two women. On his face played a myriad of emotions. Hate. Disgust. Rage. Fear. He said, "Remember the Truth. Remember our purpose. Henford is almost free of aliens, thanks to us. It won't be long until it's pure. We're stronger. We can move on and save another town. It's up to us. Remember the cause."

"Fuck the cause," said Peaches.

"Remember all Rex taught us."

Peaches tossed her head, motioned with the rifle, and lifted her chin. "We're going back to camp."

"And Rex?" Dean gestured at the naked body.

"I told you already," said Peaches. "Fuck the cause."

Chapter Thirty-one

They reached the outdoor classroom, Dean in front, Peaches and Judy side by side, Norris following. At the planked border of the clearing, Peaches looked over her shoulder and said to

Norris, "You run away, now. You know the road; you got here with no blindfold, didn't you?"

"What are you going to do?"

"What do you care? You're free. Get out of here." Peaches directed Dean to sit on a bench in the first row. The handful of newer Eagles, who had been ordered by Rex to stay behind on the benches, watched, confused. A scrawny man with a hook nose leaned forward to ask Dean something, and Peaches pointed the gun at him and shouted, "Sit still and shut up!" Hooknose sat straight. Judy crossed her arms and took her place beside Peaches.

Norris walked to the center of the clearing. The bonfire was lower now, burning blackened logs that would soon collapse into ash. He found his shoes and slid his feet into them. He heard several other Eagles, who had been stationed at the far side of the clearing, talking with each other. They had seen Peaches and the gun.

"What is this?" one called out.

Peaches said, "Come, hear the Truth sent us by Rex."

The three White Eagles came into the clearing. Two men, one woman. They stared at Norris and paused. Norris stared back. Peaches said, "Rex sent word to you."

One man said, "Where is he?"

"Come and listen, Junior," said Peaches. They went to the benches and sat.

Norris's fingers had forgotten how to tie laces. He fumbled with them and then let them go. He stood up, and looked at the brotherhood on the benches with the armed sisters before them. The bonfire was a tiny torch now, spitting a faint wash of yellow along the ground to the feet of the

Eagles. No face was alight by it. No eyes bright in its glow.

She said leave. Go now.

"What is this?" asked Junior again.

Peaches said, "Rex said go home."

There was shifting of disbelief. Dean said, "Rex would never say that, bitch."

"I got his gun, his gun speaks for him. If I say go home, then he says it. It's finished. Get your butts out of here. Take the car, the truck, walk, I don't fucking care, but leave or I'll kill you dead as Rex."

"Rex is dead?" It was Hooknose.

"Shot dead," said Peaches.

Junior's chin looked as though it would fall off. "Who shot him?"

"You shot him," said a recruit on a back bench.

"Rex shot himself," said Peaches.

"And the police gonna find us soon," said Judy.

"Goddamn," said Junior.

"Gonna come get us and inject our asses on the gurney."

"Goddamn," said Junior.

No one moved. Norris looked at the Eagles, then at the shed by the whipping tree. There were people in there.

"Police know where we are?" asked Junior.

"Fag found us, didn't he?" said Judy. "Police can, too. And Arlen ain't gonna care no more with Rex gone."

No one moved.

Peaches lifted the barrel of the rifle directly above their heads and fired. Somewhere behind the benches, a branch crashed to the ground.

"I said leave!"

The Eagles scattered.

Feathers of dead birds in the wind of panic.

Chapter Thirty-two

They were gone, fast as a roomful of kindergartners at recess. There had been twelve White Eagles in all. Norris, watching from beside the whipping tree, counted them in their flight. He had thought there'd be more, many more; power like this must boast hundreds, but twelve had been enough. Twelve converts. Twelve disciples of the god of perversity.

The truck and car held ten of them, and they were gone in a spray of grit and forest floor.

Two stayed. Dean on the bench. Peaches with the rifle. Neither spoke. Neither moved. They watched each other without emotion.

And then Norris said, "I want to let them out."

Peaches turned a half step in his direction, the gun still on Dean. "Aren't you gone, queer?"

"No." *Will she shoot me now*? Don't rock this boat.

"Anyone who stays dies," Peaches said.

"I want to let them out."

Peaches said to Dean, "Ain't it funny, that all this time there was a shitload of weapons in the trailer? That Rex never let us use them? He played with them but we weren't allowed. He never trusted us."

"The time wasn't ready," said Dean.

"You still believe that shit."

"Until I die."

"That ain't long, brother."

And Peaches put her eye to the sight and pulled the trigger. Dean fell backward off the bench. "Ain't long," Peaches said again.

Peaches turned and looked at Norris by the tree. "Fuck you, I said who stays dies."

"I want to let them out." Norris pointed a shaky finger at the shed. Peaches cocked the rifle and pointed it at him.

Death by gun or torture or strangulation.

Then she shifted the barrel and stuck it under her chin. "See you in hell, faggot," she said.

Her eyes stayed open even as bone and brain and bits of hair made a fireworks shower in the light of the dying bonfire.

Chapter Thirty-three

The shed door creaked as he pushed it open. He did not want to look inside. Of all things he feared, this was the worst.

There was no sound from inside, no movement, no talking, no crying. The smell that rushed out to greet him made his teeth chatter and his stomach clamp.

He did not want to look.

He took a step inside the shed, onto the foul straw and the darkness. His sight began to adjust.

There were eyes, wide and staring, trained on him. Then he saw the forms of faces and bodies chained to the rough wood of the walls.

They were alive.

One voice from the center of the back wall said, "Norris?"

God, someone knew his name.

"What?"

"Is it over?"

Norris moved slowly into the shed. The faces

did not turn but the eyes did, watching him without blinking.

"Norris, my name is Matt. I'm Bernie's friend."

Bernie.

Norris said, "They're leaving. Rex is dead. I killed him." They would order him out, then, certainly. They were a nonviolent group. They didn't tolerate murder. He held his breath, waiting.

"Are you all right? Please come closer."

Norris went to the voice. He kneeled down. The face before him was thin and sick and kind. The lips were cracked, the beard tangled. Norris wondered what he, himself, looked like now. It had to be pathetic. His own hair was crusted with sweat and blood from the fight. His own beard was rough like briars.

Matt said, "You came to set us free."

"Yes," said Norris.

"God brought you. Bernie said God would save us."

"No. I'm a fuck-up. I'm a screwed-up, worthless slug God wouldn't know even if I wore a name tag."

Matt smiled then. There was nothing in his tired eyes but acceptance. He said, "We love you, Norris."

Norris felt a heat of agony and relief draw from his chest. He sobbed, once. Then he put his arms around the thin, battered man and held him for a long time.

Chapter Thirty-four

Stone House United Methodist Church was full of relatives. There were no smiles, no rosebuds passed out to G-Mom. Reverend Dunn shared no happy anecdotes about family life. The front pews were reserved, and the relatives there were clothed in black. They leaned on each other and wept.

In front, on the altar, sat sprays of fall flowers. There was no casket. To the distress of Lindsay's mother and grandmother, Mandy had been cremated.

Hank was not there.

Norris did not sit with the family. He watched the funeral from a back pew. Beside him, Matt and Sandra bowed their heads and listened to Mandy's eulogy.

The service was short. Grace, the blind girl, stood up at her seat when Reverend Dunn was finished and sang a song for her sister. It was something about itsy spiders. The family in front wept openly after this.

Norris was the first outside after the service. He stood in the October sunlight on the sidewalk on Church Hill, and stared at Henford's mountains. They were in full brilliance now. In another week, the reds would fade to burgundies, the oranges to browns.

He took deep breaths of the cold air, swallowing it in deep gulps. Life was a bright fall leaf, he thought. Falling freely in the wind of whim. And people clung to it as long as they could, struggling to control its direction, wondering where the leaf would land.

Waxing fucking poetic, now aren't we, Norris? He pulled a cigarette from his pocket and lit up.

Mourners came from the church doors behind Norris. They muttered softly to each other, many walking arm in arm. Norris turned from them and stared at the mountains. He knew his family had many questions they wouldn't ask out of politeness. He knew his father would come outside, look at him, and walk away. But that was a battle for another day.

A hand touched his shoulder. He pulled the cigarette from his lips and looked around. Aunt Marla, her wrinkled face shadowed by the brim of a large black hat, said, "Norris, honey, it's so terrible." Her voice and the skin on her neck wavered. "It's so very very sad."

"I know," Norris said. And then Norris saw Lindsay's face over Marla's shoulder. Lindsay said, "Aunt Marla."

Marla turned around to look at her niece. Lindsay was holding Grace's hand. To both sides of Lindsay stood other mourning relatives, watching and waiting to see how they might be of help to the bereaved mother.

"Lindsay, sweetheart," said Marla. "How can a family stand this? We buried Bernie yesterday, and today we said good-bye to your little baby." She leaned over to give Lindsay a kiss on the cheek.

Lindsay, her face never changing expression, spit in Marla's face. "This was your fault, bitch," she said.

Marla shrieked and touched her face. Lindsay

turned on the relatives behind her. "Get away from me!"

The relatives backed away. Lindsay came forward and caught Norris's arm. "Come, talk with me," she said.

Norris, Lindsay, and Grace walked alone to the corner. They stopped at the street sign. Lindsay put her cheek on the scratched, silvery post and looked at her cousin. Grace, still holding her mother's hand, had her face pointed to the ground. Norris wondered if there would ever be a medical breakthrough to give an eyeless child sight.

Lindsay said, "Pretty bad, huh?"

"What?"

"Spitting at Marla."

"We's mature, that's for sure," said Norris.

"Yeah."

"So." Norris crossed his arms and looked back at the church. Most mourners were outside now, many moving toward their cars. Reverend Dunn stood on the wide brick stoop and shook hands. "So what are you going to do now?"

"Take care of Grace. Endure the grief of the family. Try to endure my own. And mail my letters."

"Letters?"

"I wrote letters. To editors. For Bernie. For Mandy." Lindsay looked at the sky. Her eyes tightened. She looked back down. "For all who died. I'm sending them to all the newspapers in Virginia. I'm telling about what happened here, how bigotry and ignorance killed us. It's a warning to people in other towns, other places. You didn't know where the other members of the White Eagles were going. They might end up anywhere. People need to be ready, to be watching for the signs."

"Did you send one to *The Henford Press*?"

"I sent them a personalized version. I even addressed it to G-Dad himself."

"He'll never see it."

"I know."

"The editor won't print it."

"Of course he won't."

Norris drew on his smoke and dropped the butt. Lindsay stepped on it. Across the street, Norris saw Matt and John waiting patiently beside an old Volkswagen bug.

"I've lost weight through all this," Lindsay said. "Have you noticed? I've been wanting to lose about twenty pounds, and I've done it in spite of myself."

"I never noticed you needed to."

Lindsay was silent, then she said, "And what about you, Norris? What are your big plans? Are you going back to Norfolk right away?"

"I'm not going back."

"No? Why?"

Norris wanted another cigarette. He crossed his arms instead. "I owe a lot," he said. "I have a lot of financial debts, and they've got me in trouble. But I found someone who's going to pay them off for me."

Lindsay rubbed the top of Grace's head. The girl put her face into her mother's skirt. "Really? Who?"

Norris paused. He said, "Bernie."

Lindsay's eyes widened. New tears welled to join the old tears on her cheeks.

"Through her friends. Through a trust," said Norris.

"Norris." Lindsay touched Norris arm. It did not pry, it only cared. It was a hug. *Thank you, Lindsay.*

"Will I see you again soon?"

"Maybe. I'll be at HeartLight."

"HeartLight." Lindsay smiled a small smile. "Bernie's home. With her friends."

"Yes. And I have my own letter to write, though not to a newspaper. Someone I hurt, someone I want to get in touch with again, to try to fix up the mess. Someone I hope will come visit me up here."

"The HeartLight people are very trusting, open people. They seem to care for everyone. They're nonjudgmental. Very spiritual," said Lindsay. "Not your usual group of friends, I wouldn't think."

Norris shrugged. *I never had a group of friends.*

"They care about me, Lindsay. Nothing matters to them but caring for each other. It's an amazing thing."

Norris then looked across the road at Matt and Sandra. It was time to go. He gave Lindsay a small kiss on her nose. He stepped off the curb into the crosswalk.

Lindsay said, "Do you believe what they believe?"

"You mean do I believe in God?"

"Yes."

Norris looked back at her. "No," he said. A car whipped past, then another. Then he said, "I mean I don't know. But if concern, if love is their God, I may believe already."

Lindsay nodded. "Call me."

"Of course."

Norris hurried across the street as a wind kicked up and little birds found anchor on the telephone wires overhead.

Elizabeth Massie

Sineater

According to legend, the sineater is a dark and mysterious figure of the night, condemned to live alone in the woods, who devours food from the chests of the dead to absorb their sins into his own soul. To look upon the face of the sineater is to see the face of all the evil he has eaten. But in a small Virginia town, the order is broken. With the violated taboo comes a rash of horrifying events. But does the evil emanate from the sineater...or from an even darker force?

___4407-2 $5.99 US/$6.99 CAN

Dorchester Publishing Co., Inc.
P.O. Box 6640
Wayne, PA 19087-8640

Please add $1.75 for shipping and handling for the first book and $.50 for each book thereafter. NY, NYC, and PA residents, please add appropriate sales tax. No cash, stamps, or C.O.D.s. All orders shipped within 6 weeks via postal service book rate. Canadian orders require $2.00 extra postage and must be paid in U.S. dollars through a U.S. banking facility.

Name_____
Address_____
City_____State_____Zip_____
I have enclosed $_____ in payment for the checked book(s).
Payment <u>must</u> accompany all orders. ❏ Please send a free catalog.
    CHECK OUT OUR WEBSITE! www.dorchesterpub.com

DOUGLAS

THE HALLOWEEN MAN

CLEGG

The New England coastal town of Stonehaven has a history of nightmares—and dark secrets. When Stony Crawford becomes a pawn in a game of horror and darkness, he finds that he alone holds the key to the mystery of Stonehaven, and to the power of the unspeakable creature trapped within a summer mansion.

___4439-0 $5.50 US/$6.50 CAN

Dorchester Publishing Co., Inc.
P.O. Box 6640
Wayne, PA 19087-8640

Please add $1.75 for shipping and handling for the first book and $.50 for each book thereafter. NY, NYC, and PA residents, please add appropriate sales tax. No cash, stamps, or C.O.D.s. All orders shipped within 6 weeks via postal service book rate. Canadian orders require $2.00 extra postage and must be paid in U.S. dollars through a U.S. banking facility.

Name_____
Address_____
City_____State_____Zip_____
I have enclosed $_____ in payment for the checked book(s).
Payment <u>must</u> accompany all orders. ❑ Please send a free catalog.
       CHECK OUT OUR WEBSITE! www.dorchesterpub.com

mommy

Max Allan Collins

"Chilling!"—Lawrence Block, author of *Eight Million Ways to Die*

Meet Mommy. She's pretty, she's perfect. She's June Cleaver with a cleaver. And you don't want to deny her—or her daughter—anything. Because she only wants what's best for her little girl...and she's not about to let anyone get in her way. And if that means killing a few people, well isn't that what mommies are for?

"Mr Collins has an outwardly artless style that conceals a great deal of art."
—*The New York Times Book Review*

BRASS

ROBERT J. CONLEY

The ancient Cherokees know him as *Untsaiyi,* or Brass, because of his metallic skin. He is one of the old ones, the original beings who lived long before man walked the earth. And he will live forever. He cares nothing for humans, though he can take their form—or virtually any form—at will. For untold centuries the world has been free of his deadly games, but now Brass is back among us and no one who sees him will ever be the same . . . if they survive at all.

___4505-2 $5.50 US/$6.50 CAN

BLACK RIVER FALLS
ED GORMAN

"Gorman's writing is strong, fast and sleek as a bullet. He's one of the best."
—Dean Koontz

Who would want to kill a beautiful young woman like Alison...and why? But whatever happens, nineteen-year-old Ben Tyler swears that he will protect her. It hasn't been easy for Ben—the boy the other kids always picked on. But then Ben finds Alison and at last things are going his way...Until one day he learns a secret so ugly that his entire life is changed forever. A secret that threatens to destroy everyone he loves. A secret as dark and dangerous as the tumbling waters of Black River Falls.

"Gorman has a way of getting into his characters and they have a way of getting into you."
—Robert Block, author of *Psycho*

——4265-7 $4.99 US/$5.99 CAN

SHADOW GAMES
ED GORMAN

Cobey Daniels had it all. He was rich, he was young, and he was the hottest star in the country. Then there was that messy business with the teenage girl . . . and it all went to hell for Cobey. But that was a few years ago. Now Cobey's pulled his life together, they're letting him out of the hospital, and he's ready for his big comeback. But the past is still out there, waiting for him. Waiting to show Cobey a hell much more terrifying than he ever could have imagined.

___4515-X $5.50 US/$6.50 CAN

Dorchester Publishing Co., Inc.
P.O. Box 6640
Wayne, PA 19087-8640

Please add $1.75 for shipping and handling for the first book and $.50 for each book thereafter. NY, NYC, and PA residents, please add appropriate sales tax. No cash, stamps, or C.O.D.s. All orders shipped within 6 weeks via postal service book rate. Canadian orders require $2.00 extra postage and must be paid in U.S. dollars through a U.S. banking facility.

Name_____
Address_____
City_____State_____Zip_____
I have enclosed $_____ in payment for the checked book(s).
Payment <u>must</u> accompany all orders. ❏ Please send a free catalog.
CHECK OUT OUR WEBSITE! www.dorchesterpub.com

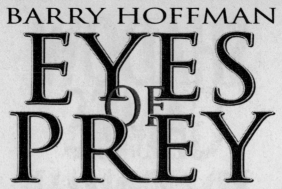

BARRY HOFFMAN
EYES OF PREY

Lysette has seen it all. As a child, she witnessed her parents' gruesome murder, and as an adult, she sees men leering at her as she works the strip clubs. But that night in the subway, the night she shoots the mugger, she sees something else. She sees the mugger, dying and bleeding, at her feet. And she sees her mission in life. That night, the Nightwatcher is born.

Barry Hoffman burst onto the scene with *Hungry Eyes,* a stunning debut that was nominated for both a Bram Stoker Award and an International Horror Guild Award. Now he takes us even deeper into the world of horror—a world of vengeance and of pity, of the natural and of the supernatural. A world in which the predator can be seen most clearly through the eyes of prey.

___4567-2 $5.50 US/$6.50 CAN

UNGRATEFUL DEAD

GARY L. HOLLEMAN

When Alana Magnus first comes to Luther Shea's office, he thinks she is crazy. Her claim that her mother is interfering in her life sounds normal enough—except that her mother is dead. Bit by bit, Alana sees herself taking on the physical characteristics, even distinguishing marks, of her mother. And the more Luther looks into her claims, the more he comes to believe she is right.

___4472-2 $5.99 US/$6.99 CAN

Dorchester Publishing Co., Inc.
P.O. Box 6640
Wayne, PA 19087-8640

Please add $1.75 for shipping and handling for the first book and $.50 for each book thereafter. NY, NYC, and PA residents, please add appropriate sales tax. No cash, stamps, or C.O.D.s. All orders shipped within 6 weeks via postal service book rate. Canadian orders require $2.00 extra postage and must be paid in U.S. dollars through a U.S. banking facility.

Name_____
Address_____
City_____State_____Zip_____
I have enclosed $_____ in payment for the checked book(s).
Payment <u>must</u> accompany all orders. ❑ Please send a free catalog.
    CHECK OUT OUR WEBSITE! www.dorchesterpub.com